Jak**e m**et her **a**ze.
"I've been way out of line. I jumped
to conclusions and made a fool of
myself."

She gazed at him, the anger subsiding as a look of
pleading burned in her eyes. "I don't care what
you think of me, Jake, but I'm begging you to
contact your father, soon, before it's too late. It
would mean the world to him—and to me."

Jake's insides twisted. It was tearing him apart to
look into her eyes and refuse her, but she had no
idea what she was asking of him.

"I'll think about it." That was the most he could
promise.

"Then I guess I'll have to settle for that for now."
She turned away and resumed packing.

A protective urge hit him hard and fast. "I know I
don't really have a say in the matter, but I'd really
like it if you'd spend the rest of the week at the
Silver Spur."

"Why?"

To keep her safe. To keep her close. He wasn't sure
exactly which need was stronger at this moment.

AMBUSH AT DRY GULCH

BY
JOANNA WAYNE

First Published in Great Britain 2016
By Mills & Boon, an imprint of HarperCollins*Publishers*
1 London Bridge Street, London, SE1 9GF

© 2016 Jo Ann Vest

ISBN: 978-0-263-91909-7

46-0716

Our policy is to use papers that are natural, renewable and recyclable products and made from wood grown in sustainable forests. The logging and manufacturing processes conform to the legal environmental regulations of the country of origin.

Printed and bound in Spain
by CPI, Barcelona

Joanna Wayne began her professional writing career in 1994. Now, more than fifty published books later, Joanna has gained a worldwide following with her cutting-edge romantic suspense and Texas family series, such as Sons of Troy Ledger and Big "D" Dads. Joanna currently resides in a small community north of Houston, Texas, with her husband. You may write Joanna at PO Box 852, Montgomery, TX 77356, USA or conncct with her at www.joannawayne.com.

To my very patient and supportive editor, Denise Zaza, who believed in me enough to stand by me during recent health problems, and to my wonderful readers, who came to love the Lamberts and the Daltons (especially Texas rounder R.J. Dalton) as much as I do.

Chapter One

Carolina Lambert shifted in the porch swing so that she could look her neighbor R.J. Dalton in the eye while they talked. He rocked back and forth in his chair, sometimes looking at her, more often staring into space.

Her heart ached at the way his body grew weaker each day. He had already beaten the odds by more than two years, but the inoperable tumor in his brain was relentless. It was only a matter of time and yet there was a peace to his spirits that she envied.

He sipped his black coffee, his wrinkled hands so unsteady that it took both of them to hold his mug. "I reckon Brit told you that you better get over here and check on the old man while she took Kimmie in for her checkup."

"No one has to coax me. Spending time with you is always my pleasure," Carolina said truthfully.

But he was right. Even with a precious baby girl to keep her busy, his daughter-in-law Brit had pretty much taken over the job of coordinating the family's schedule so that R.J. was never alone for more than a few minutes at a time.

"I swear you dropped off Saint Peter's coattail, Carolina. You're the best danged neighbor a scoundrel like me ever had. Best looking, too. Can't believe you're still running around single. Hugh's been dead what? Three? Four years now?"

"Four and a half."

"That's a long time to put your life on hold."

"My life's not on hold. I'm busy all the time with my family, friends like you and countless projects."

"Not the same as having a lover."

"Now, what are you doing even thinking about lovers at your age?"

"I'm not dead yet. If I was thirty years younger and not playing hide-and-seek with the grim reaper, I'd be after you quicker than hell can scorch a feather."

"You've done more than your share of chasing women, Reuben Jackson Dalton."

"I caught a few mighty fine ones, too."

"So I've heard."

He smiled, the wrinkles around his eyes cutting deep into the almost-translucent flesh. "Lived life on my terms, sorry as it was. By rights I ought to be drowning in regrets. Wasn't for taking your advice about what to do with my ranch, I would be."

"I can't take credit for you turning your life around."

"You don't have to take it, by jiggers. I'm a-givin' it to you. I offered to give you the Dry Gulch Ranch free and clear. You turned me down. Didn't leave me much choice except to try your idea."

"I suggested you leave the Dry Gulch Ranch to your family. That's not a particularly inventive idea."

"Sounded like crazy talk to me. Leave this ranch and what lottery winnings I had left to a bunch of strangers who wouldn't have tipped their hats if I'd passed them on the street."

"Until they got to know you."

He nodded and rubbed his weathered, bony chin. "Blessing was I got to know them. Listen at me, talking about blessings. You have really rubbed off on me. Surprise, ain't it, after me being a worthless rounder most of my eighty-plus ornery years?"

"You were never worthless."

"I done plenty of stuff I'm not proud of, but I must have done something good along the way, like pick the right women to birth and raise my kids. You gotta admit, I got me some real winners. Got the smartest and cutest durned grandkids on the planet, too."

"Next to mine," Carolina teased. "So you really do have no regrets?"

"I'd like to trade a few more years with my family for all the ones I've wasted, but I'm good with what I've got." He turned to watch a woodpecker in a nearby pine tree. "Would be lying if I didn't say I have one other regret, though."

"What is that?"

R.J. scratched his chin, his fingers poking into the loose pads of skin at his neck. "I'd just like the chance to sit around the table and chew the fat with Jake, one-on-one. At least make a stab at getting to know my firstborn, find out why he's so set against being part of the family."

Carolina swallowed hard, feeling his pain and fighting her own swelling anger. R.J. hadn't been much of a father to any of his children when they were growing up, but what kind of adult son could just turn his back on his dying father? She tried not to think ill of anyone, but Jake Dalton was the exception.

She'd gone so far as to call him herself last week, planned to beg if necessary to get him to pay R.J. a visit before it was too late. He'd been cool and aloof, until she'd pushed.

Then he'd struck out at her, accusing her of having done enough already to screw up R.J. and the rest of the Dalton clan. She might have found out what he meant by that if her temper hadn't flared to the point that she'd hung up on him.

The man was arrogant, coldhearted and infuriating. If his mother was anything like him, no wonder R.J.'s first marriage had ended in divorce.

Of course, so had his other three marriages, so she definitely couldn't absolve R.J. of fault.

"How's your friend Mildred Caffey?" R.J. asked. "Has that no-good, wife-beater ex-husband of hers tried to get in touch with her since he got out of prison?"

"He hadn't the last time we talked, but I know she's worried that he will. It's been good for her that she's been so busy working on a project with me."

"You don't think she'll go back to him, do you?"

"No. She's much smarter and more emotionally stable now then she was when they were together."

"Thanks to you." R.J. swatted at a honeybee that had been flitting among the blossoms of the potted petunias scattered about the porch. "You go around rescuing every stray you see."

"Only the ones who want my help. And Mildred isn't a stray. She just made some bad choices along the way."

"Sure as shooting, she did. I knew Thad Caffey was bad blood the first time I met him. Don't know why a nice young woman like Mildred ever married a no-account skunk like that."

"Love sometimes blinds people."

"Reckon you're right about…" He stopped midsentence, ran bony, knotty fingers through his thinning hair and stared into space.

He stayed silent so long Carolina feared he was fading into one of the spells he had far too often these days. Times when he drifted into another world, one where he didn't recognize his own family. One where he visited a woman from his past or from his dreams.

Carolina imagined this phantom as a first love, one who had carved out a space in his heart and never fully let go. Perhaps someone he'd loved the way she'd loved Hugh.

Finally R.J. turned and looked at Carolina, his eyes clearer now, as if he'd returned from the secret caches of the memories that had claimed him.

"He's gonna be out to kill you, Carolina."

"Who?"

"Thad Caffey. I was in the courtroom the day the jury found him guilty. I saw the way he looked at you, his face contorted and his eyes wild like he was a panther about to spring. I figured he blamed you for her testifying against him."

"If he thinks I encouraged her, he'd be absolutely right. I won't be intimidated by Thad Caffey."

"Or any other man around these parts." R.J. sputtered a raspy, guttural sound that might have been a chuckle or a cough. "All the same, keep an eye out for trouble."

Carolina looked up at the sound of approaching hooves and gladly let the topic drop as R.J.'s son Adam came riding up on a handsome gray mare. He tipped his hat and dismounted.

"Hope I'm not interrupting anything."

"Absolutely not," Carolina assured him. "Always good to see you."

"And you. Hadley's been talking about having you over for supper one night soon, but she says you're jumping through hoops getting ready for that summer riding-camp program you're organizing."

"I have to be in Austin for their area training session starting tomorrow. This is a busy time."

"Busy myself. Spring on the ranch," Adam said, knowing she'd understand that said it all. He joined them on the porch, stopping to lean against the railing. "Just came by to see if you want to go check out a new foal that was born last night, Dad."

"Long as you don't expect me to ride that mare of yours to the barn."

"Nope. We'll take your truck."

"Good. I'm about as steady as a cat on skates these days. Carolina can go with us. She's always keen on any kind of baby."

"Yes, but I have to beg out today," Carolina said. "Too many errands on my to-do list. But I know you'll be in good hands."

She stood when R.J. did and gave him a quick hug and a kiss on his sallow cheek. Her anger swelled again at the thought of Jake Dalton and his refusal to pay a visit to the Dry Gulch Ranch and R.J. The loss was definitely his.

The Daltons were one terrific family—second in her heart only to her own.

She said her goodbyes and went back to her black Mercedes sports car. Her phone rang before she made it back to the highway.

"Hello."

"Glad I caught you, Carolina. This is Jack Crocker, and I got a bit of bad news for you."

"What's wrong?"

"I'm going to have to back out of hosting that training session here on my ranch next week."

Her spirits plummeted. The arrangements were all made. Ten new summer riding camps opened in two weeks, their first venture into the Austin area. If they canceled the training, they had to cancel the program and disappoint one hundred and fifty young teens from the inner city.

She'd known Jack and his wife for years. They were the first people she'd thought of when she decided to branch out to the Austin area.

"What's happened?" she asked, struggling not to show her disappointment. "Are you sick? Is Betsy?"

"Nope. Me and the wife are fine. Just found out that all the kids and grandkids are coming to town to surprise Betsy for her seventieth birthday. No idea why they didn't tell me before now, 'cept they figured I'd never keep the secret."

"I understand," she said, crushed, but already trying to figure out a plan B.

"Don't you go frettin' about it, though," Jack consoled. "I wouldn't leave you stranded in a ditch without a mule to haul you out. I gave a call to Aidan Bastrop. He took over from there."

"Took over, how?" Aidan was a state representative and a friend, but this time she didn't see how he'd be able to intervene. He didn't own a ranch, and much of the training required that.

"Aidan worked something out with a neighbor of mine. You'll have bigger and better facilities than what you'd have had here."

The knots in her stomach relaxed. She should have known Jack wasn't the type to blow a commitment lightly. The relief lasted for the two seconds it took for him to mutter the name of his replacement.

The last person on earth she would have asked for a favor.

Chapter Two

Jacob Edward Dalton worried the knot in his red-striped tie for about ten seconds before jerking it off and tossing it to a nearby chair. Texas State Capitol building or not, he was going casual. Mid-June and the humidity was already battling the temperature for record highs for this time of year.

He could kick himself for letting Aidan Bastrop talk him into volunteering the Silver Spur for some project he'd never even heard of before now. Nothing like a gaggle of women descending on a ranch to guarantee his wranglers would do more gawking than work.

Not that Jake was against helping out. He gave generously to several causes important to him. But he had a ranch to run and a teenage daughter to corral, neither of which was going particularly well at the moment.

His foreman had been thrown last week when a rattlesnake spooked his horse. Granger had suffered a broken leg and bruised ribs. The man would be limited in what he could do for the next couple of weeks, though Granger would keep abreast of everything going on around the Silver Spur.

As for his daughter, Lizette, he was considering shipping her off to the Arctic until she cooled down. Her latest state of rebellion had been fueled by his forbidding her to date Calvin Owens.

Calvin was the local bad boy, two years older than Lizzie, and already had a juvenile record for vandalizing the local high school and shoplifting. And that was just what they knew he was guilty of.

Now Lizzie was constantly pushing the house rules and the limits of decency in her wardrobe choices. If her denim cutoffs got any shorter, she might as well skip them altogether. She considered curfews irrelevant and her newly acquired driver's license a proclamation of freedom.

She did a lot better when her grandmother was in the house. But Jake's mother, Mary, was on a European river cruise with a few of the other widows from their church. She was almost eighty, yet some days Jake swore she had more energy than he did. She definitely had more skill in dealing with Lizzie.

Jake headed down the hallway and stopped at the door to Lizzie's bedroom. He tapped softly and lingered a minute, though he didn't expect a response. She hadn't been up before noon once since school let out for the summer.

He took the wide staircase to the first floor and then followed the smell of fresh brew to the kitchen. "Good morning, Edna," he greeted his housekeeper as he poured himself a mug of coffee. "You're here early today."

"Not a lot of use in hanging around my place by myself when I can be up here drinking your coffee and soaking up your air-conditioning."

"Can't blame you for that." And it wasn't as if she had far to come. Jake had built Edna a cabin on his spread after her husband died almost three years ago. The tall big-boned woman had been with him ever since he'd turned his back on a promising medical career and taken over the ranching business right after...

Nope. He was not going there this morning.

Edna handed him a cup of coffee. "You don't look like you're planning to do a lot of ranching today."

"No, but I should be. Instead I'm off to Austin and the capitol building for some meeting that I don't have time for."

"Seems like all those politicians do is meet. What are they yakking about this time?"

"Some project that Aidan Bastrop enlisted my help with."

"I thought you had more on your plate than you can handle with Granger hurt."

"Yep, but this is an emergency of sorts."

Edna opened the refrigerator and started pulling out breakfast items while he finished his coffee. "What is it you've volunteered for? Giving a talk about ranching? Sponsoring an event? Making a donation?"

"I'm donating, all right. Unfortunately it's not just money. It's the ranch."

She looked at him as if he'd lost his mind—which he probably had, at least temporarily. "Donated the ranch? What in blue blazes are you talking about?"

"Actually, it's only the *use* of the ranch, our horses, corrals and some meeting space. And only for five days, starting Wednesday."

"Who borrows a ranch?"

"A group of about thirty women. But don't start having conniptions. You won't have to do a thing."

"Humph. A bunch of strange women taking over the place and no extra work. That'll never happen."

"I'll see that it does," he promised, though he wasn't

fully convinced of that himself. "The house is not included in the loan."

"What are all these women training for, some kind of trail ride?"

"Nope. It's called the Saddle-Up program, or something like that."

"Never heard of it."

"Nor had I, but then it involves teenage girls, so it's outside my realm of expertise. I have enough trouble managing Lizzy."

"Exactly what do they do with these teenagers?"

"According to Aidan's persuasive argument, they give inner-city girls from high-poverty areas one month on a real working ranch over the summer. They teach them to ride, work as a team, take responsibility—that sort of thing."

Edna's hands flew to her ample hips. "Well, why didn't you just say that in the first place? Those kids need a summer on a ranch. When does this training start?"

"Officially—Wednesday."

"This Wednesday? As in two days away?"

"Yes, but like I said. You don't have to do a thing." As if there was a chance Edna wouldn't be in the middle of things.

"You can't ignore guests," Edna said. "It's not the Texas way."

"Maybe not, but I plan to give it my best shot." Starting today. "A few of the women are coming out to tour the ranch this afternoon, just to get their bearings before the official training begins. If they show up at the house before I get back, give me a call and I'll have one of the wranglers hook up with them."

"You should be here for that," she said. "You never

know. Some of those women might be mighty fine-looking."

"I'm sure the wranglers will appreciate that. If you need me, call me."

"You're not leaving without breakfast, are you? I can whip up some bacon and eggs before you finish your coffee."

"No need. I'll grab a bite to eat in town. Best to get on the road now before traffic becomes a pain in the butt. But you can remind my daughter when she finally crawls out of bed that I expect to see her at the dinner table tonight. On time."

Edna stared at him as if he'd spoken in a foreign language. "Lizzie didn't spend the night here last night."

Irritation ground in his gut. "She was here when I went to bed."

"She left you a note on the foyer table that she was spending the night with her friend Angie."

"A note telling me—not asking. Another stunt like this and I'm going to take her keys away."

"Maybe you should just sit down and talk to her first. Take her for a horseback ride and a little teamwork of your own."

"See you at dinner," Jake said. He turned and walked away before he said something he'd be sorry for.

Edna thought talking was the answer to every problem that came along, but she had no idea what he'd been through with Lizzie. If her mother was here...

The old pain swelled inside him, followed by a surge of crusty hardness that allowed him to keep functioning. It was the only way he knew.

When he reached the foyer, he picked up his daughter's

note. *Angie broke up with her boyfriend tonight. Needs a friend. I'll spend the night. See ya.*

He'd been home. She should have asked him before she left instead of sneaking away. But then if she'd asked, he'd have said no. At sixteen, she was too young to be driving the dark country roads out to Angie's at night.

If she'd even gone to Angie's.

The sweet, adorable Lizette he'd known once had to live somewhere inside the stranger she'd become. Somehow he had to find a way to reach her.

Instead he was off to a meeting he could do without.

CAROLINA MARCHED UP the steps of the capitol building, fighting the growing agitation that she was forced to accept Jake Dalton's help, mentally debating how she'd handle their initial meeting.

"Slow down," Mildred said. "I'm out of breath trying to keep up with you."

"Sorry. I guess I'm still blowing off steam."

"You are going to be civil to Mr. Dalton, aren't you?"

"I'll try. That's the best I can promise—which is more than he was with me when I called him about paying R.J. a visit."

"You might have caught him at a bad time. Maybe this is his way of making it up to you."

"I seriously doubt that. And if it was just a matter of timing, he's had time to rethink it and contact R.J. Besides, he was the one who made this personal by insinuating I'd done something wrong."

"If he's still upset with you, he certainly wouldn't have volunteered the Silver Spur for the Saddle-Up project."

"I strongly suspect a little quid pro quo was involved.

He probably owed a favor to Aidan Bastrop—or wants one from him."

"Whatever his reason, I'm glad the training wasn't canceled," Mildred said. "Now I just hope I can continue to be part of it."

Mildred's voice hinted of angst. Carolina slowed and turned to face her. "Of course you'll be part of it. You've already put in hours and hours of work."

"I know, but…"

"But what?"

"Thad."

Carolina's irritation switched from Jake to Mildred's abusive ex-husband. "Have you heard from him?"

"Last night, near midnight. He sounded as if he'd been drinking."

"What did he want?"

"To see me. He said it's urgent."

"What gall. He almost beat you to death. You're divorced now. You owe him nothing."

"He admitted all that, but he begged me to give him another chance. He says he's a changed man."

"What did you tell him?"

"That it's over and he should go on with his life. But I know Thad. He's not going to accept that. He thinks I belong to him like a piece of property. He always did."

Mildred was clearly disturbed and with good reason. She needed to talk this out, but the meeting was due to start in minutes. "Why didn't you mention this at breakfast or on the drive from the hotel to the capitol?"

"I didn't want to upset you, but then I started to feel guilty about keeping it from you. If you want me to drop out of the training, I'll understand."

"Drop out and let Thad dictate your life. Absolutely

not. You can block him from calling you again, and you definitely don't have to see him."

"That doesn't mean he won't cause trouble."

"If he does, we'll contact Sheriff Garcia and he'll have him arrested. The law is on your side. You don't have to put up with Thad's abuse ever again. Now, let's not let Thad Caffey ruin our day. After all, we have Jake Dalton for that," she added with a smile, trying to ease Mildred's tension.

Senator Ralph Baldwin caught up with them just as they reached the door. He pushed it open and held it for them to enter.

"Good morning, Carolina. You look beautiful, as always," he said, practically ogling.

"Thank you. You look nice yourself." She stepped through the door and kept walking. She could definitely do without Ralph's seduction routine this morning.

The senator took her arm and tugged her to a stop. "Why didn't you tell me you'd be here today?"

So she could avoid awkward moments like this one. "I'm just here for a meeting."

"I have a luncheon meeting myself today, but I'm free tonight. Surely you could stay over in Austin and have dinner with me," Ralph said. "I hate to eat alone."

"I'll go on ahead," Mildred said, no doubt mistakenly thinking Carolina would appreciate the privacy.

Carolina turned back to Ralph. "You could always have dinner at home with your wife."

"She's in Midland visiting her parents." He lowered his voice. "Besides, I've told you, we're married in name only and even that will come to an end after the next election."

"Perhaps we'll have dinner then." And perhaps there would be a Dallas snowstorm in August. "I need to go now. Time for my meeting." She hurried away before he had time to reply.

No one seemed to understand that she didn't need a man in her life. She'd been married to Hugh Lambert, bigger than life, a man among men. How could she ever expect to find a man to measure up to him? If she did, it certainly wouldn't be a lowlife philanderer like Ralph Baldwin.

Carolina hurried down the wide halls of the capitol and slipped inside the conference room a few minutes before the scheduled starting time. Once she was inside, the noise level increased dramatically. A good sign that the volunteers were excited about the project.

Carolina glanced around the room, nodding and smiling at the attendees. This would be her first time to meet many of them, though she'd interviewed every volunteer by phone and had a background check run on them. In every case they were respectable ranchers' wives or experienced riders, active in their communities.

There was much more to providing an enriching summer experience to these teens than just teaching them to ride. She had to make sure the volunteers knew exactly what they were signing up for and that they had a true desire to help and bond with the frequently troubled girls.

She quickly spotted Jake Dalton, standing in a corner by himself. It was only the second time she'd seen him in person, the first being at the Dry Gulch just after R.J. had been diagnosed with an inoperable brain tumor.

The occasion had been less than joyous—the reading of R.J.'s will while he was still alive. Jake had been resentful then, and unlike his half siblings, he apparently still nurtured his grudge.

He had the same ruggedly handsome features as his

four younger half-brothers. Tall. Tanned. Broad shoul-
dered. Chiseled jaw. Lean and hard bodied. Blatantly
masculine in his ranch-cut sports jacket and shirt that
was open at the neck. A bit of gray salted the thick, dark
hair around his temples.

About her age, she'd guess, though he might be
younger than her fifty-five years. The only obvious negative to his looks was a mouth that looked as if it might
have forgotten how to smile. Probably a reflection of
having to deal with her this morning.

Only he didn't have to. He could have said no. She
knew for a fact he was good at that.

Aidan welcomed the group and talked for only a few
minutes before introducing Carolina. Jake Dalton stared
at her, looking as shocked as if someone had thrown a
glass of ice water in his handsome face.

So he hadn't known he'd be dealing with her and
hadn't recognized her before now. That explained a lot.
She could start looking forward to five days from hell.

After the introductions, Aidan and Jake excused themselves and left the room, and the rest of the meeting went
off without a hitch. The women all seemed capable and
excited about the project.

They broke at noon. Carolina, Mildred, Peg Starling
and Sara Billings, the four who planned to tour the facilities at the Silver Spur Ranch that afternoon, lingered
in the conference room.

"How is it you failed to mention our host was a hunk?"
Sara asked.

"And no little gold band on the gorgeous rancher's finger," Peg commented. "Guess that means he's available?"

"I wouldn't know," Carolina said. "Any ideas for lunch
that won't eat up too much of our afternoon?"

"There's a French bakery nearby that makes great coffee and sandwiches and the best almond tart I've ever tasted," Sara suggested. "It will be crowded, but service is fast."

"Works for me," Mildred said.

"And for me," Peg added.

"Then the bakery it is," Carolina agreed, ready to get moving before the conversation switched back to Jake's looks or relationship status.

"If you don't mind, I'll get you and Mildred to follow us to our ranch after lunch," Sara said. "It's on the way and we can change into jeans, drop my car off at home and catch a ride with you out to the Silver Spur."

"Can do. Mildred and I brought more appropriate clothes for the ranch, as well. We can change at your place."

"I would have packed much sexier jeans if I'd known Jake Dalton was so good-looking," Peg said.

"You'll be sexy no matter what you wear," Mildred assured the shapely blonde.

Carolina picked up her purse and slung the strap over her shoulder as the door opened and both Aidan and Jake stepped back into the room. She wasn't surprised to see Aidan, but she'd assumed Jake was long gone, possibly trying to figure out an excuse to get out of his commitment to the project.

"I hope everything went well," Aidan said.

"Couldn't have gone better," Carolina assured him.

"Carolina's enthusiasm gets everyone fired up," Sara added.

"I'd love to take you women to lunch," Aidan said, "but I have another meeting at one."

"What about you, Mr. Dalton?" Peg asked flirtatiously.

"I have some errands to take care of in town before I head out," Jake said, keeping his tone businesslike. "I'll give you directions to the ranch. When you get there, my housekeeper, Edna, will hook you up with one of the wranglers. He'll show you around and answer any questions you have."

"That will work out fine," Carolina assured him, keeping her tone as cool and aloof as his had been.

Directions were simple, and she was relieved when they were finally on their way. Jake was no doubt as eager to be rid of her as she was of him. He was turning them over to a wrangler for today's tour. She suspected that would be his modus operandi for the remainder of the training session.

With luck, she might not even have to see him again.

"I know you think Jake Dalton is a heartless cad," Mildred said as she walked to the car with Carolina.

"Yes, I do."

"You can't blame him too much for not bonding with a father he never really knew. Didn't all of R.J.'s sons feel that way at one point?"

"Yes," she admitted reluctantly, "but that doesn't excuse Jake's behavior. He's the oldest. He should feel some level of responsibility."

"If anyone can change his mind, you will," Mildred said.

"With luck, I won't even have to speak to him."

They were several yards away from her vehicle when Carolina spotted a man leaning against the front fender of her car. He was in ripped jeans and a black muscle shirt, a cigarette dangling from the corner of his mouth. A snake tattoo covered much of his right arm. A pair of aviator sunglasses hid his eyes, but his mouth was twisted into a menacing frown. An uneasy chill crept up her spine.

She glanced around. The parking lot was crowded with cars and pickup trucks, but the closest people she spotted were two men in suits, several rows down, walking in the opposite direction.

When the thuggish-looking man noticed her staring at him, he smiled and nodded as if in greeting.

Mildred grabbed Carolina's wrist and pulled her to a stop. "What are you doing here?" Mildred demanded.

The man flicked his cigarette to the concrete and ground it out with the toe of his right boot. "Waiting on you."

The taunting voice struck a chord and finally Carolina recognized Thad. He'd changed during his four years behind bars. Gained weight. Added a lot of muscle.

Mildred dropped Carolina's wrist and hugged her arms about her own chest, as if protecting herself from Thad's presence. "We no longer have anything to discuss."

"That doesn't sound like much of a welcome for a husband you haven't seen in four years."

"You are no longer her husband," Carolina corrected.

"Stay out of this, Carolina. This is between me and Mildred," Thad snapped.

"Please, Thad. Just go," Mildred pleaded. "I don't want trouble."

"I'm not going anywhere until we talk."

"What part of her not wanting to see you do you not understand? Either you go willingly or I call the cops," Carolina ordered.

"I'm not breaking any laws. This is a public parking lot. So you call anybody you want to."

He left the car and stepped closer, his gaze firmly

planted on Mildred, his tone switching from arrogant to loving without missing a beat. "I know I made mistakes, sweetheart, but you can't imagine how much I've missed you. We can start over now. I promise you that things will be different."

Carolina's stomach turned at his meaningless promises. Too little, too late. "Last chance, Thad. If you don't leave this minute, I'm calling 911."

"How about you let Mildred speak for herself? Or are you running her life now the way you run half of Texas?"

Mildred let her arms fall to her side. "I do speak for myself now, Thad. I hope you have changed—for your sake—but we can't go back. I've moved on."

"You know you don't mean that, baby. You still love me. I still love you. We can work this out."

"We can't. It's over between us, Thad." Her voice trembled, but she didn't back away.

Carolina put a steadying arm around Mildred's waist. "There's your answer, Thad. You can leave now unless you're looking to go back to prison."

"Go to hell, Carolina."

Fury burned in his voice now, his mood turning dark and threatening. He reached out and grabbed Mildred's arm, jerking her toward him. "Don't make me do something I'll be sorry for, Mildred. You know how I get when you make me crazy."

Carolina pulled her cell phone from her handbag. Thad let go of Mildred and grabbed Carolina's wrist with one hand while twisting the phone from her fingers with the other. She heard the clunk as it hit the concrete beneath their feet.

"Is there a problem here?"

Carolina jerked around at the sound of the strong, male voice. She gulped in a deep breath. Who'd have thought she'd ever be this thankful to see Jake Dalton?

Chapter Three

"No problem that needs your help." The thug dropped his hold on Carolina's hand and backed up a step, but his eyes burned with fury. Jake sized him up. Physically fit, probably in his early thirties.

Jake figured he could still take him in a fair fight, but brawling in a parking lot wouldn't fix anything and was definitely not his style.

He turned to Carolina. "Was this man harassing you?"

"He's stalking Mildred."

"Having a conversation with my wife is not stalking."

Mildred hugged her arms around her chest, head down, looking more like a scared child facing an angry parent than a forceful woman. "I'm not your wife, Thad. We're divorced."

So the thug was Mildred's ex. That clarified the situation a bit for Jake, even though it hadn't been Mildred the bully was manhandling.

The man reached a hand toward Mildred. "I just want to talk to you—in private."

Jake turned to Mildred. "Is that what you want?"

She shook her head and raised her eyes to Jake's, hers pleading when her gaze met his.

"I never meant to hurt you," Thad said, his tone considerably softer. "I love you. You know that. And you love me."

"You tried to kill her and almost succeeded," Carolina cut in, her words blistering. "She's through with you, so stay away from her or you'll be back in prison where you belong."

"Stay out of this, Carolina. You might own half of Texas, but you don't own Mildred and you sure as hell aren't going to order me around."

Jake struggled to contain his own anger as the situation became clearer still. The itch to punch Thad Caffey rode Jake hard.

He stepped toward Jake. "Mildred and Carolina are with me and you're through here. You have a problem with that, take it up with me now."

Thad glared at Mildred and then turned to Carolina. "So that's how it is. You got rid of me and now you've fixed my woman up with one of your rich rancher friends."

"One of my bulls would have been an improvement over you, Thad Caffey."

Thad beat his right fist into his left hand and ground it as if he were getting ready for a fight. Jake's muscles tensed. He'd never wanted to punch a guy more.

A second later, Thad turned and walked away without a backward glance. Jake watched him go, but his gut feeling was that this was far from being settled.

Jake lingered with the two women until Thad had sauntered over to an old mud-encrusted pickup truck with a rusted right fender and driven away.

"Good timing," Carolina said. "I'm not sure I could have taken him down if you hadn't shown up when you did. But I could have done some serious hair pulling and hopefully got in at least one knee to the groin."

"Ow. My bet's on you. But I'm glad I could intervene. Is there more to the story that I should know?"

"Thad is not a nice man," Mildred said.

"I got that."

"The four years in prison didn't make him any nicer," Carolina added.

"How long has he been out of prison?"

"Almost a week," Mildred said, "but last night was the first time he tried to contact me. I got a phone call from him at the hotel. I'm not sure how he found out I was here with Carolina. I don't know how far he would have pushed things today if you hadn't shown up when you did."

"Glad to help, but I seriously doubt you've seen the last of him. You should let his parole officer know he's stalking you."

"He doesn't have one. He served all his time."

"Then call your local sheriff."

"A great idea." Carolina took her car key from her handbag and pushed the unlock button. "We should get moving. Sara and Peg are probably already at the restaurant wondering what happened to us."

Jake glanced at the clouds that were rolling in. "I wouldn't dawdle over lunch," he suggested. "Weatherman may have been a little optimistic predicting the thunderstorms would hold off until evening."

He stepped past Carolina and opened the door for her. She brushed past him as she slid behind the wheel. Her skirt rode up her thighs, innocently provocative.

His senses reeled from an unexpected kick of sensual

attraction. He was still feeling the effects long after they drove away.

Carolina Lambert was even more stunning in person than she was in her society page photos. Great body. Thick eyelashes. Sun-streaked hair that tumbled past her shoulders in soft, natural curls. Hazel eyes that sparked green when she was mad. Full, beautiful lips.

None of which changed the fact that she had manipulated R.J. into writing that bizarre, manipulative will, a will that she surely planned to work in her favor once R.J. was dead and gone and the family was released from his rules and regulations.

But a deal was a deal, even though he hadn't known it was her he was helping out this week. Carolina could do her thing. She'd have his wrangler's full cooperation.

But it was a large ranch. With luck, he wouldn't even have to see her again.

Two hours later Carolina sped down the highway, barely paying attention to the conversation in the car as the four of them rolled down the last stretch of interstate before taking the exit for the Silver Spur Ranch.

The day had started with sunshine and promise. Now the sky was threatening. The cloud Thad Caffey had cast over the day was even gloomier.

If Jake hadn't walked up when he had, the situation might have turned violent. Just as frightening, Mildred might have gone with Thad in an effort to protect herself or Carolina from his rage.

Okay. Score one for Jake Dalton. She had to concede that he was not the complete cad she had figured him for. He'd been impressive in the parking lot, all the grit and virility a woman could ask for.

"I should have brought my rain slicker," Sara said from the backseat. "Looks as if it might start pouring any minute."

"It's not too late to turn around and try to reschedule the tour for first thing tomorrow morning," Carolina offered.

"We're almost there," Peg said. "Might as well see as much as we can today. If we need to check out more, we can always come back tomorrow and wade through the mud."

"The sexy ranch owner wouldn't have anything to do with your vote, would it?" Sara teased.

"No, but I can't say that I'd mind getting caught in the rain—or anywhere else with him. He is hot."

"Not to mention rich and single," Sara said.

"Better than all that, he seems like a really nice guy," Mildred said. "They're hard to come by."

It was one of the few times Mildred had joined the conversation since they left Austin. She had asked Carolina not to mention their run-in with Thad to the others, and Carolina had agreed that was for the best. Mildred didn't need a lot of questions thrown at her about her past experiences with her ex.

"How old do you think Jake is?" Peg asked.

"Maybe early fifties," Sara said. "What do you think, Carolina?"

"I'd say that's probably about right."

"I don't know," Peg said. "Those are not the biceps or butt of a middle-aged man."

"Good grief," Sara exclaimed. "What does age have to do with it? George Clooney, Kevin Costner, Colin Firth. My husband, Jess. All hunks past fifty."

"Doesn't just apply to men," Mildred added. "Case

in point: Carolina. Remember the magazine article last year that declared her one of Texas's most beautiful and altruistic women?"

"A major exaggeration," Carolina said, as the others gave her a wahoo. "And for the record, I don't plan to spend a second of my time trying to impress Jake Dalton."

"Guess that leaves him to you and me, Mildred," Peg said, likely only half joking.

"Then he's all yours," Mildred said. "I like the single life."

Carolina turned at the entrance of the Silver Spur. The double gate of entwined metal links incorporated the images of two life-size rearing horses and the name of the ranch.

Sara stretched her neck to see more. "Wow. Impressive."

Carolina lowered her car window, pressed the call button that was mounted on a metal stand and looked into the lens of a security camera.

A few seconds later, a friendly female voice responded. "Hello. Welcome to the Silver Spur."

"Thanks. I'm Carolina Lambert, with the Saddle-Up project."

"Carolina Lambert," a female voice repeated, followed by a few seconds of silence. "The real Carolina Lambert?"

"I'm not sure who you're expecting, but I am real."

"I recognize you now. You know, from the pictures I see of you in the newspaper. Just last month you hosted that big fund-raiser for the children's hospital in Dallas."

"Yes, and thanks to a lot of very generous Texas donors, we surpassed our expectations. We're here to tour the ranch," she said. "Mr. Dalton said you'd be expecting us."

"He just said some ladies were driving out from Austin. He didn't say it was you. And I'm just blabbering on. Sorry. I'm Edna, Jake Dalton's housekeeper. You ladies just follow the main road back to the house and we'll have some proper introductions. I'll put the coffee on."

"Please don't go to any trouble for us."

"Coffee's no trouble. Can't miss the main house. Two story. White. Dark green shutters. Big covered porch."

"Is Mr. Dalton here this afternoon?"

"He's not back from the city yet, but Tilson can show you around. He's young, but one of the nicest wranglers you'll ever meet and he knows the spread like the back of his hand."

"I'm sure Tilson will be more than adequate."

The gate clicked, then swung open. Carolina shifted the gearshift into Drive and eased over the bumpy cattle gap. The gate creaked slightly as it automatically closed and locked behind them.

"Nice setup," Sara said. "I can't wait to see the house."

"Only thing missing is the boss man himself," Peg added. "Bummer."

So far, so good, Carolina decided as she stared at rolling pastures and the wooded areas that bordered them. The Silver Spur without Jake Dalton would work just fine.

"A severe weather watch will be in effect for Travis, Hays and Blanco counties from 4:00 p.m. until 7:00 p.m. Be on the lookout for heavy rain and flash flooding in low-lying areas."

Jake turned down the volume on his truck radio and

used the hands-free Bluetooth connection to call Lizzie. Weather anxiety skirted the other issues of the day as he waited for his daughter to answer her phone. When she didn't, he left a message.

"Storm is rolling in fast. I should be back to the ranch in about fifteen minutes. Hopefully you're there, as well, or at least somewhere safe. Call me as soon as you get this message."

When he broke the connection, he called his house. Edna answered on the fourth ring. After a quick hello he asked if the Saddle-Up team had defied the threatening storm and actually driven out to the ranch that afternoon.

"Yes, a couple of hours ago. I nearly passed out when I looked to see who was at the gate and Carolina Lambert was staring back at me."

He knew the feeling, only he hadn't been looking at a camera image. "I take it you pulled yourself together enough to let them in."

"Of course, but I can't believe you didn't tell me she was the Saddle-Up leader."

"I didn't know you were a Carolina Lambert groupie."

"Pshaw. I'm too old to be a groupie. But she's famous. She attended a party at the White House once. I read that online."

"Guess that makes her a celebrity."

"She's not a bit stuck-up. All that money, and I swear she showed up here in a pair of Wranglers, worn cowboy boots and an ordinary white T-shirt. Just like regular people."

At least she'd changed out of that skirt that had inched up her thighs before she toured the ranch. He needed his wranglers working, not ogling.

"I hope the women left the ranch in time to make it back to Austin before the storm hits full force."

"They haven't left. They're still out with Tilson."

He swallowed a curse. Just what he needed. Carolina stuck at his house waiting out a storm. If they made it back to the house before it hit. "Did Tilson take them in one of the pickup trucks?"

"No. They wanted to go on horseback. I'm starting to worry about them, though. I haven't seen any lightning yet, but the thunder is sure rumbling and clouds are getting dark."

"Do you know where Lizzie is?"

"She's with Tilson and the ladies."

That did not sound like his daughter. "How did that happen?"

"Mrs. Lambert started asking her about the horses and the next thing I knew, Lizzie was headed to the horse barn with them. I haven't seen her since, so she must have decided to stay with the group."

Inspiring Lizzie to do anything that didn't include social media, texting or hanging out with her friends was a major accomplishment. If Lizzie was actually with them and hadn't slipped away from the ranch without mentioning it to Edna.

"I'll be home in a few minutes," he said. "Take care and stay inside. If you see Lizzie, tell her I said not to leave the house again."

"I'm sure that once she gets inside, she won't leave again in the storm."

Edna had more faith in Lizzie's judgment than he did. He broke the connection and gave his injured foreman a quick call. Granger answered on the first ring.

"How are the weather preparations going?" Jake asked.

"We're on top of things, even though I'm just able to man the phones. Winds are already gusting and blowing up whirlwinds of dust. Clouds are threatening to let loose with a deluge any minute now. Lanky's heading up to the big house to check on Edna, just in case she needs help with anything. He should be there any second."

"Sounds good. What about the livestock?"

"Got a couple of wranglers checking on the horses now. You know how spooked they get when a storm blows in. I had the cattle in pasture six moved to pasture five. Ground's higher there and will drain off a lot quicker if we get the rain they're forecasting. Feeding is taken care of."

"And the rest of the wranglers?"

"Told Fisher and Morgan to hightail it on home before the storm hits. The others are probably in the bunkhouse sipping whiskey and cooking up a bunch of fajitas by now."

"Edna tells me Tilson is still out with the ladies' tour group," Jake said.

"Just talked to him. They're on horseback and not five minutes from the big house. Lanky will help him take care of the horses after he drops off the ladies."

"That's what I needed to hear. I'm less than five minutes from the gate myself."

Streaks of lightning darted about the gray depths of the heavens as he broke the phone connection. A gust of wind made the truck shudder.

A big yellow dog ran the fence line just past the burned ruins of the old Baptist church. A shrieking murder of crows lined an electric line as if warning motorists they'd best get on home.

The first huge drops of rain began to pelt his windshield as he passed through the ranch gate. By the time he pulled into the three-car garage, the rain was falling in wind-driven sheets. He took the covered walkway to the back door.

Thankfully Tilson and the Saddle-Up group had made it back to the house, but not before the rain had hit. They were huddled in the kitchen, drenched to the skin. Carolina's gaze met his as he joined them, but it wasn't her eyes that brought him to instant attention.

Her firm breasts and puckered nipples were detailed beneath the clinging shirt. Arousal hit Jake so hard and fast it was dizzying.

He looked away quick, before the ache in his groin became a visible bulge.

He didn't even like the woman. What the hell was wrong with him?

Chapter Four

Tilson called his name and Jake jerked himself back to reality. "Sorry," he said. "I missed that."

"I was just apologizing for getting the ladies caught in the rain."

"Actually, it's our fault," Carolina corrected him. "We were so impressed with the view at Cotter's Canyon that we lingered too long."

Cotter's Canyon. *His* spot. More of a gulch than a canyon but special all the same. The place he went to get his head on straight. Now when he went there he'd most likely remember Carolina's nipples pressed against the white cotton.

Stunning even dripping wet. Sinfully sexy.

Texas was full of beautiful women. He needed to get out more, see something more intriguing than cows. A date every now and then couldn't hurt.

Edna stepped into the room, her arms filled with fluffy white towels. She passed them around, and the ladies took them eagerly.

"I'd best get back to the horses," Tilson said.

"I'll help," Lanky said, "unless you want me to hang around longer, boss man."

"No. You and Tilson just take care of the horses. Move

quickly and take cover if need be. There are some extra ponchos on hooks in the garage," Jake said. "Grab a couple."

"Too late now. Besides, a little rain never hurt a cowboy," Tilson said. "Mighty sorry for letting our guests get caught in the downpour, though."

Unwittingly Jake's gaze swept back to Carolina. She dabbed her face before wrapping long locks of dripping hair between folds of the thick terry.

"Where's Lizzie?" Jake asked, coming to his senses to realize she was missing from the group.

"Headed straight to her room to get out of her wet clothes," Edna said.

"You have a lovely daughter," Carolina said.

"Really fun to be around," Peg added.

"Thank you." Obviously they'd seen the side of Lizzie she seldom shared with him anymore.

"We're puddling your floors," Carolina said, looking down. "If you'll get me a mop, I'll clean up our mess."

"Guests don't mop," Edna said quickly. "I'm more worried about the four of you standing around in those wet clothes. Why don't I show you to guest rooms and gather some robes? You can change into them and I'll toss your wet clothes into the dryer. They'll be ready for you to put back on in no time."

All four of the women voiced their approval of that.

Jake walked over to the counter to start a pot of coffee while the women now draped in thirsty towels followed Edna to retrieve the robes. As usual, Edna was way ahead of him. The pot was full.

He was halfway through a mug of hot brew when Lizzie padded barefoot into the kitchen. Her long auburn hair was turbaned in a light blue towel. Her too-skimpy white denim shorts rode low on her hips. A blue cropped top showed far too much skin for his liking.

As tempted as he was to send her back to her room for something more suitable for guests, he decided to let it ride this time.

"Where did everyone go?" she asked.

"To change into robes so that Edna could dry their clothes."

"I'll go see if I can help." She headed for the hallway.

"Lizzie."

She stopped and turned toward him with a roll of her eyes. "What did I do now?"

"Nothing. I appreciate you helping out today. It was a..." He searched for the right words.

"Decent thing to do. I get it, Dad. Don't sound so shocked. I'm not completely heathen."

"I was simply saying thanks."

"Yeah." She nodded and left the room.

He couldn't even pull off being appreciative and make it work with her anymore. How had the gulf between him and his daughter ever grown so wide?

Jake checked the weather radar on his phone. The entire county was getting hit, but the worst was north of them, toward Austin. He stamped to the mudroom, grabbed the mop from the closet and went to work on the floor.

"Keep that up and you'll scrub the finish off the tiles," Edna said, rejoining him in the kitchen a few minutes later.

He looked down. The floor was completely dry. He eased his grip on the mop handle as lightning zigzagged across the sky, followed by a clap of thunder that shook the windows.

"Keeps storming like this and a few of those low-lying roads are sure to flood," Edna said. "Lucky we have plenty of spare bedrooms if the ladies need to stay over."

A sleepover with Carolina was exactly what he didn't need. "Storm will likely pass in a couple of hours."

"Might. Might not. I'll take some chicken out of the freezer just in case. It can be thawing while I wash their clothes."

"What happened to the plan to just throw them in the dryer for a few minutes?"

"The hems of the jeans were muddy and everything smelled of wet horseflesh."

"Nothing wrong with that. This is a ranch."

"We don't have to smell like the horses. Besides, it's not as if they have to get dressed immediately. They can't set off for Austin in this storm. I told them to slip out of everything and put the laundry outside the door. I'll pick their soiled clothes up in a few minutes and toss them in the washer while they just make themselves at home."

"You are definitely getting into this."

"Do you blame me? It's not every day we have some-one like Carolina Lambert in the house."

"Now you're knocking my friends."

"You know what I mean. She's exciting and so inter-esting. Her friends are nice, too. Even Lizzie is enjoying herself, in case you haven't noticed."

He'd noticed. He'd dated a few times since Gloria's death. None of the women had made anywhere near the impression Carolina was making.

"Did you know that Carolina is a widow with three adult sons and four grandchildren?" Edna asked.

"I've heard that."

"She doesn't look nearly old enough to have grown sons or be a grandmother."

He couldn't argue with that.

"Her son Durk is the CEO of the family oil business and her other two sons, Damien and Tague, manage the Bent Pine Ranch."

"You are just chock-full of information today."

"I like to know about the people I'll be entertaining for the next few days."

"Whoa. We are not entertaining them. They're using our facilities and our horses, but we're not involved. It's totally their show. Keep that in mind."

"That doesn't mean I can't be hospitable. You need to do the same. You never know. You might just find some chemistry with one of our guests."

"I'm not looking for chemistry."

"It might find you anyway if you'd stop being so contrary." Edna pulled a package of chicken from the freezer. "I settled the ladies into all four of our guest suites. Made sure they had plenty of that good-smelling soap, shampoo, and fresh towels and washcloths, too."

Great. So now Carolina Lambert was taking a hot shower under his roof. Naked. He swallowed hard, determined to keep his arousal level at low-key. He didn't like the woman, and with good reason. Why couldn't his manly urges get that?

"Just remember you're bringing all this extra work on yourself, Edna. Don't blame me if your good intentions turn into more than you bargained for. In the meantime, I'll be in my office if you need me—getting some work done while we still have power."

"Good thinking. I'll put out some candles and the oil lamps. Never know when the electricity will go out."

His office was down the hall on the first floor, far away from all the guest rooms—except one, which was only a few steps from his office. With his luck, Carolina was probably stripping out of her clothes in that one right now.

CAROLINA STARED OUT the window and into a torrent of rain. She should be back in her hotel room in Austin. But here she was, standing in one of Jake Dalton's guest rooms, no longer dripping, but with her damp clothes clinging to her like a clammy second skin. She looked away from the storm and glanced around the room.

A king-size bed topped with a dark green comforter was piled high with pillows. A small antique desk held a cup of pens, some note paper and several hardcover novels displayed between beautifully sculptured horse-head bookends. A floor mirror in a beautiful oak stand adorned a far corner.

The walls were painted a pale green and decorated with framed photographs of Texas landscapes, at least two of which she was certain had been taken on the Silver Spur. She recognized the magnificent views from this afternoon's ride.

A wooden rocker next to the window with a flowered cushion and a knitted afghan thrown over its arm looked cozy and inviting.

Difficult to imagine the calming decor was the rugged rancher's doing. But then, she had to admit, she actually knew little about the man other than his coldhearted stubbornness where R.J. was concerned.

Thinking about the brief phone conversation she'd shared with him a few days back still left her seething.

She couldn't understand anyone unwilling to bend a little for a dying parent—even if R.J. had been a rotten father.

She dropped the towel she was wearing sarong-style over her wet clothes and caught a glimpse of herself in the full-length mirror. She grimaced. Her wet, curly locks and runny mascara gave new meaning to the drowned-rat cliché. Her gaze fell lower.

Ohmigod. She could see every pucker of her nipples beneath the damp cotton of her shirt. The others' shirts had been just as wet—but not white. They'd clung, but she hadn't noticed that you could see right through them.

No wonder Jake had stared so hard. She might as well have stripped off her shirt.

Her cheeks burned. How was she going to face the guy again? Not without a bit of embarrassment, that was for sure. As if things weren't awkward enough between them.

No use to dwell on it now. There was no changing the facts. She undressed quickly, peeling off everything, including her bra and panties. Then she dropped the wet clothing outside her door as Edna had instructed.

She wondered if Jake knew what a jewel of a housekeeper he had in Edna. Hopefully he was a lot more considerate to her than he was to R.J.

Carolina headed to the bathroom, took a quick shower to shed the odor of horseflesh and then used a fresh towel to buff her naked body.

The overhead light flickered a couple of times but didn't go out as she padded back into the bedroom. She wrapped herself in the soft robe, though she had no intention of going back to the den until she was fully dressed.

She threw back the coverlet and slid between the sheets. It was like sinking into a cloud. The serenity lasted only until thoughts of the morning encounter with Thad Caffey returned to haunt her.

Mildred had thought her life with him was behind her. Clearly, Thad did not share that sentiment. But how far would he go to get her back?

How sad for Mildred that her marriage had deteriorated into fear and danger. Yet she must have cared deeply for Thad at one time, before the love changed to fear and heartbreak. Before she saw the man she'd vowed to share her life with as the monster he really was.

Carolina had difficulty comprehending that kind of relationship. Her life with Hugh had been loving and exciting. If anything he'd been overly protective of her. A man's man, all the way. He'd been her world, and she'd never known fear of anything or anyone when he was around.

The familiar ache set in again. As busy as her life was, as much as she loved her family, her heart still longed for the relationship she'd shared with Hugh.

Having known that kind of love, she could never settle for anything less. She had no illusions that she'd ever find love like that again.

Chapter Five

The pain was blinding, as if someone were hammering nails into his skull. Not a new pain, but one that had become excruciatingly more familiar since the day he'd been sentenced to four agonizing years in prison.

He recognized the torture for what it was, knew the only real release would come when he was back in control. When he could feel the sweet release of revenge.

He'd had four years to plan the payback. Nights of trying to fall asleep to the sounds of rants from half-insane inmates and the scratching of rats scurrying in and out of his stinking cell. Days of staring at bars and marching to the barking orders of guards whom he longed to twist apart like rotten fruit.

Four years of torture. It was time for action. The plan was all in place. The clock was clicking inside the very marrow of his bones.

He picked up the bottle of beer from the bar in front of him, took the last gulp and signaled to the waitress to bring him another.

Before she could, a platinum blonde wearing a low-cut top and inches of thick makeup got up from her stool a few down from his and walked over.

"Want some company? Looks like the rain is going to be with us for a while."

He didn't want company, but he shrugged and she obviously took that for a yes. She slid onto the stool next to his.

"I hate stormy Mondays."

"Yeah," he muttered. In prison a man lost track of the days. They came and went in a steady stream of monotonous boredom, seeing the same people, eating the same lousy food, staring at the same dull walls.

"You married?" she asked.

"Yeah. My wife is out screwing some wealthy rancher. Is that what you're looking for, too? I figure you're just another slut looking for some man to pay for your drinks and maybe get in your pants."

"You're crazy, you know that? A freakin' nutcase." She stood and walked away.

The waitress put his bottle of beer in front of him without saying a word. He threw a few bills on the bar, gulped down his beer, then got up and walked out of the nearly empty bar.

The rain needled his skin. He kept walking. The hammering grew worse. If he didn't let off some steam soon, he'd explode.

Chapter Six

Carolina was curled up beneath the comforter, trying to concentrate on a suspense novel she'd taken from the antique desk. She looked up at a light tap on her door.

She glanced at her watch. Almost five. "Come in."

Peg did, still in her robe and barefoot, since their boots probably wouldn't be dry for hours. Yet her hair was dry and shiny, makeup meticulously applied.

"Laundry's done." She handed Carolina her jeans, shirt, socks and undies.

"You even folded them. Thanks."

"Actually, Edna folded them. She wouldn't let me or Sara near the laundry room."

"We'll have to think of something nice to do for her after this week," Carolina said. "Have you seen Mildred?"

"Not yet, but Edna is taking her dry clothes to her now. She would have delivered yours, but she was afraid of waking you. She thinks you're royalty."

"That's what happens when you make the society page."

They both laughed. "I told Edna you're a workaholic and were probably in here finalizing and double-checking everything for the Saddle-Up training."

"You know me too well," Carolina answered, side-stepping the truth.

Working would have been far more productive than vacillating between concerns about what Thad Caffey might try next and trying to figure out how she could totally manage to avoid Jake Dalton, especially after her wet T-shirt display.

"Edna suggested we meet back in the den for cocktails or a glass of wine once we're dressed."

"I'll join you, but no alcohol for me. I still have to drive back to Austin tonight."

"If the roads are passable. That was a deluge for about an hour."

Peg shut the door behind her as she left. Carolina slid off the side of the bed and padded over to the window.

The wind had stopped howling, the thunder had faded into the distance and the driving rain no longer swept the windows in sheets. Only a light mist and a blanket of dark clouds remained—the clouds a lingering threat that the weather might not be through with them yet.

Carolina dressed hurriedly, finished drying her hair and put on a tinge of lipstick before heading back to the den. She heard the laughter as soon as she started down the hallway.

"Thought you'd abandoned us," Mildred said when Carolina rearranged a couple of throw pillows and took a seat on the end of a deep brown leather sofa.

"I had some paperwork to do."

Lizzie perched on the arm of the other end of the sofa. "Those camps must be a lot of work, but I bet those kids love it—or do some of them hate it?"

"Some do when they first arrive," Carolina admitted.

"But we usually convert them long before the month is over. The horses win their hearts."

"I know. When I got my first very own colt, I even slept in the horse barn a few nights. Do you teach Western saddle riding?"

"Absolutely," Carolina said. "We do the whole cowgirl experience. Riding, some minimal roping, sampling every kind of taco you can imagine and singing songs around the campfire. Of course they have to learn to clean stables and take care of the horses, too."

"Naturally. So, do you get out with the kids yourself or just sponsor the camps and the training?"

"I'm hands-on," Carolina said, "especially for the fun activities."

"She's out there every day, all day," Mildred said. "Works harder than any of us."

"Awesomesauce," Lizzie said. "The way Edna talks, you're like a queen or something."

"Those were not my exact words," Edna denied, untying and pulling off her apron as she joined them in the den. "But I'm impressed myself that you're out there with the kids getting all hot and sweaty."

Peg joined them in the den. "Looks like the gang's all here except for the boss man himself. Where did your father disappear to, Lizzie?"

Lizzie shrugged. "Who knows? He's always doing something on the ranch. Some days we hardly see him."

"Running a ranch is hard work," Edna reminded her. "Does anyone mind if I turn on the TV? I'd like to catch the early-evening news, see what they have to say about that storm that blew through here like a wailing banshee."

Of course, no one objected.

They tuned in just in time to be reminded that a little

pill could guarantee them a perfect sex life at any moment with no preparation. It had been years since Carolina had given much thought to a sex life.

The top news story of the night was the storm. The screen switched to a live shot of a male reporter in a dark blue wind jacket standing in water up to his knees. The running print dialogue below the images warned of flash flooding in low-lying areas in and around Austin.

"Looks like Austin got the brunt of it," Peg said as images of flooded streets, overflowing drainage ditches and cars stranded on the highway were shown in rapid succession.

"Good thing we didn't hang around there all afternoon," Mildred said.

"Or get out on the road during the storm," Sara added as the images and narrative skipped to the report of a six-car pileup on the interstate. "We could have been stuck out there for hours if we'd been behind that."

"Numerous fender benders and stalled cars have basically shut down the interstates in all directions around Austin," the reporter continued. "Stay off the roads unless it's absolutely necessary, but if you must venture out, watch out for rising water."

"That settles it," Edna said. "It is definitely not safe or sane for you ladies to drive back to Austin tonight. There's plenty of room for all four of you to stay right here."

"Makes sense for Mildred and Carolina," Sara agreed. "I definitely wouldn't risk flooding out Carolina's sports car if I were her. But our ranch is less than a half hour from here. My hubby will come pick up Peg and me in his four-wheel-drive pickup truck."

"Staying here works for me," Mildred said.

It definitely did not work for Carolina. Things were awkward enough as they were without adding a sleepover with Jake to the mix. "Thanks for the offer, Edna, but I'm sure the roads will be safe for travel again in a couple of hours."

Conversation stopped as the back door opened, followed by heavy footsteps. A few seconds later, Jake joined them in the den.

Jake's six-foot-plus frame and commanding demeanor dominated the scene even before he said a word.

"Any storm problems?" Edna asked.

"Some of the horses needed a bit of calming down, as usual, but no wind damage that I noticed except for a couple of limbs down in that stretch of pines along the creek."

"Did you check the entire ranch?" Peg asked.

"Not enough time for that, but we've been through enough storms to know where floods and the wind usually do their damage."

Edna straightened the skirt of her blue-flowered housedress. "You should have seen the pictures of the flooding in Austin."

"Too much rain or not enough. That's Texas."

"I invited the ladies to spend the night," Edna said. "No use for them to risk facing a flash-flooding situation."

For the first time since he entered the room, Jake turned and looked directly at Carolina, his dark eyes peering into hers. Her chest grew tight.

"If you want to stay, there's room."

That wasn't exactly what she'd call an eager agreement.

"We've already been far too intrusive in your lives,"

Carolina said. "I'm sure the roads will clear up enough that we can get back to our hotel tonight."

"Suit yourself, but the offer stands. Now if you ladies will excuse me, I need to make a few phone calls." He started toward the hallway, then stopped and turned back to face Carolina. "If you had no problems with Tilson today, I'll assign him to assist you in any way he can during the training session. If you need other wranglers, he can line them up."

She wondered if that offer was to make up for Jake's less than enthusiastic offer of hospitality.

Even so, she could use the help. "I appreciate that, and I'm sure Tilson will do fine."

"Does that mean you're neglecting us?" Peg asked, her voice bordering on outright seduction.

"I'll be around if you need me, but I'll do my best to stay out of your way." He stopped next to Lizzie and put a hand on her shoulder. "Don't even think about leaving the house tonight."

"Wasn't planning to."

"I'd better get back in the kitchen and get started on those chicken enchiladas," Edna said.

"Please don't go to any extra trouble for us."

"No trouble at all. Nothing more fun than having a full table to cook for. Is dinner at seven okay?"

"Perfect," they said in unison.

"I'll give Edna a hand," Mildred said, following the housekeeper to the kitchen.

"You know, Lizzie, I don't think your dad's as excited as Edna about having a houseful of women around," Sara said. "Not that I blame him, since he doesn't even know us."

"No. That's just how he is," Lizzie said. "He doesn't

get excited about much. But if he didn't want you here, you'd know it."

Lizzie's cell phone rang. She grabbed it and answered quickly, "What's up?"

She left the room before she said more, but it was clear from her suddenly strained expression that the phone call was upsetting.

Lizzie was vivacious and smart, but Carolina had a feeling she was also as complex and troubled as many of the youngsters who'd show up for the Saddle-Up summer-camp program.

Now that she thought about it, Lizzie, with her knowledge and love of horses and riding, would be a perfect junior volunteer for the session on Sara's ranch. Not only would the participants learn from her, but the interaction with young teens so much less fortunate than herself might do Lizzie some good, as well.

Her involvement would require Lizzie's willingness and Jake's permission. The latter might be the more difficult to obtain, but worth a shot.

Determined to face the issue before she changed her mind, she went off in search of Jake. It didn't take long to find him. He was at a wide wooden desk in his home office, staring at a table of figures on the computer screen. She tapped lightly on the open door.

He looked up. "Come in."

"Is this a bad time?"

"No. Can I help you with something?"

"Hopefully. It's about Lizzie."

His brow furrowed. "What about her?"

"She's a really nice kid. Smart and great with horses, too."

"Thank you."

"She's got a lot going for her, but she's—"

"Look, Mrs. Lambert, if you're here to tell me that she has a problem with me, don't bother. I'm quite aware. It's not for lack of trying on my part. It's just..."

"Carolina."

He frowned. "What?"

"You can call me Carolina. And I'm not here to criticize but to ask a favor of sorts. I'd appreciate it if you'd hear me out before you say no."

"Go ahead."

"I'd like your permission to invite Lizzie to be one of our junior counselors this summer. She has so much to offer, and I think it might even be good for her."

"Exactly what would that involve?"

"One month of working with the underprivileged campers on Sara and Jess's ranch. It would be voluntary, but she could stay on site with the other camp counselors so she wouldn't have to be on the highway driving back and forth."

"Have you mentioned this to Lizzie?"

"No. I wanted to clear it with you first."

Jake swiveled his chair so that he was facing Carolina. Concern etched his face. "If you can persuade my daughter to give up sleeping until noon and then spending the rest of the day either texting or hanging out with her friends, I'd say you're a miracle worker."

"I'll take that as a yes."

"Definitely. Go for it. You do the asking. If it comes from me, the answer would be an unqualified no."

Perhaps if you set a better example with the way you treated your own father.

Those were the words Carolina wanted to toss back at him. She bit them back. Lizzie needed her father, and

If they didn't find a way to connect soon, they might never find it.

"Carolina. I've been looking all over for you."

She looked up as Mildred rushed into the room, her face a pasty white. "What's wrong?"

"Thad. He's not giving up."

Chapter Seven

Jake was not surprised. He had sat out the storm at ranch headquarters, checking the internet for anything he could find about the arrest and trial that led to Caffey's conviction.

There hadn't been much. As rotten a crime as spousal abuse was, it didn't get a lot of press unless either the perpetrator or the victim was a celebrity.

The sketchy details indicated that Thad had abused Mildred throughout their three years of marriage in what the prosecutor described as mental and physical torture.

Slugging her for simple mistakes like scorching his shirt when she was ironing it or not scrubbing the kitchen floor as clean as he wanted it. Always hitting her somewhere the bruises could be hidden beneath her clothes.

On other occasions, he wouldn't tell her what she'd done wrong but would lock her in a room for days with only tepid water to drink. And yet she'd stayed with him. Now he was back again.

"I can't believe he has the gall to contact you," Carolina said, "much less to keep harassing you. On second thought, knowing Thad, of course he had the gall. What did he say?"

"Not much. It was a text this time." She handed the phone to Carolina, who read the brief message aloud.

"'Waiting for you at the hotel. Need to talk—alone. Miss my wife.'"

"He must have found out where we're staying," Mildred said.

"Good. Let him wait for us. The police will know where to arrest him for stalking you."

Jake doubted a text asking to talk to an ex-wife was grounds for arrest. Unless... "Is Caffey under any legal orders to stay away from you?"

"No," Mildred admitted. "I didn't ask for that, never dreamed I'd need it. He wrote me several times the first year, telling me that I'd turned on him and he never wanted to see me again."

"Has he written since the first year?"

"Only once, when the divorce became final. He wrote me a blistering three-page letter reminding me of all he'd done for me and saying what a thankless bitch I was. Mostly he railed on Carolina, accusing her of turning me against him."

"Naturally he didn't take any responsibility for his actions," Carolina said.

"After that, I never heard from him again," Mildred continued. "I only knew he was out of prison because Sheriff Garcia called me. He's our local sheriff and the one who arrested Thad the night he almost killed me."

"I know Garcia. Good man," Jake said, though he'd only met the sheriff once and that had been a couple of years back.

Jake hadn't actually been invited into this discussion, but having it take place in his home office should give him some rights. Besides, neither Carolina nor Mildred seemed to resent his input.

"How long did you say Caffey's been out of prison?" he asked.

"Five days to be exact."

"And last night was the first time he's tried to contact you?"

"Yes. I'm so sorry about this. I never would have come to the training program if I'd known he was going to start trouble."

"Nonsense and don't apologize," Carolina insisted. "You've done nothing wrong. Thad is the one who's out of order."

Jake agreed, but in spite of her bluster, Carolina was not the one to take on a man who fell into rage the way Caffey did.

"I think you should give Sheriff Garcia a call," Jake said. "Let him know what's going on and see what he advises. If he thinks a restraining order is called for, I'm sure he can expedite it. Then if your ex harasses you, Mildred, there's grounds for an arrest."

"Good idea," Carolina agreed.

Mildred looked uncertain. "That's only going to upset him more. Maybe I should try talking to Thad first."

Jake figured Mildred was falling back into her old ways of trying to smooth things over with Thad. "I wouldn't recommend that."

"Giving in to Thad will do nothing but encourage him," Carolina said.

"I guess you're right."

Jake was certain Carolina was right, but that still left Caffey waiting for them back in Austin. Another confrontation. A better-than-average chance that Caffey would lose his temper again.

Not going to happen on Jake's watch. He was about to invite a heap of complications into his life, but he couldn't see any way around it.

Jake stood and walked to the front of his desk, then nonchalantly leaned his backside against it. "You might want to rethink driving back into Austin tonight."

"That won't be necessary," Carolina assured him. "I'll alert hotel security. They'll see that there's no trouble."

"What if they can't?" Mildred asked. "What if Thad outsmarts them like he always fools everyone?" She wrung her hands. "I'd feel better if we stayed here— just for tonight."

"Plenty of room," Jake said. "Won't put anyone out."

Carolina's lips pressed together, as if spending the night at the Silver Spur was a major concession. Her resentment toward him was no secret, but she could show a little appreciation. He wasn't the monster forcing the change of plans.

Finally, she looked up and met his gaze. "If you're sure you're comfortable with us here?"

He was anything but comfortable with Carolina sleeping under his roof, but that was a matter between him and his libido. It would help if she weren't so damned attractive when she was playing Mama Bear.

"So what do I do about the text?" Mildred asked.

"Nothing," Jake said. "Don't answer or delete unless the sheriff instructs you to."

"Thanks. After four years of not dealing with Thad, I had forgotten how much he frightens me. But today in the parking lot and then tonight when I read his text, I got that same nauseating feeling in my stomach that I had every day and night of living with him. Never knowing which Thad would come home at night—the loving husband or the devil."

Carolina put a hand around Mildred's shoulder. "You don't ever have to go back to that again."

"I hope you're right. I'll go call the sheriff now. The sooner I can get the restraining order started, the better." She turned to go. "Thank you so much for letting us stay here, Mr. Dalton. I'm sure I'll sleep much better knowing Thad won't come busting into my room any second."

"Glad to help, and call me Jake."

"Okay, Jake."

Carolina rocked on the heels of her stockinged feet as Mildred disappeared into the hallway. "Thanks, but you really didn't have to do that," she said.

"It's just a bed for a night, Carolina. It's not that big a deal."

"Isn't it? I saw your face this morning when you realized I was the one you had to put up with for almost a week. You were anything but pleased."

"I was surprised, but not bothered at all by your being here."

Carolina was a woman used to getting what she wanted. Nothing daunted Carolina Lambert.

Best not to let her know that she daunted him, especially now that she'd be sleeping under his roof.

THE EVENING DRAGGED by for Carolina, but there were no more awkward conversations between her and Jake. He made an excuse to skip out on dinner and didn't show up again until Jess arrived to pick up Sara and Peg.

Once they were gone, she excused herself and made

her way back to the comfortable guest room, one just steps away from his office.

When she reached the room, she threw back the coverlet, sat on the bed and pulled off the thick socks she'd worn in lieu of wet boots or going barefoot. Fatigue, mental as much as physical, set in so powerfully that the tasks of undressing and washing her face seemed monumental. She stretched out on the bed fully clothed.

A little more than twenty-four hours after their arrival in Austin with high expectations and excitement, everything had gone wrong. She had Thad Caffey to thank for that. He was a beast of a man who'd intimidated and terrorized Mildred for years while pretending to love her. He apparently planned to pick up where he'd left off the night he was arrested.

No wonder he struck such fear in Mildred.

But the last person she'd expected to come to the rescue was Jake Dalton. She'd had him all figured out before she met him. Arrogant. Coldhearted. No respect for the feelings of his dying father.

So exactly how was she supposed to integrate that with the man who was so quick to come to the rescue tonight? Not that the tension between them had decreased. If anything, it was stronger, almost palpable.

She could neither understand nor deny that he had a dizzying effect on her.

A light tap at the door interrupted the troubling thoughts. Mildred poked her head in. "Mind if I come in?"

"Of course not. Is something wrong?"

"No, but I still haven't heard back from Sheriff Garcia. Maybe he didn't get my message. Do you think I should call again?"

"If you want to, but he works crazy hours, depending on what's going on in the area."

"I know. I just keep thinking of Thad in Austin, waiting on me to get there and getting madder by the second."

"We stayed here so you can get a good night's sleep."

"I know, and I do feel safer than I would back at the hotel. Even you have to admit, Jake has been a lifesaver today."

"I wouldn't go that far, but he's come through for us."

"I think he likes you."

"I think he's tolerating me—admittedly more than he's doing with R.J."

Carolina was grateful when Mildred's phone rang and killed the subject at hand.

Mildred yanked the phone from the pocket of a white chenille robe. "It's Sheriff Garcia."

Carolina pulled her legs into bed with her and sat cross-legged, her back propped against a stack of pillows, as she listened to Mildred's side of the conversation. After about ten minutes of rehashing the latest developments, she handed the phone to Carolina.

"The sheriff wants to talk to you."

Carolina took the phone and exchanged a greeting. The sheriff wasted no time in getting down to business.

"I know you always mean well, Carolina, trying to solve everybody's problems, but don't go thinking you can handle Thad Caffey the way you do one of your ornery quarter horses."

"I have no intention of dealing with Thad. That's why Mildred called you."

"Good that you did. Based on Thad's history, there will be no trouble getting a restraining order. If Thad disobeys it, I can immediately put out a warrant for his arrest."

"That's what we're hoping for."

"Surprised the heck out of me when Mildred told me where you're staying for the rest of the week. When did you and Jake Dalton get to be such good buddies?"

"We didn't. It's a long story, but we'll be using his ranch for a Saddle-Up training session."

"Mighty convenient. Does that mean he and R.J. mended fences?"

"No."

"Then you must have had some sweet change of heart."

"No." It never failed to amaze her how much everyone in the small town of Oak Grove knew about her business. Nonetheless she wasn't feeding the gossip gristmill with the sheriff.

"Anyway, long as you stay at the Silver Spur Ranch, I won't be worrying about you. You're as safe on the ranch with Jake Dalton as you'd be with me or one of my deputies."

"Do you know Jake?"

"Met him once when I had to question a guy who was working for him. Good rancher. No nonsense."

"I'm glad you approve of our living arrangements." Not that she was planning to stay at the Silver Spur on a twenty-four-hour basis until Sunday, though it might be wise for Mildred to stay here.

A matter they could discuss in the morning.

"What do your sons have to say about this?" Garcia asked.

"I haven't talked to them about it."

"Don't you think you should?"

"Mildred's ex showed up and wants to talk to her.

That doesn't seem like something I should pull them into. Besides, Durk and his wife are at an energy conference in Saudi Arabia this week. Damien and his family are spending a couple of weeks at the family fishing cabin in Colorado. Which means Tague is left to run the ranch by himself."

"Tague might be busy, but he'd want to know what's going on."

"He'd worry and there's no reason for that."

They wrapped up the conversation quickly and broke the connection. Mildred seemed much calmer now that she'd actually talked to the sheriff and they had a plan. Within minutes, she said good-night and returned to her room.

Carolina stripped out of her clothes and climbed naked beneath the crisp sheets. It had been a long, stressful day. She was bone tired. Still, when she turned off the light and closed her eyes, she saw Jake Dalton. Strong. Virile. Piercing eyes the color of dark chocolate.

A heated shimmer ran through her. She punched her pillow and forced the image from her mind.

Still, sleep was a long time in coming.

GARCIA LEANED BACK in his office chair, kicked out of his worn work boots and propped his aching feet on his desk. He ought to turn over more work to his deputies and quit putting in these ten-hour days.

Hell, a man his age should be retired. Trouble was, puttering around an empty house got boring real quick. And there were just so many old John Wayne movies a man could watch.

It wasn't like the old days, though. Then men like Thad Caffey were few and far between. Now they seemed to multiply like weeds in a pea patch. These days a lawman put his life on the line every time he approached a suspect or stopped a car for speeding.

Never understood how a nice girl like Mildred got mixed up with a thug like Caffey. Lucky for her that Carolina had taken her under her wing. Carolina could never turn down a worthy cause.

Garcia had known Carolina ever since Hugh Lambert married her and brought her back to the Bent Pine Ranch. At the time, she'd been the most beautiful woman Garcia had ever seen. It figured a man like Hugh would get her. Rich, powerful, charismatic and tough. A man's man.

That had been the first time Garcia had seriously lusted for another man's wife. He'd never stopped. But then half the men in the county were at least halfway in love with Carolina. Stunning looks. A heart of gold. An easy smile. There was nothing not to love.

Reaching into his shirt pocket, Garcia pulled out a toothpick, removed it from its cellophane wrapper and stuck it between his teeth. Chewing the strip of wood was a bad habit he'd picked up two years ago at the doctor's orders to replace an even worse habit.

He still missed his cigars. Never more than times like this when a gnawing uneasiness coated the lining of his stomach with acid.

He stared at the wall in front of him, but his mind's eye returned to the courtroom the day Thad Caffey was sentenced. There hadn't been a sign of remorse on his face. Instead his eyes had burned with rage when he stared straight at Carolina Lambert.

Mildred was likely not the only woman in danger from a deranged lunatic. Garcia needed to make one more phone call tonight.

Chapter Eight

The dull gray of predawn sneaked through the slats of the blinds. Jake rolled over and checked the time. Ten after five. His body protested the movement, craving more than the few hours of restless sleep it had been given. He could bury his head in the pillow, but chances were slim he'd fall back asleep even if he stayed in bed.

Resigned, he threw his legs over the side of the bed and walked to the window. The storm had blown over, leaving the land to soak up the water for the long, hot summer to follow. The storm of complications had only just begun.

Last night's conversation with Sheriff Garcia replayed in his mind. The sheriff's call had only verified what Jake had already surmised from his brief encounter with Caffey and what he'd read about the trial.

Thad Caffey was a man given to rage before he went to prison. There was no reliable way to judge what he might be capable of now. The restraining order was the sensible next step, but it might send him over the edge. And if it did, the wife he was trying to win back would not necessarily be his first intended victim.

Jake pulled a pair of worn jeans from his closet and

wiggled into them. The house was quiet and likely would be for another hour or two.

He'd get a head start on things, drive over to ranch headquarters and make some changes to the day's wrangler assignments. Assign a couple of guys to keep an eye on things around the house, though even Garcia had agreed it was extremely doubtful Caffey would show up here.

Cowards who beat up women didn't voluntarily tangle with armed wranglers, especially considering how fast Caffey had backed away yesterday when Jake interrupted his confrontation with the ladies.

Nonetheless, it always paid to be prepared.

But first, Jake needed a shot of caffeine.

He padded down the hallway in his bare feet. He paused at Lizzie's doorway, the familiar ache hitting again. He'd failed her as a father, was clueless as to how to bridge the gap that had grown between them.

Yet Carolina had shown up on the scene and bonded in one afternoon. Not only had she won Lizzie over, but she had the usually wary Edna more excited than he'd seen her in eons.

Far more surprising, she'd aroused him to the point it was embarrassing. Strange and scary powers, the beautiful rancher possessed.

His nostrils captured their first whiff of fresh-brewed coffee at the staircase landing. Evidently Edna was too excited over their famous guest to sleep and had beaten the sun up this morning.

He stopped abruptly at the kitchen door. It wasn't Edna but Carolina who stood in half shadows, facing the window. Her hair was pinned on top of her head, loose tendrils floating down the back of her neck and dancing along the collar of the pale blue robe. In his kitchen at daybreak, sucking up all the oxygen in the room.

He swallowed a curse as physical reactions he didn't understand and couldn't control rocked his body. He struggled to fill his lungs enough that he could make a stab at speaking intelligently.

"You're up early." Not a particularly brilliant opener.

Carolina startled at his voice and spun around to face him.

"Sorry," he muttered. "I didn't mean to frighten you."

"I didn't hear you walk up. Guess I was too lost in my thoughts."

"I trust they weren't all bad."

"They could have been better. Thad Caffey has definitely put a damper on my enthusiasm. I tossed and turned much of the night."

Jake's imagination jumped back into play. Images of her kicking off the sheets, her body stretched out across the bed, flew to his mind. Testosterone shot through his veins, accompanied by a jolt of protective urges.

Those were the urges he needed to heed. There was too much at risk to let his libido call the shots.

"Mind if I join you in a cup of coffee?" he asked.

"Why don't I take mine back to the bedroom and leave your kitchen to you?"

"I'd rather you stay for a few minutes. We need to talk."

The four scariest words in the English language. Her eyes were shadowed with dread at what might come next.

FEELING UNEASY AND INTRUSIVE, Carolina studied Jake as he filled a mug with the hot brew. He might want to talk, but she was pretty sure he hadn't expected to run into her in his kitchen this early in the morning.

His hair was mussed from sleep, one dark lock falling over his forehead. His bare chest revealed swirls of even darker hair that narrowed where they disappeared into the unsnapped waistband of his jeans.

She looked away quickly as a slow burn snaked along her nerve endings. It was hard not to be aware of a man who wore his virility like a second skin, especially in a setting as intimate as this one.

She took a deep breath and pulled the tie tighter on the borrowed robe. Next time she came downstairs this early...

Whoa. What was she thinking? There would be no next time. No matter what Mildred decided, Carolina would move back into the hotel today and stay there for the duration of the training session.

She refilled her cup, walked to the round oak breakfast table and took a seat.

Jake straddled one of the wooden chairs across the table from her. "Are you always an early riser or do you have a lot of last-minute preparations left to take care of?"

"Not too many, but I'll touch base with my guest instructors to make certain they know exactly what to expect and what we need from them."

Small talk, surely not why he'd wanted a conversation.

He sipped his coffee. "What kind of guest instructors do you need for a riding camp? Seems a couple of good wranglers could handle that."

"Actually, my lead volunteers are all excellent horsewomen, and all the ranches we're using have knowledgeable wranglers. It's handling troubled girls, most between thirteen and fourteen, that baffles them."

"That, I can identify with."

The tension began to ease. As long as they kept things simple and businesslike between them, she'd be able to pull this off. It was only when she let thoughts of R.J. take over that the resentment began to simmer. Or when one of those bizarre sensual reactions hit.

"Sounds like you could use an office to work from today," Jake said. "You are welcome to use mine, and if you need any printers, copiers, et cetera, they're available at ranch headquarters."

"I appreciate the offer, but the hotel has a well-equipped business office for guests."

"You never know how many people might be using that."

"True, but I'm sure I can schedule around them." She was starting to see where this was going, but it was hard to believe he actually wanted her here as a houseguest.

"If you're still worried about issues with Thad, you can relax," she said. "Mildred talked to Sheriff Garcia last night. She just has to pick up the restraining order forms, fill them out and fax them to Garcia."

"Actually, we can file them here in Austin. Garcia assured me he'd follow up to see that the process is expedited and that Thad is served the papers ASAP."

"When did you talk to Garcia?"

"Last night. He called after he talked to you and Mildred."

Her emotions flared. "Garcia had no right to involve you in this any more than you already are. I definitely didn't ask him to."

"He's concerned about you and Mildred. Frankly, so

am I. Caffey's dangerous and unpredictable. You can't take chances with a psycho like that."

"He's a monster, but he's not stupid. As soon as he realizes that harassing Mildred will lead to his arrest, he'll back off. He's surely had enough of life behind bars."

"Makes sense, but risky to second-guess a man like Caffey."

Carolina took a sip of coffee, adding caffeine to her rattled nerves. This was growing more complicated by the second.

If they didn't get this training session in this week, they'd be forced to cancel next month's camps in the Austin area. So many needy children would be disappointed, so many opportunities to make a difference in their lives lost.

"If you want to back out of our arrangement, I'll understand. I know this is more than you bargained for."

"And then what would you do at this late date?"

"I could possibly move it to the Bent Pine."

"I thought the whole purpose of having it in the Austin area was so the volunteers didn't have to travel and be away from their own homes for five nights."

"It was, but—"

He put up a hand to halt her words. "No backing out, not after offering to save my daughter from herself for a few weeks this summer. Besides, Sheriff Garcia and I both agree that there's no reason to let Thad Caffey interfere with your plans. We just need a few rules of engagement."

"Such as?"

"From now until the session is over or Thad is behind bars, whichever comes first, you and Mildred won't leave the ranch without me or one of my wranglers with you. On the off chance Thad is foolish enough to show up here, I or the wranglers will be sure that he's entertained appropriately until the law arrives to arrest him."

She shook her head. "I appreciate the offer, but I can't ask you to give up your privacy."

A seductive smile touched the corners of his mouth. "I have a huge house on over two thousand acres of land. I think I can find a bit of privacy if or when I need it."

It was still asking a lot, especially considering their prior relationship. "You don't have to do this."

"Sure I do. What kind of selfish rat would I be to deny kids a month on a ranch? Besides, I'm intrigued with the whole Saddle-Up project. In spite of what you think, I'm not totally heartless."

The perfect segue into his treatment of R.J., but he was saying all the right things, doing the right things. And she needed his ranch. Jumping him at this point would be ludicrous.

"My staying here would be awkward," she said honestly.

"It's six days, Carolina. Not a marriage proposal and we're adults."

"In that case, I accept your offer—until Thad is arrested. But first I have to go back to the hotel, pick up our luggage and check out. Then I need to run a couple of errands in town."

"No problem. While we're out, Mildred can stop off at Judge DeWitt's office, fill out and file the needed papers to get the order of protection started."

"Who is Judge DeWitt?"

"A friend of mine. Garcia is going to call him this morning and fill him in on the situation."

Another decision she'd been left out of. But, after all,

this was Mildred's dilemma, not hers, to micromanage. "I'm sure Mildred will appreciate that."

Jake finished his coffee, carried his mug to the sink and rinsed it.

"Edna will be here about six to cook breakfast and talk your head off. If you want something before that, help yourself to whatever you see that you want. Give me an hour or so heads-up before you're ready to go into Austin. I have to take care of a few things on the ranch first. Edna has my cell phone number."

"It really isn't necessary that anyone go with us to the hotel. Security is excellent there and you have a ranch to run."

"The rules of engagement, remember? And the cows won't miss me."

She watched as he walked away, hating that he seemed so cool with all this when she knew he didn't want her here. Hating that Garcia had enlisted him as their protector.

Hating most of all that she was starting to like the man.

Six more days. Avoiding him was no longer an option. He'd made the decision to force them to engage.

So before she left the Silver Spur on Sunday afternoon, the issue of his treatment toward R.J. would come to a head. The elephant in the room could not be ignored forever.

CAROLINA CLIMBED INTO the backseat as they left Judge DeWitt's office, leaving Mildred to sit in the front with Jake. She had to admit that Jake was good for Mildred, managed to pull her into conversations that didn't center on Thad. He'd even coaxed laughter from her a few times.

In the bright light of day with life in full swing all around her, Thad Caffey felt more like a bump in the asphalt to Carolina than the roadblock he'd seemed last night. There was a good chance they'd all overreacted, a fact that would no doubt please Thad.

"Filing the restraining order was liberating," Mildred said as they pulled back into traffic. "Not that I want Thad to go back to prison. I know it sounds crazy, but I hope he has changed and that he is able to go on with his life as a decent citizen—just not with me."

"Doesn't sound crazy to me," Jake said. "You loved him enough to marry him. He must have had some good qualities."

"I was convinced of it at the time. However, I was seventeen, living on my own after years in foster care, and had never had anyone tell me they loved me."

"Where were your parents?"

"There was never a dad. I mean, there had to be one, but his name wasn't on the birth certificate. Mother was addicted to heroin and crack cocaine. She overdosed when I was six."

"That had to be rough."

"The saddest thing of all is I barely remember her. Foster care was never terrible. My marriage to Thad is the incomparable nightmare chapter of my life."

The nightmare chapter of life.

Unbidden, the words triggered memories that never failed to drag Carolina back to her own darkest days. One phone call from an unfamiliar voice and her world had plunged into darkness.

The private jet carrying Hugh and his friends home from a Dallas Cowboys game had crashed in an isolated area of West Texas. There were no survivors.

She'd forced herself to go on, calling on all the energy she possessed to plow through each day.

And then God dropped a miracle into her life. Her son Damien found a frightened and injured woman named Emma and baby Belle wandering across their ranch in a rare Dallas area snowstorm. Damien had become Emma's hero.

Baby Belle had become Carolina's. Having a baby in the house to love and cuddle had revived her as nothing else could have.

Life had changed a lot since then. Now all three of her sons were happily married and the big house overflowed with love and children. She'd never stopped missing Hugh, but she'd moved on, just as Mildred was doing, though their situations weren't the least bit similar.

The most poignant difference was that Carolina had known true love, the kind no one should ever expect to find more than once in a lifetime.

Fifteen minutes later, Jake pulled up in front of the hotel. He stepped out of the truck and scanned the area, no doubt making certain Thad had not made good on his threat to be waiting for their return.

Carolina half expected to see Thad step out of the midday shadows, but fortunately there was no sign of him.

In minutes they were walking through the hotel and taking the elevator to the two-bedroom suite.

"All clear," Jake said, as they approached the door.

"Don't count on that," Mildred said. "It would be like Thad to be inside, stretched out on the bed watching TV, waiting, just as he said."

Mildred's voice trembled, a reminder to Carolina of how much she feared her ex.

Carolina linked her arm with Mildred's. "The hotel would never give him a key."

"I'll stick my head in first and make sure there are no surprises," Jake assured them. Carolina handed him the key.

Jake entered, walked across the spacious living area and opened the drapes, letting in a golden sweep of sunshine and revealing the breathtaking city view. Once he'd taken a peek into the bedrooms and bathrooms, he came back to the door and ushered them inside.

"Nice digs. No wonder you weren't excited about leaving this place."

"All the comforts of home," she said—a huge exaggeration. As luxurious as the suite was, she was never as at home as she was on the Bent Pine Ranch. But she would have been far more at home here than she was going to be sleeping in Jake's guest room and risking running into him every time she ventured out.

She did a visual sweep of the area. Everything looked exactly as they'd left it. For all they knew, Thad might not even have been in Austin when he sent the text, much less waiting for them at the hotel.

Wife beaters tended to also play fast and loose with the truth. That was just one of the many facts she'd learned about spousal abuse since befriending Mildred.

"It won't take me but a few minutes to pack," Mildred said. "I'd like to get out of here as quickly as possible, just in case Thad is outside and was watching when we arrived." She went into her bedroom and closed the door behind her.

Jake followed Carolina into the other bedroom. "Do you need some help with packing, perhaps take care of the hanging clothes?"

"No. I can handle it."

"Now, why does that not surprise me?"

"You make independence sound like a bad thing."

"It can be, if it's taken too far."

"We're not still talking about packing, are we?" Carolina asked.

"Not necessarily."

"The truth is I'm only taking a few things with me," she said. "Garcia's rules of engagement are only in effect until Thad is arrested or no longer a threat. I expect that to be long before I drive back to Oak Grove on Sunday afternoon."

"Is accepting my hospitality that unpleasant for you?"

She took a deep breath and exhaled slowly. "Can you honestly say you want me at the Silver Spur after the accusation you hurled at me on the phone a week ago?"

Jake stepped closer, in her space, his stare piercing. "We're getting nowhere talking around this. We're both adults. Hit me with your best shot and then hopefully we can move past R.J. and deal with the situation at hand."

Her best shot. Why not? She might not get this chance again. Still, she should play this smart.

But once the words started coming, her emotions took over and all her frustration spilled out.

"What kind of coldhearted, merciless, intolerant, unforgiving man would deprive his dying father of even hearing his voice on the phone?"

Chapter Nine

Jake winced at the bombardment of adjectives. "Don't mince words on my account."

"You said to hit you with my best shot."

"I wasn't expecting it would be from a shotgun."

"I may have gotten a bit carried away," Carolina admitted, "but I'm being honest. I understand why you don't have a lot of love or respect for R.J. He was a failure as a father and a rotten husband. He admits that."

"He couldn't very well deny it."

"No, but people can change."

"By screwing up his adult children's lives—as if he didn't do enough of that while we were kids?"

"He's not screwing up their lives. He's reached out and reunited with every one of his six children but you. They've become a loving and close-knit family. If you weren't too contrary to visit them at the Dry Gulch, you'd see that for yourself."

"I have no desire to be part of R.J.'s attempt at guilt resolution."

"What about Lizzie? Doesn't she deserve the chance to get to know her grandfather?"

"So she can be part of the trap?"

"What trap?" Carolina demanded.

"That bizarre will he concocted."

"I admit the original will was a bit unorthodox, but it's not as bizarre as it seems and certainly not a trap."

Not surprising that she'd back the will, since she'd likely been in on the idea from the beginning. "What do you call it when all you have to do to be included in his will is give up your lifestyle and career and move onto the Dry Gulch Ranch to pay homage to a man who never gave two cents about you when you needed him?"

"A second chance."

"A second chance for R.J. For everyone else it's a train wreck, or it will be when the money runs out and the infighting starts. The Dry Gulch can't possibly support that many families over the long haul. Imagine the bitter resentment when it blows up in their face. Of course R.J. will be long gone by then."

"Think what you want to. You will anyway." Carolina walked over to the closet and began removing clothes from their hangers and placing them on the bed.

The conversation had solved nothing. This whole R.J. thing had become a crusade with her.

She tossed several shirts to the bed. "You have everything wrong. In the beginning, the will might have been overly demanding, but none of that matters now. All the manipulative demands of the will have been eliminated one by one."

"Were the changes your idea, too?"

Her hands flew to her hips. "What did you say?"

"R.J. admitted from the beginning that you were behind the will. I just wondered if you authorized the changes, as well."

She stared at him as if he were speaking Greek. "So that's why you accused me of screwing over the Daltons?

You think I talked R.J. into all that. For the record, R.J. came to me when he was diagnosed with an inoperable brain tumor and said he wanted to leave the Dry Gulch to me to keep it out of the hands of developers. I suggested he leave it to his family. The will itself was all R.J.'s doing."

R.J. had wanted to give her the land and she'd refused. That bit of new information blew the hell out of his theory that she was looking to step up and buy the ranch when the family-ties fiasco fell apart.

Carolina stopped for a quick breath and then seemed to gain steam in her verbal assault. Nothing he didn't deserve.

"You should get your facts straight before you make snap judgments about people or situations, Jake Dalton. The Dry Gulch doesn't have to financially support all the Daltons. Leif is a defense attorney. Travis is a Dallas homicide detective. Cannon is raising rodeo bulls and broncs. Jade lives with her navy SEAL husband, who's stationed in San Diego. Adam is the one who actually manages the ranch and does a great job at it."

"I stand corrected." And feeling extremely guilty.

Not for misjudging R.J. Jake's reasons for resenting his biological father ran a lot deeper than the manipulative will. Reasons he would not indulge to Carolina today or any other day.

But he had been a real jerk where Carolina was concerned.

He met her steely gaze. "I've been way out of line. I jumped to conclusions and made a fool of myself. I'm sorry for crediting any of that will to you."

She looked at him, the anger subsiding as a look of pleading burned in her eyes. "I don't care what you think of me, Jake, but I'm begging you to contact your father, soon, before it's too late. It would mean the world to him and to me."

Jake's insides clenched. It was tearing him apart to look into her eyes and refuse her, but she had no idea what she was asking of him.

"I'll think about it." That was the most he could promise.

"Then I guess I'll have to settle with that for now." She turned away and resumed packing, leaving more behind than she was taking.

A protective urge hit hard and fast. Caffey hadn't been waiting today. That didn't make him any less a threat in Jake's mind. "I know I don't really have a say in the matter, but I'd really like it if you'd just take everything and spend the rest of the week at the Silver Spur."

"Why?"

To keep her safe. To keep her close. He wasn't sure exactly which need was stronger at this moment. "Because if you leave the Silver Spur, I'll be forced to move into the hotel to watch your back, and I truly hate city life and hotels."

"For once we agree on something."

NINETY MINUTES AND a full stomach later, Carolina was still second-guessing her decision to check out of the hotel. If Caffey was arrested, there would be no logical reason for her to infringe on Jake's hospitality.

When she lost her cool and unloaded her frustration and anger on him back at the hotel, she'd half expected him to immediately renege on his offer of the Silver Spur Ranch. Instead his protective edge had taken over.

He'd even apologized for assuming she'd had something to do with R.J.'s will. She didn't fully understand why he was so angered by the will, though the terms had pretty much excluded him.

He had the Silver Spur to run. There was no way he'd have left his ranch to help manage the Dry Gulch. Then again he didn't need the money or the land, so why let the will keep him from doing the right thing by R.J.?

His resentment had to be triggered by something more. At least a promise to think about connecting with R.J. had come out of the confrontation. That was an improvement over where they were before the heated discussion this morning.

At any rate, Jake didn't appear to be harboring a grudge against her. If anything, he seemed more relaxed since they'd brought everything into the open. And it definitely hadn't had a negative effect on his appetite.

The first stop after leaving the hotel had been a neighborhood Italian trattoria with checkered tablecloths, mismatched chairs and mouthwatering odors. Mama Giada, the plump matron of the Italian family, had greeted Jake with laughter and a warm hug. He was obviously a much-liked regular in the restaurant.

They weren't offered a menu. Instead Mama Giada and her staff served them family-style, the round table laden with overflowing platters of antipasto, lasagna, and spaghetti and meatballs—all apparently Jake's favorites. And then Mama Giada had insisted they stay for dessert—huge servings of creamy tiramisu and steaming cups of cappuccino.

Jake was the only one who'd done the food justice. Like her sons, he had that ravenous rancher's appetite. Not that you'd guess that by looking at Jake's hard, lean body and six-pack abs.

"That will keep me fueled for a few hours," Jake said as they left the restaurant. "What's on the agenda for the rest of the afternoon?"

"For starters, we need to stop somewhere and stock up on bottled water, soft drinks, instant tea and lots of ice. Beverages will be in high demand in this heat and humidity."

"Snacks and fruit, too," Mildred added.

"Before we buy all that, we need to give Edna a call. I suspect she's had the oven full of cookies all day and probably already called Gus's market and ordered bottled drinks and lots of extra ice."

"Surely not," Carolina lamented. "I already feel terrible that she's having to deal with unexpected houseguests."

"I told her you could handle it, but I can't guarantee she listened. In case you haven't picked up on it already, Edna works for me in name only. In actuality, she runs the house and orders everyone around—except Mother. Mother is the queen, thankfully a benevolent one who adores her granddaughter and tolerates me."

His mother, Mary, R.J.'s first wife, though she was the one wife Carolina had never heard R.J. mention. Not that he ever talked much about any of his ex-wives. The only woman whose memory still seemed to haunt him was someone he called Gwen.

They weren't even sure Gwen was real, since R.J. asked for her or talked to her only when he fell into one of his confused states.

But it would be interesting to meet R.J.'s first wife. Getting to know her might explain Jake's treatment of R.J. The queen might even be the tipping mechanism that could change Jake's mind about contacting R.J.

"I can't wait to get to meet your mother," Carolina said.

"You'll get your chance tomorrow."

"I thought she wasn't coming home until the weekend."

"Change of plans. New York is also hot and muggy, so they decided they might as well head back to Texas— after they see *The Phantom of the Opera* tonight."

"Good for them. She'll love it."

"She knows. This will make about her tenth time to see it."

"Sounds like a woman who knows what she likes. But a ranch full of women and two unexpected houseguests. That might upset a Texas queen."

"Not this queen. She rolls with the punches, occasionally delivering a few of her own."

"Then I'll definitely stay out of her way."

Jake pulled into traffic before he made the call on the car's speaker system. As soon as he made the connection, Edna burst into her own agenda.

"I've made blackberry cobbler for dinner tonight. I hope you two ladies like cobbler. I picked the berries myself."

"Love it," Mildred said.

"I love all kinds of cobblers, but blackberry is my favorite," Carolina said truthfully. "But I hope you didn't go to all that trouble for us."

"Wasn't a bit of trouble. Made so many cobblers in my life I could do it in my sleep and still have the crust come out a golden brown."

"And delicious, I'm sure."

"Don't get many complaints around the Silver Spur," Edna admitted.

"Is that all you baked?" Jake asked.

"No use to heat up the oven for just one cobbler. I baked a few dozen chocolate chip cookies and some blueberry muffins. I figured the volunteers will need some nibbles. That store-bought stuff is hardly fit to eat."

"I'm sure we'll love anything you make, but you're going to spoil us and wear yourself out. Keep this up and Jake won't ever let us come back to the ranch after the training session is over."

Not that she ever expected to.

"I'm through with the baking for today, and I'm not a bit tuckered out," Edna continued. "Oh, and before I forget, I ordered a few cases of bottled water and soft drinks from Gus's market. He's gonna have his grandson deliver them in the morning, already iced down and ready to quench the thirst."

"You keep this up and Carolina's going to fire me as the training leader and hire you," Mildred said.

"Not a chance. But I like helping when I can. Doing for others is good for the soul."

"I agree," Carolina said. "But now you've done more than enough."

"What will you do about lunches for the volunteers?" Edna asked.

"The food is all ordered from a caterer in Austin—simple lunches that we can eat picnic-style on the ranch. One of the volunteers will be picking that up on her way here every morning. Really, the food situation is under control."

"I didn't mean to go steppin' on your toes," Edna said. "If I do, you just tell me. I can call Gus back and cancel that order if you want me to."

"Absolutely not. You just saved us an hour of shopping. I can't thank you enough, but please don't do more. I hate putting you out like this."

"Don't you go fretting a minute about that, Mrs. Lambert. I'm tickled pink to be busy. Nothing I like better than cooking for a full table of hungry folks."

And after the lunch they'd just eaten, Carolina might not be hungry again until this time tomorrow.

They finished the conversation, and Carolina went back to her to-do list. "I think we can bypass grocery shopping."

"So, where do we go from here?" Jake asked.

"Sheplers, to pick up one hundred and fifty white straw Western hats."

"Now you're talking," Jake said. "Can't be a cowgirl without the appropriate hat and boots."

"Unfortunately, the budget didn't stretch to boots," Mildred said. "But we did get jeans, shorts, T-shirts, undies and socks, and one authentic Western shirt for each girl in the program."

"I'm impressed."

"It's as much necessary as generous," Carolina admitted. "Many of the girls don't have appropriate clothing. Having them all dress similarly avoids hurt feelings and worries about fitting in. And it keeps the counselors from having to outlaw some of the more revealing shorts and tops the girls show up in."

"Like the ones my daughter wears," Jake said.

"Sometimes far worse, believe me," Carolina said.

"Hard to imagine." Jake took the freeway ramp. "Still seems like the girls need cowboy boots, especially if they try kicking a cow chip on a hot day."

"That's a gross thought. Actually, we usually do have

to buy a few pairs of shoes for the girls who show up with nothing but flip-flops."

"And everything is bought with donations?"

"Yes, and most of that donated by Carolina," Mildred said. "And that's only a smidgen of all the contributions the Lamberts make to worthy causes around the state and the globe."

"So I've heard." He flicked on the lane change signal. "Is it too late for another donation, one that would cover the cost of a hundred and fifty pairs of cowboy boots?"

"It's never too late to accept boots if you're buying."

"I'm buying. Never count a coldhearted, ruthless man out."

Now he was mocking her, but she could handle that. "I'm not sure we can find that many boots in the right sizes on such short notice."

"Are you kidding? It's Texas. And I can be very persuasive when I need to be."

"I've noticed."

"How will you fit all the girls?" Mildred asked. "Western hats only come in a few sizes and we get a variety that usually works. But shoes have to be a good fit."

"If I'm buying one hundred and fifty pairs of boots, the company can send someone out to fit them."

"All the girls attend orientation at Sara and Jess's ranch a week from next Monday," Carolina said. "That would be a good time to fit them into the boots. After that, they'll be scattered to ten different ranches for the duration of the month."

"We'll work it out one way or another," Jake said. "I don't want it said I let cowgirls go without boots."

He was doing it again, screwing with all Carolina's preconceptions about him. He was both protective and generous, a caring father and close to his mother—all traits she admired.

It must have been something more than a will that turned him against his father. Whatever it was, it was time to let it go—for his sake and R.J.'s.

True to his word, once they arrived at the Western shop, Jake made all the arrangements to purchase the boots, though some would have to be shipped directly from the supplier to Sara's ranch. Salesmen would show up the day of the fitting to make sure every girl got boots.

Apparently Jake had a great deal of clout with the shop and no shortage of attention from the female clerks. Widowed, wealthy, gorgeous and not totally heartless— it was amazing he'd managed to stay single for so long.

Carolina perused the shop while Jake helped load the boxes of hats into his pickup truck. When he rejoined them inside, his cell phone was stuck to his ear and he did not look happy.

Dread knotted in her stomach. Her first impression was that this must be Thad again.

Chapter Ten

As soon as Jake had broken the connection with Sheriff Garcia, Carolina was at his elbow asking if anything was wrong. He wouldn't lie to her, but he managed to put her off until they were in the truck and headed back to the ranch. Unfortunately that reprieve only lasted until he'd started the engine and backed out of his parking space.

"So, what is it you didn't want to talk about in the shop?"

"The call was from Garcia. Nothing terrible, so don't go jumping to conclusions."

Carolina groaned. "What is Thad up to now?"

"No one's exactly sure. That's the problem."

"Has he been served with the restraining order?" Mildred asked.

"Not yet. Have to find him first."

"I gave them his address."

"He wasn't there. They ran into a problem locating him."

"Then he must still be in Austin," Carolina said, "still hoping to lure Mildred into meeting him."

"At this point he could be anywhere," Jake said. "What made you think he was living at his hunting camp?"

"I just assumed it," Mildred admitted. "It's the only

property he owns. It's where he went when he claimed he needed alone time, so it would have been natural for him to go there long enough to get his act together."

"According to Garcia, it doesn't appear that he is living in the camp now or that anyone else has stayed there in a very long time."

Carolina leaned forward, a hand on the back of Jake's seat. "How did he reach that conclusion?"

"No clothes in the closet or the drawers. No food in the house. No electricity. Spider webs across the doors. Several scorpions crawling along the uneven floorboards."

"Spiders and scorpions. Throw in some rats and Jake should have felt right at home," Carolina said.

"How did they get in the cabin if Thad wasn't there?" Mildred asked.

"They didn't have to break in. Half of the windows were broken or missing and the back door was ajar. Basically it's a deserted camp house. Do you know of a friend Caffey might be staying with?"

"No. He didn't really have friends. He got along with people at the feed store where he worked the stockroom, but he didn't see them after work. He was always a loner. The defense couldn't find even one person to attest under oath to his good character."

"Well, he has to live somewhere unless he's sleeping in his car," Jake said. "Or does he even have a car?"

"He was driving the same old truck he had before he was convicted when we were accosted by him at the parking lot. I'm guessing someone kept that for him while he was in prison."

"So they found nothing at the camp to indicate Thad had been there?" Carolina said, more statement than question.

"It's doubtful he's been living inside the camp, but it is possible that he's been living in his truck on the property—maybe even likely."

"Why do you think that?" Carolina asked.

"Garcia and his deputy found dozens of empty beer cans and cigarette butts near the camp house. It was clear they hadn't been there long. There were also empty shell casings scattered around the dirt area behind the house as if someone had used the area within the last few days for target practice."

"How would Jake get a gun?" Carolina broke in. "He's committed a felony. I'm certain no one around Oak Grove would have sold it to him, and the authorities definitely didn't let him keep his hunting guns after he was found guilty."

"An Oak Grove resident had his house broken into four days ago. Nothing was taken but some cash, an electronic tablet and two guns—a rifle and an automatic pistol. That syncs with the recently fired shells they found on the property, though there's no forensics available on that."

"Burglary and the illegal possession of guns," Carolina said. "That's enough to arrest Thad right now without waiting for him to break the rules of a restraining order."

"*Suspected* burglary and possession of firearms," Jake reminded her. "That's only a theory at this point. There's no concrete evidence as yet to back that up."

"And that doesn't change the fact that they can't arrest him if they can't find him." Angst reduced Mildred's words to a shaky whisper. "It's not hunting season. If Thad stole guns, he plans to use them either to force me to get back together with him or to pay me back for the testimony that sent him to prison."

Jake had to agree with her logic. But why steal guns

to shoot Mildred when he'd always resorted to using his fists against her before?

"That settles it," Mildred said. "My continuing problems with Thad will be a distraction for the Silver Spur and the training program. It's time for me to go home."

"You can't just go home without a bodyguard at this point," Carolina said. "Maybe we should cancel the training program."

Jake's chest tightened, his muscles bunching beneath his shirt. Carolina belonged to one of the wealthiest families in Texas. All the protection money could buy was hers for the asking. He should be glad for her to take all these problems off his hands.

But he could hear the anxiety in her voice. She clearly hated disappointing those kids, but she was torn between that and putting anyone in danger.

Only he had worries of his own where her safety was concerned.

"If protection is the only issue, I can't imagine you'll find any place safer than the Silver Spur," Jake said. "Caffey is a stinking coward who beats up women. He's not going to come charging onto the ranch with as many wranglers as we have to take him on. If he does, we have him."

"Having your wranglers doing duty as bodyguards hardly seems fair to you," Carolina said. "What will your mother think of this?"

"You can ask her yourself tomorrow, but I guarantee she'll tell you not to dare let a man like Thad Caffey shut down your program."

"It's not that I'm afraid," Carolina argued. "I was giving you an out."

"I'm not looking for one."

"Are you sure?"

"Wouldn't say so if I didn't mean it."

"In that case, there really is no reason for Mildred to leave or for us to cancel."

Relief relaxed Jake's strained muscles. He had no doubt that he could keep both Mildred and Carolina safe—as long as they were here on the Silver Spur.

But he couldn't make them stay forever. Five more days and Carolina would be gone.

Off his ranch. Out of his life. Exactly what he'd wanted yesterday morning.

So why was the prospect of her leaving sounding so damned upsetting now?

LIZZIE TURNED UP her radio and began twirling around the room to the beat of the latest Taylor Swift tune. The summer she'd already given up on as being a monotonous drag was looking up.

Carolina Lambert had surprised her at dinner tonight by actually inviting her to work not only with the women this week but as a junior counselor for the whole month of July. Even more surprising, her father had agreed to let her do it.

It might not be the most exciting summer she could have had, but it beat hanging around here all day. Her three best friends were either traveling or working. And her dad would ground her forever if he found out she'd sneaked out to see Calvin.

Her phone rang. Calvin—again. She started to ignore it, but if she did, he'd only keep calling until she answered.

"Hello," she said, already wary, knowing what he wanted.

"Hi, baby. Where are you?"

"In my room."

"By yourself?"

"Yeah. Just hanging out and watching MTV."

"You'd be having more fun hanging out with me."

"Until Dad killed me."

"Tell him you're going to Angie's."

"I can't keep lying to him."

"You won't have to. I might be gone from this boring town soon. That's why I gotta see you, baby."

"Are you in trouble again?"

"Same old stuff. The sheriff still thinks I had something to do with breaking into Bilson's Liquor Store last weekend."

"Did you?"

"No. I told you that already. But Mom is on the warpath and threatening to send me to live with my dad and his new wife up in Oklahoma."

"For the summer?"

"For good." He spit out a stream of foul language that made her cringe. "Don't worry, baby. I've got a plan. I'm not staying with that tyrant and his bitch. And I'm not going anywhere without you."

The comment made her uneasy. She definitely wasn't running off with him. "What kind of plan?"

"Meet me tonight and I'll tell you all about it."

"I can't. We have houseguests. My dad expects me to help entertain them," she lied.

She hated lying to anyone, especially Calvin or her dad, but she seemed to be doing it more and more lately. She'd love to tell Calvin her news, but it would seem kind of heartless with his life in such a mess.

"Are you coming to meet me?" he urged.

"I said I can't."

"So you're just going to let your dad run your life?" he challenged.

She let the question go unanswered. At sixteen she didn't have a lot of choice. If Calvin had listened to his mother she wouldn't be sending him away. Pointing that out would only make him mad at her.

"I'll be waiting for you at our secret spot just north of your gate," he said. "Make it happen. You know you want to, Lizzie." He broke the connection without bothering to say goodbye.

Typical Calvin. Everything was about him. He'd be furious if she didn't show. Dating the school bad boy had been exciting at first, but when things didn't go his way, he could be downright scary.

She felt shaky inside as she tossed the phone to the bed. She walked over to her dresser, picked up her lip gloss and took a good look at herself in the mirror.

It was a wonder Calvin had ever asked her out in the first place when he could have dated almost any girl in the school. She wasn't beautiful, not the way her mother had been.

Lizzie's long reddish-brown hair curled at the ends, whereas her mother's had hung straight to her narrow shoulders. Lizzie's nose was sprinkled with freckles and there was always a pimple waiting to pop up on her face.

Her mother's skin had been flawless. The picture of the two of them Lizzie kept on top of her chest was a constant reminder of her mother's beauty. It was the other memories that were slowly slipping away. The memories that had held her together in the horrifying days and months after her death.

Poignant images of her mother holding tight to her hand the first day of kindergarten. Echoes of her mother's laughter as they baked cookies on cool Saturday afternoons or rode their bikes to the park. Warm, fuzzy memories of her mother sliding into bed beside her and cuddling when she'd wake up screaming from a nightmare.

Sleep well and sweet dreams, princess. Love you.

Those were the last words Lizzie would hear before her mother turned off the light each night.

They were the last words she ever heard her mother utter.

An old familiar ache settled inside her, not so much for the mother she could barely remember, but for the mother who wasn't here now.

The lip gloss fell from her fingers and rolled onto the floor. Not everything was about Calvin. Lizzie had needs, too. If her mother were here, she'd understand.

The mother who only existed in a picture frame on Lizzie's dresser.

BY ALL RIGHTS, Jake should be miserable this morning. He wasn't. In fact he was feeling a lot like his old self—confident, energetic and ready to tackle the world, including Thad Caffey.

There was no easy explanation for it, at least not one he was ready to examine closely. But Lizzie definitely had something to do with it.

She'd shown up for breakfast this morning in a good mood and actually engaged in table conversation. Well, primarily she'd talked to Carolina, but still, she'd been pleasant and involved. He didn't understand the rapidly developing bond between them, but he wasn't knocking it.

Right after breakfast, Jake had called a conference

with all the wranglers. They'd met at headquarters for coffee and some of Edna's homemade muffins. She'd made enough he could have shared with the entire neighborhood and still have more than enough left for Carolina's gang.

He'd presented the basics, and his workers had reacted as expected—exuberant and loud. Dealing with a wife beater on their turf was obviously a lot more exciting than the routine ranch work they were used to.

Jake couldn't locate any pictures of Caffey on the internet that resembled the man they'd run into at the capitol, so he was forced to rely on an oral description. Not perfect, but close enough they'd recognize him if they caught him sneaking around the spread. Not that they wouldn't have checked out any man who showed up where he had no business.

Jake had full control of gate security today. The automatic monitor would send the entrance request directly to his cell phone. If the system was tampered with in any way, he'd also get a signal. The gate wouldn't open without his knowing it.

The strings of barbwire fences were another story. They did a great job of keeping in the cows, but needless to say the wire could be cut or crashed through without too much trouble.

Not a problem in this situation. If the yellow-bellied coward was crazy enough to trespass, he'd never get anywhere near the Saddle-Up team or the house before he was noticed and apprehended.

Protection was taken care of. Unfortunately, Jake's unexpected attraction to Carolina was giving him more problems than ever. When they accidentally brushed shoulders in the kitchen that morning, he'd felt another hit to his libido. He couldn't just avoid her, so he had to find some way to put this in perspective.

Jake was almost back to the horse barn now. He'd get one of the wranglers to take care of Riley and then put the stallion out to pasture until afternoon.

He tugged on the reins and circled around a cluster of scrawny mesquite trees until he had a good view of Carolina's meeting spot. He had offered the air-conditioned conference room at headquarters for their kickoff that morning, but Carolina had decided that a pine-strewn, shady spot near the horse barns would be more in keeping with the atmosphere of the camps they'd be conducting in the heat of summer.

She was definitely not the wealthy, pampered socialite he'd thought her before he got to know her.

The thirty women had brought and set up their own chairs like soccer moms ready for a big game. Carolina was standing in front of the group behind a metal folding table Tilson had brought down from headquarters.

Jake's cell phone rang—the automated gate security system letting him know someone was requesting entrance. He changed it to the security-camera view and the image of a middle-aged guy with a receding hairline, a sprinkling of dusky-colored facial hair and a pair of wire-rimmed glasses.

Definitely not Caffey.

"Good morning. Welcome to the Silver Spur. How can I help you?"

"I'm Dr. James Otis. I'm supposed to meet Carolina Lambert here this morning. Actually I'm running a bit late. Drove right by the turnoff to this place and had to double back. I do believe this is officially rural living."

"Yep. Home, home on the range, a half mile from the end of nowhere."

Jake recognized the name from the list Carolina had provided him. Otis was an Austin psychiatrist who specialized in helping parents cope with unruly teens. His teen boot camps had gained national attention.

"When the gate opens, just follow the main blacktop road back to the big house. I'll meet you there and walk you out to where Carolina's group is meeting. It's only a short walk."

"I'd appreciate that, unless it's the walk that leads anywhere near those giant Texas longhorns I saw on the way here. Oh, and no snakes, either, especially the ones who carry their own rattle. I find them to be extremely antisocial."

"You drive a hard bargain, but I'll try to accommodate you."

And then he'd go back to dealing with his livestock. He didn't need a shrink messing with his mind. He had a good mood going. No reason to risk losing that.

CAROLINA WELCOMED DR. OTIS and then turned him over to Mildred for introduction to the group. When she stood back and looked around, Jake was already walking away.

She ran to catch up with him.

"If you have some time, you should stay and listen to the doctor's talk. You might get some insight into the communication problems you're having with Lizzie."

"Communication problems? Is that what you call it when your daughter rolls her eyes at everything you say?"

"I've never had a daughter, so I won't begin to pretend I know what you're dealing with. But I've heard Dr. Otis speak before. I think you'd get something out of his talk."

Jake looked back toward the group. "One man in a group of women. I'd feel like the lone rooster at a hen party."

"You're not worried about damaging your manhood, are you?" she teased.

"Nope. Worried about the teasing from a group of macho cowboys. Tell you what, why don't you listen and then we'll go horseback riding when you finish up with your meetings today and you can share what you think I need to hear?"

"It doesn't work that way."

"It could. But don't worry about it. I know you're busy. I'll get out of here and let you get back to work."

She should let it go at that, but the truth was she wanted to go riding with Jake. She couldn't come up with a reason for it, but she knew she wanted to spend time with him. Away from Mildred. Away from constant talk of Thad Caffey, which had basically been the center of almost every conversation up until now.

"I'd like to go riding with you, but we don't finish until after four. What time are you expecting your mother?"

"Not before six thirty, but that's okay. It was just a thought."

"Are you reneging on your invitation?"

"No," he said. "Just giving you an easy way out."

"In that case I'll meet you at the horse barn a few minutes after four."

He tipped his hat and smiled. "See you then."

Her pulse raced. It must be from too much sun.

CAROLINA CHOSE A packaged chicken and an avocado/spinach/goat cheese wrap from one of the caterer's baskets and a soft drink from a large cooler. A few of the women took their food back to their chairs. Most wandered over to one of the wooden picnic tables a few of the wranglers had set up while they were role-playing problem situations with Dr. Otis. Carolina had no idea where they'd obtained the tables on such short notice.

Carolina took her sandwich and walked to a huge tree stump near the fenced corral where a half dozen magnificent horses were grazing contentedly. All in all it had been a successful but busy morning, leaving her little time to fret about Thad Caffey or contemplate her promised afternoon ride with Jake.

He'd certainly been quick enough to back off when he thought she wasn't interested. Only she'd wanted to accept and her motivation hadn't just been her love for riding. She liked him. There was no denying it any more than she could deny that he got to her on some inexplicable sensual level.

It was the first time she'd experienced anything like that since Hugh's death.

She wasn't ready for that. She might never be, but definitely not yet. Nor had Jake given any indication that he was interested in her as a woman.

"Mind if I join you?"

Carolina looked up at Lizzie's voice. She'd been so lost in her own thoughts she hadn't realized Lizzie was there.

"Of course I don't mind. I'd love to hear what you thought of Dr. Otis and the morning's activities. Unfortunately you can't just pull up a stump, but we can move to a table."

"I'd rather stay here where it's private. I don't mind standing, since the grass is too wet to sit on."

"Then by all means, let's chat. What is it you want to talk about?"

"Dr. Otis. He's really smart. I don't know how he knows so much about teenage girls, but I could relate to a lot of what he said."

"Good. Anything in particular?"

"That stuff about boyfriends, how you get all these mixed emotions when you're with them."

"The war between your hormones and your judgment?"

"Yeah. I guess that's it. At first guys like you the way you are, but then they want to own you."

"That works both ways. Sometimes it's the girls who want to control the guys. Either way you have to figure out who you are and what's important to you."

"I suppose. I'm not sure I know who I am or what I'm feeling."

"No one fully does at sixteen." Sometimes not at fifty-five, not even when you'd thought you had it all together.

"Sometimes I wish no guys liked me, so I didn't have to even think about dating," Lizzie said.

"Have you tried talking to your dad about your emotions? Sometimes parents are more in tune than you think."

"Maybe a cool parent like you, but not my dad. He thinks I'm a kid and not a very smart one at that. Everything I do is wrong."

"It may seem that way to you at times, but I'm sure he loves you very much. He just worries about you."

"It doesn't feel that way. Sometimes I think he hates me."

"He may have trouble relating to you, but I'm sure he doesn't hate you. Why would he?"

"I was only nine years old when I caused my mother's and grandfather's deaths. Not literally, but Mom,

Grandpa and Grams were on the way to see my dance recital when a drunk driver in an SUV swerved into our lane and crushed them against a bridge railing."

Carolina stood and put an arm around Lizzie's shoulders. "Oh, sweetheart, what a terrible thing for you to go through. I know it was traumatic for you, but it certainly wasn't your fault. I'm sure your father doesn't blame you for that, and you must never blame yourself."

"All I know is our life changed after that. Dad practically became a zombie. Sometimes we'd be sitting in the living room, not talking or anything, but when he looked at me I'd see tears in his eyes."

"I'm sure your father was heartbroken. I know I was when my husband died. Grief can rob all your happiness for a while, sometimes for a very long time. But that doesn't mean he blamed you, not even subconsciously. You have to talk to him about this."

"I was thinking that maybe I could talk to Dr. Otis, you know, as a patient."

"I think that would be an excellent idea."

"Would you talk to Dad about it for me? I'm afraid he'll just start badgering me with questions about what's wrong and things will only get worse."

"I'll talk to him."

"Thanks."

Lizzie was dealing with far more than Carolina had realized. Counseling could be beneficial, but Lizzie might not be the only one who needed it. The problems she had with her father had been brewing for a long time.

Her conversation with Lizzie had accomplished at least one thing. She knew what she and Jake would be talking about that afternoon.

Chapter Eleven

The early-afternoon sun was searing into Thad's back, burning right through the thin cotton of his T-shirt. He took a shortcut through a maze of tombstones, wilted flower arrangements and cheap plastic remembrances.

He had come here often at first, when the pain had still bled into the thrill of the kill. This was the first time he'd been here in years. He wasn't exactly sure where the poorly marked grave was now.

But he'd find it, the same way he'd found the information he needed last night when he searched through the confusing maze of the internet.

The rancher's name was Jake Dalton. He lived with his mother and his teenage daughter. That information had been easy to discover after Thad had followed Jake, Mildred and Carolina to the Silver Spur Ranch.

Actually, he'd followed them from the time they'd left the hotel. Mildred had ridden in the front seat beside the rancher as they drove around Austin in his fancy black truck. They'd lingered for over an hour at an Italian restaurant and then gone shopping as if she'd never given another thought to responding to his text.

There would be no more texts. He'd dropped that phone from an overpass into the Colorado River. Even if his lying, cheating ex-wife wanted to get in touch with him, it was too late now.

Mildred had squandered her chance to do this peacefully, but that didn't mean she wouldn't have to pay for her sins. And once they were across the border, there would be no interfering bitch like Carolina Lambert for her to run to, crying for help.

There would be no Carolina Lambert anywhere—at least not alive. He could almost taste the sweetness of his revenge. For four years, he'd planned how he'd kill her. Each step of her murder was indelibly etched in his mind as if it had happened a hundred times before.

She thought she was on top of the world. He would drag her into a bottomless pit of shame and degradation. Her body would be ravaged, her dignity trampled. And then finally, when she was too destroyed to even beg for mercy, he'd put his hands around her neck and squeeze until her face turned blue and her body went limp.

He closed his eyes and let the ecstasy flow through him.

The ringing of his new, untraceable cell phone shattered the moment. There was no caller ID, but he didn't have to wonder who was calling.

The only man who had this number was his former prison mate Mateo Salinas. Adrenaline shot through Thad's veins as if it had been injected with a giant needle.

"What's up?"

"Your first job for the man."

He hadn't expected this to come so soon. "What kind of job?"

"There's a female border-control agent in Brownsville who needs to be taught a lesson and made into an example."

"You want me to kill her?"

"No. Want her alive so she can tell people who was responsible for the beating. Just beat the bitch up real good, whatever kind of torture turns you on. I know that's your style. But make sure she knows it's not a random act but what happens when you mess with the cartel."

"This bitch got a name?"

"Melissa Green. She lives alone, but there's a guy who hangs out at her house a lot. He drives a red, souped-up '92 Mustang convertible. Make sure his car isn't there when you make your move. And be aware, she has a weapon and won't hesitate to use it if you give her the chance."

A gun changed the odds. "I could get shot."

"You want a job or not?"

He didn't have a lot of choice. It would be way too risky for him to stay in the country once he'd whacked Carolina. "I want the job—as long as you keep your word to get me across the border safely."

"I told you. The boss takes care of the ones who take care of him. Get the job done. Then contact me immediately. We'll have only a few hours to sneak you over the border before every law enforcement officer in Texas is on your tail."

"All I have to do is rough her up?"

"Put the hurt on her big-time. Mess this job up and I never heard of you. I don't protect men I never heard of. Get the picture?"

"Got it. There won't be any screwups on my end, but like I told you back in the clinker, there will be two of us crossing the border."

"Fine. Bring your own poison. I don't give a damn

who you share your bed with, but there will be plenty of senoritas when you're craving fun."

"I may need a few more days."

"No problem." Mateo laughed as if they'd shared a hilarious joke. "Take all the time you need, long as the job's done by midnight Sunday. Maybe sooner if the boss says so. Whatever the boss says goes."

Thad's hands knotted into fists, anticipation running hot inside him as the pressure swelled in his brain.

Killing Carolina was now on countdown.

But first he had to tell someone goodbye.

Chapter Twelve

Carolina dismounted when Jake did, without waiting for his help. Touching his hand to the butt of his holstered pistol, he scanned the area before leading the horses to drink from a spring-fed creek.

It was next to impossible that Caffey would show up out here. But if trouble of any kind came calling, Jake was ready for it.

He turned his attention back to Carolina, who was already making the rocky climb to the nearby ledge. Even with unsteady footing, she was graceful.

Not surprisingly, she had demonstrated that same skill in the saddle. Self-assured, confident, trusting the horse he'd picked for her, she'd kept up with him easily as he'd taken Riley from a trot to a full gallop.

When they reached the open range, she'd urged her horse faster, looking back only once to make sure Jake was following.

He'd taken advantage of the view. Her hair had caught the wind, dancing behind her, trapping rays of sunshine and casting them off like ribbons of gold. Her back straight, her head high, her long legs hugging the saddle, she'd looked positively regal.

Leading the horses back to the shade, Jake tethered

them to the low-hanging branch of a sycamore tree and hurried to catch up with Carolina.

"First time to ride?" he teased.

"First time today." She smiled and did a 360-degree turn, slow enough to soak in the scenery. "It's beautiful here."

"Not the best view on the ranch, but it's close."

"The Bent Pine is beautiful, too, but in a different way. More pines. Not totally flat terrain, but it doesn't rival this."

"Every part of Texas has its own charm," he said, "but the Hill Country is my favorite. The Big Bend area runs a close second, though."

Carolina nodded her agreement. "We used to camp out there when my sons were much younger. To my mind some of the best hiking trails in the world."

The path grew steeper, the rocks beneath their feet less stable. Jake reached for her hand to help steady her. She took it, her fingers curling around his. A perfect fit.

The crazy dizzying attraction hit again. Nothing he could adequately describe but somewhere between watching the birth of a new foal and getting kicked in the gut by a bull.

He struggled to ignore it. He hadn't asked her to go riding to seduce her.

Or had he? Was his libido ruling his subconscious?

"You must love the Silver Spur," Carolina said.

"Always have," he admitted, "since the day Mom married for the second time. I was on top of the world the day we moved into the big house. I got not only a dad I loved but a ranch to live on."

"My husband used to say that ranching wasn't an

occupation, that it was a calling and that the love of it seeped into your blood."

"I get the feeling you think the same. A good thing I guess since you own one of the largest and most productive ranches in the state."

"I do love the Bent Pine, but I don't actually own it. My link to the land is strictly bound by heartstrings."

That surprised him. "Is that how your late husband framed the will?"

"No, but everything would have eventually gone to my three sons, so I made the decision a few years back to give them full legal possession of Lambert, Incorporated, which includes the ranch, the oil company and its subsidiaries."

"Sounds a little risky to me. You must have a lot of faith in them not to fear they'd lose it all through bad business decisions or perhaps even sell it."

"They won't do, either. They're honest, hardworking and savvy. And they love the ranch as much as I do or more."

And ownership apparently meant little to her. Which made his first assumptions about her encouraging a will that would lead to her eventual acquisition of the Dry Gulch Ranch even more ludicrous.

The last few yards to the top of the ledge were the steepest of all, the trail narrowing so that they were forced to go single file. Even so, she didn't let go of his hand until they reached the top.

"Wow! What a view," she said.

"Worth the climb?"

"Absolutely."

The top of the ledge was fairly flat before falling off

again on the other side. Jake took a seat on a large rock with smooth edges.

Carolina found a rock of her own. "Did you invite me riding today to show me this?"

"Not entirely."

"So why did you invite me?"

A weak moment. A need to find out if she was genuine. An attempt to find something about her he didn't like. All were at least partially true but nothing he was willing to share with her.

"With all that's been going on over the past three days, I thought we should at least have a chance to talk one-on-one," Jake said. "I also figured you could use a break. Nothing like a good ride to soothe the mind and soul."

"It worked, to a point," she admitted. "I wouldn't say I'm completely soothed, but I'm glad we're having this chance to talk."

"So what advice do you have for me from Dr. Otis?"

"Nothing from Dr. Otis, but I would like to talk about Lizzie."

"What about her?"

"I had lunch with her today. I was sitting by myself and she walked over to join me."

"Did she tell you I'm an overbearing ogre who's cramping her lifestyle?"

"No, it's a bit more serious than that."

His mind went off on a tangent. Serious like being dragged into trouble by that hoodlum he'd forbidden her to see? Taking drugs? Pregnant. He reined in his fears. This was his Lizzie they were talking about.

He gulped in a lungful of air. "How serious?"

"She's dealing with a lot of emotional issues, Jake. She

was impressed with Dr. Otis today and thinks he could help her deal with them."

Jake found that difficult to believe. "Lizzie is volunteering to see a shrink?"

"Yes. She asked me to talk to you about the possibility of private counseling."

His spirits plummeted. So this was what it had come to. His own daughter felt she had to have an ally to deal with him.

He buried his head in his hands. "I try. I really try, Carolina, but she turns away from me or gives me that eye roll to suggest I'm irrelevant. I guess the truth is I'm a lousy father."

"You're not a lousy father. Lousy fathers don't worry the way you have, the way you're doing right now. But from what she said, it seems the problems between you go back a long way."

"How far?"

"To the death of her mother."

He muttered a curse beneath his breath. That was the last place he'd wanted to go today. "What did she tell you?"

"I don't want to betray her confidence," Carolina said. "Besides, the issues have to be dealt with between the two of you, possibly with Dr. Otis's intervention."

"I probably wasn't the help I should have been to Lizzie at the time of Gloria's death. I was barely holding on to sanity myself. I'm sure I made bad decisions."

"Grief does that, especially in the early stages. But a child of nine has even fewer coping mechanisms."

"Lizzie amazed everyone at the time with how well she handled everything. I guess she kept the real hurt buried inside."

Carolina put a hand on his shoulder. "Lizzie is amazing, Jake. I'm sure she was then, too. But she still has issues that need to be faced, and she still needs you."

He stood and walked to the edge of the ledge. His whole world stretched in front of him. A few minutes ago the serene, pastoral landscape had made him feel on top of the world. Now he felt as if the huge rock he'd been sitting on was resting on his shoulders.

"Don't beat yourself up about this, Jake. It's not that unusual for teenage girls to go through a rocky period, even ones who haven't lost their mothers. Luckily she has you and her grandmother to center her world with love, even though she might not see it that way now."

"I hate the prospect of having a shrink crawling around inside my head digging up the past, but if it's what Lizzie needs, I have no choice."

"In the long run, you won't be sorry. I can almost promise you that."

"You would have been a good psychiatrist yourself, Carolina Lambert."

"No way. I'd never be able to stay subjective. I'd jump headfirst into everyone's problems."

The way she had done with Mildred. The way she was doing now with Lizzie. The way she was doing with R.J.

Jake had misjudged her seven ways to Sunday. She really was the kind to want to step in and rescue a neighbor with no thought of what she would gain from it.

"I'm sorry I put such a damper on our beautiful outing," Carolina said.

"Me, too," he admitted honestly. "You know how we cowboys are. We're tough enough to face angry bulls and untamed stallions, but throw in an emotional factor and it scares the wits out of us."

"You're tough enough, Jake. I have no doubt of that."

"Thanks for that vote of confidence."

"We should get started back," Carolina said. "Your mother will be arriving soon, and I don't want her mad at me if you're not there to welcome her home."

"About that, I need you to do me a favor when you're with her."

"What kind of favor?"

"Don't mention Thad Caffey to her, and ask Mildred not to mention him, either. I'll tell her about the situation if need be, but I don't want to get into it on her first night back."

"That makes sense."

"And don't mention R.J. to her."

"What if she brings him up?"

"She won't."

Neither of them spoke as they made their way back down to the waiting horses. Today hadn't worked out as planned. But at least Carolina had left him with a possible route back to his daughter.

"Same time tomorrow?" he asked as he helped her mount. "Only without the psychology session."

"It's a date."

In that case, he'd bring wine.

"YOU SHOULD HAVE seen him after I poked that cone of gelato in his face. He was standing there sputtering like crazy, ice cream dripping from his mustache and a strawberry stuck to the end of his nose. My friend Katherine was laughing so hard, she swore she peed in her pants."

Lizzie reached across the table and gave her grandmother a high five. "Way to handle a pickpocket."

Carolina wasn't about to wet her panties, but she

couldn't remember when she'd laughed harder or enjoyed an evening more. Mary had fascinated them with tales of their European adventures and had them in stitches over some of their misadventures.

"I'd like to travel with your group," Carolina said, "except I don't know if I have the energy to keep up with you."

"Sure you can. Just get you a cane like I carry. People give me a wide path. Guess they figure if they don't get out of my way, they might get tripped or clobbered with it."

"Tell me you don't go around tripping people who get in your way," Jake said.

Mary's eyes twinkled, lighting up her smile. "Hardly ever."

Jake shook his head. "I don't want to go on a trip with you. I'd probably end up in jail."

"Anyone for more dessert or another cup of decaf?" Mildred asked.

"None for me," Mary said. "It's past my bedtime, or at least I think it is. Hard to tell with that jet lag playing havoc with my body clock."

"If you're tired, it's bedtime," Jake said. "I'll walk you back to your room to say good-night."

"No, I'd like Carolina to walk me back to my room. We should get to know each other better."

"You're back a day and I'm already replaced."

"Temporarily. Besides, I have a cane that Carolina might want to borrow in case you get too bossy."

Everyone stood when Mary did. She was like a beloved queen in a way. After knowing her for only a few hours, Carolina could understand why.

She was joyous to be around and didn't hesitate to

say what she was thinking. She must have been a good match for R.J.'s stubbornness. No wonder their marriage hadn't lasted.

Mary made her way around the table, giving Mildred a warm hug and hugging and kissing both Jake and Lizzie on the cheek. The house was much more like a home with Mary around.

Mary linked her arm with Carolina's as they walked to her first-floor suite. It was at the far end of the hall, past Jake's office.

When she opened the door, Carolina breathed in the faint odor of lavender.

"I'm glad you're here," Mary said. "You're good for my son."

Oh, no. Somehow she'd gotten the wrong idea about her and Jake. "I'm only here for a few days. Jake is letting us use the Silver Spur for the Saddle-Up charity project."

"I know, dear. He told me. But that doesn't change the fact that you're good for him."

"Thank you, Mary. He's also good for me."

She hadn't realized how true that was until the words slipped from her lips.

But she was only here until Sunday.

IT WAS AFTER ten when Carolina finally climbed between the sheets. Her body was tired, but her mind was churning. Tomorrow's Saddle-Up activities, her talk with Lizzie, Mary's words—and Jake.

Their relationship had become a conundrum. She wasn't sure exactly what she felt for him, but it was nothing like what she'd experienced with any other man since Hugh's death almost five years ago.

She'd liked riding with him today. When he took her

hand, awareness had hummed inside her. When she'd had to tell him about Lizzie and witnessed his pain, it was all she could do not to wrap her arms around him.

She shouldn't feel any of those things. She'd loved Hugh with all her heart. How could she think of any other man as more than a friend?

Her cell phone vibrated. She didn't recognize the number on the caller ID. A rush of dread swept through. *Please don't let it be Thad Caffey causing more trouble.*

"Hello."

"Is this Carolina Lambert?" A woman's whispered voice.

"Yes. Who's calling?"

"It doesn't matter. I just need to warn you."

"About what?"

"Thad Caffey. He's planning to kill you soon. You need to go away somewhere he can't find you."

"What makes you think he is going to kill me?"

"He said so. Not to me. He didn't see me. When I heard him talking, I hid. But I heard him tell his sister, Jane, that he was going to kill you. I couldn't live with myself without letting you know."

"Is that all he said?"

"I have to go now. But he means it. He's killed before, you know?"

She hadn't known. She still didn't. This could be some cruel hoax perpetrated by Thad. "Who did he kill?"

The connection went dead. Carolina hit call back. The phone rang. And rang. And rang. No one answered.

She shivered and pulled the coverlet over her.

She would not let Thad Caffey get to her. She was safe here.

She'd tell Jake about the call in the morning and call

Sheriff Garcia, as well, but she wouldn't let Thad's threats control her life.

With luck he'd be back in prison where he belonged in a matter of days or even hours.

Get ready for that, sister Jane.

Chapter Thirteen

Jake paced his small office, so angry he could barely make sense of what Carolina was saying. "Go get Mildred. We need to get to the bottom of this."

"I don't think she's even out of bed yet."

"It's seven o'clock. Go wake her," he insisted.

"Isn't there any way we can leave her out of this?" Carolina pleaded. "When I've asked about Thad's life before they married, she's never seemed to know much."

"If she knows anything, I want to hear it."

"I guess you're right." Carolina stopped to pick up their two empty coffee cups from the corner of his desk. "I'll be right back—with Mildred and more caffeine."

The fact that Thad Caffey wanted Carolina dead wasn't a shocker. Nor was the notion that Caffey was capable of murder. This might even be the lead they needed for the police to find and arrest him. The coward might still be hanging out with the mystery sister, Jane, bragging on what he planned to do while waiting on the chance to catch Carolina alone.

It was the fact that Carolina had to deal with any of this that made Jake's blood boil. He was not a violent man, but if he'd known Monday at the capitol what he knew now, he wasn't sure he could have kept from beating the son of a bitch to a pulp. Not that Jake's going to jail would have helped anything.

But he was damn tired of that two-bit criminal calling the shots. It was time for action. He was still pacing and considering his next move when Carolina returned with Mildred ten minutes later.

"I should have left the second he confronted us Monday," Mildred said. "I'm so sorry about this."

"I only told her I'd received a threat by phone from an unknown source," Carolina said.

"Good. Forget the recriminations, Mildred. I didn't call you in here to blame you," Jake said. "I just need some facts about Caffey's family."

"Of course. I'll tell you anything I know, but that won't be much. As far as I know, it was just him, his mother and a sister."

"A sister named Jane?"

"Yes. How did you know?"

"The caller mentioned her. Do you know where Jane lives?"

"She's dead. She was murdered several years before we were married. Thad did tell me that much."

That added a twist. "Who killed her?"

"No one was ever arrested for the crime. Thad didn't talk about her much. When I asked about his family, he'd get upset, so I would just let the subject drop. I got the impression he and Jane were very close."

"But you're sure she was murdered?" Carolina asked.

"I'm sure he told me that. I never knew anything for sure with Thad. He lied to me more than once, sometimes about things that didn't really matter. He'd just lie instead of admitting the truth."

"How old was she when she was murdered?"

"Nineteen. She was two years older than Thad. Like I said, he didn't talk about her much, but…"

"But what?" Jake coaxed.

"I think I reminded him of her. Sometimes he'd call me by her name without seeming to realize it. I feel weird even saying this, but sometimes he'd call out her name when we made love. That would really creep me out."

"That would creep anyone out," Carolina said. "Did you question him about that?"

"I did the first few times, but he'd deny that it had happened and say I was making things up to hurt him. I stopped asking after he slapped me across the face so hard my vision was blurred for hours."

And yet Mildred had stayed with Thad. Jake didn't get it, but then he'd never walked in Mildred's shoes.

"He sent me a huge bouquet of roses later that day to say he was sorry," Mildred added, almost as if she were still justifying his barbaric, abusive actions.

"You mentioned his mother," Jake said. "Did you ever meet her?"

"No. He said she was so upset over Jane's death that she died from a heart attack. I always thought the trauma of losing both of them was what made him so erratic.

"At least that's how I excused his behavior. The truth was that I was more afraid of being alone again than I was of living with him. It wasn't until Carolina got me hooked up with a counselor in Dallas that I was able to see that."

Carolina had a habit of saving people. A reminder that he'd have to be careful not to read too much into her being there for him and Lizzie.

"Where were they living when Jane was murdered?" Carolina asked.

"Gunshot, Texas. It's about a hundred miles west of

Dallas, so small it's not even on most maps. West of nowhere and east of hell, Thad used to say. You only pass
through it if you're lost. I wanted to visit there, just to see
where he grew up, but he wouldn't go back."

East of hell, but close enough Thad could easily have
driven there yesterday and talked to Jane—if her murder
had been another of his lies.

Jake asked a few more questions Mildred couldn't answer. It might not have helped if she could, since there
was no way of knowing how much Thad had told her
was actually true.

But there were ways of finding out.

"Thanks for the help, Mildred."

"I just wish I knew more."

"You gave me a place to start," Jake said. "So now go
out there and get those volunteers in shape."

"I'll do my best."

When she left, Carolina walked over and dropped into
his chair. "I think we should call Sheriff Garcia and give
him an update."

"Agree."

"And then we should take a drive to Gunshot, Texas,
if we can find it."

"If it exists I can find it. But I want to do a little investigating before I go running off chasing after a woman
named Jane who may be dead. But let's start with a phone
call to Garcia and see where we go from there."

If he did go on a field trip to Gunshot, she was not
going with him. He'd fight that battle when he came to it.

"WHERE IS THAT damn sock?"

It had been there a minute ago. Garcia scooted over

to make sure he wasn't sitting on it and then shoved the top sheet back to see if it was entangled in the covers.

He would have thought it was a sign he was getting old if he hadn't been losing a shoe or a sock or a shirt he'd laid out ever since he became sheriff.

Too many problems cavorting about in his hard head. Too many nutcases out there with nothing to do but cause trouble. Song should have said "Mama, don't let your babies grow up to be criminals."

His phone started vibrating. He reached over to the bedside table to get it. It was hiding under the dad-burned sock. Maybe he was getting old.

He checked the caller ID. Had to be more trouble if Jake Dalton was calling this time of morning. "What's Caffey done now?" he answered, sure that the deadbeat thug was the reason for the call.

"Talking to the dead, from what we've heard so far."

"Likely can't find nobody else to talk to him. But you gotta be clearer than that for me to help you."

"Carolina got a phone call last night from an unidentified woman. I'll switch the phone to speaker and let her tell you about that."

"Nothing Caffey's up to would surprise me," Garcia said when Carolina finished with her story. "But he wasn't talking to his sister, June, any time lately. She's been dead for years."

"According to Mildred she was murdered," Jake said.

"That she was. Brutally murdered and her body left to be eaten by the buzzards. The prosecutor dug up that information while preparing his case against Caffey."

"And the killer was never apprehended?" Jake questioned.

"Nope."

"Do you know which detective investigated the murder?"

"Not off hand, but that's a rural area. I s'pect it was the sheriff's office that handled the investigation. But sometimes in a murder case like that, the Texas Rangers or one of the big-city police departments will be called in to help. The sheriff's name is Lonnie McDowd. He's been there a long time. He'll know how the case was handled."

"I'll give him a call."

"You can do that, but you might get more out of him if you talk to him personally, that is if you've a mind to get that involved."

"I've a mind to," Jake said.

"Then go face-to-face with him. Not that I'm recommending you get involved at all. There's a warrant out for Caffey, and I still s'pect him to be arrested any minute now. I'll let you know soon as that happens."

"We'd appreciate that," Carolina said.

"I reckon you've called your sons and told them about last night's phone call," Garcia said.

"No," Carolina admitted. "Tague is the only one on the ranch right now, and I'm sure he has his hands full running the Bent Pine. You agreed that I'm in good hands, so there's really no reason to bother him."

"He'd want to know."

"I'll be home on Sunday. I'll tell him all about it then."

"He's gonna blow a gasket when he finds out you waited so long to tell him."

"I'll give it some thought." Garcia figured that statement was to humor him. But he knew Tague. He wouldn't take kindly to being left out of the loop where his momma was concerned.

Garcia would do what he thought was best. He was still the sheriff.

ONCE THE CALL was over, Carolina stood and walked to the door. "What time do we leave for Gunshot?"

She'd caught Jake off guard. "Did you forget that you have approximately thirty women showing up here in about two hours to partake of your expertise?"

"Not today."

News to him. "Did you cancel the training?"

"No, but today is devoted to team-building activities— a very important part of the campers' experience. We have a specialist coming in to teach the methods, and Sara and Mildred are coordinating the activities. They don't need me."

"Good. You need a day with fewer responsibilities. But you're still not going with me. It isn't safe or necessary."

"Sorry, Jake. I appreciate all you've done, but either I go with you or I go by myself. Your call."

Fear for her safety battled his admiration for her spunk. The fear won out. "The deal was that you stay on the Silver Spur until either Caffey is arrested or you return to the Bent Pine. But I promise that I'll share everything I learn with you when I get back."

"The deal was I don't leave the ranch alone. The question was when do we leave. It would work better for me if I have time to get the day's session started, but I can leave earlier if we need to."

Problem was he believed her when she said she'd go with him or go alone. Not a chance he was willing to take. "Let's shoot for ten."

She gave him a little salute as if he were in charge, though she'd just won the battle. She was the most independent, exasperating woman he'd ever met.

He'd keep her safe or die trying. No. He'd keep her safe and Thad Caffey was going back to prison. Hopefully Jake would get at least one good knockout punch to Caffey's gut in the process.

Now all he had to do was go explain all this to his mother and tell her that she was not to leave the ranch today without an escort just in case Caffey was in the area waiting to cause trouble.

Carolina had complicated his life to the max. Now he was forced to deal with two fiercely independent women before breakfast. And still he liked having her around.

GARCIA PADDED TO the kitchen, one sock on, one foot bare. He needed a shot of caffeine bad. He had faith that Jake Dalton could protect Carolina Lambert, and he had all the respect in the world for her. But he was friends with all her sons, too. Good men. Solid. Cowboys to the core.

Tague was the youngest of the three, funny, good-natured, seldom seen angry. But he'd get his dander up for sure if he found out his mama's life was being threatened and she hadn't told him anything about it.

Tague would be plenty riled at Garcia, too, if he found out he knew and didn't pass on that information. No need to get on the bad side of the Dalton men.

As soon as he got his coffee, he went back to the bedroom and finished getting dressed while he considered the risks in going against Carolina's wishes. He didn't even get the khaki shirt of his uniform fully buttoned before he'd made up his mind.

He sat back down on the edge of the bed and made the call.

SHERIFF MCDOWD LOOKED to be in his midsixties, going bald, needed a shave and to lose about fifty pounds. He leaned back in his desk chair and gave his whiskered chin a good rubbing.

"What can I do for you?"

"There was a woman named Jane Caffey murdered in Gunshot, Texas, several years back."

"Yep." He gave Jake and Carolina a good once-over. "Are you two in law enforcement?"

"No. I'm Jake Dalton. I have a ranch south of Austin. And this is Carolina Lambert."

McDowd clicked his tongue and gave Carolina another studious look. "You part of the Lambert Incorporated bunch?"

"I am."

"Thought you looked familiar. Now, what's your interest in the Caffey case?"

Jake explained the situation.

"So Thad Caffey finally went to prison. Good to know, even if he is out for the time being. You know he was the prime suspect in his sister's murder for a while."

"We had no idea," Carolina said. "What made them suspect him?"

"I don't remember the details. Neighbors reported him as strange, stuff like that, but no solid evidence. He was never arrested. No one was, so whoever killed her is still walking around a free man."

"Is there someone who might remember more?" Jake asked. "The lead investigator, maybe."

"Likely so. Donald Morgan handled that case. He was retired from the FBI when he signed on with us. He'd been in profiling for years and had a real knack for it. He was convinced Thad was guilty. Like I said, he never found enough evidence to convict him. After Mrs. Caffey had her stroke, Thad quit school and left town. Never heard of again until now."

"I thought Thad's mother died of a heart attack a few days after his sister died," Carolina said.

"No, she had a stroke about a year after the murder. Lived a few months and then died of a heart attack while in a rehab center."

"Are you certain?" Carolina asked.

"It's the way I remember it, but Donald can tell you more. He followed that case for several years."

"Is Donald Morgan still with your department?" Carolina asked.

"No, he got shot in the leg two years ago trying to stop a crack-high thug who was robbing a liquor store. He retired for good then. Built himself a lake house on Lake Johnson. He and his wife moved up there, and I haven't seen him since."

Lake Johnson. In the Hill Country. Much closer to Austin than Gunshot was. "Do you have a number where I can reach him?" Jake asked.

"No, but I'll see if I can get it for you. I know one of my deputies has stayed in touch with him."

"I'd appreciate that, the sooner the better. Time is of the essence here."

"I get that. Leave me your card and I'll have him get in touch with you."

Jake pulled a Silver Spur Ranch card from his pocket and slid it onto McDowd's desk.

"One more question," Carolina said as they were getting up to leave. "Do you know where Jane was buried?"

"I reckon right there in Gunshot. There's an old cemetery there behind the remains of a Baptist church. Church hasn't been opon for the soul-saving business in years, but I think they're still burying folks behind it."

"Thank you."

Jake didn't have to wonder where they were going next.

CAROLINA WALKED SLOWLY, admiring the remains of what must have once been a beautiful old country church. The highways and back roads of Texas were sprinkled with those, many still standing, still cradling the dreams of generations, though they'd weathered hurricanes, tornados, floods and fires.

This one had not fared nearly as well. The bones of the building were mostly bare, the wooden planks lying on the ground in rotting piles. A bell tower still reached to the sky, but the bell was missing and the cross that topped it was cracked.

Jake walked at her side, stopping when she did, often with a hand at the small of her back. She was growing comfortable with his touch. She wasn't sure if that was good or bad or even what it meant. For now, she was just thankful to have him with her. And for the fact that he was licensed to carry the pistol he'd just holstered at his right hip.

"It may take a while to find Jane's grave," Jake said.

She looked past the ruins to the row upon row of tombstones of every size and shape imaginable.

"Maybe they're in order by date of death."

"Doesn't look that way. I see bouquets of fresh flowers a few feet from a crumbling tombstone that looks like it's been there for a hundred years."

"Well, at least we have the place to ourselves."

"Just us and the ghosts."

"If you think you're going to frighten me out of searching for Jane's grave, you're mistaken."

"It was worth a try." He took her hand and they walked the maze together, occasionally stopping to read and smile at a humorous epitaph left on a tombstone. A few brought the quick burn of tears to Carolina's eyes.

"Only a few hundred left to go," she said after forty minutes of heat and humidity and swatting at honeybees and mosquitoes.

Jake took a handkerchief from his back pocket and wiped beads of sweat from his brow. "And then you owe me a beer."

"Icy cold," she said. "Plus lunch if you find the grave."

"Now, that's what I call incentive."

They were near a dirt road in the back west corner of the cemetery when she spotted it. Not a tombstone, but only a small cement marker that read Jane Dalton and the words Till Death Do Us Part, followed by the dates of her life span.

"Dead at nineteen," Carolina said. "Brutally murdered. So sad. Maybe Thad was perfectly normal before that and the trauma pushed him over the edge."

"You do like to look for the good in people. Personally I think it's more likely he beat her to death the way he almost killed Mildred."

"I don't deny that sounds plausible," she admitted.

"Do you think he's the one who came up with the epitaph? It doesn't read like something a brother would say about his sister."

"No," Carolina agreed, "but Mildred did say they were very close."

Carolina studied the other markers in the area. "I don't

see her mother's grave. You'd think it would be nearby, since she died so soon after Jane."

"There's probably a story there, too. Hopefully not as depraved as Jane's murder."

Carolina jumped, startled by a rustle in the grass. She was immediately aware of Jake's hand flying to the butt of the pistol. Her heart jumped to her throat.

"Over there," Jake whispered, pointing to an elderly woman shuffling through a row of graves a few yards from them. A basket of blossoms swung from her arm.

She showed no sign of noticing them as she stopped and knelt at a grave. Scattering red and yellow peonies, she began to hum an old hymn that was one of Hugh's mother's favorites. Grams sang it often while she knitted.

Carolina turned to Jake. "Do you think she could have been the one who called me last night?"

"I'd say it's doubtful, but anything's possible at this point."

"I'm going over and talking to her."

"I'll go with you."

She shook her head. "I think she might be more receptive if I go alone."

To her relief he didn't argue the point, though she knew he'd be steadily scanning the area. He hadn't said it, but she knew he was as aware as she was that if Thad had been overheard talking to his sister's grave, he could still be in the area.

"Hello," Carolina called before getting too close so as not to startle her.

The woman looked up and smiled. "Hello. I didn't think anyone was around. There seldom is."

"I'm here with a friend."

The woman looked over to where Jake was standing.

"Got yourself a cowboy. Mighty fine-looking one at that. Better hold on to him if he's as good as he looks."

"I'll tell him you said that. Your flowers are beautiful."

"Thank you. Charles loved working in the garden. I don't like it much myself. Too many bugs and too hard on my back. But I've managed to keep his peonies alive."

Carolina looked at the new tombstone. Charles had been dead for six months. "Was Charles your husband?"

"He was—my second husband. My first is buried two rows over. He never liked peonies, but he grew lots of delicious vegetables. Both men as good as gold."

"Were you by any chance here yesterday?"

"I was, last night about dark. I come here often when my arthritis isn't misbehavin'." She pointed to the dirt road. "If you look down there, you can see the roof of my house."

"No wonder we didn't see your car. When you were here last night, did you see a man standing over by where my friend is right now?"

The woman didn't answer, but her face twisted into a frown, her loose skin tightening around her mouth but spilling over her chin. Carolina was sure that was fear shadowing her eyes.

"Don't be afraid. No one is going to hurt you. I'm Carolina Lambert. If you're the one who called me last night and warned me about Thad Caffey, I want to thank you."

The woman looked around, her gaze still fearful. "I called you. My son found your number for me on the internet somehow."

"Then you saw Thad Caffey in this cemetery last night?"

"And heard him, too. He was talking to his sister's grave like he thought she was still listening. Things he said he was going to do to you made me so sick I almost threw up in the grass."

"Did he see you?"

"No. He thought he was alone or he wouldn't have said such depraved things. I scrunched down behind that big tombstone just behind us and stayed hidden until he left."

"How did you know the man talking was Thad Caffey?"

"He called Jane his darling sister, and that was the only sister he had. He killed her, you know."

"How do you know that?"

"Everybody around here knows that except the police. If he hadn't left town when he did, somebody around here would have killed him and that's a fact."

"Then we'll pray he's gone for good this time," Carolina said. "Can we give you a ride back to your house?"

"No. I can use the exercise. But you stay close to your cowboy over there. He'll keep you safe. I can tell by the way he's watching over you now."

"I do believe you're right." Carolina gave her a quick hug and hurried back to where Jake was waiting.

"Let's get out of here," she said. "By the way, do you like peonies?"

"What are peonies?"

"Never mind. It's time to go get that beer."

Chapter Fourteen

They stopped at a backwoods diner a few miles off the interstate whose sign heralded the best catfish in Texas. Carolina had doubts about the claim's veracity, since dozens of eating establishments in the state made that same promise.

When the hostess welcomed them, Jake pointed out the table he wanted. It was in the far corner of the room, one that would offer plenty of privacy to discuss what they'd learned about Thad Caffey this morning.

Mainly it boiled down to the facts that Caffey had been a suspect at one time in the death of his sister and that he'd been back in his small rural town of Gunshot last night. Both facts had already been passed on to Sheriffs McDowd and Garcia.

Carolina excused herself to go to the restroom while Jake was being seated. By the time she returned, an amber-colored beer in an icy mug was waiting for her.

She took a sip and licked her lips. "You ordered well, cowboy."

"I thought you might like that. It's a Texas craft brew they carry on draft."

"Good choice, though the heat and humidity have me so parched, stump water might taste good."

"Maybe for an after-dinner drink."

He was doing his best to break the tension of the morning. Amazingly, it was helping.

She perused the menu and settled on a grilled-chicken salad. Jake ordered the fried fish. He was halfway through his beer before he leaned back in his chair and broke the easy silence that had settled between them.

"No offense intended, but you're a tough babe to be one of Texas's rich and famous socialites."

"I raised three Texas boys and was married to a man who was bigger than life. I had to be tough or be lost in the machismo."

"With me it's just the opposite. With Mom, Lizzie and Edna in the house, I have to feign a rugged masculinity to keep from having someone paint lipstick on me."

"You do a good job of feigning."

"Thanks."

"Tell me about your family," he said.

"You probably know the basics. I'm a widow and a grandmother with three sons, three grandchildren and another on the way. We own a ranch and Lambert Oil. That covers it."

"That's the surface. Tell me the good stuff. Who's your favorite daughter-in-law? Do you ever have big family brawls over who gets the chicken legs? Which grandchild do you spoil the most?"

"You do want the dirt. I truthfully don't have a favorite among my daughters-in-law. They're all special in their own ways and they make my sons very happy."

"Then tell me about the grandchildren you've spoiled rotten."

"They're not rotten, but not from lack of trying on my part. Belle, Emma and Damien's adopted daughter, is absolutely adorable and so cute you just want to hug her till she squeals. She's almost five. Their son, Zachary Hugh, is a toddler, into everything and gives the best kisses in the world.

"Then there's Tommy, Alexis and Tague's adopted son. He'll be in the first grade in September and already a cowboy at heart. He loves the rodeo and riding his pony. And he can climb like a monkey. He's on top of everything.

"And Meghan and Durk are expecting their first child in October. I can't wait for another baby in the house. Did I leave anything out?"

"The chicken-leg fights, but I admit that is rather personal."

"No chicken-leg fights. An occasional riot over who gets the last bite of banana pudding or slice of chocolate cake, but that's as rough as it gets. Well, unless Aunt Pearl drinks the last of Grams's sherry. Then the fur—or at least Pearl's horrid black wig—has been known to fly."

"Do you all live on The Bent Pine?"

"Yes, but not all in the big house. We're a regular commune. Durk also has a high-rise condo in town for nights he has to work late or any of the family wants to stay over in Dallas for the theater or a ball game. Then there's Grams, my late husband's mother, and her widowed sister, Aunt Pearl. Never a dull moment."

"Sounds like you have it all."

She'd thought so, or as much as she could hope for after losing Hugh. Surely it was still true, but there was something about being with Jake that made her realize for the first time what she'd missed by not having a man in her life.

Not just for sex, but for moments like this—quiet talk

and sharing a beer. Like the touch of his hand on the small of her back or his hand reaching out for hers.

Like the way he was looking at her right now, as if he could devour her but still he didn't push for more.

By the time the waitress brought their food, her insides were quaking. Was all the craziness with Thad Caffey making her delusional? Or was it possible she was actually falling hard for Jake Dalton?

LIZZIE TOOK THE steps two at a time and swung through the back door. She'd figured losing driving privileges would totally ruin her summer, but today had been really fun. She couldn't wait to help with the team-building games when she was a junior counselor. The heat she could do without.

The air conditioner felt heavenly. She gulped in the cool air and tugged her sweaty shirt away from her body. She'd planned to head straight for the shower, but odors wafting in from the kitchen waylaid her.

Edna was pulling a sheet of snickerdoodles from the oven.

"How was your day?" Edna asked without turning to see who was there.

"Good. How did you know it was me?"

"The smell. You need a shower, young lady."

"And cookies. I need energy. I'm a working girl now."

"I'll wrap some in a napkin for you to take with you, but you wash your hands before you eat them."

"Naturally. Do you know where Mrs. Lambert is? She didn't show up for the training session today. I asked Mildred about her, but she just said Mrs. Lambert had some business to take care of."

"She went somewhere with your dad. They didn't say

where they were going, but your dad said he'd call if they weren't going to be home for dinner, so I expect them anytime now."

"Mrs. Lambert and Dad. That's weird." Lizzie wondered if they'd talked about her seeing Dr. Otis. She didn't think her dad would be mad, but he'd want to talk it out and that never got them anywhere.

"Where's Grandma?" Lizzie asked.

"She said she was going back to her room for a nap a couple of hours ago. I haven't seen her since. I reckon it's the jet lag making her so tired in the middle of the day and the napping all afternoon that keeps her from sleeping through the night."

"Okay. I'll see her later. Off to shower."

"Use lots of soap."

"I know and wash behind my ears. I'm not three." She nabbed a cookie from the napkin, stuffing half of it in her mouth as she raced up the stairs.

When she got to her room, she grabbed another cookie and checked her cell phone. Ten missed calls from Calvin. He'd be steaming she hadn't called him back, but Mildred had stressed no phone calls except emergencies during team building.

Her phone started to vibrate. Him again. Ignoring his call, she shimmied out of her jean shorts and kicked them and her shoes into the corner. He'd waited all day; he could wait until she'd showered.

He was only going to growl at her anyway.

The phone was ringing again when she got out of the shower. She wrapped herself in a towel and tied another turban style around her hair.

Eleven phone calls. Maybe he'd had an emergency.

A wreck on his motorbike or been arrested. A surge of guilt sent her flying across the room.

"Hello," she said breathlessly.

"Where have you been all day?"

"Working. I told you I'm training to be a junior camp counselor."

"Oh yeah, that. Well, you should have called me. It happened."

"What happened?"

"I'm getting sent to live with my dad. Not that you'll miss me. You'll be off camping."

"I'll miss you, but I'll bet you'll be back before school starts."

"Nah. I'm not coming back, not staying there, either. I'm heading off on my own."

"You can't just run away."

"Sure I can. Thousands of kids do it every year."

"It's dangerous."

"I can take care of myself. Anyway, I just called to say goodbye. I plan to be gone in the morning before Mother wakes up."

She couldn't let him do this, not without at least trying to talk him out of it. Even Dad would understand that. Some things were more important than rules and grounding.

"Do you want to meet for a few minutes at our usual place?" she asked.

"Aren't you scared of your dad?"

"Not scared, but I don't like getting in trouble."

"Does that mean you want to meet me or not?" he quipped.

"I do. In fifteen minutes. But I can't stay long, and if you're not there I can't wait."

"I'll be there."

She hung up the phone and threw on some clothes. All the better if she could get there and back before her father got home. But if she didn't, she'd just have to hope he understood—and then be grounded for life.

THAD CAFFEY SLOWED as he reached the gate of the Silver Spur. It was the second time he'd driven by in the past thirty minutes, but time was running out and he was tired of waiting.

He'd made up his mind. It wasn't the way he'd planned things, but he could live without Mildred. As Mateo had said, there would be plenty of available senoritas once he got to Mexico.

But he couldn't leave without getting even with Carolina Lambert. It had been gnawing at his guts for four years. He'd lived on thoughts of what he'd do to her, how she'd scream for mercy. All she would get was justice. No one wronged him like that and lived to tell about it.

No one. Not even his Jane.

Thad was practically to the gate when he saw a car approaching it from the other side. The driver had long hair and sunglasses. The venom of revenge rushed through Thad's veins.

The gate opened and the car sped through it. He only got a quick glimpse, but it was enough to know that the female behind the wheel wasn't Carolina. He followed close behind and then passed slowly.

The driver looked right at him as he passed. She was young, around the age of Jake Dalton's teenage daughter.

Adrenaline rushed through his blood at a murderous pace. Carolina would never turn down a cry for help from a teenage girl.

He might have just accidentally found the way to get Carolina to come rushing into his trap.

LIZZIE STARED BACK at the driver of the blue sedan as he stayed even with her instead of passing. At first she thought he must be someone she knew. Few people drove this back road whom she didn't know.

She didn't recognize him, and the way he glared at her freaked her out.

Finally he sped past. She breathed easier—but only for a minute or two. Once they'd crossed the bridge over Cotter's Creek, he slowed to a crawl. She slowed down, too. Whatever crazy game he was playing was dangerous.

Driving at ten miles an hour, she still caught up with him. She'd have to pass him and pray he didn't chase after her. She might be able to outrun him on a straight stretch, but there were blind hills and dangerous curves ahead.

Still, she had to pass. She put on her blinker. He stuck a hand out his open window and gave her a thumbs-up, as if she'd joined his treacherous antics. She was starting to get really scared. If this was what breaking her dad's rules came to, she was never breaking another one.

She fumbled in the side pocket of her tote bag for her cell phone. The blue sedan began to weave. The driver had to be drunk or high.

Suddenly he threw on his brakes. She swerved around him, missing him by inches. Her heart pounded in her chest. The cell phone slipped from her fingers. She leaned over and tried to retrieve it, but it had fallen between the seats.

She hit the gas. Her only hope was to get away from him. In seconds the blue sedan was in the wrong lane, driving even with her, so close she could have reached out and touched it. He swerved closer, scraping her brand-new car and ripping her side mirror from its bearings. The mirror dangled precariously, bouncing against the sides of the car.

He was going to run her off the road. Panic swelled inside her until she could barely breathe.

His car raked hers again, harder this time, the metal making a crunching noise that hammered in her ears. She lost control and had to steer frantically to keep from skidding off the shoulder and into a ditch.

She slowed as she fought to get the car back on the road.

Please just let him drive away. If she got out of this alive, she'd never break her dad's rules again.

The sedan slammed into her again, this time hitting the left fender so hard the car spun fully out of control. She held on to the wheel and braced for the ditch.

Instead the car rolled along the grassy area just off the shoulder until it sputtered to a stop. Smoke was pouring out from under the crinkled hood and through the vents. She had to get out before the car caught fire and blew up with her in it.

She struggled with the seat belt. It wouldn't budge.

Someone was beating on the door of her car, but when she looked up, all she could see was smoke.

She opened her mouth and screamed. She wanted her daddy. But Daddy was nowhere around.

Chapter Fifteen

The car door flew open. Coughing and struggling for oxygen through the smoky haze, Lizzie instinctively tried to shove away the man who was trying to pull her from behind the wheel.

She spotted the knife through her clouded peripheral vision. She tried to squirm away as he struck with it. Expecting pain, she shuddered with relief as the seat belt gave way and the man pulled her toward him. Her feet hit the ground.

She tried to break loose and run, but the man swept her into his arms like a bag of groceries and started running away from the smoking car.

"Are you okay?"

No. How could she be? The man's arms were holding her tight, and she was too dizzy and nauseated to even try to escape. The smell of smoke was still stringent, her throat dry and choking, but nothing like what it had been inside the car.

"Take deep breaths," the man coaxed. "You're going to be okay. Just relax and breathe. I've got you and I'm calling 911 now."

Lizzie's eyes burned and watered as she heard him requesting emergency help, firefighters and an ambulance. She blinked repeatedly until she finally gained focus. She began to shake uncontrollably.

The man holding her in his arms was not the leering lunatic who'd run her off the road. He was the hottest, hunkiest cowboy she'd ever seen in her life. She was hallucinating. Maybe dead.

Only he was much too real to be an illusion. Her mind cleared fast. "My car. It's on fire. I have to save it."

"Too late for that, but firefighters might get here in time to put out the fire before the car explodes and sets someone's pastures on fire."

"My dad is going to kill me."

"I promise you he won't, sweetheart. When he finds out what happened out here, he's just going to be thankful you're alive." He put her down, holding on to her until she was steady. "Now, are you sure you're okay? Nothing hurting? Nothing bleeding?"

"My knee," she said, realizing for the first time it was aching. "I must have banged it against something when the other car knocked me off the road."

He bent over for a closer look. "It's red, but the skin isn't broken. Guess I should introduce myself. I'm Tague Lambert."

"Lambert? Are you kin to Carolina?"

"She's my mother. Who are you?"

"Lizzie Dalton. I'm Jake Dalton's daughter. Your mother is staying at our ranch, the Silver Spur. Did you come here to see her?"

"I did. Good timing, if I do say so myself."

"Yeah, if you hadn't come along when you did, I might be dead."

"We don't even want to go there."

Lizzie looked around. They were standing next to a

white pickup truck that must belong to Tague. Lizzie's car was on the other side of the road and several yards back. It was still smoking, but not as bad as it had been when the car first hit her. The blue sedan was nowhere in sight.

"I saw the crash," Tague said. "It looked as if that blue Honda intentionally ran you off the road?"

"It did. The driver had been messing with me ever since I left the ranch. If I slowed down, he slowed down. If I sped up, he'd catch up, pass me and then slow down again. He sideswiped me once before slamming into my fender. Thankfully we weren't going very fast when he hit me."

"Road rage?"

"No. If it was, I didn't do anything to cause it. He just started following me."

"And you have no idea who he was?"

She shook her head. "I'm pretty sure he's not from around here."

"Did you get a good look at him?"

"Very good. I think I'd know that face and the slithering snake tattoo on his arm anywhere."

Approaching sirens screamed in the distance. Within minutes, a fire truck sped up to the smoking car.

One of the firemen rushed over to them. "Anyone trapped in the car?"

"No," Tague answered.

"Positive?"

"Positive," Lizzie assured them. "I was in the car alone, and Tague pulled me out before he even called you."

"Good man." The fireman looked back to Lizzie. "Are you injured?"

"Just a bruised knee."

An ambulance arrived and pulled off the road in front of her car. The firemen already had the blaze under control.

"Forget the gurney," the fireman said, waving the paramedics over.

Deputies from the sheriff's department were the next to arrive. Lizzie was starting to feel guilty that she wasn't hurt, since she'd caused all this commotion.

Over it all, she heard the familiar knock and growl of Calvin's motorbike. With all that was going on, she'd forgotten all about meeting him. He slowed when he passed, looked her right in the eye but didn't even acknowledge her. He just kept on going.

He no doubt figured he had enough problems of his own without getting bogged down in hers. But you'd think he'd have at least stopped to make sure she was okay. Some tough guy he'd turned out to be.

And this was all because of him.

Well, actually it was the fault of the lunatic in the blue car, but Lizzie wouldn't have been here if it wasn't for Calvin.

The paramedics began insisting she should go to a hospital and get checked out. She assured them over and over that she was fine. The deputies wanted her story but kept interrupting for details she couldn't give them.

"I can give you the license number of the blue Honda that ran her off the road," Tauge said.

All the attention turned to him.

And then a new vehicle joined the circus. Jake and Carolina had arrived on the scene. Lizzie's heart sank as the real truth settled in.

She was definitely going to be grounded for life.

CAROLINA STOOD ON the front porch, staring down the road that led to the gate, wondering what was taking Jake and Tague so long. The men had waited around to get the damaged car towed, but how long could that take? She'd driven Lizzie back in Tague's truck almost two hours ago.

Tague had saved Lizzie's life, appearing on the scene totally unexpected at exactly the right moment. It wasn't the first time Tague had been a hero. He'd met his wife when he saved her son from a carjacker. It was the first time Carolina had put him in a situation that required his heroism.

When they'd talked at the accident scene, it was clear Tague was agitated to have to hear about a credible threat on her life from Sheriff Garcia.

He'd made the drive from Oak Grove to see and hear firsthand what was going on and take her home with him, if necessary. He wouldn't have to do any convincing with that. She'd done enough damage here.

All she could think about was what if Tague hadn't driven up when he did? What if… She shuddered. The what-ifs were too scary to think about.

Carolina was certain from Lizzie's description that Thad was the man who'd forced her off the road. Since she was the one Caffey was out to kill, she was the one who needed to leave the Silver Spur immediately.

Mildred could stay here, and with Peg and Sue's help they could finish the training without Carolina. Her belongings were already packed.

Carolina had come here thinking that working with Jake would be next to impossible, a vexation to be endured. She would leave knowing that she would miss him far more than she would have ever dreamed.

All her previous perceptions of him had been wrong.

Instead of being heartless, he was generous, honest, strong, loving and funny. She felt safe with him.

Carolina didn't understand his reluctance to reconcile with R.J., but he must have his reasons. She just wished he'd change his mind about them.

She was just about to go inside and see if she could help with dinner preparation when she spotted Jake's truck, kicking up dust on the road to the house. She walked down the steps to meet them, wondering how the two men had got along after she and Lizzie left.

Jake reached out to her, taking her hand and squeezing it hard. The contact felt good, natural, reassuring after the trouble she'd caused.

They dropped hands after that, but she was sure Tague had noticed.

"How's Lizzie?" Jake asked.

"Physically, she seems fine except for a bruised knee. Emotionally, she's a bit of a wreck and has every right to be. She talked a mile a minute when we first got here, telling her grandmother, Mildred and Edna every detail. She was even more descriptive than she'd been with us."

"How did Mom take it?" Jake asked.

"Great at first, but then she wiped tears from her eyes and we all started crying. Therapeutic for all of us. That was followed by lots of hugs, and then Lizzie rushed off to her room to call her friend Angie."

"Guess there's no use trying to keep any of this quiet," Jake said. "It is what it is. All comes down to the facts that we've got to stop Thad Caffey and I owe Tague big-time."

"Glad to help, though like I said, I don't think Caffey had any intention of letting her die."

"How can you say that?" Carolina questioned. "She was trapped in a car that could easily have exploded."

"Let's talk about it inside," Jake said. "How about the three of us meet in my office as soon as I have a chance to say hello to Mom and check on Lizzie?"

"Works for me," Tague said. "Will give me a few minutes to wash up."

No one waited for Carolina's vote before rushing off. Perhaps they'd already decided it was best for her to go back to the Silver Spur and the meeting was to tell her.

The thought stung. It was one thing for her to decide to leave. It was another for Jake to want her to go.

Now she was being ridiculous. It wasn't as if they were romantically involved or even that she wanted to be.

But she did like him. She liked him a lot. It was a very scary admission.

CAROLINA WAS ALREADY waiting in Jake's office when Tague arrived.

"Nice setup," Tague said, dropping to the tan leather couch on the opposite wall from Jake's large oak desk. "I wouldn't mind an office like this in my house except that Alexis hates it when I take care of ranch business at night."

"I don't blame her. You need family time. I probably should follow that advice myself," Jake said.

"What did you mean when you said you didn't think Thad would have let Lizzie die?" she asked Tague, getting back to the issues at hand.

"Thad jumped out of his car like he was in a big hurry and started running toward Lizzie's wrecked, smoking vehicle. I can't imagine him rushing to get her out of a car that looked like it might explode any second if he was just planning to kill her."

"But he didn't rescue her," Carolina argued.

"No. Once he saw me he got scared and took off like he had a rocket under his hood."

"And you rushed to the car that could have exploded any second."

"Any decent man would have done the same."

She wasn't so sure of that. "Then why do you think Thad ran her off the road?"

"Maybe to use her as bait to get you to run to her rescue. Maybe just to scare you. Who knows what goes on in his sick little mind?"

Jake joined them in the room. "I plan to do everything I can to put him and his sick little mind back in prison where he belongs. I don't care what it takes."

"He must realize that," Carolina said. "Maybe he'll move on now."

"I doubt that," Tague said. "After hearing what he said at his sister's grave, he's obviously obsessed with getting revenge. But he did prove once again what a coward he is. He couldn't get away fast enough when he saw me get out of my truck."

"He'll wait until he can get Carolina alone," Jake said. "I'm almost sure of that, but I'm not taking any chances."

"I can see that," Tague said. "I came here to persuade Mom to come home with me, but I don't know that our ranch is any safer than the Silver Spur. At least here, she has the training session to keep her mind occupied with something other than a depraved maniac."

They were leaving out one very real concern, one that had just occurred to her. "If Thad came after Lizzie to get to me, what's to keep him from coming after some-one in our family, Tague?"

"Me. I've already upped security at the Bent Pear and made sure everyone knows the new rules. I did that as soon as I got off the phone with Garcia this morning."

"The sheriff definitely didn't waste any time getting in touch with you."

"It was the right thing to do," Tague said.

"It certainly turned out that way," she agreed. "There's still the volunteers to consider. They have to drive the same back road for a few miles every morning to get to the Silver Spur. Some of them ride alone and unarmed."

Though she knew many did carry a weapon in their vehicle. Women in rural areas had been protecting them-selves and their families from beasts for generations. This particular beast walked on two feet instead of four, but that wouldn't detract from their aim if they were threatened.

"I think you can forget about Caffey showing up out here again," Tague said. "He's whacko but not stupid. He has to figure local law enforcement will be on constant lookout for him."

"And if desperation and revenge rule, I still have it covered," Jake said. "I called a charter bus service while Tague and I were waiting for the tow truck to arrive. A coach driver will pick up the women at Carl's Diner on the interstate, a few miles from our exit. He'll chauf-feur them to and from the ranch. Actually I should have thought of that sooner. It will save that backup at the gate every morning."

Jake and Tague had taken over with no input from her. But she still had a say.

"I've already made up my mind to cancel the rest of

the training and go home," she said. "I've put you and your family out enough, Jake. You never signed on for this."

"I signed on to host the training session. It's not over."

"It is for me."

"What happened today was not your fault, Carolina. There's no reason for you to leave. Even Tague agrees with that."

"Don't you think you better ask the rest of your family how they feel about my staying?" Carolina asked.

"No, and it wouldn't change things if I did. No one wants you to go, Carolina." He stepped closer, his dark gaze mesmerizing. "No one."

She swallowed hard. How would she say no to that look?

"If that's settled, all we need now is an arrest," Tague said, breaking at least some of the fiery tension. "I figure that's only a matter of time. In the meantime, I'll keep in close touch."

"You may as well stay the night," Jake said, "or at least for dinner."

"No can do. We're inoculating cattle in the morning. I like to be home on the ranch to oversee that myself."

The men shook hands, and Jake thanked him again for jumping to Lizzie's rescue. It was surprising how well they'd bonded in one afternoon, almost as if they were old pals.

Carolina walked out with Tague.

"Am I picking up some romantic vibes between you and Jake?" he asked teasingly as they approached the truck.

A slow burn crept to her cheeks. "I have no idea what you mean by that."

He put an arm around her shoulders. "It's okay if you are, Mom. I'm not pushing, just saying it wouldn't bother Durk, Damien or me if you found someone."

She laughed and pushed him away. "Go home and don't worry about me or my love life." As if she had a love life.

He gave her a warm hug and kissed her on the cheek. "Me thinks you protest too much."

JAKE WAS ABOUT to go looking for Lizzie when she wandered into his office.

She walked over and perched on the corner of his desk, the way she used to do when she was a little girl and wanted him to stop what he was he doing and go outside with her. He hadn't done it often enough. Opportunities he could never regain.

"I'm really sorry about this afternoon, Dad."

"You should be. Do you know how much it scared me to see your car wrecked and surrounded by firemen and an ambulance?"

A stupid, rhetorical question. Of course she didn't know. Words couldn't begin to describe the hell he'd gone through in those few minutes until he knew she was safe.

"I shouldn't have broken your rules. I hadn't planned to, but then Calvin called and he was so upset about having to go live with his dad, I didn't know what to do."

"You could have called me."

"You would have said no."

"And you would have been safe."

"I didn't know there was some crazy guy stalking our gate. I thought everyone was worried about security because there were so many volunteers around or because

Carolina is so famous. No one told me there had been a threat on her life."

"You were grounded. There was no reason to share those gory details with you."

"I know. I did everything wrong again. I do try, but I keep disappointing you."

None of the things he'd nagged her about seemed important now. All that mattered was that she was safe. All that mattered was that his heart hadn't been ripped from him again.

He had to find a way to bridge the gulf between them.

"Carolina told me that you want to see Dr. Olson as a patient," he said.

"I'd like to."

"I'll call him tomorrow and set up a couple of appointments. One for you and one for me."

"You're going. Why?"

"I've obviously made a lot of mistakes as a father. Whatever I'm doing wrong with you, I want to start doing right."

She walked around the desk, dropped into his lap and gave him a big hug. "I love you, Daddy."

Seconds later, she was gone.

His eyes were wet with tears when Carolina stuck her head in his door. He tried to whisk them away with his sleeve, but he didn't fool her.

"What's wrong?"

"Nothing." Nothing that wasn't better when she walked into the room.

"Then I guess we'd best go to dinner. Your mother said if you're not there in three minutes, she's starting without you. Said you know she hates it when her potatoes get cold."

"Queen Mary can wait."

Jake walked to the door, tugged Carolina inside and then kicked it shut behind her.

He wrapped his arms around her and slowly touched his lips to hers.

Chapter Sixteen

Carolina's heart leapt to her throat. She was being kissed. On the mouth. With passion. She hadn't even remembered what it felt like. Or that it could turn you inside out.

Right or wrong, desire flamed inside her.

Their breaths mingling, she sucked in the essence of Jake, reveling in the taste of his lips. She should pull away. But she couldn't. The need raging inside her was far too strong.

His hands tangled in her hair, his thumbs riding the column of her neck. Every part of her body responded as her breasts pushed against his chest. She couldn't reason and didn't want to. All she wanted to do was feel the sensations that were setting her on fire.

A knock on Jake's door broke the spell. She jumped away quickly, straightening her blouse, raking her fingers through her mussed hair.

"What do you need?" Jake asked. His voice was husky, almost gravelly.

"Dinner's ready," Lizzie called back. "And we can't find Carolina. Have you seen her?"

Carolina walked over and opened the door, praying the glow she felt inside wasn't showing on her face. "I'm here. We were just rehashing the day," she said. "But I'm starved. Let's eat."

She glanced back at Jake, half expecting him to look as changed as she felt. But it was the same Jake looking backing at her. Just a man. So why was he turning her life upside down? Why was desire strumming through every part of her body?

"Give me a minute to finish up something and I'll be right behind you," Jake said.

"Well, hurry. Grandma already said grace."

Carolina wondered if the minute he needed was to regroup after the kiss that had knocked her for a loop or if he was simply regretting it.

Was she regretting it?

Should she be regretting it?

Should she run as fast as she could from the primitive hunger that had driven her reaction to something as simple as a kiss?

She had never expected to feel that kind of passion with another man again. She'd given her heart so completely to Hugh. Was there enough left to build a new relationship?

A kiss, she reminded herself. Only a kiss, not a commitment.

It might mean nothing at all to Jake.

IT WAS THE perfect summer night.

Katydids and tree frogs competing to see which could be the loudest. Nocturnal creatures rustling through the grass. Leaves fluttering in the breeze. The occasional haunting hoot of an owl. The eerie howl of a coyote. The creak of the front-porch swing as Carolina gently nudged it into movement with her foot.

Even the heavens were enchanting. The moon was a silver crescent, surrounded by stars so brilliant they looked as near as the fireflies darting in and out of the shrubbery that bordered the right side of the porch.

All sounds and sights that Carolina was so accustomed to that she seldom noticed them except on nights like this when her mind craved the familiar.

As familiar as home. But this was Jake's home, not hers. His world. His family. His past. Even if she wanted to, could she ever fit in here?

Once again she was jumping way ahead of herself, but she couldn't get the kiss out of her thoughts. For a few breathless minutes, desire had exploded inside her. A hunger so strong it had consumed her. An eruption of passion that she'd thought was lost to her forever.

The front door opened. To Carolina's surprise it was Mary who stepped out, her long white nightgown fluttering around her narrow ankles.

"I didn't realize anyone was out here," Mary said. "Would you mind a little company?"

"I'd love some company." Not completely true, but she scooted over to make room beside her in the swing. "I thought you went to bed a couple of hours ago."

"I did, but I woke up and couldn't get back to sleep. This old porch swing has soothed my worried mind on many a restless night."

"Jake said you've lived here since he was a young boy."

"Yes. We moved here when I married my second husband. I had no intention of ever marrying again after my divorce. Reuben gave forever a bad name. John made it a dream. Unfortunately, our forever ended much too soon."

"But you married again after your second husband died?"

"Yes. I've been married three times. That makes me sound a bit risqué, doesn't it? I admit, I did like to have a good time back in the day."

"From what I hear, you still do," Carolina teased.

Mary chuckled. "So, how is Reuben doing—though I hear he goes by R.J. now?"

Carolina remembered Jake's warning and hesitated.

"You can talk about him to me," Mary said. "What happened between us happened a long time ago. The statute of limitations on divorce issues was reached an eternity ago."

"He's not doing well," Carolina said. "I heard from one of his daughters-in-law after dinner tonight. The doctor gives him another week or two at the most, but R.J. has fooled the doctors before."

"Is he still living at the Dry Gulch?" Mary asked.

"He is. The family plans to keep him there until the end."

"It's amazing that so many of his children reconnected with him after such bad beginnings."

"All of his children except Jake," Carolina said.

"Really?"

"Yes, even Jade, the daughter of a woman he'd never married. He'd offered, but Jade's mother turned him down."

"Smart woman."

Carolina hated to push the issue, but after all Mary had started this conversation. "Why do you think Jake refuses to take even a stab at getting to know his father?"

"That's between my son and R.J. You'll have to ask Jake that question."

Carolina had asked him, but she'd do it again. It would have to be soon. A few more days and it could be too late.

They talked a few more minutes, mostly about the Saddle-Up project, before Mary yawned and decided to try sleep again.

Carolina stayed—a mistake since it was the kiss that claimed her mind when she was alone again. She put her fingertips to her mouth. She could swear the heat from his kiss still lingered on her lips.

With a madman out to kill her, it was a kiss that would rob her of sleep tonight.

JAKE WOKE EARLY on Friday morning, as he always did. But running the ranch was no longer ruling his activity schedule. Thad Caffey and Carolina were.

Top of the list was to find Thad Caffey before he struck again. Jake had lain awake for hours last night, considering the facts and where he should go from there. He had a plan.

He'd stayed awake half the night thinking of Carolina, the taste of her, the flowery scent of her hair, the way she'd felt in his arms. He did not want her to walk out of his life on Sunday when she left the Silver Spur. He had no plan for how to ensure that.

He left the house at six, walked to the horse barn, saddled Riley and rode up to Cotter's Canyon. He'd come here daily when he first returned to the ranch after Gloria's death. The little solace he'd found he'd discovered here.

He slowed Riley to a walk. The horse easily maneuvered the rocky trail. A doe stepped out of a wooded area. It stopped and stared at Jake with its big brown eyes, then walked into the clearing. Two spotted fawns joined her, and they went about foraging for their food as if they knew Jake presented no danger.

Jake didn't stay long. The canyon seemed to have lost all its ability to clear his mind. By seven he was in the headquarters office making a call to a bounty hunter named Brad Pacer who'd made a name for himself in the Austin area locating missing persons who didn't want to be found.

The phone rang six times before it was answered.

"This better be damned important if you're calling this time of the morning."

"A matter of life and death," Jake answered.

"Then my help must be worth a lot of cash to you. Who am I talking to?"

"Jake Dalton. I'll pay you what you're worth, a whole lot more if I get quick results."

"Start talking, Jake Dalton."

Jake explained the situation.

"So all you want from me is to find this Thad Caffey, whose whereabouts you know as of yesterday."

"You got it."

"My price is three thousand dollars plus expenses."

"Locate him in forty-eight hours and hold him until the cops get there to arrest him and I'll triple that fee."

"You got yourself a deal. Now tell me everything you know about Thad Caffey."

Jake filled him in. "I'm also trying to get in touch with a retired law officer who lives in the Lake Johnson area named Donald Morgan."

"Formerly an FBI profiler?"

"That's the man."

"A friend of mine. I can give you his phone number now. You got a pen handy?"

"In my hand."

When they finished the conversation, Jake checked

off hiring a private eye and obtaining Donald Morgan's phone number from his list of urgents.

His next call was to Donald Morgan. His greeting was much friendlier. As soon as Jake mentioned Thad Caffey, Morgan became extremely cooperative. Jake made an appointment to meet with him at a coffee shop in Marble Falls at eleven o'clock. Check off item number three.

Before he could leave the office, he got a call from Sheriff Garcia, who obviously thought of him now as the contact person for all things dealing with Caffey.

"Good morning, Sheriff. Hope you're calling with some good news for a change."

"I have information, some obtained from your local sheriff's department. I don't know that it's particularly good. In fact, you may have already heard it."

"No. I haven't talked to anyone from the sheriff's department this morning."

"It turns out the blue sedan that ran your daughter off the road yesterday was stolen from a retirement home in Austin."

"That figures," Jake said. "He no doubt assumed he could outrun little old men in their walkers if they came after him."

"I've seen some who would give him a run for the money. But the rest of the story is that the stolen car was abandoned in a parking lot in Austin last night."

"Then they should have fingerprints to prove it was Thad who was responsible for the hit-and-run."

"They also have film from a security camera," Garcia said. "We should end up with at worst a grainy image of whoever parked and left the car. And I have the fingerprint report from the Oak Grove burglary on my desk this morning."

"Is it a match with Caffey?"

"It is. We have more than enough evidence to arrest him and make it stick. All we have to do is find him."

"About that, I want to offer a reward of ten thousand dollars for any information leading to his arrest and capture."

"That's a mighty steep reward considering we'll likely have Caffey under arrest in the next day or two."

"Every minute he's out there looking for a way to get to Carolina is a minute too long."

"It's your money."

"Right." But there was still one thing that didn't quite add up. "Why do you suppose he's not worried about leaving fingerprints and getting caught on camera? Is it possible he wants to go back to prison?"

"Makes more sense to think he's planning on disappearing, likely across the border."

As soon as he got his revenge. But the way he was leaving tracks, he must know his time was running out. He'd strike soon and go to any extreme to exact his revenge against Carolina.

The only way he could do that was over Jake's dead body. Jake had no intention of dying just when he had a chance at starting to really live again.

Chapter Seventeen

Thad Caffey had gotten the word. The assignment had changed. The saucy little border-patrol agent named Melissa was to be left bleeding and in agonizing pain sometime within the next twenty-four hours. The time range was nonnegotiable. She was off duty tonight and should be at home alone.

Caffey picked up the bottle of whiskey he'd bought with his last few dollars. He didn't like the taste of whiskey. Had never cared for any kind of alcohol. It was the drink of the devil. It had made Thad's mother beat him when he was little and kneel on rice until he cried.

He put the lip of the bottle to his mouth and swigged, letting the burn eat its way to his stomach.

Jane had never drunk, either. She didn't have hardly any faults, not until that filthy-minded preacher had come to town. He'd put some kind of spell on her, made her turn against Thad and tell him to never touch her again.

The preacher was the reason Jane had turned against him, the same way the rich bitch Carolina Lambert was the reason Mildred had turned against him.

Ten years ago Thad had made a terrible mistake. He'd killed the wrong person. He wouldn't make that mistake again.

He picked up the whiskey bottle again.

One woman to assault and torture. Another to kill. Twenty-four hours to finish both jobs.

He threw the half-empty whiskey bottle against the wall of his dingy motel room. The devil's juice sprayed the walls like amber colored blood.

Thad grabbed his shirt from the back of a chair and poked his arms through the sleeves. The shirt smelled of sweat from two days of wearing it in the humid heat. It didn't matter.

He'd buy new ones when he reached Mexico.

Chapter Eighteen

As soon as they got past the handshakes and introductions, Donald Miller jumped straight to the topic of Thad Caffey.

"I figured he'd killed his sister even before he'd answered my first question. After an hour I was sure. But come on in. I should at least offer you a cup of coffee before I get started on Thad Caffey."

"Sure, but don't worry about the coffee. It's information I'm after."

Jake had checked Morgan's credentials a bit more on the internet before driving out. He'd been a big-time FBI profiler, aiding in identifying several infamous serial cases in the Northeast.

Jake hadn't found any indication as to how Morgan had ended up working for a primarily rural sheriff's department in Texas. Probably a story there somewhere, but Jake was only interested in the topic of Thad Caffey this morning.

However he'd landed in the Lone Star State, Donald Morgan had retired well. This was not what Jake had pictured when Sheriff McDowd called it a lake house.

It was in a gated community of homes that probably started at around four hundred thousand and ranged upwards of several million. Morgan's looked to hit at least the half-million mark.

The retired detective led Jake straight through the den and kitchen to a glassed-in sunroom that extended across the back of the house.

"Fabulous view," Jake said, looking out over a well-manicured lawn that led down to a dock and an expanse of water that sparkled in the sun like diamonds.

"That's what sold us on the place. Sit down. Make yourself comfortable. How do you take your coffee?"

"Black but don't go to any trouble."

"No trouble. It's already made. Unless you'd like something stronger."

"Coffee's fine."

All he really wanted was to get back to the topic of Caffey. Information about his past might not help with what was going on today, but it was always wise to know your enemy. And identifying clues into what makes a madman tick seemed to be Morgan's specialty.

Morgan was back in a minute with the coffees. Jake had taken a chair. Morgan took a seat on the couch, kitty-corner from him.

"You're not in law enforcement," Morgan said, repeating what Jake had told him earlier on the phone. "So exactly how are you involved with Caffey?"

Jake filled him in from the beginning, starting with his imprisonment for the brutal attack on Mildred and finishing with the hit-and-run yesterday. Morgan listened without interruption, though his facial muscles seemed to grow more strained with each sentence.

"I hadn't heard he was out of prison," Morgan said. "I tried to put all my unresolved cases behind me when I retired. Had to find some way to sleep at night."

"I understand. I'd just like to know your impressions of Caffey. I'm not looking for anything specific, because I don't know what that would be. His weaknesses, his patterns of behavior. Anything to help us apprehend him before he gets to Carolina Lambert."

"She's in imminent danger," Morgan said. "Any guy who'd kill his sister and then later whack his own mother is capable of heinous crimes."

"I heard his mother died of a heart attack after suffering a stroke."

"That was the best the authorities could come up with. I never bought it. Caffey nursed a maddening mixture of love and hate for his mother."

"He told you that?"

"Not in those exact words, but it was obvious. One minute he'd vehemently defend his mother against any suggestion that she could have been implicit in her daughter's murder—not that she was ever a credible suspect. Five minutes later, Caffey would go off on her alcoholism and how cruel she was when she was drunk."

"There must have been an autopsy when Mrs. Caffey died."

"There was. The part about her dying of a heart attack brought on by damage from the stroke checked out. It's the stroke story I have my doubts about."

"Why is that?"

"Medical reports indicated the stroke was most likely bought on by a lack of oxygen to the brain."

"Such as suffocation might cause."

"You got it. Caffey called 911 at two in the morning reporting that he'd found his mother in her bed, blue in the face and not breathing. When the ambulance arrived, the paramedics were able to revive her."

"So he called too soon?"

"The end result would have been the same," Morgan said. "She never spoke again."

"So if your theory is right, he got away with murder."

"Got away with it twice."

"And only got four years in prison for almost making it three," Jake said, thinking aloud. "What do you know about Thad and Jane's relationship?"

Morgan leaned back and crossed a foot over one knee. "That's where things really get interesting. A hodgepodge of information from various family members, neighbors and school personnel painted a clear picture of Thad's dependence on Jane. I can't say it was incest, but they were unusually close, almost always together, frequently holding hands when they thought no one was watching."

"Did anyone speculate why they might be so close?" Jake asked.

"Reports from friends and neighbors suggested Jane was his protector from their abusive, alcoholic mother, who was rumored to have frequently switched her son, occasionally hard enough to leave welts and cuts on his body."

"People knew and did nothing to stop her from beating the crap out of her young son?"

"Several of his teachers reported it. According to the records, their complaints were followed up on by the state's social services department. Thad was seven when they received the first complaint, small for his age, quiet and withdrawn.

"Both Thad and Jane denied any cruel and unusual punishment to the social worker and Mother Dearest must have wised up and quit leaving bruises anywhere they'd show. The case was eventually dropped."

"Basically the same pattern of behavior Thad displayed when he was married to Mildred, only this time he was the one with the power. Like a vicious cycle," Jake said.

"Happens that way sometimes, but not always."

"You must also have a theory for what sent Thad into the rage that left Jane Caffey dead."

"Actually, I don't, which left us with no motive. Partner that with no solid evidence that he did it, and there was no case. But I was so sure he did it that I followed him for years after that. Not as closely after he moved to the Oak Grove area, but I wasn't surprised to read that he'd gone to prison for almost beating his wife to death. Too bad they didn't sentence him for life."

"I second that one," Jake said.

He'd got what he came for—information that helped explain the monster Thad Caffey had become. What he didn't discover was how to stop him for good.

"At least we know Caffey's a coward who only attacks when the odds are greatly in his favor," Jake said.

"So far," Morgan agreed, "but don't count on that always being the case. If he's desperate enough, he'll take more chances. That appears to be what happened in his encounter with your daughter on a public road. The only way you can protect Carolina Lambert is to get him back behind bars or kill him."

"Both options look good to me at this point," Jake admitted.

"Just be careful. Never take anything for granted where he's concerned. Predictability can never be depended on when you're dealing with someone like Caffey."

That pretty much said it all. Ten minutes later, Jake

was on the road and heading back to the Silver Spur with nothing solid in his pocket to lead him to Caffey and even more evidence of how dangerous he was.

He'd have to tell Carolina about his visit with Donald Morgan. She'd be furious that he'd gone without her, but she deserved to know Morgan's take on Thad Caffey.

It would be his first time alone with her since they'd kissed. He didn't know what to expect from her, but he did know she'd kissed him back. Not any perfunctory gesture but a mind-numbing, electrifying kiss that had turned him into mush.

They'd missed their date to go horseback riding yesterday. He'd make up for that today with wine and cheese and some of those fresh raspberries he'd seen in the fridge this morning.

And hopefully they'd wash it down with kisses—or more.

But he wouldn't push and scare her away. He was falling hard, and he wasn't going to blow this if there was any way to give their relationship a chance.

THEY HAD RIDDEN a different route today, one that skirted acres of hay fields, and then meandered through a wooded area before they rode at full gallop across rolling pastures. They finally stopped at the bank of a shimmering pond where two deer were drinking.

The startled deer looked up and then quickly disappeared into the forested area beyond the pond.

Carolina took a few seconds to rein in the exhilaration she'd experienced riding with Jake before dismounting. There was no explaining the way he affected her. There was no denying it, either.

With all she had to deal with, it was Jake's kiss that

had kept her awake until the wee hours of the morning. She was over fifty, a widow, sensible—a grandmother, for God's sake. She didn't become giddy from riding horses with a sexy cowboy. Didn't get weak-kneed from a man's touch, certainly didn't get heart palpitations from a kiss.

But then it had been years since she'd been kissed like that. Plenty of sweet kisses from her grandchildren. Frequent pecks on the cheeks from her sons. And that New Year's Eve when Gillian Casey had grabbed her and placed that disgusting, slobbering smack on her mouth.

Still, she had to get her emotions under control before she made a fool of herself over a man she hadn't even liked a few days ago.

She'd be going home in two more days. After that, she'd likely never see Jake again. Her life would go back to the predictable. In the meantime, she had to get her emotions under control.

Jake walked over as she dismounted, took her reins and tethered them to the branch of an oak tree whose roots crawled into the earth like knotty fingers.

"You were right," Carolina acknowledged. "The ride was just what I needed to get the kinks out of my body and mind. Usually these training sessions are busy but fun. Thad Caffey has made this one an ordeal."

"Yes, and unfortunately I need to bring him up again."

"If you're going to tell me about the car Thad was driving being stolen and then abandoned, I already know. One of the deputies who investigated Lizzie's incident called me today. After that, I called Garcia to be sure he knew. He did and also told me they'd verified Thad's fingerprints were at the scene of the gun burglary."

"That takes care of two issues."

"There's more?"

"I've offered a reward for information leading to Caffey's arrest."

"That the sheriff didn't tell me."

"I'd asked him not to. I wasn't sure how you'd react, and I thought it might be better coming from me."

"I think it's a great idea. Only I can't let you do it. I'm the one Thad Caffey wants dead. If any reward is paid, the Lamberts will pay it."

"Fine. You pay the ten thousand. I'm not getting into a money fight with you. Obviously, the Lamberts would win. But I'm not exactly on poverty row out here."

"I didn't mean it that way."

"Good. Then that's settled."

It wasn't with her. "Do you have any more bombs to drop on me?"

"I met with Donald Morgan today."

"Without even asking if I wanted to go with you?"

"You had obligations here."

He was right, of course, but he could have asked. If he thought one kiss gave him the right to run her life, he was mistaken. Her emotions took off on another roller-coaster ride, this time all downhill.

She turned and walked away, with no particular destination in mind. He caught up with her quickly. He reached for her hand but she jerked it away.

"What did you learn from Morgan?" she snapped. "Or do you think you have to protect me from that, too?"

He grabbed her wrist and this time didn't let go when she tried to pull away. "If my worst sin is protecting you, I can live with that. But protecting you from a crazed madman is all I'm doing. I'm not trying to usurp your independence. Not that I could if I wanted to."

He let go of her wrist and she stepped away. This time she only walked over and leaned against the spindly trunk of a young elm tree. She took a deep breath and exhaled slowly. She had to stop letting every interaction between them—good or bad—affect her so strongly.

"Tell me what you learned about Thad from Donald Morgan," she said, struggling to keep her voice calm.

"Okay. Let me warn you, it's ugly. But I know you can handle it," he added quickly.

Now he was pandering to her as if she were an unreasonable shrew. Not without reason, she reminded herself.

Jake went through the details quickly, not making judgment calls or dwelling on the gore. Even the filtered version of Thad's past was disturbing.

"That's about it," Jake said.

"Scary, but horribly sad, too. It's no wonder Thad turned into the monster he is now."

"Sad, but lots of children go through traumatic childhoods and end up decent, responsible, even loving adults. Thad Caffey chose violence, and now it's consumed him. His reign of terror has to stop."

"I know," she agreed. "But think how tragically twisted and evil his mind and soul have become if he actually killed his sister and his mother."

"Right now I'm having a hard time mustering any sympathy for the guy. What do you say to a pact not to mention Caffey's name for the duration of our outing?"

"An excellent idea, but I can't guarantee clearing him from my thoughts."

"I have a bottle of wine to help with that."

Wine with Jake; just the two of them in an idyllic setting. A seduction scenario that would almost surely lead to another kiss.

"I don't think that's a good idea."

"Why not? Are you afraid of me?"

"No, of course not."

"Then I'll open the wine." He walked back to where the horses were tethered and unloaded a saddlebag that she hadn't even noticed before.

She watched nervously as he spread a blanket over a carpet of pine straw and then pulled a bottle of wine and two crystal flutes from a padded carrier. Only he didn't stop there. He opened individual containers of crackers, raspberries and cheese.

"Is this the typical Jake Dalton entertainment package?"

"Nope. This is the cowboy way to taking a lady's mind off her problems. Well, this and letting her help shovel out the horse barn."

"Then I'm glad you decided to go this way." The humor helped, but her insides were already quaking. If she was smart, this should be where the cowgirl rode away.

She couldn't bring herself to do that.

She joined him on the blanket and took the glass of wine he held out to her. Their fingers brushed. A heated sensation swept from her head to her toes, leaving her giddy before she'd even sipped the wine.

He held his glass up for a toast. "To beautiful beginnings," he said.

She clinked her glass with his. She sipped slowly, afraid of where this was going even while desire had her all but unglued.

He picked up a raspberry and slipped it between her lips. She chewed and swallowed, but it was not raspberries she was craving.

He trailed his fingers down her arm and then back up again, letting them dance across her shoulder until his thumb massaged the nape of her neck.

He was going to kiss her. Once he did, she was going to lose all control. Fear overrode the passion that was burning inside her. She backed away.

"What's wrong now?" he asked, frustration deepening his voice.

"I'm not sure what's happening with us."

"I figured it was pretty clear that I'm crazy about you."

"I like you, too," she admitted. "But I don't see where this can go."

"It can go wherever we want it to. We don't have to rush. If you don't want to make love, if you don't even want me to kiss you yet, I can wait."

Make love. She hadn't even considered that. If his kiss had sent her into ecstasy, what would making love with him do? The idea of it was exciting—but scary.

She'd loved Hugh. She'd been certain she'd never become drunk on another man's nearness, become giddy at another man's touch. That she'd never hunger for another man's kiss. That she'd never ache to sleep in another man's arms.

This time she was the one who leaned in close and claimed Jake's lips with hers. And then she was lost in the thrill of it all.

JAKE WAS TAKING a cold shower back at the house, trying to tamp down the sexual drives that would never be satisfied with just kisses. He might never be satisfied. He couldn't even imagine getting enough of Carolina.

But was Carolina really ready for this, or was it the

danger intensifying her feelings? When she was safe, would she back off, be hesitant to fall in love again?

He had to admit that until this week, he'd never seriously considered falling madly in love again.

But at some point, you had to go on with your life. He'd reached that point as long as he could move on with Carolina. If she needed time, he'd give it to her, even though it would mean a lot of cold showers and sleepless nights.

His phone rang. He rinsed the soap from his hair and body, stepped out of the shower and grabbed a towel. Still dripping, he knotted the towel around his waist and dripped his way to the phone.

"Hello."

"Brad Pacer here."

"Great. Dare I hope you're calling with good news?"

"I don't have your man in hand, but I do have some credible sightings reported. Seems he's working his way down south, driving an old beat-up gray compact car. Don't have the make or a license plate number yet."

"How far south are we talking?"

"A few miles south of Corpus Christi. My guess is he's heading to the border. I alerted Border Patrol to keep an eye out for him, but they already had him on their watch list."

"You're sure these sightings are credible?"

"At least three of the four are. The last one was at a truck stop on Highway 77. I showed the waitress his mug shot and tried to explain how he looked now. She jumped in and described that snake tattoo exactly as you did."

"I find it hard to believe that Caffey is going to give up on getting to Carolina," Jake said. "So if he is planning to cross the border, it won't be for good. The bastard will just be waiting it out until he feels it's time to strike again."

"You could be right."

Which would leave the danger hanging over Carolina indefinitely.

"What's next?" Jake asked.

"I called the state police and let them know where he was last spotted," Pacer said.

"Did they even know there was a warrant out for his arrest?"

"They did after they looked it up. I wouldn't hold my breath waiting on them to arrest him, though. Considering what they deal with every day in the border towns, a threat and a hit-and-run is about as high on their priority list as stealing a box of Girl Scout cookies."

"I'm sure it is, but finding Caffey is on the top of my list. Do you need more men to get the job done?"

"Not at the moment," Pacer said. "I'll let you know if that changes."

"Keep me posted."

"Will do. One other question. Have you ever heard of Mateo Salinas?"

"Not that I recall. Why?"

"He was in prison with Thad Caffey. I questioned one of the guards who said Caffey and Salinas buddied up before Salinas was released."

"What's Salinas's claim to fame?" Jake asked.

"He's involved with a Mexican drug cartel. I'm thinking Caffey might be headed down south to join up with him. In the meantime, I don't think you need to worry about Caffey showing up at the Silver Spur."

If Pacer was right and Caffey had cleared out of the area for now, at least they had some breathing room. Not that Jake was planning to let up on any of the security measures they had in place.

But he would need to tell Carolina the news, which meant bringing up the fact that he'd also hired a bounty hunter without discussing it with her.

He'd soft-pedal it later, when they were alone—whenever that turned out to be. He started pacing. The knot worked loose and the thick terry towel slid to the floor. He kicked it aside and kept walking, arousal rearing its head again as a plan began to formulate in his mind. Too bad bedtime was still hours away.

Chapter Nineteen

Carolina dipped her fingers into the jar of lilac-scented body butter. With long strokes, she rubbed the moisturizing nourishment into her arms until it was absorbed completely, careful not to get a glob of it on her clean pink nightshirt. Creaming her whole body was a nightly routine she'd initiated years ago, having learned soon after marrying Hugh that spending too many hours in the hot Texas sun could wreak havoc on her skin.

The prospect of becoming a rancher's wife had been scary. She'd known nothing about cattle or horses. Had never even been close to a tractor, much less driven one.

Now she couldn't imagine living anywhere but on the Bent Pine Ranch. Her sons and their families were there. Her memories were there. Her heart was there.

Jake Dalton's life was here, in this house, on the Silver Spur, raising his troubled daughter, managing his mother, who at eighty was clearly a handful. Spry, independent and delightful. Still sharp enough that nothing got past her.

Which meant she had probably sensed the sparks between Jake and Carolina, just as Tague had. Surprisingly the idea of her being romantically involved with another man hadn't seemed to bother Carolina's youngest son at all.

She screwed the top back on the rich cream and walked back into the bedroom, closing the bathroom door behind her. She climbed into the king-size bed and slid between the crisp sheets.

A bed in Jake's house. On Jake's ranch. With the taste of Jake's kisses still on her tongue. With a hunger growing inside her that she longed to satisfy with a man she barely knew. She was falling in love. She wouldn't even try to deny that anymore.

She just couldn't fathom where the relationship could go. She had her life. He had his.

She turned off the lamp, wrapped her hands around one of the three spare pillows and hugged it to her chest. She was sensible. Mature. Responsible. But even knowing the odds were stacked against them, even knowing that when she left on Sunday this infatuation would likely end for him, even having a madman who wanted her dead to deal with...

She still wished she were sleeping in Jake's arms tonight.

A tap on the door startled her but only for a second. It was probably Mildred with a last-minute question about tomorrow's schedule or just wanting to talk.

She flicked on the lamp. "Come in."

The door opened and Jake stepped in, dressed only in jeans and carrying an overflowing tray.

"What in the world are you bringing me?"

"Normalcy. A first movie date. Like people have who aren't dealing with a madman."

"It looks more like food and drink to me."

"Hot chocolate, popcorn, Edna's homemade oatmeal

cookies and movies." He set the tray on the desk and tossed a half dozen movies onto the bed.

"It's ten o'clock," she cautioned.

"We don't have to watch all of them. I wanted you to have a choice."

"Lonesome Dove? Hangover? Die Hard? The Good, the Bad and the Ugly?"

"Well, you weren't expecting me to own chick flicks, were you?"

"Absolutely not." She shoved the pillow she'd been hugging behind her and propped herself up to a sitting position.

He handed her a cup of the chocolate. "What's your movie choice?"

She patted a spot on the bed next to her. "I'd rather talk."

"As long as it's not about Thad Caffey."

"Who?"

"Atta girl." He crawled into bed beside her, on top of the coverlet, still in his jeans. "What shall we talk about?"

She knew she was probably about to blow the moment, but they couldn't always just get lost in the physical. If this had a chance of going anywhere, they had to really get to know each other.

"Tell me about your past, your life as a surgeon, your life with Gloria."

Jake frowned, his whole demeanor changing. "Do we have to go there tonight?"

"We have to be able to go there if we're going to keep having movie dates. I'm not asking for your darkest or your most personal secrets. I just want to understand you better."

"I'm not a complicated man. I am what you see, Carolina. No pretenses. No lies."

"How did you and Gloria meet?" she asked, moving him along before the desire to be in his arms overpowered her need to talk.

"We were both freshmen at the University of Texas. She was the superior student, determined to be a doctor since she was a kid and taking her classes very seriously. I had no idea what I wanted to do with my life. I was there to party."

"Then you didn't always want to be a rancher?"

"I did when I was growing up. From the day Mother married John Dayton and we moved onto the Silver Spur, I considered myself a full-fledged cowboy."

"What changed that?"

"John was killed in a hay-baling accident when I was fifteen. In my mind John was my real father and always will be. With him gone, I found myself hating ranching.

"That might have passed except a couple of years later Mother remarried. Butch Dickens wasn't a bad man, but he wasn't my dad. Looking back, I probably didn't give him much reason to like me. At any rate, we clashed at every turn. I couldn't wait to leave home."

"That must have upset Mary."

"She took it in stride. I think she figured I had a lot of growing up to do and I'd do it better out on my own. And I'm sure it was a lot more peaceful around here with me gone."

"What made you decide to become a doctor?"

"Gloria. From the moment we met, things started falling into place for me. We both knew we were meant to be together. I worked my tail off. It was a champagne-guzzling day for everyone when we were both accepted into medical school."

"And both of you went on to become doctors. That's quite an accomplishment for a bona fide cowboy."

"You better know it. Gloria loved kids. Becoming a pediatrician was a natural for her. I had to search a little harder to find my niche."

"What finally made you decide to become a surgeon?"

"The idea of cutting out the diseased tissue and being done with it appealed to me. I chose general surgery. Figured I'd lose fewer patients on the operating table than the specialist surgeons. I liked saving patients. Was never good at telling someone they weren't going to make it. I never missed that part of being a doctor."

"What did you miss?"

He lay back, letting his head rest on a pillow as he stared at the ceiling. "I missed my life with Gloria. After the car accident, after she died, I couldn't go on as if life still had any meaning. Besides, Butch was dead and Mother was in a coma. They didn't give me much hope she'd ever come out of it. I came back to take care of the ranch. It was the only thing I had to hold on to."

"You had Lizzie."

"And she was the only bright spot in my life. I was so lost in my grief that I'm sure I didn't give her enough attention. I can't help wondering now if that is what's at the root of our current inability to connect."

"You'll have a chance to work that out with Dr. Otis," Carolina offered.

"I hope he helps."

"Even if Dr. Otis doesn't have all the answers, you'll find a way to reach Lizzie. I'm sure of it."

Jake rolled over on his side and propped himself on

his left elbow so that he was facing her. "I don't want to lose you, Carolina. What we have together doesn't come along every day. You must know that."

"I can't replace Gloria, Jake. No one can."

"I don't expect you to, no more than I can replace Hugh. What we build together won't diminish what we shared with them. We'll carve out space in our hearts and minds for us. Shared moments that are ours alone. A favorite movie. A song that belongs to us. All I'm asking is a chance."

All she knew was that she'd be crazy to walk away without giving them both that chance. She rolled into his arms and kissed him. Tender at first, then wild with passion.

"Keep this up and we're never going to get to that movie," she murmured.

Jake picked up the movies and slid them onto the floor. "In that case, Carolina Lambert, we are wearing way too many clothes."

CAROLINA WOKE TO a sweet ache in her thighs and the sound of Jake's rhythmic breathing. One of his arms was thrown over her naked abdomen. One of his legs crossed hers.

She hadn't been dreaming. They had made love, more than once. She'd never imagined she'd find this kind of magic a second time in her life.

He stirred, his leg sliding up hers. Delicious desires danced through her again. But it was morning and she had a training session to conduct.

She tried to slide from the bed without waking him. Instead he pulled her into his arms, his body spooning hers. His erection pressed hard against her.

"I thought you were asleep," she said.

"I was. Now I'm awake. Wide awake."

"Good because you need to get up and go back to your room before someone realizes you slept in here with me last night."

"I was thinking maybe I'd just shout it from the rooftop."

"That would create a stir." She pushed him away, threw her legs over the side of the bed and pulled on the nightshirt that had ended up thrown over the lamp.

"I have an idea," he said. "Why go home on Sunday? Why not spend at least a few more days here? Or we could go away. Colorado's nice this time of year."

"I have a better idea," she said, speaking as the idea formed in her mind.

"Let's hear it."

"You go home with me for a few days. Meet my family."

"I think I might be able to handle that."

"We could stop off at the Dry Gulch for a few minutes. You could say hello to R.J."

He stretched out across the bed. "You're never going to let go of this until I do, are you?"

"I might if you tell me why you're so set against even talking to your father."

"In the first place, I don't consider him my father. More important, he let me and my mother down when she needed him most."

"When was that?"

Jake got out of bed, wiggled into his jeans and walked to the window. "She kept calling for Reuben when she was in the coma. It took a few days for me to realize she was talking about her first husband. It had been years since she'd even mentioned his name."

"Did you call R.J. and let him know?"

"I did better than that. I paid him a visit. He was so drunk he didn't even know who I was when he came to the door half dressed in the middle of the day."

Carolina couldn't begin to make excuses for R.J. He'd had his demons. Alcoholism had been one of the worst. But he'd changed. He'd found redemption. His body was giving up. His heart had turned to gold. "Did you try to talk to him?"

"No. A woman half his age came staggering down the hall wrapped in a dingy sheet. I left without saying another word. My mother came out of the coma sixteen days later. She never mentioned Reuben again, and I never told her what happened."

"I can understand how you feel, but I still think you should see him—for both your sakes."

"I don't need anything from him."

"Then what do you have to lose?"

"Okay, Carolina. You win. But I'm doing this for you, not R.J."

She walked over, stopped behind him and rested her head on his shoulder. She'd never felt closer to him than she did at this second. "Thank you."

He turned and pulled her into his arms. This time she didn't push him away.

JAKE STRETCHED HIS legs under Granger's small kitchen table and studied the printout his foreman had just handed him. "I don't see a charge for that new feed blend I ordered when I was in San Antonio last week."

"They haven't shipped it," Granger said.

"They promised immediate delivery. Check with them on Monday. If they don't have a good reason for the delay, cancel the order. I don't want to start doing business with a company if I can't depend on their word."

"I'll take care of it."

Jake scanned down a few inches. "Looks like Dan Stinson robbed me again with those tractor repairs."

"He swears that everything except the two-hundred-dollar labor charge went into the parts."

"He always does," Jake said. "He's the best tractor mechanic this side of Austin, though, and I can't afford to have that big John Deere sitting idle this time of the year."

"And Stinson knows it," Granger agreed.

Jake pushed back from the desk. "Everything else looks good to me."

"Lanky says the engine on the Yamaha four-wheeler sounds like it's chewing rocks," Granger said.

"Have Tilson take a look at that on Monday. He's got an ear for those ATV engines. Better than those diagnostics they run at the shop."

"Will do."

Expenditures and ATVs. Jake was going through the motions but having a devil of a time wrapping his mind around anything to do with the ranch. Carolina claimed too many of his brain cells.

He'd been with other women since Gloria's death. Beautiful women. Successful women. Women who'd made it clear they'd like nothing better than to become Mrs. Jake Dalton.

He wouldn't say he'd never enjoyed being with them, but there were none he'd wanted to be with when the sun came up the following morning.

He could have stayed in bed with Carolina all day.

He could see himself having lazy breakfasts with her on Saturday mornings in the future, lingering over coffee and then going back to bed and making love until noon.

He could see himself curled up beside her watching the movies they'd never gotten around to last night or even a chick flick. He could picture the two of them cuddled in front of a roaring fireplace on a frigid January night, or dancing in the moonlight beneath a star-studded sky.

He could see spending the rest of his life with her.

He'd only felt that way about one woman before. If you'd asked him last week, he'd have bet the ranch that kind of magic could never happen twice. He might well be the luckiest man on the planet.

"You ever think about getting married, Granger?"

"All the time. But then I think about it some more and decide against it."

"Why?"

"I've seen too many men who let wives wreck their lives. Want to go hunting? The little lady wants you to spend the weekend with the in-laws. Want to go fishing? Wifey wants you to work in the yard. Want to have sex? She has a headache. My dog, my horse and my pickup truck. And a few cold beers on Saturday night. That's as good as it gets."

"Sounds like you got your philosophy of life from a country song."

"You can do worse."

Jake was hoping for a whole lot better.

"I need to let you know that I'll be away Sunday night," he said.

"Leaving when the crew of women do?"

"About the same time, hopefully around three thirty tomorrow afternoon."

"So what about all this extra security we have in place? Want me to call the dogs off with the exit of Mrs. Lambert and those Saddle-Uppers?"

"No. Leave it in place until I give the word. I'd like at least two men watching the house at all times while I'm gone. Move Tilson into the house. He can stay in one of the guest suites."

"He's gonna lap up that luxury like a starving dog."

"That's okay, as long as Mother and Lizzie are safe."

"So Thad Caffey is still on the loose?"

Jake nodded. "For now. Hopefully not for long."

But the odds of his crossing the border to freedom grew greater every minute. Jake glanced at his watch. Almost ten. He'd expected to hear from Brad Pacer before this. If Brad was as good as his reputation, he should have found Caffey and turned him over to the police by now.

"Anything else you want me to take care of while you're gone?" Granger asked.

"Yourself. Don't do anything to aggravate that leg."

"I'm watching it. This hobbling is getting old fast."

"You can reach me by cell at any time," Jake said. "Don't hesitate to call, especially if it concerns Mother or Lizzie."

"I'll see they're watched over. Don't you worry none, boss man."

He'd stop worrying when Caffey was behind bars. He waited until he was back in his truck and then made a call to Brad Pacer. No answer. He left a message for Pacer to call him back.

And he still needed to tell Carolina about the bounty hunter. Last night had not been the opportune time.

He placed a call to Sheriff Garcia's private cell phone to see if he had any news on Caffey's whereabouts. He was about to break the connection when the sheriff finally answered.

"Damn, Jake. You must be psychic. I was about to call you."

"With good news?"

"Not good for a young woman in Brownsville, Texas. Thad Caffey struck again."

"I'm not following you."

"Melissa Green, a young Brownsville woman, had her house broken into in the wee hours of the morning. She was savagely attacked, beaten and kicked until she passed out. She's in the hospital now, undergoing surgery for internal injuries."

"I know Caffey is capable of beating up women, but how did they tie Thad Caffey to Melissa Green?"

"It was all caught on a security camera that he obviously didn't see."

"And it's a quality image, clear enough that you're sure the attacker is Caffey?"

"That's the word I'm getting."

"Attacking a stranger has never been his modus operandi. He must have some connection to her, perhaps in his past, in Gunshot or maybe in prison."

"Possibly. She works for Homeland Security with Border Patrol. She's not talking yet. If she does, we may find out more."

"By if, do you mean she may not make it?" Jake asked.

"Her condition is listed as critical."

"Has Caffey been apprehended?"

"No, but Brownsville is crawling with cops searching for him. If he's there, they'll find him."

"And if they don't?"

"Then it's possible he's already escaped into Mexico

and free to travel to all points south," Garcia said. "He won't have changed, but he may be someone else's problem and not ours."

Jake reminded him of the obvious. "We can never rule out his sneaking back into the country."

"If he does, and Melissa Green dies, he'll face murder charges. If she doesn't, he's still earned himself a return trip to prison."

When and if they caught him. As long as Caffey was free, Carolina would never be safe.

Jake hated to interrupt her, hated even more to tell her the sickening new developments. But he couldn't wait. If she or Mildred had ever heard of Melissa Green either directly from Caffey or during his trial, Jake needed to know now.

If Caffey had any ties with anyone in Brownsville, he needed to know that, too.

All he asked was one solid clue to lead to Caffey's arrest. One more miracle. And he needed it soon.

"THERE HAS TO be a tie between Thad and the assaulted woman," Carolina insisted, seething at Jake's revelation of Thad's latest horror. "I can't imagine he drove to Brownsville to attack a random woman."

"I agree," Jake said. "That's why I asked Lanky to bring you and Mildred to headquarters to meet me. I'm hoping one of you has heard of her before."

"The only Melissa I ever heard him mention was the clerk at the market," Mildred said. "That was just to complain that she held up the checkup line chatting with the customers."

"What about Brownsville?" Jake asked. "Did he have family or friends there that you know of?"

"Not that he ever mentioned to me," Mildred said. "Don't you think he was just in Brownsville to cross the border into Metamoros?"

"And may already have," Jake said. "But if he hasn't, then he's hiding out in the area. If we knew his ties to Melissa Green, it might help us track him down."

"And they're sure that it was Thad who attacked her?" Carolina asked. "Because this sounds a lot like the work of one of the drug cartels, payback against a border agent."

"Another possibility," Jake said. "Did he ever mention any prison mates with ties to a drug cartel?"

"I don't remember him ever mentioning but one friend in his letters."

"Do you remember his name?"

"Salinas. Give me a minute. Salinas Mata? No. That's not it."

"Maybe Mateo Salinas?" Jake offered.

"That sounds right. Thad was impressed with him. Said Mateo was going to get him a job when he got out of prison and that we'd be clearing out of Oak Grove for good. That was before I filed for divorce and he stopped writing."

"Do you know Mateo Salinas?" Carolina asked.

"No, but I've heard of him from a contact of mine," Jake said. "Apparently he is connected with a drug cartel."

"You have friends in low places," Carolina said.

"Actually the contact is a bounty hunter that I hired to find Caffey."

"You hired a bounty hunter without even talking to me about it. Is that even legal?"

"He's legal and licensed," Jake said. "A retired navy

SEAL who has a reputation for getting his man. He doesn't arrest anyone. He just locates the guy and makes sure the police know where to find him."

"How long has he been looking for Caffey?"

"Since yesterday morning. He'd followed Caffey's trail to Corpus Christi yesterday and suspected he was heading to the border. I haven't heard from him since then."

"So it could be that he beat up the woman in exchange for Salinas giving him a job or at least helping him sneak across the border illegally," Carolina said.

She shivered as chills crept up her spine. "That's why he didn't care if he left his prints. He was planning to kill me first, drive to Brownsville, attack Melissa Green and then it was adios, America."

"And there's a good chance he would have killed you if Jake hadn't convinced us to move to the ranch," Mildred said. "I can't believe I made excuses for Thad's violent behavior for three years, right up to the moment he attacked me the way he did Melissa Green."

"You were lucky you got out of that marriage with your life," Jake said.

"What about Melissa?" Carolina said. "Will she live?"

"Her condition is listed as critical."

"I'm glad you hired a bounty hunter," Carolina said. "I want to be in the courtroom when they sentence Thad Caffey to life in prison."

"So do I," Jake said. "So do I, but if he gets shot first, I can live just fine with that, too."

Chapter Twenty

It was an hour later before Brad Pacer returned Jake's call.

"Sorry to be so late getting back to you. I've been investigating in an area with no cell phone service."

"Where is that?"

"I can't give away trade secrets, but suffice it to say, it's a place where you'd never turn your back on anyone."

"Have you heard that Caffey brutally attacked a female border-patrol agent in Brownsville sometime during the night?"

"I didn't hear about it until it hit the morning news. I contacted my sources and that's when I went way undercover to investigate."

"What did you learn?" Jake asked.

"The attack was payback for her shooting one of the cartel members in a shootout along the Rio Grande last month. Border Patrol claimed it was self-defense. The cartel called it murder."

"But you don't have any leads as to where Caffey is hiding out now?" Jake asked.

"It's almost certain he's across the border by now, not legally, of course. They would have been watching for him at the checkpoints. But the cartels run people across like cattle whenever it suits them. The only laws they follow are the ones they make."

"But it is possible he could still be hiding on the American side of the border," Jake said.

"It's possible," Pacer admitted. "I haven't run into evidence of that. Sounds like you're not ready for me to give up the search."

"I won't be ready to do that until Caffey is in jail or dead."

"If I work both sides of the border, my price triples."

"Not a problem. I just want results."

"Then you're in luck. When restrictions are off the table, I always get my man."

LIZZIE PLACED A plate of sliced tomatoes on the table Jake had set up on the wide back porch. "I can't believe you two are leaving tomorrow. It seems like you just got here."

"But I'll be seeing a lot of you when you're a junior counselor," Mildred said. "I'll be helping Sara out."

"Fun. What about you, Carolina?"

"I'll be coordinating the camps in the Dallas area. They will keep me very busy, but you can always come visit me at the Bent Pine."

"Did you hear that, Dad?"

Jake flipped one of the steaks he was grilling a few feet away. "I heard. I figure we can work that out one day."

Mary joined them on the porch, a pitcher of icy lemonade in hand. "What are you two working out?"

"Lizzie's visiting Carolina's ranch."

Mary's eyebrows rose. "Tell me more."

"We don't know when yet."

"Before the end of summer," Carolina said.

Jake said nothing. For a man who wanted to shout their relationship from the rooftops, he'd suddenly become suspiciously silent.

"What about you, Jake?" she prodded. "Do you want to visit the ranch, too?"

"He never does fun stuff," Lizzie complained. "He works on the ranch, goes to meetings and reads thick, boring books with no story."

"It's called nonfiction," Jake said. "But I guess I may as well tell you all that I'm going to follow Carolina and Mildred back to Oak Grove when they finish up the training session tomorrow."

"That's a surprise," Mary said. "And a long drive there and back, especially getting such a late start."

"I won't be driving back tomorrow night."

"Why not?" Lizzie asked. "I heard Dad say that Thad Caffey escaped into Mexico. You're not still in danger, are you, Carolina?"

"No, and thankfully neither are you. Thad Caffey is nowhere near here." No use to frighten her again. She'd been through enough.

"Are you planning to see R.J. while you're so close?" Mary asked.

Matter-of-fact and straightforward. Mary must have always been that way. She and R.J. were probably a wild match, but Mary didn't hate him. Clearly she hadn't discouraged Jake from talking to his father.

"Who's R.J.?" Lizzie questioned.

"R.J. was my first husband," Mary said. "He's your dad's father."

"I thought John Dalton who got killed baling hay was Dad's father. How many husbands did you have?"

"Only three, dear." Mary sat down beside Lizzie and patted her hand. "And only one at a time."

"If R.J. is my grandfather, why have I never heard of him?"

"I'll take care of this from here," Jake said. He moved the steaks from grill to platter and joined them at the table. "It was John Dayton, not Dalton, who was killed in the hay-baling accident. Mother left R.J. when I was very young. John was the only father I ever knew, so it's natural he's the one you heard me refer to as Dad."

"If I have another grandfather, I want to meet him."

Jake put a hand on Lizzie's shoulder. "He has brain cancer, sweetheart. He's dying. You don't want to see him like that."

"I don't want to wait until he's dead. Why can't I just go with you and Carolina tomorrow?"

Jake looked at Carolina. She nodded her approval.

"I don't think it's a good idea," Jake said, "but if you really want to meet him, you can go with us. Just remember, he's very ill. I don't expect him to recognize me or understand that you're his granddaughter."

"Sometimes he doesn't even recognize me, and we're very close friends," Carolina said, knowing Jake was right to prepare Lizzie for the worst.

"You know, I think I'll go, too," Mary said. "You don't mind, do you, Carolina?"

"No. The more the merrier."

Jake groaned.

Carolina smiled and gave one of Lizzie's hands a squeeze. R.J. wanted to get to know all his family. He might be about to get more than he'd bargained for.

She just prayed he was alert enough to know that his oldest son was finally coming home—even if it was for only a day.

Chapter Twenty-One

"A spokesperson from the hospital just informed KRGV-TV that Melissa Green, the border-patrol agent who was brutally beaten in her home last night, has died from her injuries."

Thad reached for the nearest thing he could find. His fingers closed around the cheap lamp. He picked it up and threw it as hard as he could at the TV. The screen shattered. The sound went silent.

He'd screwed up. Mateo had warned him not to make a mistake. Melissa Green was not supposed to die. Mess up with Mateo's boss and you didn't live to do it twice.

Mateo and some guy he didn't know had picked him up after the attack and brought him out to this run-down mobile home so far from civilization that no one could find him, and he had no idea how to find his way out.

They'd brought him clean clothes. Brought him fast-food hamburgers and a couple beers. Took the rifle he'd stolen back in Oak Grove. Would have taken the automatic pistol if they'd found it on him. And then they told him they'd be back for him when they had everything in place to sneak him across the border.

He'd thought he had it made. He hadn't given up on

killing Carolina Lambert. He was only giving her a reprieve.

They'd come for him just like they said. Any minute now they'd come for him. But he would never see Mexico. He'd never even see another dawn.

He had to get out of here. If he kept walking he'd have to eventually come to a road or a house or a railroad track he could follow. He went to the kitchen, searched the drawers and came up with a jagged-edge hunting knife, a screwdriver and an ice pick. It never hurt to have more than one weapon.

He'd never used an ice pick to kill and torture a woman. He'd never thought of it as a weapon—until now. The perfect weapon to plunge through the center of Carolina's heart.

He wouldn't get to Mexico, but he would get his revenge.

Chapter Twenty-Two

R.J. sat in his favorite chair and tried to keep up with the conversation going on around him. One-on-one, he could communicate with his sons, but when they all four got to talking together, it was just too dadgum confusing.

Adam walked over and stood by the arm of R.J.'s chair. "Do you remember who's coming to see you tonight?"

"Dog me if I don't. You done told me enough times. Jake outta be here by now. Do you think he got lost?"

"Carolina's with him, Dad. I'm sure she didn't get lost coming here."

"Probably had to hog-tie him to get him here," R.J. said.

"I doubt that," Cannon said. "More likely she used her womanly wiles."

Carolina and Jake. Be something if they were a couple. He'd always thought it would be nice if one of his sons ended up with her. Not that he didn't love the daughters-in-law he had.

But Jake was a widower with a teenage daughter. He needed a wife. He was about the right age for Carolina, too.

But R.J. wasn't sure Jake was good enough for her. He'd know after they talked unless he fell into one of those confusing spells where he had trouble even remembering where he was.

"Jake's mother is coming, too," Leif said. "And so is his daughter."

"You done told me that a dozen times, too."

"Sorry about that," Leif said. "You know how I tend to repeat myself."

"Do you remember Jake's mother?" Travis asked.

"Hell yes, I remember her. I fell in love with that prissy girl back in high school. Of course, every other boy in school did, too."

"But you were the one who ended up with her," Travis said.

"I dated her our senior year. I didn't end up with her. You don't see her around here anywhere, do you?"

"Not yet," Cannon admitted. "Did you two marry right out of high school?"

"Lands no. That girl wasn't even thinking about settling down. She couldn't wait to go away to college. She begged me to go with her, but I barely passed high school. Besides, Daddy needed my help running the ranch."

"Well, you had to get together at some point," Cannon said. "You married her."

"You guys are worse than a bunch of cackling hens."

"How did the two of you get back together?" Cannon asked.

"Best I remember, she just showed up back in Oak Grove one day. Got tired of living in New York, I s'pect."

"She sounds like an interesting woman," Adam said.

"She was that."

But those days were long gone. It was Jake he was interested in seeing now. He couldn't make things right with Jake. He'd been a terrible father and that was a fact.

The drinking and gambling had taken him down. Nobody's fault but his own.

But he could say he was sorry.

R.J.'s eyelids felt heavy. He was getting sleepy. "Reckon they changed their mind about coming," R.J. said.

"They'll be here in a few minutes. Carolina would have called if there had been a change of plans."

R.J. got up and walked back to the kitchen for a glass of water. He took a glass from the cupboard and held it under the faucet. The water filled his glass and ran over his fingers. The water just kept coming.

The room started to spin. Faster and faster. He stumbled to the table and fell into a chair.

"Gwen," he called again. "Gwen. I can't turn off the water."

Gwen didn't come. She was never here when he needed her. There was something he was supposed to do tonight. He put his head on the table and floated away.

JAKE STOPPED IN front of R.J.'s house. Three pickup trucks and one car were parked in the driveway. Carolina was certain they were all eager for Jake and R.J. to get together.

"It looks like a party," Jake said.

"No one but the Dalton brothers are supposed to be here tonight," Carolina said. "And Brit and the baby. She and Cannon live in the house with R.J. The others have their own cabins scattered about the ranch."

"A grandfather, uncles, aunts and cousins by the dozens," Lizzie said. "I can't wait to meet everybody."

"Not this trip," Jake said. "This is to meet your grandfather. We won't be staying long enough for a family reunion."

They got out of the car. Carolina led the entourage with Lizzie right beside her. Jake and Mary brought up the rear. Carolina's nerves were on edge. She so wanted this to go well.

R.J.'s son Adam met them at the door and then led them to the family room for introductions.

Carolina looked around. "Where's R.J.?"

"He was in here and looking forward to seeing you until about ten minutes ago," Cannon said. "He had one of the spells that are occurring at least once or twice a day now."

"That breaks my heart," Carolina said, "I know he really wants to see Jake. Maybe if I talk to him, he'll snap out of it."

"I don't think that's a good idea," Adam said. "He's in bed, resting if not asleep."

"I'm sure you know best," Jake said. "Mom, Lizzie and I are staying the night at the Bent Pine. We'll try this again in the morning. For now I think we should just get out of here so we don't disturb him."

"Sorry to say it," Leif said, "but I think that would be for the best."

Mary made no move to leave. Instead she walked to the center of the spacious room. "You know, I remember dancing with Reuben in this very room. Furniture was different. Old fireplace looks the same, though.

"He had a Dean Martin song spinning on his old Victrola." Mary started singing. "When the moon hits your eye… Sorry," she said. "I just got carried away."

Jake heard shuffling footsteps in the hallway. A minute later R.J. appeared at the door.

"Gwen, quit that squawking. Turn off that music and come to bed."

Carolina rushed over to take R.J.'s arm so as to help steady him.

"I'm sorry," Cannon apologized. "Dad frequently asks for someone named Gwen when he sinks into a confused state."

"He's not that confused," she said. "Reuben always called me Gwen. He didn't think Mary was a fancy enough name for me."

"Are you coming to bed?" R.J. insisted.

Tears moistened Mary's eyes. "No, you old fool. I'm not coming to bed. We're going to dance."

She walked over and put her arms around him. They swayed for a few seconds in each other's arms. "Now we're going to bed," she said. They walked away together, arm in arm.

"Well, I'll be damned," Adam said. "All this time we've been trying to figure out who the mystery woman Gwen was. Now it turns out she was his first wife."

Tears burned at the back of Carolina's eyes. R.J. and Mary, lovers from the past. R.J. called for Gwen when he faded to a place where he lost all sense of time and reality. Mary had called for R.J. when she was in a coma at the point of death.

Their marriage hadn't made it, but they must have loved each other very much at some point in the past.

Mary joined them a few minutes later. "Rueben's back in bed. I think we should go now. We'll come back in the morning. If he feels better I may even make him finish our dance."

CAROLINA AND MARY stood on the front porch at Dry Gulch waving goodbye to Adam, Jake, Lizzie and R.J. Carolina was thrilled with how the morning had gone so far. She should have known Jake and R.J. would have something to talk about. They were both ranchers.

R.J. couldn't wait to give Jake a tour of the Dry Gulch Ranch. That was where they were off to now, with Adam in the driver's seat.

Mary slapped her cheek lightly. "Wouldn't you know I walked right off and left that basket of peaches I brought for Reuben on your kitchen table back at the Bent Pine? I picked them myself just yesterday from my own trees."

"I can go back and get them," Carolina said.

"That's not necessary. He probably gets enough peaches from around here."

"Not ones that you've picked yourself."

And he would like that. It was easy to see he was excited about seeing her again.

"Are you okay here by yourself?" Carolina asked. "If not, you can ride back to my house with me."

"I'm just fine. Funny the little things I'm remembering just sitting here. The night I went into labor with Jake and we couldn't get our old car to start."

"What did you do?"

"Jake rode his horse over to a neighbor's in the middle of a thunderstorm and borrowed their car."

"Did you make it to the hospital in time?"

"About three days too early. It was false labor. Reuben didn't think it was nearly as funny as I did."

"I bet not. I'll drive over and pick up the peaches and be back long before the guys."

"Take your time, dear. I'll be just fine."

Carolina was already in the car and almost to the highway when she remembered that Jake had told her not to leave the ranch alone. He was still worried about Thad, but that was only because he was overprotective.

Even Sheriff Garcia had dropped by the ranch earlier this morning to tell them that Border Patrol had issued a statement saying they had credible evidence that Thad had escaped into Mexico.

The gate at the Dry Gulch was not automatic. She got out, pushed it open and then got back in the truck to drive through it. Then she had to get out and close it again.

She tuned the radio to one of her favorite stations that played a mixture of standards and light jazz. She liked driving her car again. Liked being home again, too.

If she and Jake were to marry, there would be a million changes she'd have to make in her life. She wouldn't see her grandchildren nearly as often. Most of her close friends lived nearby. Her doctors were all in Dallas. Her hairdresser was in Oak Grove. All the people she relied on for repairs or catering or altering clothes were in this area.

She glanced behind her as she neared the turnoff for the back road to the Bent Pine. A car was coming up on her fast. Too fast and it wasn't slowing down. She took to the shoulder to avoid being hit.

The car slammed into her. Her car skidded down the shoulder a good quarter of a mile before she could get it under control. When she looked in her rearview mirror, she could see the car was hanging back, as if the driver was waiting for the opportunity to hit her again.

This could not be a coincidence. Not on this road, where they had never had trouble like this before. Not so soon after Thad had run Lizzie off the road.

There was only one logical explanation. Thad Caffey wasn't in Mexico. He was in the car behind her and determined to run her off the road, the same way he had done to Lizzie.

Not very creative, but he'd probably figured that his best chance to get her alone was on this lonesome back road, either leaving or returning home. She had ignored Jake's warnings and played right into Thad Caffey's evil, murderous hands.

She floored the accelerator and steered hard around the curve. Just a few more miles, but she was approaching an even sharper curve.

She held on to the wheel with both hands. She was almost through the curve when she heard a gunshot. A second shot hit the back window of her car, shattering the glass into a million tiny fragments.

A new spray of bullets splattered the back of the car.

He was going to kill her, mere miles from the Bent Pine. She hit the curve going as fast as she could. The car practically went into orbit. It flew across the shoulder on the opposite side of the road and then started to roll. When it stopped, she and her car were upside down.

Vertigo struck with a vengeance. Her vision grew fuzzy and then went black.

By the time she revived and could focus again, she was on the ground, her hands bound at the wrists. Thad Caffey was standing over her, an ice pick clutched in his right hand.

Chapter Twenty-Three

Jake held on to R.J.'s arm to steady him as they walked to the truck from the horse barn. Lizzie was still bonding with every horse in sight.

"You've got some mighty fine horses," Jake said.

"That's my only claim to fame around these parts."

"Maybe not your *only* one," Jake said.

"Well, except for my bad reputation."

Jake's phone rang. It was Brad Pacer.

"I'm afraid I have to take this call," he said.

"Don't worry about me. I can still walk."

Albeit not very steadily. Fortunately, Adam came to the rescue.

"Morning, Brad," Jake said as Adam and R.J. walked away. "How are things in Brownsville?"

"I'm no longer in Brownsville. As of about two minutes ago, I'm on my way to Oak Grove."

"Why?"

"Thad Caffey was recently spotted in a service station about ten miles south of there."

The pressure swelled, pushing against Jake's chest.

"I'm not sure how credible this particular sighting is," Pacer admitted, "but I stopped everything to alert you."

"Thanks. I'll call you back later, but right now I need to make sure Carolina is not in danger."

He punched in Carolina's mobile phone number. There was no answer. His throat tightened. He called his mother. Thankfully she answered on the first ring.

"I'm trying to get in touch with Carolina. She's not answering her phone. Is she with you?"

"No, she drove back to the Bent Pine to pick up some peaches I forgot to bring with us this morning."

"How long has she been gone?"

"About ten minutes. You sound upset. Is anything wrong?"

"I don't know. Stay put, Mom. Don't leave that house."

He called the Bent Pine. Carolina's aunt Pearl answered. "Is Carolina there?" he asked.

"No, she left with you over an hour ago."

"You're sure she's not there."

"I'm sure I haven't seen her."

"Can you look in the kitchen and see if there's a basket of peaches on the counter?"

"They're still here."

"Thanks, Pearl."

Jake ran to Adam's truck. "I need to borrow your truck. It's urgent."

"Take it. I can get one of the wranglers to pick us up and drive us back to the house." Adam handed him the key. "Is there anything I can do?"

"Call Sheriff Garcia. Tell him Thad Caffey is in Oak Grove and Carolina is on her way from the Dry Gulch Ranch back to the Bent Pine. Send backup to the area ASAP."

"Did you say Thad Caffey has Carolina?" R.J. asked in a quivering voice.

"Hopefully not. But I'm taking no chances. I'm out of here now."

"Damn straight, you gotta go. Don't you dare let anything happen to Carolina. You kill that Thad Caffey. Do you hear me?"

"I hear you loud and clear."

Jake jumped into the truck and took off, following the dirt road all the way to the gate.

If anything happened to Carolina... No, he couldn't indulge in horrifying possibilities. He would not lose Carolina.

STILL DAZED, CAROLINA was only vaguely aware of the sticks and rocks scraping her back through her clothes as Thad dragged her through the woods.

"What do you want from me?" Carolina asked. "Why are you doing this?"

"You know why, you rich bitch. You meddle in other people's lives because you've got no life of your own. You talked Mildred into pressing charges against me and then divorcing me. I spent four long years in prison because of you. But you won't meddle in my life or Mildred's any longer."

There would be no reasoning with him. She had to outsmart him or find a way to break free. If she could run, at least she'd have a chance.

Finally he stopped walking and dropped her head and shoulder to the hard earth so hard she felt her brains had been scrambled.

Still, she tried to roll away from him. He yanked her back toward him by her long hair. Before she could try to fight him off, he straddled her and began running the tip of an ice pick along her neck and then down to the swell of her breasts.

A prick here. A prick there, painful, bloody reminders of what the ice pick could do if he pushed with more force.

She could see the evil burning in his eyes and she knew for certain what no one had been able to prove. He had killed his mother and his sister. Nothing in his past could justify that.

And now he was going to kill her. She screamed, but there was no one around to hear her.

She should have listened to Jake. And she should have told him she loved him. She did love him, so very much. Now all those unfulfilled dreams were about to die at the hands of a madman.

She closed her eyes, and as the tip of the ice pick slid between her breasts and down her belly, her mind escaped to the thrill of Jake's kiss and the joy of waking up in his arms.

ADRENALINE AND FEAR pushed Jake into overdrive the second he saw Carolina's ditched car. He searched the vehicle to make sure she wasn't still inside it, injured or…

No. She was alive. She had to be alive.

Convinced she wasn't still trapped in the car, he headed to the woods, his pistol at his hip, ready. He found their trail in seconds. One person walking. One person or thing being dragged. Did Jake dare call out or would that only startle Caffey and spur him into doing something desperate?

Jake kept walking, listening for any sound that might lead him to Carolina. The sound was a bloodcurdling scream. He took off, running as fast as he could. If Caffey had hurt Carolina, he'd kill him.

He reached Carolina just in time to see Caffey's hand raised high above his head, a bloody ice pick clutched in his fist. He was in position to plunge that thing right through her heart.

Acting on instinct, Jake dived into Caffey like a plane coming in for a crash landing. They struggled for the ice pick until Jake was able to subdue him. Jake was on the verge of finishing Caffey off with the same deadly kitchen utensil he'd been about to use on Carolina.

"Don't," Carolina begged. "Please don't. He's the one lost to the devils in his mind. We're the sane ones."

Jake's hand trembled, but he forced himself to lower his arm. He tossed the ice pick into the wooded area, but kept Caffey pinned to the ground, sputtering curses.

Jake turned to Carolina. "Are you okay, baby?"

"I am now."

"You're bleeding."

"Just barely. He was still into the torture phase."

"You need an ambulance."

"I won't turn one down, but it's strictly precautionary."

A few seconds later, Sheriff Garcia arrived on the scene. Tague was a few steps behind him.

"You're too late for the action," Jake said, "but I could use some handcuffs over here." Jake left Thad in the hands of Garcia. He sat down on the damp, pine-strewn earth beside Carolina and freed her wrists before pulling her into his arms. Jake buried his face in Carolina's hair. "Let's make a pact. Don't ever scare me like that again. My heart can only take so much."

"It's been a rough morning. As soon as I finish getting checked out at the hospital, I'll be ready to go home," she whispered.

"Where is home?"

"Anywhere you hang your Stetson on the hat rack and park your boots under my bed."

His heart hammered against his chest. "Do you mean that?"

"I've never meant anything more. I love you, Jake Dalton. I never thought I'd ever love again. Never imagined I could fall this hard so quickly. But when I thought I might die tonight, I knew that I had already given you my heart."

"I love you, Carolina Lambert. Now, who do I ask for your hand in marriage?"

"My three sons. I'll make sure they say yes."

Miracles. Sometimes you wait and wait for one that never comes. Other times one's right there when you need it. But on really rare occasions, they rain down on you like a spring shower.

This was one of those times.

* * * * *

"I have a question for you. You had arranged to pick me up at five o'clock, in just a few hours, for a date. Doesn't it seem weird for you to ring the doorbell and announce that you're moving in with me?"

"A valid question." He translated her concern: "You want to know if it's unprofessional for me to agree to act as bodyguard for a woman I'm attracted to."

"Are you?" She brightened.

"Attracted?" He regretted the use of that word. "You're a good-looking woman. I'm a single man."

"And you're my bodyguard. If we're dating, isn't that a professional conflict?"

"I considered asking somebody else at TST to take this assignment." For about three and a half seconds, he'd considered. "It's not a problem. I can control my personal feelings. At five o'clock, I can quit being a bodyguard, and we'll have our date. Or not."

"How do you decide?"

"We'll know," he said.

MOUNTAIN BODYGUARD

BY
CASSIE MILES

First Published in Great Britain 2016
By Mills & Boon, an imprint of HarperCollins*Publishers*
1 London Bridge Street, London, SE1 9GF

© 2016 Kay Bergstrom

ISBN: 978-0-263-91909-7

46-0716

Our policy is to use papers that are natural, renewable and recyclable products and made from wood grown in sustainable forests. The logging and manufacturing processes conform to the legal environmental regulations of the country of origin.

Printed and bound in Spain
by CPI, Barcelona

Cassie Miles, a *USA TODAY* bestselling author, lives in Colorado. After raising two daughters and cooking tons of macaroni and cheese for her family, Cassie is trying to be more adventurous in her culinary efforts. She's discovered that almost anything tastes better with wine. When she's not plotting Mills & Boon Intrigue books, Cassie likes to hang out at the Denver Botanical Gardens near her high-rise home.

To Khloe Adams and her brilliant advice.
And, as always, to Rick.

Chapter One

The hotel was a bodyguard's nightmare. Mason Steele fidgeted beside French doors that opened onto a flagstone terrace. With extreme impatience, he watched while Admiral Edgar Prescott, tonight's honoree, made his way through the stragglers who were toasting the crimson glow of a June sunset and finishing off their complementary glass of Colorado merlot.

Number one security problem: isolated mountain location. This seven-story structure was surrounded by national forest with only two viable access roads. Never mind that Aspen was less than forty minutes away, this site was remote. An attacker could assault the hotel, dash across the ninth green and vanish into the forest before Mason and his colleagues figured out where they were hit. To prevent such an ambush, his firm, TST Security, had stationed their own snipers on the roof.

This charity banquet was all hands on deck for TST. They were using five regulars and six part-timers, plus had a helicopter pilot on standby.

Security issue number two: though the styling of the hotel was meant to resemble a hunting lodge from the early 1900s, the interior of the banquet hall featured a wall of windows and another of French doors. The design was an open invitation to long-distance shooters.

Issue number three: the people. Too many had been invited. The circular tables reached almost to the walls, which meant a sure pileup if they had to evacuate quickly. The well-dressed guests had all passed through metal detectors, but that was no guarantee of safety in this era of plastic firearms. Potential weapons were everywhere. Prime rib was on the menu; steak knives were on the tables. The centerpieces blocked sight lines, and the tall Art Deco arrangements on either side of the dais were large enough to hide a couple of AK-47s.

As soon as the admiral stepped over the threshold from the terrace, Mason signaled to one of his men to round up the last few people that were outside and lock the French doors. As for himself, he took a position against the wall where he could watch the crowd. Most of them had settled into their assigned seats. Some had already been served. Others table hopped, chatted and chuckled and showed off photos on cell phones.

A woman in a sleeveless blue jumpsuit approached him. He'd been introduced to her before, had noticed her thoroughly and had paid particular attention to the way the clingy blue fabric hugged her curves. She was part of the entourage for the admiral, his movie star wife and their several children. When the lady in blue sidled up next to him, the top of her head was only as high as his shoulder. Lights from the chandeliers glistened on her curly auburn ponytail.

She nudged his elbow. "Whose body are you guarding?"

"The admiral's." He dropped a glance in her direction, expecting to quickly look away. Instead, she seized his attention with her big brown eyes and the constellation of freckles that spread across her nose and cheeks. The corners of her mouth naturally turned upward as though caught on the edge of laughter.

"Your friend across the room," she said with a nod toward Scan Timmons, who was the first *T* in TST Security, "must be in charge of watching Helena Christie Prescott's body. How did he get the good assignment?"

"Seniority." The admiral's glamorous dark-haired wife showed a lot of cleavage, and the slit on her skirt was thigh high. Watching her was kind of a treat.

"You're Mason, right?"

"Yes, ma'am." Mason Steele was the *S* in TST Security. "And you're Francine Alexandra DeMille."

"Call me Lexie."

"Why not Francine?" he asked. "Or Franny?"

"Because of my job. I take care of the Prescott kids."

Which made her Franny the nanny? He stifled a chuckle. "There are six of them, right?"

"Two teenagers from the admiral's first marriage. The ten-year-old twin boys come from Helena's union with the hunk who's in that stripper movie—a deadbeat dad, but, oh, those abs."

"I know who you mean."

She stared intently at him. "You look a little bit like him. With the buzz haircut and the cool blue eyes and those big, muscular...arms." She squeezed one of his biceps and immediately yanked her hand away. A pink blush colored her cheeks. "And the six- and four-year-old are from this marriage."

When he forced his gaze away from her and checked out the children's table, the littlest girl stood up on the seat of her chair and waved at him with a golden magic wand. He fought the urge to laugh. On the job, he couldn't afford to be distracted by cuteness, but this little golden-haired girl was irresistible. He grinned back at her and winked.

Mason had always thought a big family would be fun.

He was his parents' only surviving child. Thanksgiving was no picnic. And Christmas? Forget about it.

"Here's my problem," Lexie said. "The younger kiddos are restless and on the verge of turning into a nuisance. The older ones are bored. And we're at least a half hour away from the speeches. Do you have any security issues if I whisk them out of here in a few minutes?"

He was glad she'd asked before dashing out the door. TST provided extra security when children were part of the scene. Mason looked around the banquet room, trying to spot the bodyguard who was responsible for keeping an eye on the Prescott offspring.

"Strange," he muttered. "I don't see Carlos."

"Nope." Lexie shook her head, and her curly ponytail bounced. "He introduced himself earlier, and I would have gone to him, but I lost track of where he was, which is kind of hard to do, since good old Carlos is the size of a side-by-side refrigerator-freezer combo."

A former pro football linebacker, Carlos was six feet five inches—only a little taller than Mason, but Carlos outweighed him by nearly seventy-five pounds. The big man was good at his job and wasn't the type to wander off.

Where the hell was he? A twang of apprehension jangled Mason's nerves. "It might be a good idea to get the kids out of here."

Immediately, Lexie picked up on his mood. Her grin disappeared. "Is it dangerous?"

Always. There was always danger. He didn't want to tell her that; didn't want to point out the obvious fact that his security firm had been hired to protect the admiral and his family from an imminent threat, which meant a threat existed.

"Let's see what I can find out." He gave her a light pat on the shoulder. His intention had been to reassure her, but when he touched her bare skin, a spark ignited. Like wildfire, an unexpected heat crackled though his nerve endings and turned his blood to lava. For an instant, he was struck dumb. He had to drag his focus away from Lexie before he spoke into his headset to Sean.

After a quick, quiet conversation with his partner, Mason regained his self-control. There was no room for further distraction; tonight was important. TST was there to protect Admiral Prescott, a man he respected and admired. Though the admiral had been retired for three years and wasn't in uniform tonight, his posture bespoke military discipline. Mason's brother, an expert in naval intelligence, had known the admiral personally.

Lexie cleared her throat. She looked to him for an all-clear signal. He wanted to give her a thumbs-up so she'd reward him with that cute upturned smile of hers. When she lifted her hand to brush back a wisp of russet hair, he noticed her delicate charm bracelet. The silver chain shone brightly against her tanned forearm. One of the charms resembled a ninja throwing star.

Sean's voice came through his earbud. "I found Carlos. I knew I'd seen the big guy headed this way. He's in the bathroom, puking his guts out."

"What's wrong with him?"

"Might have the flu," Sean said. "One of his kids is sick."

Or he could have been drugged, could have been poisoned. Several scenarios flipped through Mason's mind, ranging from an attempted abduction of the children to a full-on assault with fiery explosive devices. In every possible circumstance, he needed to get the children to safety.

Keeping his voice calm, he spoke to Lexie. "Tell the kids we're leaving. We'll go out through the terrace. It's the closest exit."

"Should I be worried?"

Not wanting to alarm her, he didn't offer an explanation. "I thought you wanted to get the kids away."

"True, and I don't mind missing those speeches myself."

With a toss of her head, she pivoted and returned to the circular table where the Prescott brood was sitting. The teenagers were texting, the younger kids were playing with their food and the princess with the magic wand was waving to everyone.

In a hushed tone, Mason informed Sean that he'd take over Carlos's job, guarding the children and moving them upstairs to their bedrooms. The hotel had provided extra security guards on the seventh floor, where the entourage was staying. "While I'm gone, you watch the admiral."

"I'm worried," Sean said. "What if Carlos was drugged?"

Mason was about to ask if Carlos had eaten anything or had anything to drink. Before he spoke, he realized that it was a dumb question. Carlos was always eating and drinking. "Let's hope it's just the flu."

He scanned the crowd. As more people were served, the sound of conversation was replaced by the clink of silverware against china. The situation was under control. Earlier today, they'd come up with several possible evacuation plans. But what if the attackers had outthought them and were already waiting outside? Mason contacted his snipers on the roof, letting them know that he intended to exit with the kids.

He seriously doubted that the bad guys had gained entrance to the banquet hall. The guests, cooks and servers had all been vetted and the TST Security computers were a foolproof system, protected by something Dylan Timmons, who was the second *T* in TST Security, called the mother of all firewalls.

Mason's gaze flicked around the room. Could he

trust computer clearances? Doubt assailed his judgment. "Maybe we should shut this operation down."

A voice in his head—which was actually Sean —advised, "It's your call, Mason."

At TST Security, the three partners had their areas of expertise. Dylan specialized in computer security. Sean was former FBI, more of a detective and a profiler—a deductive genius. And Mason was the muscle—the man in charge of action and strategy. "First, I'll get the kids to safety."

As if he needed another complication, the admiral had left his banquet seat and was coming toward him. Smiling and genial, the admiral picked his way through the crowd and stood beside Mason. "What's the problem?"

"The bodyguard protecting the children has a suspicious case of the flu." He kept his voice low so the other guests wouldn't take notice. "It's probably nothing, but I recommend escorting the kids to their rooms on the seventh floor."

"Agreed. I don't take chances with my children's safety." He beckoned to Lexie, who began moving the kids in their direction. "I'll help."

"My men can handle the situation, Admiral. It's not necessary for you to leave the banquet."

"I'm retired, Mr. Steele. You can drop the admiral and call me Prescott. But make no mistake—I still give the orders."

The expression on Mason's face didn't change a bit. Inside, he was cheering for the old warrior who was still man enough to take care of his children, marry a movie star and lead the charge into battle. Still, he said, "Sir, let me do my job. If you come, I need to pull other security. Please, stay here."

Their gazes locked. Each man took the measure of the other.

Prescott grinned. "I worked with your brother."

"I know."

"Carry on, Mr. Steele."

While Prescott returned to his seat, Mason signaled his man who had earlier locked the terrace door and instructed him to accompany them, bringing up the rear. When the children and Lexie had gathered, Mason opened the door onto the flagstone terrace and stepped outside into a rose-colored dusk.

He led the way down a wide set of stone stairs to a wooden door. Like the rest of the hotel, this entrance was less than a decade old, but had been aged to look antique. What did they call it? Distressed. The wood had been distressed to make it seem as though this door and the stone wall were part of a hundred-year-old hunting lodge. In contrast, the door was opened by a computer pad that required Mason to enter a code. He opened the door and led them into the parking lot under the hotel.

The sound of their footsteps made a hollow echo in the concrete structure filled with vehicles. Many of the guests at the banquet were also staying at the hotel. Tomorrow, some of them would play golf with Admiral Prescott, which was another complicated scenario for TST Security.

Mason had already checked out the parking garage. With four separate exits on each level and six elevators, it was a good place to bring the kids for an escape. He hustled his little crew toward the elevators.

The teenagers were mature enough to know that something wasn't exactly copacetic. The oldest girl held the youngest boy's hand. These were military kids; they knew how to behave. Not so much for the Hollywood twins—handsome ten-year-olds with shaggy blond hair and dark eyebrows. They were punching each other, whining about how they wanted pizza and making growling noises interspersed with high-pitched squeaks.

Lexie hustled the gruesome twosome forward. Throughout this whole process she'd kept her cool and followed instructions. Mason noticed that she was carrying the emergency alert equipment Carlos had given her. If she ran into a threat, she was supposed to hit the red button and all TST Security personnel would respond.

He wondered if she'd had any specialized training to protect the kids. She was in good shape, had an athletic stride and her arms were well toned. But did Franny the nanny do kung fu?

He wanted to know more about her. Maybe tonight after the kids were in bed, they could get together. Maybe they'd talk, maybe laugh, maybe she'd allow him to glide his fingers down her smooth, tanned shoulders and arms. At the elevators, she shot him an over-the-shoulder glance before turning her full attention to the twins, who were trying to expand their obnoxious behavior to include the other kids. She moved quickly to separate the twins from the rest of the herd.

But one of the twins shoved into the teenage boy, Eddy Jr., who was at the age when he was almost manly. In a voice that was significantly deeper than that of the twins, he muttered, "Watch what you're doing, dork face."

"You're not the boss of me."

"But he's bigger than you." His twin poked him in the back. "He could kick your—"

"Enough," Lexie said.

She stepped between the twins and Eddy Jr. Both elevators dinged as the doors opened simultaneously. Lexie entered one elevator and dragged the twins with her. "The three of us will take this one. We'll meet the rest of you on the seventh floor."

"Wait!" Mason said. This wasn't procedure. The kids should be accompanied by a bodyguard at all times.

She flashed him a wide grin. "Don't worry. I've got this."

The elevator door snapped closed, and he was left with a vision of her dark eyes sparkling. Her expression was full of mischief and something more. There was something mysterious about her, and he wondered what she knew that he didn't. She seemed to be laughing inside as though she had the punch line to an untold joke.

Chapter Two

In the elevator, Lexie stood between the twins and glared at the wood-paneled walls. The boutique hotel's impersonation of an old-time hunting lodge was beginning to annoy her. She didn't mind the elk and moose heads mounted on the walls in the lobby. After all, her dad and three older brothers had taken her on her first hunting trip when she was eight years old, and she understood their desire for occasional taxidermy.

But a real hunter would never stay at a place like this. Not with the golf course, the fake Persian rugs, the ornate imitation antique furniture and the kitschy Old West touches, like brass spittoons. Spittoons? This pricey hotel didn't allow smoking, much less chewing tobacco.

"You ticked off that bodyguard," said the twin named Caine.

"He'll get over it."

The other twin—who she always thought should have been named Abel but was actually Shane—tilted his head to one side and gave her a freakishly mature look. "I think you like that bodyguard."

How could he possibly know that? The kid was right, of course. She was drawn to Mason like a spinster moth to a muscular flame, but she didn't intend to discuss her personal feelings with the kids. "Mr. Steele seems like a nice man."

Caine tugged her right arm. "You really like him."

Shane snickered. "You want to marry him."

Ignoring the twins, she stared at the lighted numbers for the floors as they passed the fourth. An interruption would be most welcome, but she wasn't having any such luck. The twin monsters prattled back and forth about how she wanted to kiss Mason and "do it" with him, about how she was in love with him.

Though tempted to respond with a childish and extra loud "am not," she kept her voice trained to a calm level. "That's enough."

"But we got more, lots more."

"If I hear another word from either of you, there will be no pizza tonight, no ice cream, no TV, no computer games, no nothing. We clear?"

They went silent, nodded and stood up straight. Though the boys were only ten, they'd had a growth spurt and were almost as tall as she was at five feet three inches. Like golden retriever puppies, their feet and hands were too large for their gangly bodies. Someday they'd be huge, handsome dudes like their matinee idol father.

She liked big men, but not big babies like the twins' irresponsible daddy. She preferred a guy like Mason who was physically fit and in the business of protecting other people. A steady, stable guy, someone she could count on, a man she could trust.

Rein it in, Lexie. Sure, Mason was handsome with his buzz haircut and his square jaw and his butane-blue eyes. But she knew nothing about his character. He might be a cheat or a liar. Being drawn to him wouldn't be the first time she'd been fooled by a man with a pretty face and muscular shoulders.

With a scowl, she reminded herself that she had no proof that Anton Karpov had betrayed her. He'd disappeared while doing a job that might be connected with the admiral. That was what he'd told her. Most likely, he'd been lying. The admiral had never heard of Anton and didn't recognize him from photos.

At the seventh floor, the elevator dinged and the doors swept open. A man in a security guard uniform assigned by the hotel stood waiting, but she didn't recognize him. He didn't look like an employee, not with that stubble on his face.

She sensed a threat. She could smell it. Spreading her arms, she kept the twins on the elevator. Down the hall on the left, she glimpsed a body on the floor.

Backing into the elevator again, she said to the phony security man, "Oops, I forgot something."

When she reached back and hit the elevator button for the lobby, he reacted. His arm blocked the door from closing. He grabbed her shoulder. "You ain't going nowhere."

Lexie hit the red alert button for TST Security and said to the twins, "Go to the lobby."

She shoved the guard in the chest, keeping him away from the twins. Lexie went on the offensive. Her first flying kick was aimed at the guard's midsection. He bent double. She fired another kick at his right kneecap.

Behind her back, she heard the elevator doors snap shut. The twins were safe. Good, she'd do anything to keep these kids from harm.

The fake guard clutched at his gut. His knee bent sideways as he made a gurgling noise in the back of his throat. Then he collapsed onto the fancy Persian carpet and rolled around while grabbing his injured leg.

She had to move fast. Where there was one thug, there would be others, and she didn't want to take on the whole gang with no other weapon than her karate skills. Lexie delivered another sharp kick to the head of the first thug. He went limp, unconscious. Since she'd chosen flats instead of pointy-toe stiletto heels for tonight's event, this fake guard might survive.

She dropped to her knees beside him and yanked his gun from the holster. Aiming high, she fired at two other men who were running toward her.

Her warning shots had the desired effect. The phony hotel guards sought cover, which gave her a few seconds to locate a better position.

MIDWAY THROUGH HIS elevator ascent with the children, Mason heard the warning squawk from Lexie's emergency alert button. What the hell? Had she run into trouble on the seventh floor? The sound of gunfire overhead was his answer.

He jabbed the elevator button, stopping the car on the sixth instead of the seventh floor. When the doors opened, he spoke to the other bodyguard. "Take the children to the lobby."

"What about you?"

"I'm going up."

Leaving the elevator, he listened to the babble of confused voices coming through his headset. They had all gotten the alert from Lexie. He heard Sean take control inside the banquet hall. Following procedure, Sean ordered most of the other TST guards to the front lobby, where Dylan— who was stationed at the reservation desk—would organize their operation.

The gunfire from above had not abated. What the hell was going on up there? He gave Sean an update. "It's Mason. I'm going up to the seventh floor where shots are being fired."

"Copy that," Dylan responded from the lobby. "I have the twins and the other kids. All secure."

The children were safe. Good. "What about Lexie, the nanny?"

"The twins say she's on the seventh floor."

Mason's gut clenched. If anything had happened to her because he'd let her take the elevator alone, he would never forgive himself. He spoke into the headset. "I'll be out of touch for a few minutes."

He unscrewed the earbud and welcomed the attending silence. His entire focus needed to be on Lexie.

Drawing his gun from the shoulder holster, he sprinted down the hotel corridor and through the door below the red Exit sign. He rushed up the concrete staircase to the seventh floor and eased his way through, moving carefully until he got his bearings.

The difference in decor on each floor was as subtle as the varying shades of beige on the wallpaper above the waist-high wood wainscoting. Antique-looking picture frames held sepia photos from the early 1900s, including many of Theodore Roosevelt, who was known for hunting in the Colorado Rockies and for establishing the National Park Service. Against the wall opposite the elevators was a claw-foot table with a floral arrangement and a teddy bear with the stuffing blown out of its chest. An unconscious man in a hotel uniform lay on the floor. Good guy or bad?

There was no sure way of telling. Down the hall was another unconscious man wearing only his underwear. Quick conclusion: the men who had been stripped were the real guards. The uniforms were being worn by impostors.

The *rat-a-tat* of automatic gunfire came from his left.

There were only fourteen rooms on this deluxe level, including a massive suite for the admiral and his wife. The floor plan was a B-shape with the elevators in the middle.

Peering around the corner, he spotted the backsides of two uniformed men. When they tried to advance, a single shot repelled them. Lexie? Where did she get the gun?

Mason fired twice and got two hits. Both men reacted but neither went down. They must be wearing Kevlar vests under their uniform shirts. When they turned toward him, he saw Lexie dash across the end of the hallway. He hoped she'd run to the relative safety of her room.

No such luck.

While he and the impostor guards exchanged fire, she circled all the way around and came up behind him. "Mason, do you have another gun?"

"Not for you."

"Don't be a jerk. I've only got one bullet left."

"Where's your room?" he asked.

She pointed behind them and waved her key card. "It's over here. I'm not sure it's safe. There are two other thugs who aren't wearing uniforms. They could be hiding inside."

They were outnumbered, and the bad guys had more firepower. The best option was to retreat. "Take me to your room, unlock the door and I'll enter first to make sure it's safe. Then you follow me in."

"You and me in the bedroom? Well, that's the best offer I've had in a long time."

He didn't take his eyes off the two men who were laying down a steady barrage of gunfire; he didn't need to look at her to know she was grinning. Calm under pressure, he liked that. What he didn't like was the way she squatted down and tugged at his pant leg. "What are you doing?"

"Looking for your ankle holster. Aha!" She undid the snap and took his second weapon. "Thanks, I need this."

She hustled down the hallway, and he followed. At her room, she unlocked the door and stepped aside. He entered, holding his gun with both hands as he searched the bathroom, the closet and under the beds. "All clear."

Instead of obeying his instructions to follow him inside and lock the door, she braced herself in the doorway and dropped to one knee as she fired down the hallway. It was obvious that she knew what she was doing. Earlier, he'd been wondering if she had self-defense instruction. The answer to that question was a resounding yes. Lexie was dangerous.

When he pulled her inside and closed the door, he noticed the slash of red across her upper arm. "You're bleeding."

"Just a graze, but it really stings." She looked down at the angled cut that dripped blood down to her elbow. "That's going to leave a scar."

He dragged a heavy silk-upholstered chair and positioned it in front of the doorway. He added a desk. The barricade would slow down any attacker long enough for him to get off a couple of accurate shots.

From the bathroom, he grabbed a fluffy white hand towel and brought it to where she was sitting on a carved wooden bench in front of a mirrored dressing table. He wrapped the towel around her wounded arm and brushed escaped curls off her forehead. Under her freckles, her complexion had faded to a waxy pale.

"Are you all right?" he asked.

"Sure. Fine."

When the energizing effect of adrenaline wore off, he expected her to crash like a rock slide. And he wanted to be there when she unwound, to catch her before she fell, to hold her and tell her that life was going to get better. There was something about her that awakened his protective instincts.

As a rule, he kept his distance from other people and

avoided committed relationships. Losing his brother had torn a hole in his heart and made him wary of deep connections. But Lexie's grin repaired his pain. He wanted to be close to her.

He held her hand, marveling at her slender fingers and the delicate turn of her wrist. His gaze lifted to her dark eyes. "I won't let anything bad happen to you."

"I know you'll do your best." She shrugged. "Sometimes there's no way to prevent the bad stuff."

Though she was acting nonchalant, the hollow echo in her voice surprised him. He could tell that this woman had experienced more than her fair share of tragedy. Immediately curious, he wanted to hear more about her life, her dreams and her plans for the future.

But this wasn't the right time. Gently, he removed his gun from her clenched fingers. Her vulnerability touched him, but he also appreciated her strength. When she'd needed to be tough, she held off four bad guys—five including the unconscious one outside the elevator. Now she could relax.

He didn't have that respite. An aggressive burst of gunfire echoed in the corridor like a call to duty. He stuck his earbud back in. Sean was screaming his name, demanding an update and informing Mason that they had a group ready to storm the seventh floor.

Gun in hand, he turned his attention to TST Security business.

Chapter Three

Leaving Mason to growl orders on his intercom, Lexie slipped into the bathroom, locked the door and leaned against it. Stillness wrapped around her. Inside this pristine tile and marble cubicle, the gunfire seemed far away.

Exhaling a sigh, she slid down the wall. *Sanctuary!* Not that she was truly safe. This peaceful feeling was akin to being in the eye of a tornado while danger continued to swirl, but she was glad for the momentary respite—especially glad she'd made it into the bathroom before she swooned like some kind of whimpering Southern belle.

Mason didn't need to know she was scared. She liked him and wanted him to like her. And something told her that he wasn't the kind of guy who enjoyed being around girlie girls. She'd seen the gleam in his eye when he watched her taking aim and when he tended to her bullet wound. As if on cue, the red-stained towel fell from her arm. Oozing blood smeared and saturated the blue fabric of her jumpsuit.

"Bummer." This was one of her favorite outfits.

It didn't hurt. Not much, anyway. But her body was having a reaction that was out of proportion to the injury. Was this some kind of panic attack? She was acutely tense. Her muscles twisted into knots. Her gut clenched. Other symptoms slammed into her, one after the other. She was light-headed. Her breathing was labored, and she smelled the odor of rotting meat. The inside of her mouth tasted like ash. Shivers twitched across her shoulders.

Her spine buckled, and she ratcheted down to the floor. She lay on her side with her wounded arm up, the white marble cooling her cheek. She tried to breathe deeply and calm herself. But she was too tense...and too cold, ice-cold. Her fists clenched between her breasts. Her pulse pounded. She pinched her eyes closed, hoping to blot out the terrible fear that threatened to overwhelm her.

She had to get control. *I'm going to be all right.* No matter how many times her conscious mind repeated those words, a deeper place in her soul didn't believe it. *I won't die.* Post-traumatic stress squeezed her in a grip so tight that her bones rattled. *Everything is going to be all right.* She wasn't in mortal danger, not this time. *This isn't like the accident.*

Her memory jolted. Flung backward in time, she heard a fierce metallic crunch and the explosion of the air bag from the steering wheel. Her brother's little bronze sedan had been thrown onto its side and was skidding toward the edge of the cliff near Buena Vista. Cringing, she heard the grinding screech of her car door against the pavement. *Should have taken the truck.* Jake was going to kill her for wrecking his car. *Not my fault.* The other car—black with tinted windows—had crossed the center line and hit her front fender.

Her mouth opened wide as she desperately tried to scream. The air bag had stolen her breath. She could only gasp. And then her brother's car was falling, crashing end over end, down the steep hillside and into the trees.

Other people had told her that they couldn't recall a single moment of their accidents. In the midst of their traumatic events, they experienced amnesia. Not her. She felt every twist and turn as the car plummeted. Fully conscious, she braced herself for what would surely come next: the gas explosion that would tear her limbs apart and the flames that would scar her flesh.

That wasn't the way it turned out. Though the driver who had hit her fled the scene, there was a witness in another vehicle. She was rescued, taken to the hospital and stitched back together. The doctors fixed as much as they could.

Replaying the accident—the worst moments of her life—lessened her current panic. The terror that had threatened to smother her receded into the shadows of her mind. She forced her thoughts back to the present reality and focused on what had just happened. She'd been attacked by five armed men.

Instead of sliding deeper into fear, she chuckled to herself. This definitely wasn't like the horrible feeling of helplessness in the car accident. When it came to self-defense, she did okay. Not a big surprise, as she'd been trained by her three older brothers, who ran a karate dojo. And her dad, a Marine Corps sergeant, had insisted that she know how to handle rifles, pistols, handguns and other weaponry.

Thinking of the DeMille men calmed her. Even though they were a thousand miles away in Austin, Texas, they were watching over her. They'd made her into what she was today: an independent, stubborn, kick-ass tomboy. A survivor.

When she'd encountered the first man outside the elevator, she knew—without the slightest doubt—that she could take him down. Lexie had earned her brown belt in karate when she was fifteen.

Shooting at people was more difficult; she didn't want to kill anybody. If Mason hadn't shown up, she had no idea what she would have done. He'd taken a risk by charging onto this floor to help her. Of course, security was his job…but still, she was grateful.

There was a tap on the door. "Lexie, are you all right?"

She scrambled to get her legs under her. "I'm fine."

"Are you sure? It's quiet in there."

"I'm fine," she repeated.

She should have turned on the shower. Mason wouldn't have knocked if he'd heard water running. Struggling, she lunged to her feet and hit the faucet in the sink. There! Was that enough proof enough that she was fine and dandy?

Her reflection in the mirror confronted her. Not a pretty sight! Her arm dripped blood, her makeup was smudged and her ponytail was tangled like a bird's nest. What she needed was a shower, but stripping off her clothes while bad guys were on the prowl seemed like an invitation to more trouble—naked trouble.

She went to the bathroom door, pressed her ear against it and listened for the sounds of battle from the outer corridor. There were distant pops. This wasn't the kind of cheesy motel where you heard every cough and sputter from the neighboring room, but gunfire was loud. She expected to hear somethi—

"Lexie?" Mason knocked again.

She jumped backward with a yelp. Off balance, she stumbled into the wall beside the huge Plexiglas shower with four separate spray nozzles. "Fine," she shouted. "I'm perfectly fine."

He opened the door.

"I locked that," she said.

"And I picked the lock." He strode toward her.

Whether she wanted his protection or not, Mason was here. He guided her across the marble floor and lifted her onto the counter with double sinks. "Do you want the out fit on or off?"

"On, of course." She pushed at his chest, accidentally staining his light blue shirt with blood. "Jeez Louise, I'm sorry."

"Jeez Louise?" He lifted an eyebrow.

"I don't swear. It's a nanny thing."

"Did you used to?"

"Hell, yes." She felt a grin spread across her face, and she was amazed by how swiftly her mood had transformed. Mason was magic. "I have three brothers."

He nodded. "Every other word was obscene."

"Not as much as you'd think. Dad didn't tolerate bad language."

"Was he a religious man?"

"Worse. A marine sergeant. Discipline was his middle name."

"My older brother was in the corps. He worked with the admiral in the Middle East." His shoulders flexed in a tense shrug. "I'd like to think that one of the reasons TST Security was hired was the admiral's good opinion of my brother."

Being from a military family, she was sensitive to the fact that he spoke of his brother in the past tense. "I wonder if your brother knew my dad, Daniel DeMille? He was stationed in the Middle East, too. He retired five years ago."

"My brother was killed six years ago in Afghanistan."

"I'm sorry."

"So am I." He peeled off his suit jacket, tossed it into the bedroom and started rolling up his shirtsleeves. "Now I'm going to clean your wound."

She pointed toward the open bathroom door. "What about those thugs in the hallway?"

"My partners have it under control. The local police and

sheriff are on the way." He tapped the listening device in his ear. "TST Security has rounded up all but one of the bad guys. He locked himself in a room down the hall and thinks he's safe."

His full lips quirked in a wry smile that told her the criminal hiding in one of the rooms was making a big mistake. She asked, "What's going to happen to him?"

"While he's watching the door to the hallway, one of the snipers on the roof is going to bust through a window."

"And you'd like to watch," she said.

"Oh, yeah."

His tone reminded her of the DeMille men, but there was nothing brotherly about the tingling she felt when he touched her arm. He moistened a washcloth under the hot water she'd been running in the sink. Holding her arm below the elbow, he cautiously wiped away the blood.

"The cut isn't too deep," he said. "I don't think you'll need stitches, but you should have a doc take a look."

"Sure." While he focused on taking care of her, she studied him. Her father would approve of his buzz cut and no-nonsense attitude, but she was more impressed by his deep-set dark blue eyes and high cheekbones. His tanned forearms showed that he spent time outdoors, but her thoughts about him required an indoor setting… A bedroom scenario, to be specific.

He lifted his gaze. What would it be like to wake up and see those eyes looking back at her? He was almost too handsome, too good to be true. *Please, Mason, don't be a liar or a cheat.*

Using a clean towel, he patted her arm dry. When he reached behind her head, unfastened her ponytail and let her curly hair fall to her shoulders, his face was near hers. If she tilted her head and leaned in, their lips would touch.

Impulsively, her fingers snatched his striped silk necktie, and she held him in place. He was mere inches away from her, so very close that she felt the heat radiating from his body. She smelled his aftershave, a citrus and nutmeg flavor with a hint of something else…the indefinable scent of a man.

"You smell good." She hadn't intended her voice to become a purr, but that was what happened.

"So do you."

Her gaze twined with his, and she tugged at his necktie to pull him a half inch closer. She wanted to kiss him, but the situation was messy. She was sitting on the countertop at a weird angle. If she pressed her body against his chest, she'd smear the blood all over his shirt. More important, she barely knew this man and could be setting herself up for a world of embarrassment.

He ended her indecision. She should have known that he would. Mason was a take-charge kind of guy. He buried his fingers in her untamed hair and held the back of her skull so that he was supporting her. Then he kissed her.

Crazy, wild sensations bloomed inside her. He kissed the same way he seemed to do everything else: with skill and finesse. His lips were firm, and he exerted exactly the right amount of pressure.

His tongue traced the line of her mouth, slipped inside and probed against her teeth. She opened wider for him. Her tongue joined with his and—

There was a hammering noise from the door to the hallway. A deep voice shouted, "Mason, you in there?"

They broke apart so quickly that she bit the inside of her cheek. "Bad timing," she muttered.

"I have to go."

Twenty questions popped inside her head. *Can I see you again? Will there be another kiss? Can I give you my phone number?* She said only one word aloud. "Thanks."

"For what?"

"Saving my life."

He dropped a light kiss on her forehead. "My pleasure."

As she watched him walk out the door, she whispered, "The pleasure was all mine."

PEERING THROUGH THE infrared scope of his rifle, Anton Karpov scanned the windows on the seventh floor of the mountain hotel, trying to catch a glimpse of Franny. Earlier tonight, he had watched her through the crosshairs on his scope. She'd been outside on the terrace, meeting and greeting, laughing and smiling. She looked good—damn good. Until tonight, he hadn't paid any attention to the nanny.

But now he knew. Anton had positively identified Franny DeMille, the chick he'd almost moved in with. Why was she calling herself Lexie? How the hell did she get to be a nanny?

The Franny he knew was a kick-ass daredevil who couldn't care less about kids and didn't know a damn thing about taking care of them. When he was dating her, she'd told him—flat out—that she didn't want babies. Hey, great news for him. He wasn't meant to play daddy. He wasn't serious about her, either. Still, it made him mad when she dumped him. It was supposed to be the other way around. He made sure she knew that.

His cell phone vibrated in his pocket, and he answered.

The voice on the other end was the leader himself. There had been a lot of talk at meetings about how no single person was more important than another. They were equals. Some had special skills or areas of expertise, but their group didn't operate within the structure of a hierarchy.

Anton didn't buy in to any of that phony, mealy-mouthed philosophy. While others talked about all for one and "the greater good," he held his silence. There was only one truth he believed in: dollars and cents. He'd been associated with the leader for almost ten years, performing special tasks for decent pay.

Quietly, the leader said, "Move out. I'll contact you later, Tony."

Long ago, Anton had Americanized his name to Tony Curtis after the old-time movie star. He even looked kind of like that Tony, with his curly black hair and blue eyes. The real Tony Curtis was usually cast as a pretty boy hero, and that didn't suit Anton Karpov, not at all. He only changed his mind when he saw the movie star play the role of Albert DeSalvo, widely believed to be the Boston Strangler.

"Are you sure I should go, sir?" He was one of the few who knew the leader's real name, but he seldom spoke it. "I have a couple of angles for a clear shot."

"I'm tempted, Tony. I'd like to kill those idiots who got caught."

"Is there any chance they won't spill their guts?"

"Oh, they'll talk. The admiral's men are skilled interrogators."

"Is that a problem?"

"They don't know enough to worry about. They're unimportant."

The leader didn't seem concerned about losing five men. The less influential members of Anti-Conspiracy Committee for Democracy, also known as AC-CD, had access to a limited amount of information. They were assigned simple jobs. Tonight, the only thing they'd been required to do was disable the hotel security and fill in for them, leaving the way open for more experienced operatives. The trained, experienced staff, led by Anton/Tony, would have kidnapped the admiral.

Anton/Tony slung his rifle over his shoulder and rose to his feet. "It was the nanny who messed up the plan."

"How could a little girl like that be such a big problem?"

The leader didn't know her. For a couple of seconds, Tony felt superior to the man who usually gave the orders. For a change, it was Tony who had the ace up his sleeve, information the leader wasn't privy to, and he was tempted to hold back.

But he didn't care about showing how smart he was and gaining power in AC-CD. He was after a quick payday, and the best way to separate the leader from his cash was to show him something he might want to buy. Franny was a prize he could set before the leader.

"She says her name is Lexie, but I recognized her tonight. The nanny is a karate expert. It's Franny DeMille, my old girlfriend."

"You don't say." The leader's voice dropped to a low, thoughtful level. "If you asked her to help you, would she?"

"We didn't break up on good terms, but I could always get her to do what I wanted." Not exactly true, but he wished it so. When he'd been with her, he was a better man. "She'll do what I say."

"I'll be in touch."

Before leaving his sniper nest, Tony pulled up his balaclava to cover the lower part of his face. Silently and stealthily, he made his way through the forest. His experience as a hunting guide was why he'd been pegged for this assignment. He could be trusted to blend with nature and not be seen. And his skill at marksmanship was worthy of a world-class assassin.

Chapter Four

In the rustic-style foyer outside the banquet hall, Mason conferred quietly with his partner Dylan, whose tall, wiry frame had been transformed from nerdy to sophisticated by a tailored black suit and a striped silk tie. Likewise, his messy brown hair had been tamed in a ponytail at the nape of his neck. They were waiting for the admiral's wife to leave the hall and join them. Prescott had asked them to escort her to the conference room, where he and several branches of law enforcement and the military had gathered.

"NSA, CIA, Interpol, army and navy intelligence," Dylan said. He pushed his horn-rimmed glasses up on his nose. "The gang's all here."

"How do you know their affiliations?"

"They were all at the banquet." As part of security procedure, he had vetted the invited guests and used facial recognition software to make sure they matched their stated identity. "Some of these guys are high-ranking hotshots. On six of them, I got an 'access denied' message when I searched for further info."

"Did you?" Mason asked. "Tell me the truth. Did you dig deeper?"

"Not yet."

But he could if the need arose. Dylan was a skilled hacker, capable of breaching NSA or CIA security without leaving a trace. He'd already patched Admiral Prescott through to the offices of the Secretary of the Navy on a video server so that SecNav could join the meeting in the conference room.

The sound of laughter erupted from inside the banquet hall. For the past hour, the guests had been watching a PowerPoint presentation that outlined the medical and sanitation needs of children in sub-Saharan Africa.

Mason glanced over at his partner. "We did good."

"How do you figure?"

"All five bad guys have been taken into custody."

"Have they?" Dylan arched an eyebrow in a skeptical expression that irritated Mason to no end. "The so-called baddies are still in the hotel."

The local sheriff, Colorado law enforcement and NSA were all fighting over who would take possession of these low-level thugs. "Arresting them isn't our problem."

"What if there are others?"

"We'll handle it. This assignment still counts as a success for TST Security." And for him, personally. Not only had he shown Admiral Prescott, a man he admired, that he was competent, but he'd also met Lexie. Her grin lifted his spirits. Their kiss elevated the evening into noteworthy; he'd remember that short, sweet contact for a very long time.

Dylan slouched and jammed his fists into his pockets, distorting the crisp line of his suit. "I don't like this, Mace. Too many questions. Not enough answers. We don't know why those guys invaded the seventh floor or what they were after."

"Whatever it was, they didn't get it. We stopped them. We met our objectives." Mason ticked off their achievements on his fingers. "The admiral and his family are safe. None of the good guys, not even the hotel guards, were seriously injured. And the people who came here for a banquet are still having their coffee and chocolate mousse dessert."

"I'd approximate that eighty-five percent of the guests are oblivious of the attack."

Though he had no idea where Dylan got his percentage, Mason assumed that his computer-geek partner was correct. Most of the guests had remained in their chairs while the servers cleared away their plates and refilled their wineglasses. Some of them might have looked around when they heard the sound of approaching police sirens, but the flashing red-and-blue lights weren't visible from the banquet hall, and the hotel management people were doing everything in their power to make sure their guests weren't aware of the mayhem on the seventh floor.

The door swept open and Helena Christie Prescott charged toward them. She was a classic beauty with long raven hair and a killer body, but all Mason saw were her flared nostrils and the flames shooting from her green eyes as she demanded, "What the hell is going on?"

"Your husband asked that I bring you—"

"Edgar is all right, isn't he?"

"Yes, ma'am."

"That's good, because I'm going to hurt him, hurt him bad." She had morphed from fiery dragon into sinister assassin, a role she'd played in a movie Mason saw. The assassin might even have used that line about hurting him bad. "And the children?"

"Everybody's okay." Mason gestured toward the hallway. "Come with us to the conference room, where your husband can brief you."

"Lead on." She strode along beside him, leaving Dylan in their wake. In her five-inch heels, she almost matched

Mason's six-foot-three-inch height, and she hiked up the side of her gown opposite the slit so she could move faster.

Dylan—the coward—had cleverly fallen back, leaving Mason to deal with Helena. He was certain that any comment from him about not worrying or calming down would not be prudent.

"We're almost there," he said. "It's on this floor."

She came to a sudden halt. "I'm not being the least bit unreasonable. But what am I to think? My husband gets called away by his assistant, then the military guys and four agents—two CIA and two from some weird NSA department—slide out the door. What the hell is happening? Has Aspen been invaded by terrorists?"

Mason couldn't have been happier to see Lexie step out of the elevator and come toward them. A short while ago, he'd saved the nanny's life. Now it was her turn to save him.

She'd changed into casual clothes: sneakers, jeans and a long forest-green sweatshirt. Her wild auburn hair was held back from her face by a yellow band.

Helena spotted her and flung both arms around Lexie in a dramatic hug. "Thank God you're here."

Though jolted back on her heels, Lexie recovered her balance and spoke calmly. "Everything is going to be fine."

"Is it? Is it really?"

"Sure," Lexie said. "The kids are okay. They're all together in your suite. I left the hotel babysitter to keep an eye on them. Plus two of the TST bodyguards." She glanced at Mason and mouthed, *Is Carlos all right?*

He gave her a thumbs-up. The big guy had recovered and was sheepish about being sick. Since there didn't seem to be a connection between his stomach flu and the ambush on the seventh floor, he doubted that poison was involved. Carlos was once again in charge of guarding the children.

"Why wouldn't the kids be fine?" Helena asked. "Has there been a threat?"

Lexie turned to him. "You haven't told her?"

"The admiral wanted to explain himself."

A ringtone—a song from *Mary Poppins*—sounded, and Lexie retrieved her cell phone from a sweatshirt pocket. After a glance at the caller ID, she looked back at the admiral's wife. Her eyes narrowed. "Your husband has some serious explaining to do. Where is he?"

Mason opened the door to the conference room and stepped out of the way as the two women marched inside. Most of the people seated around the long table were men. One of the two women wore US Marine Corps dress blues, while the other was super chic, probably a higher-up in the CIA who shopped in Paris. In keeping with the early-1900s hunting lodge theme, the conference room was wood-paneled with elk, deer and bear heads on the walls. The snarling grizzly over the stone fireplace matched Helena's fierce expression.

Prescott leaped to his feet. "I believe you all know my wife, Helena Christie Prescott. And this is our nanny, Lexie DeMille."

The chic older woman applauded Lexie. "Impressive job, young lady. If you're ever looking for a job, contact me."

"She's not looking," Helena said curtly. "Edgar Prescott, step outside with me, please."

Without saying a word, Mason sent the admiral a mental warning. *Do what she says, man. Your wife is ticked off enough to play an assassin in real life. And you're her target.*

Apparently, Prescott's antennae were working well enough to pick up on the message. He excused himself, stepped away from the table and went into the hallway. As soon as the door to the conference room closed, he apologized to his wife.

Though this was a private conversation, Mason and his partner had to be there. It was their job to guard these two bodies. They were far less uncomfortable than Lexie who shuffled her feet and stared into the distance, pretending to be somewhere else.

"I didn't want to upset you," the admiral said to his wife. "There were gunshots fired on the seventh floor."

"Our floor?"

"Lexie was involved," he continued, "and, as you can plainly see, she's fine. TST Security rounded up the bad guys and took care of the threat. We're safe. There's nothing to worry about."

Not quite true. Mason found the situation worrisome, but that might just be his naturally vigilant nature. Overall, he was satisfied that they were safe. Choppers were airborne and searching. Local law enforcement had set up a perimeter around the hotel and would be escorting those who were leaving to their cars. There were enough armed officers patrolling in the hotel that Mason and TST Security were almost redundant.

"Very well," Helena said as she linked her arm with her husband's. "Come back to the banquet hall with me and give your speech."

"I should stay here." He looked over his shoulder at the closed door to the conference room, and then he turned to his wife. "Is there any way I can convince you to give my speech for me?"

"My dah-ling, don't be absurd. These people want to hear from you. I've only visited Africa a few times. You lived there. You know what this charity is all about."

He lifted her hand to his lips and kissed her manicured fingertips. "On our last trip to Madagascar, I remember how you took over the school and taught the kids how to sing."

Mason made eye contact with Dylan, who was being so unobtrusive that he was nearly invisible. He and his partner, both of them single, could take lessons from the admiral as he wove a charmed web around his formerly furious wife.

Helena rubbed against his arm like a slinky panther wanting to be stroked. "I had fun with my little friends, my little *marafiki*. And I loved the midnight spice market in Madagascar. But the people at this banquet have contributed a great deal of money, and they deserve the full package."

"I'm playing golf with the big investors tomorrow."

"Everybody else expects to hear a talk from you."

"Fine." He kissed her hand again. "I'll come in with you and give a brief hello. Then I'm heading back to the conference room and you can talk."

"About what?"

"I think you know," he said. "These people are educated, philanthropic, intelligent and discerning. They'll want to know about Hollywood."

"They always do," she said as she adjusted his necktie and patted his bottom.

Before they went into the banquet room, the admiral turned toward him and said, "Mason, wait for me out here."

Applause sounded as the door closed behind them. Dylan dodged around him, grabbed Lexie's hand and gave a firm shake. "From what I hear, you kicked butt. Martial arts?"

"My brothers run a karate dojo in Austin. I was starting to teach a couple of classes of my own before I became a nanny."

Mason liked the way her eyes crinkled at the corners

and her mouth turned up at the edges. He didn't so much like to see her grinning at his partner. "Dylan, I thought you were anxious to return to the front desk."

"I am?"

Mason wanted her all to himself, even though they only had a few moments and limited privacy. He tapped Dylan's arm a little bit harder than necessary to drive home the point. "Don't you need to be somewhere else?"

"Actually, I do." When he nodded, his glasses slid to the tip of his nose. "I have an audio and video recorder set on the conference room and it needs monitoring. So, I should go." Suiting the action to the words, he started walking backward while waving goodbye and mumbling about how busy he was.

Lexie turned that pretty smile on Mason, which was where it belonged. "Your partner is kind of a goofball."

"That's what happens with these genius types. They trip over their shoelaces because their brains are occupied with complicated problems."

Her gaze flicked toward the doors to the banquet room and then focused on him. "I need to talk to Prescott. Do you think I'll get a chance? I just need a few minutes."

"It shouldn't be a problem." He gently took her left arm—the one that wasn't injured—and escorted her across the open space outside the banquet hall to an antique-looking red leather love seat. "How's the bullet wound?"

"Just a graze," she said. "I'm fine. The hotel doctor patched me up and slapped on a bandage."

She perched nervously on the edge of the small sofa. On duty, Mason seldom allowed himself to sit; he needed to be on his feet and ready to move at the first sign of a threat. But the man he was guarding was inside another room where there were at least three other TST Security men. He sat beside Lexie, thigh to thigh. It would have been easy to rest his arm on the back of the love seat, but he exercised restraint.

"Prescott will talk to you," he assured her. "He's got to be grateful to you for keeping his kids safe."

"I hate to bother him with my problems. He put up with a lot of mistakes from me when I was learning the ropes. Being a nanny is more than babysitting, you know, especially when you're working with smart kids."

When she spoke, she gestured with her hands, but most of her animation came from her face. She punctuated her sentences with lifts of her eyebrows, scowls and grins and even a twitch of her freckled nose. The light makeup she'd worn at dinner had been wiped away, but she still looked good. He could watch her for hours and not get bored. "Did you get training on how to be a nanny? Did you go to nanny school?"

"I have a degree in psychology. Not that my studies help when Shane and Caine are punching each other. Or little Stella loses her magic wand." She grimaced and smirked at the same time. "I could probably use some instruction. I kind of lucked into this job, just showed up on Admiral Prescott's doorstep with no expectations. I didn't know they needed a nanny and didn't know I could be one."

"Tell me more."

"It was about a year ago. I was twenty-four, finished with college, living with my dad and working at the dojo. I didn't know what I wanted to do next. It needed to be something where I helped people, but I didn't know how or where. I liked the idea of working for something like the admiral's charity in sub-Saharan Africa." She tossed her head, setting her reddish curls into motion. "Or maybe not."

Somehow she'd gotten distracted. He pulled her back to the main topic. "Why were you on the admiral's doorstep?"

"There was this guy…" She paused and laughed. "How many wild stories have started off with those words? Anyway, this guy—his name was Anton—was kind of my boyfriend and he wanted to move in with me. Did I mention that I lived with my dad? Being the only girl in the family meant I did most of the cooking and shopping and laundry. In exchange, I didn't pay rent."

Once again, she'd gone skipping off on a tangent. He could feel her tension. Nervous energy had her running on high speed, making it hard to rein in her thoughts. He wanted to hold her and calm her down. Even though they had kissed, he had the feeling that this wasn't the right time. "When you were with your dad, did you like the arrangement?"

"I love my family. Living with Dad was comfortable. I'd work at the dojo, come home, cook dinner and handle a couple of chores. Then I'd do pretty much whatever I pleased. My biggest worry was that I'd get too cozy. On some fine day, I'd wake up and find out that I was seventy years old and never left home."

"Did you move in with Anton?"

"It was the other way around. He wanted to move in with me, with my family, which was a little creepy. And I couldn't imagine asking my dad. No. Way."

"Glad to hear it."

"Don't get me wrong," she said. "My dad liked my boyfriend. The two of them bonded over their guns. Anton worked as a hunting guide and had some high-profile positions. He'd even worked for the admiral, which impressed my dad because he knew the Admiral Prescott, too. Anyway, I wanted to—"

"Wait."

He held up a palm, signaling her to stop. Lexie seemed to be bounding over the relevant portions of this story.

She'd already mentioned that her father was stationed in the Middle East but never said he knew Prescott...and now her former boyfriend?

"Problem?" she asked.

"Your father, my brother and your boyfriend were all buddies with the admiral. That's an unbelievable coincidence."

"In the first place," she said, "I wouldn't exactly say they were buddies. More like acquaintances."

"You're right," he admitted.

"As for your brother and my dad, they were both in the Marine Corps, and both were stationed in the Middle East, where Admiral Prescott was one of the top guys running the show."

"What about the boyfriend?"

"He came looking for us because Prescott mentioned that he knew my dad and my dad lived in Austin. I met Anton through my father. I remember when I walked into the house and he saw me for the first time. His jaw dropped...literally. He thought I was something special."

Though Mason had never met the guy and probably never would, he didn't like this Anton character. What kind of man tries to move in with the father of his girlfriend? "When he asked to move in with you, did he propose?"

"I wouldn't let him. He hinted and I shut him down. I wasn't looking to settle down and get married. I told him he couldn't move into my dad's house and he should think again about our relationship." She gave another one of her adorable shrugs. "He left me without saying goodbye. He left a note that told me to kiss off."

When she met his gaze, Mason saw anger and determination in her chocolate-brown eyes. Her expression was similar to when she was shooting at the fake security guys.

Apparently, nobody told Lexie to kiss off and got away with it.

Now he understood how this twisted little story fit together. "You went looking for Anton."

"I wanted him to know that I broke up with him. Not the other way around. And I also wanted to get out of Austin for a while."

"You came to Colorado. To the admiral's doorstep."

"No sign of Anton. Prescott didn't remember him very well at all. Still, he invited me to stay for as long as I wanted, because of my dad." Her gaze drifted as she recalled. "I was surprised. I didn't think my dad was a big deal in the military, but I guess he was important enough for the admiral to think of him as a friend."

"And while you were there," Mason said, "you became the nanny."

"The nanny who was there when I arrived decided to quit. And I stepped in. I've never regretted it."

Her cell phone rang again.

She pulled it out and stared at the caller ID before she leaped to her feet. "Hi, Dad."

Chapter Five

Lexie's dad spoke in tough, uncompromising tones. Sure, he was retired, but he still hadn't stopped being the ultimate hard-ass Sergeant Major Daniel DeMille. "You listen to me, Franny, and you listen good."

"I'm not going by Franny anymore." She walked a few paces on the patterned hallway carpeting. "Call me Lexie."

"Your mother and I named you, and I'll call you whatever I damn well please, Miss Francine Alexandra DeMille."

The use of her full name was not a positive sign. Nor was the mention of her mother, who had divorced Daniel when Lexie was twelve. After Mom left, Dad didn't often link them together. In doing so, he seemed to be summoning up the ghost of a past that no longer existed. Perhaps it never had. Perhaps they had always been a dysfunctional family. With Mom gone, Grandma took over. And Dad was usually stationed on the other side of the world.

He growled. "You haven't returned my phone calls."

"I talked to you once and gave you my answer." She paced farther down the hall, noting that Mason kept a discreet distance but stayed with her.

"That answer, your answer, is unsatisfactory."

"I'm not going to change my mind," she said. "I won't quit my job and run home because you're worried about me."

"Either you get your rear end back to Texas or I'm coming to get you."

"I'm putting you on hold."

"Why?"

Because I'm furious and don't want to say something I'll regret later. "Excuse me, Dad."

She clicked him to silence and shook her fist at the cell phone. Her lips pinched together in a tight knot. Then she exhaled in a whoosh, blowing through her pursed lips like air coming out of a balloon.

She whirled around and looked at Mason. "My dad is treating me like I'm five years old. He's ticked off about what happened on the seventh floor."

"Did Prescott call him?"

"It was his assistant, Josh Laurent. You've probably met him. Long, pointy nose. Beady eyes. Stooped shoulders. He looks like a woodpecker."

"Yeah." Mason wiped the smile off his face. "We've met."

"Good old Josh didn't do a very good job of telling my dad what happened." She stopped beside a tiny desk with carved legs and a brass spittoon to one side. "He made that stupid ambush sound terrible and dangerous."

"It was dangerous. Those were real bullets. The blood on your arm? That was real, too."

"Really real," she muttered under her breath.

"What?"

"There's real life, which is what life is supposed to be. And really real life, which is how it actually is. Okay, for example, I'm a nanny in real life. In really real, I'm also an assistant, a nurse, a secretary and a teacher."

"In these real and extra real worlds of yours, where do you put the bullets?"

"Whose side are you on?"

"Yours," he said without hesitation. "But if you were my daughter, I'd be worried about you."

Men! They were all alike, thinking that women were helpless creatures who couldn't survive without one of them standing at her side and flexing his biceps. She was an adult. Not daddy's baby girl. Lexie could take care of herself.

She hadn't always been so independent and strong. When she came home from the hospital after her accident, she'd had serious nerve damage. Some docs had predicted that she'd never walk again. Her internal injuries had resulted in life-altering surgeries. She was scared, so deeply scared that she'd prayed to go to sleep and never wake up. It had seemed that life was too much to handle.

That was when her father stepped up and faced the challenge. Whether she needed him or not, he was there. Day and night, he watched over her and nursed her back to health. His gentle manner kept her spirits up. His firm encouragement reinforced her progress in physical therapy, where she literally started with baby steps.

After four weeks of recovery, when she'd been able to walk with crutches, she found out that he'd retired so he could take the time to be with her. Though he'd put in enough years with the military to qualify for a very nice pension and had plans for his retirement, she felt guilty about taking him away from a career he loved. The very last thing she wanted was to be a burden to her family.

She looked into Mason's steady blue eyes. "Why do you think my dad should worry about me?"

"Because he loves you."

Her tears sloshed and threatened to spill over her lower eyelids. Though the male of the species could be overbearing and pushy and demanding, they could also be achybreaky sweet. All that blustering and flexing was the way they showed that they cared.

Once again, she was stabbed in the gut by guilt. She didn't want to upset her dad. "In your professional opinion, do you think it's dangerous for me to stay with the Prescott family?"

"I can only assess one situation at a time. Right now I'm pretty sure that everybody's safe. Do you want me to talk to your father?"

"Not a good idea. Right at the moment, he doesn't think much of your abilities, even though I mentioned that you saved my life. And I explained how I ignored your advice to ride up on the elevator by myself."

He pointed to the phone. "You can't keep him on hold forever."

"I'm going back to my original plan." She tapped on the cell phone screen. "Dad, I'm going to have you talk to Admiral Prescott. He can explain why it won't be dangerous."

"I'll be waiting for that call."

She rolled her eyes at the phone. "I know you will."

PRESCOTT EMERGED FROM the banquet hall in full sail, leaving cheers and applause in his wake. There wasn't time for Lexie to ask him to talk to her father or to do anything else. With long determined strides, the admiral charged down the hall toward the conference room with the animal heads on the walls.

Before entering, he paused and straightened his necktie. "Be ready to move, Mason. I intend to get out of here ASAP."

"I understand," Mason said.

"Do you?" Prescott lifted an eyebrow.

"I'm not a police officer, but I'm sure there hasn't been enough time for thorough questioning and investigation.

Since you made the decision to stay at the hotel tonight, it seems wise to wait until morning, when you have enough information to know what needs to be done."

"My thoughts exactly."

Lexie felt like cheering. Mason's rational assessment made the crazy situation seem manageable. Not like her father, who was probably out by the barn shooting tin cans off the fence.

Mason said, "Lexie has something she needs to talk to you about."

"Of course." He pivoted to face her, held her at arm's length and peered into her eyes. "How are you holding up?"

"Good." She gave him what she hoped was a confident smile. "The problem is my dad."

"Danny-boy DeMille? He's a problem solver, not the other way around." He dropped his arms and raised his eyebrows. "Is he worried about you?"

"He's overreacting, right? I'm better equipped than most people to take care of myself. I'm good with a gun and an expert in karate and other martial arts."

"Sorry, kiddo, logic doesn't apply when it comes to family." He rubbed his chin. "On the off chance we might have some clear intel that your dad would want to hear, I want you to come into this meeting with me and Mason. After that, I'll make the call."

"Thank you."

"This is as much for my benefit as yours. I don't want to lose you as the kids' nanny."

The compliment was nice to hear. She followed Prescott inside and took a seat near the end of the table beside Josh. What a jerk he was! She felt like punching him but held back. Instead, she smiled and nodded to several of the people at the table whom she'd met before when they visited the Prescotts' home in Aspen.

Sitting to the admiral's left was Hank Grossman—a slouchy, sloppy, middle-aged man with hair that looked like steel wool. Instead of waving, he pointed at her as though his fingers were a gun—a gesture that was particularly inappropriate given the circumstances. Did he mean to threaten her? Was he working with the bad guys? Lexie copied his gesture and pretended to shoot back at him. *Take that, Grossman.*

He was with the NSA. She knew his job was top secret but had no idea what he did or what his title was or anything else about him, other than he couldn't get through a meal without dribbling a smear on his necktie.

Beside Grossman was Sam Bertinelli, also NSA, who was dark with classic features and much more pleasant. He gave her a nod and a wink. His buttoned-down appearance was well suited for a junior executive, but Bertinelli was a little too old to be a junior anything. Certainly too old for her, which was basically what she'd told him when he'd asked her out on a date a few months ago. They had both been polite, but she'd seen the flare of hostility in his hazel eyes. The two NSA dudes were a little scary.

Josh's pointy woodpecker nose jabbed in her direction. "I spoke to your father."

"I'm aware," she said in a low voice oozing with sarcasm. "You made it sound like we were under assault from terrorist madmen. He's freaked."

"Odd. He's a marine. I didn't think he'd get upset."

She hated the insinuation. Her dad was tougher than nails; he could handle anything. "Are you saying that my dad is a wimp?"

"Hush, now."

"Take it back."

"Fine."

His head swiveled so he faced the head of the table.

Again, he reminded her of a bird with virtually no neck and a round, soft body. Why did Prescott keep him around as an assistant? Josh was neither smart nor funny nor pleasant. He did, however, fulfill whatever he was ordered to do without question or hesitation. She supposed there was something to be said for blind obedience.

Including Josh, there were seven men seated around the table and two women, one in uniform and one in a body-hugging cocktail dress with one shoulder bare.

At the head of the table, next to the bared shoulder, was a slick, good-looking guy. He rose to his feet and buttoned the front of his tux. He wasn't as tall as Mason, who was standing behind the admiral, and he wasn't as muscular. But a lot of women would have found his sweep of glistening blond hair and brilliant blue eyes appealing. The tux helped.

She leaned toward Josh. "Who's that?"

"Robert Collier, CIA."

His voice was a bit higher than she expected and had an interesting accent. Maybe French? Lexie had gotten accustomed to these suave, international men who came to visit at the Prescott home in Aspen. She suspected Collier would be a hand kisser.

"The woman next to him," she whispered to Josh, "is also CIA?"

Josh nodded.

Apparently, Collier had been waiting for the admiral to return. He addressed the group. "In my interrogation of the four men in custody, I have learned that they are part of a group called the Anti-Conspiracy Committee for Democracy, or the AC-CD."

The name of the group didn't sound dangerous. Nobody in this room was against democracy. And who wasn't anti-conspiracy? Resting her elbow on the table, she leaned forward and focused on Collier.

He pointed to the flat screen mounted on the wall behind where she was sitting. She turned to look over her shoulder. The screen was blank. Mounted on the wall near the door was an elk head with an impressive ten-point rack. On the other side of the screen was a seriously ugly boar with curly tusks.

"I would usually have photos and a logo," he said in his lilting accent, "but the members of the very loosely organized AC-CD pride themselves on being anonymous. They meet in groups of no more than five. The head of AC-CD is referred to as the leader, and sometimes different people take that responsibility."

Bertinelli nudged the shoulder of his NSA boss as he pointed out the obvious. "For a group opposed to conspiracy, they have a lot of secrets."

"That is why," Collier said with a cold glance toward the NSA contingent, "it is complicated to compile facts and information about the AC-CD."

"How did you get them to talk?" Bertinelli asked.

"They would hardly shut up. I have never had an interrogation like this. They were eager to tell me that their job was vitally important on a global level. They all used the same words—'vital importance' and 'international repercussions' and more of those catchphrases."

He swore in French and stuck out his jaw. His icy blond hair shimmered under the overhead lights.

"Excuse me," said the uniformed woman, "but what was the job they were assigned to do?"

"To kidnap the admiral."

All eyes focused on Prescott. Unperturbed, he shrugged and said, "Then they weren't after my children. Is that correct?"

"Correct, sir."

"Or my wife."

"Just you," Collier said. "Their plan was to drug your wife's bedtime drink so she would sleep soundly. When everything was quiet, they would slip into your bedroom and abduct you. Under no circumstances were they supposed to hurt you."

"Why?" Prescott asked.

"They are searching for the Damascus Cache, and they believe you have knowledge of its whereabouts."

Prescott scoffed. "The Damascus Cache was destroyed years ago."

Beside her, Josh wriggled in his chair like a schoolboy who had the right answer to the teacher's question. She gave him a nudge. "Go ahead and speak up."

"I better not." That was why he was a woodpecker and not an eagle. To her, he whispered, "I've heard chatter. People talking about the cache."

Her cell phone buzzed. A text was coming through from Megan, the oldest Prescott kid. It said, Hurry back. The brats won't go to bed.

It was kind of amazing that Lexie had been away for as long as she had without a minor crisis or two from the children. It looked as though she'd have to wait until later to get Prescott to talk to her dad.

She stood and pointed to her phone. "Please excuse me. Duty calls. I need to go upstairs and tell some bedtime stories."

"I'll be up soon," Prescott said. "Mason, accompany her."

He was at her side so quickly that he was turning the doorknob before she could touch it. In the hallway, he closed the door and spoke into his headset.

When he was beside her, she asked, "Who were you talking to?"

"Dylan. He has cameras in the conference room so he can keep an eye on things until I get back."

"Do you need to go back?"

"Prescott asked me to stay close."

She didn't like the way that sounded. "He doesn't trust the people around him."

"Do you blame him?"

"Not really."

The men and women in that conference room were spies, spooks and feds—high-ranking members of the intelligence community. It dawned on her that she'd met several of these people. "Do you think my dad is right? Am I in danger?"

"Not right now."

As they strolled to the elevators, his vigilant attitude relaxed, and he seemed to shed his bodyguard persona. She liked being with him. And he must like her, too. He'd kissed her, after all.

She pushed the elevator button. "Should I stay with the Prescotts or should I quit?"

"Do you like your job?"

"I do. It's not a career I want for the rest of my life, but I like it."

"Are you scared?"

She thought for a moment before answering. In the bathroom upstairs, she'd had a few moments of intense panic when she'd fallen through a time warp to relive her accident. But her fear had dissipated. "I'm cautious but not frightened."

"Cautious is good," he said as they boarded the elevator. "There's no glory in taking risks."

"I don't know what to do."

The elevator doors closed. They were wrapped together in a wood-paneled cocoon. She caught a whiff of his citrusy aftershave. She slowly blinked. In her imagination, their clothes melted away. In another long blink, they twined in each other's arms. A gush of passion swept through her.

An elevator bell dinged when they hit the seventh floor, and she focused on him. He was watching her with a wary but bemused expression. "You checked out. What were you thinking?"

She stepped into the hallway outside the elevator. The teddy bear on the side table that had been gunned down earlier had already been replaced by a new stuffed animal. No way would she tell him that she'd fantasized about him. Instead, she switched direction. "You haven't answered me. Stay or go back to Texas?"

"I don't think there's a logical solution," he said. "What does your heart tell you?"

Lexie didn't usually think of things in touchy-feely terms; she wasn't raised that way. But she did have feelings about her job. Going back to her father's house felt like admitting defeat. Along that line, she wasn't one to be scared off.

Her heart also told her that she liked being part of the Prescott clan. With them, she shared intimate family moments that had never been possible with her brothers and father.

And there was one more heartfelt reason. She thought of it as she watched the two littlest Prescott kids dashing down the hallway toward her with the huge Carlos in pursuit. If she left Colorado, she would probably never see Mason again.

She turned to him and gave a decisive nod. "I'm staying."

Chapter Six

The next morning at nine o'clock, Mason climbed into the passenger side of a golf cart beside Admiral Prescott. Following an asphalt path, Prescott drove from the practice putting green toward the first tee. In normal circumstances, Mason enjoyed the game and was a couple of notches under par. From a bodyguard's perspective, he hated golf. Everybody on the course was carrying a bag filled with metal implements, providing a handy hiding place for a gun or rifle. Though Mason would be sticking tight to the admiral for close-in protection, they were surrounded by forested hills where an army of bad guys could be lurking.

The local sheriff had his deputies combing through the trees and rocks, and helicopters made occasional swoops, but there was no effective way to shield against an assault from a sniper with a long-range precision rifle. Those babies were accurate at a thousand yards.

Mason took comfort in the knowledge that the Anti-Conspiracy Committee for Democracy plan was for kidnapping and not assassination. Also, if the guys they picked up last night were any sample, the AC-CD was a committee of numskulls.

Last night he'd heard more details from CIA Agent Collier's interrogation. The AC-CD thugs had broken into the admiral's room and downloaded the contents of his computer and his wife's computer onto memory sticks. They'd readily admitted to Collier that they didn't think the admiral was careless enough to transport the Damascus Cache on his personal computer, but they needed to look everywhere.

Their kidnapping plot was foiled when Lexie showed up too early on the seventh floor. Her appearance caught them unprepared; they'd only had time to get changed and drag a couple of the real guards into a vacant room to hide their unconscious bodies. The real guards had been zapped by stun guns and none of them were seriously injured. The only person to require an ambulance was the guy Lexie had karate kicked into dreamland.

The thought of the petite, auburn-haired nanny beating up an armed bad guy brought a smile to Mason's face. This mental image of Lexie was a pleasant distraction. Behind his sunglasses, he kept his eyes in motion, scanning the hillsides, anticipating threats before they became real.

"I'm glad you and your men are here," Prescott said.

"You're the boss. We'll stay as long as you want."

"Good to know." He checked his wristwatch. "In about an hour, I'll need to pull away from the rest of the foursome and take a meeting on the computer."

"A face-to-face meeting?"

"Yes, your partner Dylan set it up for me. He says all I have to do is turn on the laptop and push one button."

"I'll make sure the meeting stays private." Mason glanced over at Prescott. His close-cropped white hair was covered by a dark blue cap with *NAVY* written in gold. He was tanned and looked healthy in khakis and a lightweight gray sweater. "Lexie said you were keeping TST around because you don't trust these other guys."

"She's a very perceptive young woman—her father's

daughter." Prescott frowned. "My conversation with him last night could have gone better. I get it. The man is concerned. Hell, I'd feel the same way if one of my kids had been attacked. But I believe these idiots were after me, not the nanny or Helena or the children. They should all be safe."

"What did her father say to her?"

"He was willing to have Lexie stay."

And that was fortunate, because she'd already made up her mind about what she intended to do. "Do you mind if I ask a personal question?"

"Go ahead."

Mason cleared his throat. "Is Lexie dating anyone?"

"When she first came to us, she asked about a boyfriend by the name of Anton. But she's forgotten him. And she's only gone out on a couple of dates." He gave a sly grin. "Any other questions?"

"When is her next day off?"

MASON ACCOMPANIED THE FOURSOME: Prescott, Collier and the two NSA guys—Hank Grossman and Sam Bertinelli. Predictably, Collier was a superb golfer with picture-perfect form. Bertinelli wasn't half bad, but took way too long to set up each shot, testing the wind direction and picking bits of grass out of the way. The admiral played solid, par-level golf. And Grossman cheated.

Since they were zipping around in golf carts, the only chance for conversation was on the green. Collier, Prescott and Bertinelli followed golf etiquette and kept their voices low so they wouldn't disturb the putter. Grossman wasn't so polite.

"Listen up, boys," Grossman growled. Mason guessed that the gray-haired, stoop-shouldered man was older than the admiral, definitely north of sixty. "Let's take advantage of this time alone to talk about the Damascus Cache. We all know what it is. Don't pretend that you don't."

"I've heard talk," Prescott said, "about a comprehensive list of personnel and weapons in the Middle East and sub-Saharan Africa. A cache of information, compiled several years ago at the end of the Bush administration."

"More valuable than a cache of gold," Grossman said.

"Not all of it." Prescott's ball was in a bunker, farthest from the hole. Therefore, he was first to shoot. After selecting a wedge club, he positioned his feet in the sand, straightened his shoulders, glanced at the flag and hit a perfect chip shot. The ball stopped a mere six inches from the hole.

As he tapped his ball into the cup, he continued, "There were lists of supplies, locations of arsenals and maps of supply lines. At least, I'd guess the cache included that information—details that are now worthless."

"It is about the people," Collier said.

The next to putt was Bertinelli. His ball was about thirty-five feet from the hole, and Mason guessed it was going to take five minutes for Bertinelli to test the wind and tamp down divots. A waste of time—this average golfer wasn't going to make such a long putt.

"I agree about the danger posed to the people on this list," said Prescott. "I'm not saying that I've ever seen the cache or that I even know it exists, but I'd guess that it would give details about intelligence operatives for the military, the CIA, NSA and Interpol. Many were undercover."

"Many still are," Collier said. "These are people who may or may not still be involved in espionage. Some have dropped off the grid and are leading normal lives. They are married. They have children."

"Ha!" Grossman exploded with a loud, humorless laugh.

"I'm guessing that these former spies sure as hell don't want their names made public."

"Exposure would be a death warrant."

Finally in position over the ball, Bertinelli looked confused. "Why would AC-CD want the list?"

"Hurry up and putt," Grossman said. "As for the AC-CD, they claim to be anti-conspiracy. So they might think they're doing the world a favor by causing trouble for spies."

"An altruistic motive," Prescott said.

"Yeah, yeah, they're shining a light on the truth. That kind of phony-baloney."

Mason pinched his lips together to keep from blurting out his ideas and opinions. His college degree was in international relations. Because his brother had been stationed in the Middle East, he'd focused on that area and on Africa. These were lands where espionage ran rampant, lands where bribes were more common than taxes, lands of genocide. Heinous battles were motivated by politics, religion, ethnicity and plain old greed. He seriously doubted that AC-CD wanted the Damascus Cache to expose the truth.

Bertinelli tapped his ball. It traveled slowly but steadily and...plink! He sank the putt and gave a victorious arm pump. This guy wasn't the sharpest tool in the shed, but he shouldn't be counted out.

"I got the answer," Grossman said. "Destroy the damn list. Delete it from all servers. Encrypt the hell out of it."

While he babbled about how they could destroy the cache, he misfired on a four-foot putt. His ball was about as far from the hole as Collier's, which was good enough for Grossman. He scooped it off the green and into his pocket. "That's a gimme."

Collier spoke in his smooth, lightly accented voice as he lined up his putt. "We cannot destroy something that we do not have. The Damascus Cache, whether it exists or not, is nowhere to be found."

The stroke of his putter was as elegant as his tailored black trousers and cashmere sweater. When the ball dropped into the hole, he casually removed his sunglasses. His blue-eyed gaze zeroed in on Prescott. "I wonder, Admiral, why do these people believe that you are in possession of the cache?"

"A damned good question," Grossman bellowed. "I know you worked in intelligence with the navy SEALs, but you're retired."

Not to be left out, Bertinelli added his two cents. "You're a surprising target, sir. You have a reputation for not being comfortable with computer technology."

"True," Prescott said. "I still have trouble figuring out how to make my phone send texts."

"Why you?" Collier repeated.

The admiral didn't even attempt to answer. He shrugged, checked his wristwatch and started walking toward their cart. "Play the next hole without me. I'll catch up after I take a meeting."

"We're going to miss you," Grossman called after him.

"I'll bet."

The admiral drove the cart toward a grove of aspens that were several yards off the fairway. Apparently, he wanted privacy for this meeting. Not only did he put distance between them and the others in the foursome, but the outdoor location made it difficult for anyone else to overhear. Mason knew that his buddy Dylan would have set up a computerized meeting that was nearly impossible to hack.

"I need you to keep time," Prescott said as he handed Mason the Luminox wristwatch preferred by the SEALs. "I need to log on at precisely 10:44 and log off at 10:59."

Mason took the watch. Three minutes until log-on. The

admiral had the computer open on his lap. He flexed his fingers and cleared his throat. And then...

"Trouble approaching," Mason said.

A golf cart with a distinctive pink top bounced across the fairway toward them. In the driver's seat, Helena hunched over the steering wheel like a speed racer and squealed wildly on every bump. Riding shotgun, Lexie clung to the fringed pink top and laughed.

The admiral shook his head and grinned. "That's my woman."

A lot of men, especially those in positions of authority, would have been annoyed by Helena's wild driving, but Prescott was amused, even a little bit proud of his flamboyant wife.

"Sir." Mason tapped the face of the watch. "It's time."

Prescott touched the correct computer key, and the laptop screen showed a broad-shouldered man sitting at a desk. His face was easily recognizable from television talk shows—a lantern jaw, heavy brows and thick black hair with silver streaks at the temple. He was the Secretary of the Navy, Thomas Benson.

"Good morning," Prescott said.

"Maybe where you are it's morning." Benson's jaw lifted, and he scowled into the screen. "Here at the Pentagon it's past my feeding time. What's happening, Prescott? Tell me about these anti-conspiracy whack jobs."

"Not much to tell," he replied. "My concern is the Damascus Cache. I thought we'd destroyed every copy."

Mason took note of the change in Prescott's attitude. With the other golfers, he'd been cagey about whether or not the Damascus Cache even existed. While he was talking to the SecNav, a veteran officer who was a peer and an equal, there was a total lack of pretense. These two spoke truth to each other.

The SecNav shook his head. "I can't be certain that one copy didn't get away from us."

"Who was responsible for getting rid of this intelligence?"

"Your old buddy, Al Ackerman."

"I was afraid you'd say that."

With one last squeal, Helena parked next to them in the shadow of the aspens. She bounded from the cart and came around so she could see over her husband's shoulder. The instant she recognized the man on the screen, she fluttered her fingertips in a wave. "Hello there, Tommy."

"Helena." His smile was so broad it looked as if his jaw would unhinge. "Lovely as ever, and who's that with you?"

"Our nanny, Lexie DeMille," she said as she dragged Lexie into the camera range.

Mason noticed how Lexie's posture went from relaxed to as stiff as steel rebar, almost as though she was standing at attention. He understood why she straightened up. No matter where she went or what she became, Lexie was a military brat. SecNav was a man of the highest rank and authority.

"It's a pleasure to meet you, sir," she said with a slight quaver in her voice.

Prescott said, "She's Danny DeMille's daughter. As long as I'm making introductions, my bodyguard is Mason Steele. His brother was Matthew."

To his amazement, the SecNav saluted him. "Matthew Steele was a hero. His quick thinking saved thirty-seven children. My condolences to you and to your parents."

"Thank you, sir."

Mason was reeling. The SecNav knew his brother. More than that, he knew something about the circumstances of Matthew's death. He had posthumously been awarded a Purple Heart, his second such award, so his family had known that he'd died honorably. Still, hearing the details would mean a great deal to Mason's parents.

With a start, he realized that Prescott was talking to him, telling him to move the ladies out of the way while he finished his conversation. Mason herded Lexie and Helena deeper into the aspen grove while leaving a clear route back to the admiral in case he needed to get back there in a hurry.

"Wow," Lexie said. "Thomas Benson knows who my dad is. I can't believe it! And I met him, too."

"He's just good old Tommy," Helena said. "The man is a sweetheart and a ham. Did you know that he was a pilot?"

Both Mason and Lexie nodded. Though he was interested in her story, he kept one eye on Prescott. Mason was curious about the "old buddy" named Ackerman. Why had the admiral expressed concern when the SecNav mentioned him?

"At a karaoke bar in DC," Helena continued, "Tommy and Prescott serenaded me. Can you guess what they sang?"

Lexie nodded. "The SecNav was a top gun. I'm guessing they sang 'You've Lost That Lovin' Feelin'.'"

"Of course, you're right."

Helena started singing, and Lexie backed her up. Damn, they were cheerful. If he hadn't known better, he wouldn't have believed that Lexie had recently been in a firefight and Helena's husband was under threat of abduction. Was the singing and smiling a front? Showing a brave face so the kids wouldn't be scared?

He took a long moment to study Lexie. Her black jeans fit smoothly. On the top, she wore a white shirt with an eyelet trim under an embroidered denim jacket. Once again, her curly hair was yanked up in a high ponytail.

He liked the casual version of Lexie. If she was faking this carefree attitude, he'd have to nominate her for an award.

Prescott motioned for them to join him as he powered down the laptop and closed it. Still singing and snapping her fingers, Helena approached him and kissed both cheeks, leaving a scarlet imprint of lipstick.

"Are we okay?" she asked.

"We're fine," he assured her. "But I'm going to need to spend another day or two at the Pentagon next week."

"Next week is the start of our summer schedule. We're all taking off in different directions, and I want to get packed and organized."

Prescott looked around her shoulder to make eye contact with Lexie. "How about it—are you ready to organize the Prescott troops?"

"Ready to try," she said.

"How's the arm?"

"Doesn't hurt a bit. At the worst, I'll have another scar to add to my collection."

Mason had wanted to ask the same thing. What did she mean about a collection of scars? There was so much more he wanted to know about her.

Prescott took on a serious expression. "I want to promise you, Lexie, that we will find and destroy any existing copies of the Damascus Cache. But I know better than to make guarantees that cannot be fulfilled with certainty."

"I'm sure you'll do your best." Her lips twisted in a confused smile. "But I'm not sure why this would be important to me."

"The cache is a list of undercover operatives in the Middle East. It was generated several years ago." He took her hand and squeezed. "Your father's name is on it."

Chapter Seven

Tony Curtis blended in with the valets handling parking at the boutique hotel. He'd grabbed a uniform—a black vest and a bolo tie—from the garage, and he found a name tag in the top drawer of a beat-up desk by the lockers. The name was Andy. Not entirely accurate, but close enough. He sidled up the drive to the desk at the front entrance, where guests were checking out and demanding their vehicles.

Though he was probably fifteen years older than the other valets, his build was as lean and wiry as an eighteen-year-old's, and he'd plucked the few gray hairs from his thick black mane. It was no problem for him to pass himself off as a young dude with a hard-luck story.

Along with the rest of the crew, he hustled back and forth to the underground parking to retrieve the Escalades, Bimmers and Hummers. He let the other guys do most of the work. They didn't care. This was a job that ran on tips.

Tony made no effort to be secretive or to hide. Instead, he acted as if he belonged. He played his role as a guy who was too old to be making a living as a valet…doing it anyway but not even trying to do it well.

A job like this might have been his really real life. He smirked at the thought, acknowledging that the person who had babbled about really real life was Franny, who now wanted to be called Lexie. Hell, why not? Lexie rhymed with sexy, and that suited her. She was hot, sexier now than when he'd known her. He was almost glad he hadn't killed her.

What set him apart from the other valets was his intense training with firearms and his instinct for murder. In the past few moments, he'd been tempted to lash out. Taking gratuities made him feel like a servant. When a pompous, red-faced rich man dribbled a one-dollar bill into Tony's outstretched hand and stood waiting for a "thank you, sir," a homicidal urge boiled up inside the not-really-a-valet.

Since metal detectors were all over the hotel, he hadn't hidden a gun up his sleeve. Nor was he carrying the well-honed hunting knife he used to gut and clean a deer in five minutes. Tony had two weapons strapped to his chest under his vest. One was a stun gun. The other was a razor-sharp plastic chef's blade.

He locked gazes with the pompous hotel guest. Tony could kill this fool in ways that didn't require a weapon. With a deft twist, he could snap the rich man's neck. Eye gouging was an option. Or a quick, lethal chop to the trachea.

The rich man must have recognized Tony's deeper nature, because he peeled off a ten to accompany the one-dollar bill, quickly dived behind the steering wheel of his shiny SUV and drove away.

Nobody paid any attention when Tony edged around to the side of the hotel and pulled out a cigarette. From this vantage point, he could see the admiral and his buddies playing golf. Life would have been so much easier if he could have just killed the admiral. The kidnapping scheme meant the admiral had to be incapacitated and then removed from the scene. Neither would happen while the bodyguard protected him.

Tony traced the edge of the leather knife sheath fastened to his chest. He came to the conclusion that the only way to abduct the admiral required killing the bodyguard.

THOUGH THE DAY was sunny and clear, Lexie felt cold shadows closing around her, tweaking her shoulders and sending shivers down her spine. Standing on the balcony outside her hotel room, she stared into the warm blue Colorado sky and thought about Texas, the closest place she had to a home. Like most military families, the DeMilles had moved from base to base around the country while her parents were together. After the split, she and her brothers had been raised by her grandma in Austin while her dad was stationed far away. And working as a spy?

She hadn't even known that the marines had spies, but of course they did. Every branch of the military had intelligence officers, and the SEALs were totally involved in undercover ops. Still, she didn't think of her dad as a secret agent. How could that be? Suave wasn't part of his vocabulary. He was loud, demanding and straightforward… just about as subtle as a charging Brahman bull.

But the SecNav and Admiral Prescott wouldn't lie to her. According to those two, Danny DeMille was not only a spy, but in danger of being outed by something called the Damascus Cache. What could she do? How was she going to keep her dad safe?

The smartest move would be to rush home, throw a fence around him and shoot anybody who got too close. As if he'd put up with that? His lifestyle didn't exactly lend itself to the efforts of a bodyguard. Why couldn't he be a typical retired dad who stayed at home and puttered and watched football on TV?

When he'd left the marines and come home to nurse her back to health, she felt bad about making him change his whole life. He confided that being a soldier hadn't been his number one choice, anyway. His cherished goal in life was to be a cowboy. After she was mostly recovered, he made his dream become really real when he found a job with a buddy who owned a dude ranch. The work suited him. Her dad was the Marlboro Man without the cigarettes.

She heard a rap on the door and turned. "Come in."

Mason pushed open the door. She hadn't expected to see him again but was glad he'd shown up. Last night, she'd experienced a wonderful, luscious sleep filled with X-rated fantasies about this tall, muscular man with the sky blue eyes and the buzz-cut hair. Whether her dreams were a result of the pain pills the hotel doctor had given her or came from a deeper need, she hadn't wanted to wake up this morning.

With his hand on the knob, he stood framed in her doorway like a cover photo. He looked great in his khaki trousers, collared shirt and the dark blue sports jacket he wore to cover his gun holster. And what would she call this portrait? Casual stud? Golfing bodyguard? Husky, handsome hunk?

She cleared her throat. "Are you done with your golf round?"

"Prescott only played the front nine. He wanted to come back here and talk to Helena before she took off with you and the kids."

"So you left the two of them—the admiral and his wife—alone in their bedroom suite," she said. "Is that proper bodyguard procedure?"

"Not really." With the door to Lexie's room still open, he turned his head and looked down the hall toward the suite. "I should be right outside his door, but I wanted to catch you before you left."

She truly enjoyed hearing those words. The chill of fear

that had been poking at her melted a bit. Mason warmed her in many different ways. She floated across the room, stood beside him and whispered, "What did you want to say to me?"

"Prescott said you'd talked to your dad. Are you going back to Austin?"

The apprehensions that had been momentarily swept aside surged to the forefront of her mind. "Do you think I should?"

"If you're scared, my answer is yes." Parallel lines creased his forehead as he considered. "However, I don't think you need to feel nervous or afraid. The AC-CD is after the admiral, and he's planning to fly straight to the Pentagon after one more round of golf with big donors."

"Hold on there. He's supposed to return to the house with us." She followed Mason's glance toward the suite. "Oh, I see. He's trying to explain. I don't think Helena expected him to go to the Pentagon so soon. He's retired, supposedly."

"He mentioned that I might want to protect him from her."

"Indeed," she said.

Helena had a temper, and she'd be plenty angry that her husband was escaping the hectic hassle of getting ready for the summer season. During the next few days, the kids would be taking off in different directions for different projects. Even Helena was busy—scheduled to be filming in Toronto.

"The admiral has to fend for himself when it comes to his wild and crazy wife," Mason said. "I'm worried about you."

"Me?" She pulled one fist to her waist and thrust the other forward in a karate pose. "I can take care of myself."

"You are wise, Lexie-*san*. Not going back to Texas?"

"I didn't say that." She dropped the pose. "I'm nervous about my father being named in the Damascus Cache. He's done so much for me. He stayed with me when I thought I was going to die. At the very least, I should run home and watch his back."

"I thought you had brothers in Austin."

"I do." Unfortunately, contacting her brothers and telling them about the threat wasn't possible. The admiral had made her promise not to tell anyone else. "The Damascus Cache is top secret."

"Right."

"I could try to convince my dad to go into hiding. Maybe he'd qualify for witness protection."

She seriously doubted that he'd agree to any form of protection, even if it made sense. Whether he was wearing his dress blue uniform or riding the range in his favorite Stetson, her dad was a manly man. He believed in uncommon valor and never ran from a fight.

"Best-case scenario," Mason said, "Prescott locates the existing copy of the cache—if there is such a thing—and he destroys it."

She didn't understand why it should be the admiral's job to deal with the cache. He was retired. Why didn't the AC-CD understand that? Why had they come after Prescott? And why wasn't she taking this conversation with Mason to a more interesting place? "Enough about my dad."

"Talking about him is important. If you leave to watch over him, I have to drive over nine hundred miles to take you out to dinner."

"And if I don't go?"

"It's a mere two hundred miles from Denver to Aspen. When's your next day off?"

"Thursday," she said quickly. In her mind, that date was

lit up in neon party colors. Five days from now on Thursday, the Prescott family would be pursuing their summer adventures. She'd have the house to herself.

"I'll pick you up at five." With most guys, hand kisses were smarmy. Not Mason. He lifted her hand and lightly pressed his full lips against her knuckles. The resulting angle of her arm was a bit uncomfortable. She winced.

"Does it hurt?" he asked. "The bullet wound?"

"I hardly feel it." There were light twinges when she moved her arm a certain way, and she intended to baby herself for a couple of days—not lifting children or carrying luggage.

"What did you mean when you said it was another scar for your collection?"

"I was in a car accident. Operations on both legs left some interesting marks, and I've got a couple of surgical scars on my abdomen."

"That sounds serious."

"A hit-and-run," she said dismissively. Her accident was definitely *not* something she wanted to talk about. Instead, she concentrated on the fun she'd have going out with Mason. "Where should we eat?"

"Do you like German?"

"Ja, ich liebe Strudel."

"You love strudel. Me, too." He chuckled. "Tell me more about this car accident. How old were you?"

"Fresh out of college." She shook her head. No more about the accident. "Five o'clock is an early start for a date."

"We'll have a couple of German beers before we eat." He cocked his head to one side. "I want to hear more about this accident."

"There's not much to say. Another car clipped my fender. I lost control and drove my brother's car over a cliff. While I was crashing, I was more scared about how mad he'd be that I broke his car."

"And was he?"

The familiar ache crept over her. Her brothers had been only concerned about her. In fact, the one whose car she'd been driving blamed himself for not having a safer vehicle. "You know, Mason, I don't want to talk about the accident. I should have died, but I didn't. That's all."

He gently glided his hand down her uninjured arm and held her hand. "You don't mind having another scar?"

"Not from a bullet wound." She lifted her chin and looked up at him. "It's kinda cool. That's what the kids say."

"The twins caught a glimpse of you doing a flying kick on the armed man outside the elevator. Impressive move!"

"Yeah, they think I'm awesome until the next time I tell them they can't drink a gallon of their favorite high-octane energy drink before bed." She knew it wouldn't take long for the kids to slot her back into the boring-nanny category.

"Kids keep you grounded. The Prescott gang doesn't care that their father is an international consultant. Mom is a movie star? So what?"

Those were perceptive observations for a guy who was essentially an only child and didn't have regular contact with children. "How come you're not a daddy?"

"I haven't found the right mommy." Still holding her hand, he pivoted slightly to face her. His gaze bored into hers. "I wouldn't mind settling down and having a family. Not that I'm looking…"

But he was, she could tell. She felt him peering into her eyes, trying to discover a sign that she was the one he was looking for. Could she be the right mommy for his children?

Part of her wanted to fling herself into his arms and tell

him that she was the one. *Yes, pick me.* But motherhood wasn't in her future. It was cruel to lead him on. Dating her would be a waste of his time.

Before she could say anything, the door to the Prescott suite opened and the admiral stepped out. His gray sweater was askew. He was carrying his hat and his shoes. Helena appeared in the doorway behind him, wearing a sultry smile and a filmy black negligee with a feather trim that made it over-the-top.

Mason whispered, "Looks like they're done fighting."

"And have moved on to makeup sex." Lexie was familiar with this pattern. Passionate arguments followed by what she could only assume was equally passionate lovemaking was typical. "Here's what's strange about the movie star/love goddess. She's kind of a prude."

"Hmm." Mason wasn't actually drooling, but was clearly mesmerized by the voluptuous body under the sheer black fabric. "You don't say."

"But I do." She pulled her hand back and punched his arm. "Here's how Helena rolls. After marriage, anything goes. But she won't allow unmarried couples to sleep in the same bedroom in her house. That might explain why she's been married five times."

"Probably," he agreed.

Prescott waved to him as he stuck his toe into his right shoe. "Let's go, Mason."

"Apparently, we're done playing golf. The admiral isn't wearing his spiked golf shoes, just sneakers." He took a step away from her. "There's another alternative—something else you could do about your dad."

She followed him, taking two steps in his direction. "What is it?"

"Do you remember how I said this could all be over

if the admiral found copies of the cache and destroyed them?"

"Yes." Of course she remembered. It had only been a few minutes ago.

"Admiral Prescott isn't the only one who has access. I'll bet you've overheard more top secret intelligence than most high-clearance agents are told."

"Me?" Her voice was a squeak. "You think I could figure this out?"

"It's better than sitting around doing nothing."

As Mason hustled down the hall to the admiral's side, she watched his retreating form. She liked the breadth of his shoulders and his athletic stride. If she'd had a clear view of his bottom under his jacket, she probably would have liked that, too. More than anything, she appreciated the way his mind worked.

Someone had to locate the mysterious Damascus Cache. Why not her? Mason was correct when he said that she'd overheard a lot of high-level intelligence. Most people didn't pay much attention to the nanny. She'd have to put it all together and figure it out. She was good at puzzles. The solution couldn't be that complicated. She could do it.

Her father had devoted much of his life to protecting his home and country. He had always kept her safe. Now it was her turn.

Find the cache. Save her dad.

Chapter Eight

Given her new agenda about searching for and ultimately destroying the Damascus Cache, Lexie looked forward to the fifty-minute drive from the hotel to the family's home near Aspen. She'd have a chance to talk with Helena and get the inside scoop. No matter how much Lexie had overheard during the last couple of days, those meetings, discussions and consultations weren't the same as private conversations.

The admiral often chose to confide the most important details to his wife. He didn't blab about troop movements or spy craft or undercover operations, but he told her the human stories—the incidents that affected his heart.

More than once this morning, Lexie had noticed Helena studying her with a goopy, sympathetic expression on her beautiful face. Neither of the Prescotts was the sort of person who treated the nanny like a piece of furniture, but they weren't all buddy-buddy. Lexie's wild ride across the golf course with Helena was an exception to the rule. They were always friendly, but didn't hug each other every five minutes, which was exactly the way Lexie liked it.

How come Helena kept looking at her and exhaling a massive, dramatic sigh? What did she know? And how could Lexie get the admiral's wife to open up? There were a lot of distractions, but that was inescapable with six children.

At the front of the hotel, the kids fought about who got to sit where. Lexie moved closer to Helena, watching as the hotel porters loaded suitcases into the back of the second SUV.

"Ridiculous," Helena murmured. "We have too much stuff."

"No way around the baggage," Lexie said. "Including me, there are suitcases for ten people. Six kids, you and the admiral, plus me and Josh."

"Some days, it feels like all we do is pack and unpack."

"So true." Impatiently, Lexie waited for the right moment when she could change the topic from luggage to espionage.

"I told Josh he couldn't ride with us."

"Good." Let the woodpecker use his own car. "What about the admiral?"

"Edgar will be taking a chopper. Top Gun Tommy decided that my husband needs military protection, so he has a couple of stiff-neck men in uniform tromping along behind him."

Lexie didn't bother correcting her about the top gun status; the SecNav ranked way higher than that. But she had another concern. If Prescott had military bodyguards, he didn't need TST Security, which meant that Mason wouldn't be coming back to the house with them. Damn it, she missed him already. "What are the driving arrangements for you and me?"

"You drive the car in front with the older kids, and I'll take this one with the twins and the babies, and I'll use a driver from the hotel."

Lexie had wanted time alone with Helena, but that wasn't going to happen on this ride with only the two of them to handle all the kids. Later she'd find a time for a private talk with Helena.

The twins positioned themselves on either side of Lexie. Caine rested his shaggy blond head against her shoulder. "I want to ride with you."

Shane did the same with the opposite shoulder. "I want you to protect us."

"What about me?" their mother asked. "I'm a straight shooter, and I'm great at hand-to-hand combat."

"In the movies," the twins said together.

The oldest boy, Edgar Jr., popped into the conversation. "I'm almost old enough to drive. I could use the practice."

"I don't think so," Helena said.

Lexie knew what was going on with the kids. They were swarming, taking advantage of their mom being tired and a little bit frazzled. It was time for Lexie to turn into Bossy Nanny and take charge. She shook off the clingy twins.

Her first order was directed at them. "Shane and Caine, take your little brother and sister and put them in the car seats in the back SUV. You will also ride in that car."

"With you?"

"With your mom and a driver from the hotel." She made a quick pivot and pointed to the oldest girl. "Meggie, you ride with me and Eddy in the second car."

Eddy beamed, and she could see the beginning of a resemblance between the teenager and his father. "I get to drive."

"If you're really good, I'll take you out later. For practice."

"No fair. Meg gets to drive all the time."

"She's a year and a half older than you."

"But I need to drive."

Meggie said, "And I want to ride with Justin."

"Who?"

"The driver from the hotel."

Lexie was sympathetic when it came to Meggie and her potential boyfriends. The young man in question seemed polite, clean and he was a local with a job. She nodded to Meggie. "I think I can change the seating arrangements."

"You're the best."

She took over the rest of the preparations for departure, instructing the hotel staff on where to put the suitcases and herding the kids and their mother into the cars. She went to the head valet to get the keys.

There was no need to tip; Helena had given the concierge a huge gratuity to cover their departure. Lexie could tell from the giant grin on the valet's face that he was aware of the bonanza tip that would be his. He gushed over his goodbye and added, "Hope you enjoyed your stay."

She was about to make a snarky comment about how it was hard to enjoy herself when she was being shot at. Then she caught a glimpse of another one of the valets. Tall and lean with curly black hair, he was walking away from her. There was something familiar about the way he moved. Before she could ask his name, Mason rushed up beside her.

He spun her around to face him. "Thursday night at five."

"If there's a problem, I have your phone number."

"No problems." His blue eyes commanded her attention. "I'm not going to let you slip out of my life."

Her defenses went up, and the smile froze on her lips. She wanted to tell him that she wasn't part of his life, they weren't in a relationship and she was the one who decided whether she was staying or slipping. But the kids were bouncing in the cars. Little faces pressed against the windows. She had to go.

"Thursday," she said.

He ran back into the hotel, and she trotted around the two SUVs. Her mind flashed back to that valet. Someone she knew? Surely not one of the guests. But he might have been a server at the banquet. She shrugged off the vague impression.

The final arrangement in the cars put Meggie and Eddy, Jr. and the twins in the second vehicle. Lexie was driving the lead car with Helena in the passenger seat, which was exactly what she'd wanted. The two youngest were in the rear in their car seats. She started up the engine and turned to Helena.

Her gleaming black hair tumbled loosely to her shoulders as she covered her green eyes with sunglasses. Lexie knew for a fact that Helena had gotten up with the kids, had breakfast, chased after her husband with a golf cart and made love. But she still managed to look like a movie star in her leopard-patterned Windbreaker and skinny black jeans with strappy platform heels. Considering her gorgeous appearance, Helena spent remarkably little time fussing with her hair and makeup.

"It's hard to believe," Helena said, "that you don't have special training as a nanny. You're quite effective at getting everyone organized."

"That's how I was brought up. I had three older brothers and we were a handful. Organization was essential. I learned spit and polish from my Marine Corps dad."

Helena exhaled another dramatic sigh. "Your dear, sweet father."

"Clearly, you don't know my dad." He was seldom described as "dear" or "sweet."

"Edgar told me all about him. He's a good man. When you were hurt in that terrible car crash, your father came home to take care of you. He taught you to walk again."

Though she could have argued that it was her own

strength of character and—as her dad readily admitted—her own damned cussedness that got her back on her feet, she agreed. Her father was a truly good man. Sometimes he was overprotective with "Daddy's baby girl," and other times he was a total hard-ass. But he was a decent human being who had done right by her. Her question was: Why were the admiral and Helena talking about Danny DeMille?

She gazed through the windshield at the beautiful spring day. The gleaming white cap of snow on Mount Sopris stood out against the clear blue sky. Fresh green buffalo grass and bright wildflowers in red, blue and yellow covered the fields. She'd miss the mountains if she had to go back to Texas.

Lexie asked, "What else did your husband say about my dad?"

"They worked together in the Middle East. They were both in attendance at Al Ackerman's wedding to that Saudi princess."

Her dad never mentioned a Saudi wedding. She was beginning to think she didn't know the man at all. "Anything else?"

"I know what you're doing, Lexie." Helena adjusted her seat belt across her breasts and glanced into the back, checking on the kids. The two little ones would quickly fall asleep in their car seats. "You're probing me to get information about the Damascus Cache."

"You got me. There's no way I can trick you into telling me everything you know. You're an actress, a good one. If you decided to stonewall or fake me out, you could easily play those roles." And Lexie couldn't compete. She was a terrible liar, incapable of manipulating. "If you don't want to talk to me, you don't have to. But I'm going to lay my cards on the table."

"Go ahead."

"Before yesterday, I'd never heard of the Damascus Cache. Then your husband was targeted for kidnapping because of it. And then I find out that my dad's name is on it. He's in danger." She caught Helena's gaze and stared hard for a second before turning back to the road. "I want to do whatever I can to find the list and destroy it."

"How can I help?"

"Tell me what you know."

"Oh, dear, where should I start?" Helena twisted a strand of ebony hair around her finger and stared out the window.

"At the beginning."

"The first time I met Edgar was in Paris. He wore a tuxedo, not a uniform, and he seemed to know everyone. He spoke fluent French, German and Japanese. And when he took me in his arms to dance the tango…"

Her voice took on a resonant, lilting tone. Helena made her real life sound like a romantic movie with perfect moonlight and fragrant gardens and a beautiful couple falling deeply and passionately in love at first sight. Lexie had heard this story before and didn't mind hearing it again.

In this retelling, Helena ended her story with an unexpected twist. "To summarize, I knew Edgar was a spy before I realized he was an admiral."

"Wow." Lexie stared through the windshield at the two-lane road that stretched before them. She knew that Prescott had worked with navy intelligence in the Middle East and western Africa, but she'd never thought of him as a spy. "Why haven't I heard this before?"

"My dah-ling Edgar wouldn't be much of a spy if everybody knew about it. And he doesn't participate in an active way. Not anymore."

"Not until this stuff with the Damascus Cache."

"Ah, the cache," Helena said. "I don't have many details."

"That's fine. Simplified works best for me."

"At one time, years ago, Edgar was one of the authors of the Damascus Cache. It contained information about supply lines, weapons, contractors and undercover contacts. The names listed represented all the various groups from the military to the CIA to MI6 to Mossad and Interpol."

"It sounds like a large document. Did they reduce it down to a flash drive?"

"Indeed, there were several copies. Here's what Sec-Nav told Edgar." She leaned across the console and whispered, "These crazy anti-conspiracy people think Edgar has hidden the cache."

"Where? At the house?"

"Apparently."

The Prescott home was twelve bedrooms on seven acres. Though the setting was secluded, the house was a hive of activity. For the past two weeks, the entire family had been in residence, which was an unusual synchronizing of schedules for a movie star, an international consultant and six active children.

The idea of searching that sprawling house for something as tiny as a flash drive was daunting. Not to mention the barn for the horses and the outbuildings. Lexie had lost pairs of shoes and pillows and notebooks that had never been found.

"Here's what I don't understand," she said. "If the cache is at the house, why come after him at this event?"

Helena shrugged. "This is where it starts getting complicated. They might have already searched the house. Probably they have. There's evidence that someone sneaked into Edgar's office and the town house in DC."

"Wait a sec. Are you saying that these AC-CD people

have broken into the house in Aspen? Where we have intense electronic security and lots of people milling around?"

In addition to the family, there was a cook, a housekeeper and a couple of assistants like Josh. Also, the Prescotts did a lot of entertaining and had frequent houseguests. Lexie thought of all the people who came and went: groundskeepers, wranglers for weekends when they had horses, maids, delivery guys who handled groceries, firewood, dry cleaning and late-night pizza. Then there was Helena's staff, including a personal trainer and her hair and makeup people.

"Maybe they joined the parade of people who are always coming through." She chuckled.

"Their search of the house failed," Lexie said. "Then, their plan was to kidnap your husband. Not a clever scheme. Admiral Prescott would never give up classified information."

"Of course not. Nor would you."

"Not a chance."

"You're very brave, Lexie. That's something else you learned from your father."

Why did Helena bring up her father again? She'd delivered an important nugget of information by telling Lexie that the cache might be hidden at the house. But what else? "Is there something I'm missing? Something about my dad?"

"As an actress, I like to observe characters and character traits. Your father fascinates me. What happens when a dedicated military man is faced with trouble at home?"

"You mean when he came home to take care of me." She'd wondered about that, too. "I never understood why he retired. He could have taken a leave and then returned to active duty."

"Guilt stopped him. Your father blamed himself for what happened to you. He would never leave you unprotected again." She smiled and gently patted Lexie's arm. "When you came to work for us, he made Edgar promise on his life that he'd take care of you."

"Why would Dad feel guilty? It was my fault. I should have done more to avoid the car that hit me."

"It wasn't an accident, Lexie. The car that hit you was sending a message to the entire espionage community. If your father and my husband didn't cooperate and turn over the information they wanted, people would die."

Starting with me. Lexie's sense of what was really real had just adjusted a few notches. Someone had tried to kill her and had almost succeeded.

Helena continued, "We'll understand if you want to go back to Texas."

She'd never give up. "I'm staying."

Chapter Nine

Alone, at last! On Thursday at noon, Lexie perched on a stool at the marble-topped counter in the kitchen and savored a mug of free-trade coffee from Colombia. The stillness was pure luxury. Her eyelids lowered and lifted in a slow blink as her breathing regulated to a less frantic pace. Ever since the Prescotts had returned from the hotel on Sunday afternoon, she'd been running in high gear, racing madly to prepare the family for their summer activities.

Her lazy gaze slid around the huge French country-style kitchen with quaint white cabinets, double-sized stainless steel appliances and gobs of gadgets neatly arrayed on marble countertops. The curtains and trim were slate blue. French doors opened onto a huge cedar deck, which was perfect for entertaining and offered a wide view of Henscratch Valley, where three small rivulets combined into one wide creek that flowed into the Roaring Fork River. From a bird's-eye view, the joining of the rivulets resembled a hen's claw. Hence, the name Henscratch.

Though the Prescotts employed a cook for entertaining, grocery shopping and those occasions when Helena was on a special diet, Lexie or one of the other adults usually cooked for the family. Lexie was teaching the older kids how to make basic survival food, not that these youngsters would ever need to survive on omelets and ramen noodles.

At present, the kitchen was well stocked, thanks to a massive shopping trip by the cook, who was taking a month off…as was the housekeeper.

Lexie swung around on her stool and gazed into the huge family room. On the wall above the shelves and storage for toys was a large flat screen that served as a calendar to outline the various activities of each member of the family for the next six weeks. Each person had a horizontal line. The weeks were broken into seven vertical days. This screen synced with her handheld tablet and contained all contact information, locations and names. All she had to do to find the details for one of the kids was tap the appropriate space on the screen and the information popped up.

The first row was dedicated to Edgar. Currently, the admiral was in DC, staying at the town house he'd owned for years.

Helena had taken the twins for a weeklong visit to her ex-husband in California. Afterward, she'd drop the kids off at a horseback riding camp on Catalina Island. She would then proceed to a movie set in Toronto for six weeks of filming.

The two littlest kids were at summer camp for eight weeks. Though the family could easily afford the finest camping experience available for the munchkins, Prescott had convinced Helena that the kids could use a dose of reality in the woods. They were at a camp run by former SEALs where they would learn survival skills. *For four- and six-year-olds? Really?* The side benefit to this camp was that the entire staff were trained bodyguards. If there was danger, the little Prescotts were safe.

Thinking of safety reminded Lexie that being alone in a house that bad guys wanted to search might not be the smartest plan in the world. A shiver prickled her spine. She looked down at the coffee mug and saw that her hand was trembling. Ever since Helena had told her that her accident wasn't accidental, fear had been creeping around the edges of her consciousness. She kept looking over her shoulder. Remembered pain tensed her muscles.

Over and over, she told herself that there was nothing to worry about. This house had been searched by the CIA, the NSA and the admiral's assistant, Josh. They'd used an array of equipment designed to locate miniaturized circuits or magnets or whatever went into a flash drive. Josh had attempted to explain the technology before Stella grabbed the search probe and waved the long rod like a magic princess wand.

The thought of adorable blonde Stella brought a smile to Lexie's face. That was what she needed. Confidence and cool detachment were essential if she was going to figure out a way to use her special perspective to find the Damascus Cache. Mason might help. He'd be here by five o'clock, fewer than five hours. She could last until then.

The alarm on her watch went off, reminding her that she needed to make a phone call to check on the two oldest kids, who were staying with their mother in Seattle and taking a sailing trip on the Strait of Juan de Fuca. Taking her phone from the pocket of her jean shorts, she hit the speed dial for Meggie. The girl was far more likely to answer than Eddy Jr., who didn't like to be monitored.

The young woman's voice took on the chilly, whiny tone she used when adults were being annoying. She reported, "Our plane got in okay, but Mom's running late to pick us up. You'd almost think she wasn't thrilled to see us."

"Sarcasm?"

"What do you think?"

"More sarcasm."

"We only see her for an extended time twice a year. You'd think she'd make an effort. Oh, wait." Her voice lightened; she almost sounded happy. "Here she is. It's Mommy. 'Bye, Lexie."

"Have fun."

Her words were lost in Meggie's haste to get off the phone, and she wondered if Edgar had warned his former wife about the potential danger to the kids. Meggie was old enough to date, to be out on her own. The experts thought no one was in danger except for the admiral, but her experience had been different.

The image of her own car crash appeared in her mind. She mentally replayed those few seconds before impact. Could she have pumped the brakes or cranked the steering wheel harder? Had that bastard deliberately targeted her?

She didn't know. The perpetrators had never been identified, mostly because her dad had done what they wanted and quit the military. According to Helena, the car crash had nothing to do with the Damascus Cache. Nor was the anti-conspiracy group involved. The leader of AC-CD might have been using a different name at that time or she might even have been attacked by some other hater.

The attack was meant as a warning to men like her dad who dabbled in secrets. By hurting her, the bad guys were showing that their evil could reach all the way across the ocean and hurt loved ones in the States. She was a pawn to them. She meant nothing.

Yet that crash had changed her life and destroyed her future. In addition to the broken bones and torn muscles in her legs, the internal injuries were devastating. A collapsed lung, a punctured spleen and there had been nerve damage. She had required a hysterectomy.

The fragile dreams she'd had of a husband and family had been shattered. It wasn't fair for her to date or form a serious relationship. Maybe she should call Mason and tell him not to come. Clearly, he was a man looking for a settled-down relationship with the standard wife and kids. That was something she could never do.

A burst of rage spread from her belly to her chest. A flush crawled up her throat. Her cheeks flamed.

When she was taking care of the kids, she couldn't allow her emotions to get the better of her. She'd been holding back this outburst since Sunday. Now she was alone. So. Very. Alone.

She leaped from the stool onto the wood parquet floor. Her red sneakers thudded as she ran to the spacious entryway with its two-story ceiling and modern silver chandelier. A sweeping staircase going up led to the master suite and four other guest bedrooms, along with another suite for special guests. The kids had a wing of their own at the northern end of the house. Lexie slept there, but that wasn't where she was headed.

In the hallway beyond the foyer, she took the staircase to the lower level of the house. Tension kept building inside her. And the heat—she was on fire as she darted down a long hallway, passing storage spaces and the twenty-four-seat home theater. The southern-most room in the house was the home gym.

Too bad the swimming pool was empty! It would have been a relief to dive into the long narrow lap pool that stretched along the farthest edge of the room. The pool was surrounded on three sides by triple-pane bulletproof windows and had a fitted cover that matched the empty hot tub. With two young kids running around, the open water was too dangerous.

But the kids weren't here. Lexie was free to play rough. On the admiral's side of the gym were gray metal weights, a heavy punching bag, dumbbells, mats and a speed bag. Helena's side focused on movie-star exercises, like yoga and stretching. She had mirrors and a ballet barre and sometimes worked out to the music from Tchaikovsky's *Nutcracker* Suite. The admiral preferred Sousa marches played by the Marine Corps band.

Lexie took her cell phone from her pocket and placed it out of the way, then kicked off her sneakers and went through her karate warm-ups, starting by bouncing on the balls of her feet and progressing to stretches, squats and light kicks. Ever since she first started training with her brothers, she'd done this routine, and the repetition of familiar motions helped her get centered. Her tension wasn't gone; that would be far too simple. But she was beginning to loosen up. She added shouts to her kicks. "Ha. Ha. No fear. Ha."

She bounced over to the sound system. Amid the marches and the operas, there was a sound track of mixed selections that both the admiral and Helena liked. Lexie picked one. The first song: "Sweet Caroline." With the music cranked up loud, she sauntered toward the heavy punching bag suspended from the ceiling. With a fierce yell, she unleashed a series of kicks first with one leg, then the other. She expanded her attack to include a freestanding kick bag that popped back up when she knocked it down. She rolled down onto the mats and up again. Now she was singing along with the music. "Good times never seemed so good..."

Whirling and leaping and kicking, she made a circuit around the gym, practicing her poses—*Kihon Waza*—building her adrenaline, working off fear and dread. She came to a halt in front of Helena's wall of mirrors and stared at herself.

Under her freckles, her skin was flushed. She tore off her light sweatshirt. The T-shirt she wore underneath had sleeves too short to cover the puckered pink scar left by the bullet graze. She studied it. "What does one more matter?"

In the mirror, she had a full view of her legs. Her tan was marred by a faint patchwork of scars. The broken bones in her ankle had required surgery and both knees had had arthroscopic work done. More than once, she'd tried to tell herself that they were like tattoos. The difference was that she hadn't asked for these marks. It didn't matter that they weren't all that noticeable; she didn't want them.

"Those bastards," she muttered. How dare they come after her? She almost wished that her dad hadn't given in to them. If he'd kept up the fight, what would have happened to her? Would they have come after her in the hospital? After racing around the gym, she was pumped, energized, feeling no fear. She threw a couple of karate jabs and high kicks at her reflection in the mirror.

On the other side of the gym, she heard her cell phone ring. She dashed across and answered. It wasn't a number she recognized.

The voice on the other end of the call was patchy. "Are… surprise…ready."

"I can't hear you," she yelled. The loud background music didn't help. "Let me turn this down."

Quiet descended.

"There," Lexie said. "What did you say?"

"Are you alone?"

"What did you say?" Her breath froze in her lungs. "Who is this? What do you want?"

The call disconnected.

In spite of the static, she knew what he'd said. *Are you alone?* Anticipation of danger was often worse than the actual threat. She didn't scare easily. If somebody was coming for her, she would be prepared to take them on.

She peered through the wall of windows on the other side of the lap pool. Outside, there were trees and boulders, leafy bushes and shrubs. A stand of pine obscured the view down the slope to Henscratch Valley. When she saw movement, she jumped. A scrawny black squirrel darted across the top of a flat granite boulder.

Though certain that she'd locked the doors and set all the alarms, Lexie left the exercise room and went down the hallway to an unmarked door. Inside was a small room that the admiral called Command Central, which contained an impressive and extensive array of surveillance equipment. Monitors on sensors showed that none of the doors or windows had been opened or broken or compromised in any way. Outdoor cameras covered seven different angles. She studied each of these approaches to see if anything was out of place.

Nothing. She stared more closely. It all looked fine. That weird phone call was a fluke. Then she saw it. A rope dangled against the wall at the far north end of the house. Was it left over from a game the kids had been playing? *The roof?*

If an intruder intended to break into the house through the roof, he'd have to go through a window, which would set off an alarm. She'd heard nothing. The cameras didn't show anyone creeping through the surrounding forest. But there was that phone call…

She needed to go outside and take a look at the rope, and that meant she needed to be armed. Her karate skills were useful for surprise attacks, but she needed a gun for protection. She headed up the stairs to the main floor, where there was a locked gun cabinet.

In the front foyer, sunlight from high windows splashed against cream stucco walls and the gray tile floor. The overall style of the house was clean and modern with high ceilings and windows, so many windows. The branches of trees always seemed to be moving. Shadows changed and shifted.

Her ringtone sounded. She heard the breathiness in her voice. "Hello?"

"Are you alone?"

"Who is this?"

Chapter Ten

"If you're by yourself, I'll come to the front door." Mason heard the tension in her voice through the phone. "If somebody else is in the house, meet me by the garage."

"Come to the front," she said.

"I'll be there in five minutes."

When he'd gotten the call that morning from the admiral, hiring him to stay at the mansion in Aspen with Lexie for the next few weeks, Mason hadn't asked for much information. There was no need to question the best stroke of luck he'd had in years. He'd pounced on the chance to stay at a mansion in Aspen. Oh, and would he object if an attractive auburn-haired woman stayed with him? Mason couldn't say yes fast enough. He'd just won the lottery!

The edginess he'd heard in her voice gave him second thoughts...not enough to make him drop the assignment. No way would he back out. This job was fate, kismet, the way things were meant to be. Ever since he saw Lexie, he'd been thinking about her, trying to figure her out. The woman was a wealth of contradictions. She was optimistic and quick with a smile. But she was equally speedy with a karate kick to the groin and had done serious damage to that guy who attacked her outside the elevator. She was smart and had a degree in psychology. She kissed like an angel. But she had secrets—dark secrets—that gave her depth and complicated his job as a bodyguard.

He drove his Land Rover past a long building that had to be a garage designed to house a fleet of vehicles and ascended a sloping driveway toward a large structure with clean, bold architectural lines. It butted up to the granite hillside. Two stories in most places and three in others, the house was made of light cedar planks and accented with rectangular walls of concrete or natural stone. The angle of the entryway made him think of a boat, and the doorbell played a familiar sea chantey: "Yo ho ho, and a bottle of rum."

The door swung inward. Barefoot, Lexie dashed to the wall pad and punched in the code to deactivate the alarm. He noticed that she'd gathered a stockpile of weapons on the stairs: a rifle, two handguns and a hunting knife.

He glanced from the arsenal to her and back again. It was a little bit disconcerting. "Is there something I should know?"

"Never call a woman who might be alone and ask if she's alone."

"And why is that?"

"It's scary. You sound like a stalker." A smile played at the edges of her lips, but her dark eyes held a shimmer of real fear. "Or a pervert whose next question is going to be, 'And what are you wearing?' You should have explained."

"It was a bad connection."

"That's no excuse," she snapped. "Do I have to teach you phone manners? Like I do with the kids?"

I've been a naughty boy, nanny. Spank me. But she wasn't joking around. What had happened to the cute, funny, teasing Lexie? "You've made your point."

"Why did you want to know if I was alone?"

Her accusatory tone bugged him. Maybe he hadn't handled that phone call the right way, but it was time to let it go. She liked him, he knew it. Why else would she agree to a date? He pushed the door closed and dropped his backpack on the foyer floor. "The admiral suggested that—"

"The admiral? Why are you talking to him?"

"This morning he contacted TST Security and hired me for two weeks. It was his suggestion that I call ahead and see if you could meet me at the garage to open the door. I wanted to know if you were alone. If you were, I didn't want you running around outside."

"Why? Is there some kind of danger?"

Their earlier meetings had been natural, pleasant and encouraging. Now every word that came out of his mouth ticked her off. He didn't know how to approach her. If he told her to settle down or take a few deep breaths, she'd be insulted and then angrier. If he hid behind a fake smile and told her that there was nothing to worry about, she'd know he was lying.

There was only one approach that worked for him. "I'm going to tell you the truth."

She took a backward step. "Oh, my God, there is danger."

"I don't know," he said. "I need to do an assessment of the real and potential threat. That's what I always do when I come to a house as a bodyguard."

"You're guarding my body?"

Guarding wasn't the only thing he'd like to do to that slender, athletic body. He glanced at the scar from the bullet wound on her upper arm, which seemed to be healing well. Her snug coral T-shirt outlined her high, round breasts. Her cutoffs were frayed at the edges and short enough to display muscular legs with fading traces of scars that stood out against her tan.

It said something about her that she didn't try to hide the

scars. Lexie was comfortable with who she was. Unapologetic and tough, she was the sort of woman he liked. She didn't take herself too seriously, as evidenced by the fact that each of her ten toenails was painted a different hue.

"I like your feet," he murmured.

"For a guy who wants to tell me the truth, you're very slow to say anything."

"Is there danger?" He repeated her question. "The admiral doesn't expect an attack on the house. Apparently they've done a lot of searching. Correct?"

She nodded and her curls bounced. "Mobs of technicians with special instruments have poked in every corner and crevice."

"So the house is clean. The Damascus Cache isn't here," he said. "But Prescott didn't want to take any chances in case the bad guys didn't get the word and tried to break in. It's better to be safe than sorry."

She pinned him with a gaze. "Did he say that?"

"As a matter of fact, those are his exact words."

"My dad says that all the time. Better to be safe, better to be safe, it's better to be safe than sorry."

The last time Mason saw her at the hotel, she'd had an issue with her dad being overprotective. Did that explain her current hostility? "Have you talked to him?"

"Not yet. It's kind of a big deal between us. I'm not sure whether I'm mad at him or whether I feel guilty or what…" Her voice trailed off. "You haven't heard the latest development between me and my dad, right?"

"I haven't."

She pivoted and marched down a hallway. "Do you want something cold to drink? We have soda, water, lemonade and beer."

Mason didn't follow obediently behind her like one of

the Prescott kids. "You can't leave these weapons lying here."

"I'll clean up later."

Not good enough. He went to the staircase and picked up the rifle, handguns, ammo and knife. Even if no one else was in the house and the weapons weren't loaded, they needed to be returned to where they belonged. Taking a guess, he went down the hall behind the staircase. A light wood door stood open to his right, and he entered a very masculine office with an ornate, antique wood desk that looked as though it was seldom used for actual paperwork. The walls were lined with bookshelves. He spotted the gun cabinet behind the desk. The glass door stood unlocked and wide open. After he returned the guns to their places, he found the key in the middle desk drawer.

When he turned, he saw her leaning against the door frame with her arms folded below her breasts. She asked, "How did you know the key would be there?"

"It's the most logical place. Also the most obvious. I suggest hiding the key somewhere else. Better yet, put the gun cabinet in a room that isn't so easily accessible."

She exhaled in a huff. "You're right, of course. I've said the same thing to Prescott myself. With the kids getting into everything, we need to practice extreme gun safety."

"For now, I'll put the key back in the middle drawer. Tomorrow, we'll make adjustments."

"So you're going to be here two whole weeks."

He closed the middle drawer and came around the desk to stand before her. He was tired of her evasions. "Is that a problem?"

"Let's get you a drink."

When she turned, he grasped her uninjured arm above the elbow and held her gently but firmly. "Don't run away from me."

"I'm not." But she avoided looking at him.

It wasn't easy to protect anyone, much less a woman who was treating him like—what had she called him?—a stalker or a pervert. "If this is going to work, you have to trust me."

"It's not you, Mason. It's me."

"That's the oldest line in the book."

"Give me some time." Her gaze lifted, and he saw the pained vulnerability in her dark brown eyes. "I need to relax."

He released his hold. "Ten minutes."

"Fine."

This time, he followed her when she went down the hall and across the foyer to the kitchen. She still hadn't put on shoes. Her hips twitched in a way that was both athletic and sexy. Though she wasn't any taller than five feet three or four inches, her proportions were perfect and her legs were both slender and shapely.

In the kitchen she pointed to the stools at the counter. "Sit there. Now, what can I get you?"

"You mentioned lemonade."

She went to the side-by-side refrigerator, found the pitcher and poured a glass for each of them. She slid his across the marble-topped counter. It didn't escape his attention that she stayed on the opposite side rather than taking the stool next to him. She was keeping a distance between them.

He checked his wristwatch. He had promised ten minutes for her to relax. Only four minutes had passed, but he was too impatient to wait. "You said there was a development with your dad. I'd like to hear more."

"I have a question for you first."

When she took a sip of her lemonade, a bit of pulp stuck to her lip. She delicately removed it with the tip of her pink tongue…like a cat. An apt comparison, he thought. Like a cat, she captivated him with her graceful, clever moves. Like a cat, she turned her back without showing the least bit of interest in his response.

"Okay," she said. "You had arranged to pick me up for a date. But that's not why you're here right now. This is a job. Which is it?"

"A valid question." He translated her concern. "You want to know if it's unprofessional for me to agree to act as bodyguard for a woman I'm attracted to."

"Are you?" She brightened.

"Attracted?" He regretted the use of that word. "You're a good-looking woman. I'm a single man."

"And you're my bodyguard. If we're dating, isn't that a professional conflict?"

"I considered asking somebody else at TST to take this assignment." For about three and a half seconds, he'd considered. "It's not a problem. I can control my personal feelings. At five o'clock, I can quit being a bodyguard, and we'll have our date. Or not."

"How do you decide?"

"We'll know," he said. "Now it's my turn to ask you a question. Why did they leave you at the house alone?"

She pointed to a flat screen mounted on the wall in the room behind the kitchen. Unlike the rest of the sleek, stylish house, the family room had a more lived-in appearance. Toys were pulled off their shelves. A gang of stuffed animals sat side by side on the sofa facing the regular television. The blue and green colors with an occasional splash of yellow were cozy and welcoming.

He looked at the display on the flat screen. "A schedule?"

"It lists summer activities for all the kids and the admiral and Helena. There are camps and training programs.

Helena will be filming in Canada. And the older kids are visiting their mom."

The closest Mason had ever come to a summer activity was when his brother, who was seven years older, took him camping in the mountains for a weekend with borrowed sleeping bags and beat-up cooking gear. The total cost for one of these weekends was almost nothing, but he had loved every moment. He wondered if these rich kids appreciated what they had. "Do the kids enjoy their activities?"

"Last summer, they seemed to like it a lot. Couldn't stop talking about it." Her gaze narrowed. She could see his attitude, his judgment. "You think the kids are overprivileged and spoiled."

"These kinds of activities are costly."

"I won't lie to you. It's a difficult balancing act to keep them grounded. The admiral makes sure that the older kids understand that they've received a lot and need to give back. They're involved in charity work."

Mason expected the admiral to raise responsible children. He also knew that it was easy for him to criticize someone else's child-rearing tactics when he didn't have kids of his own. Someday that would change, and he'd become a father. Someday soon, he hoped. He was ready for that challenge. "If everybody else is busy with activities, why do you need to stay at the house?"

"Two reasons. First, somebody needs to watch the house. Second, these schedules don't fit together seamlessly. I'm here to cover the downtime after one activity ends and the next begins. Sometimes Helena will fly in with some movie friends for an impromptu party. Or her husband will hold a weekend conference with movers and shakers."

"But mostly you're at the house alone."

"Poor me," she said with a melodramatic rolling of the

eyes. "Here I am…all alone in a multimillion-dollar mansion amid some of the most spectacular scenery in the world."

He tried to find something objectionable. "What about housework? Or special projects that the family wants you to do?"

"The maid service comes in once a week. If there's a special project, the housekeeper has already hired someone to do it. For cooking, all I need to do is make a phone call. The chef lives in town and is happy to come out and prepare a single meal or a whole regimen for any of Helena's crazy diets."

"Why doesn't the housekeeper live here in the summer?"

"The summer house-sitting used to be her job," she said. "But she's sixty years old and likes to travel. I wanted to do it, and the housekeeper gets much-deserved time off. She's taking two of her grandchildren to Australia for the month."

He looked down at his watch, and then held it so she could read the dial. "Time's up. You said that you needed ten minutes to relax before you could talk. Ready?"

Resolutely, she lifted her chin. "What do you want to know?"

"You're different." He could tell that she was scared, but mentioning her fear seemed confrontational. "Something has changed from the last time I saw you."

"I learned that somebody tried to kill me." Her voice was eerily flat, as though she'd repeated those words a hundred times. "And they very nearly succeeded."

Chapter Eleven

When Mason showed up on the doorstep and said he'd been hired to be her bodyguard, Lexie had been relieved. The possibility of another attack had made her nervous. A deeper fear arose when Helena told her that the car crash hadn't been a random event. She'd been targeted. For the first time in her life, she'd felt like a victim.

Her life had been irreparably damaged. She'd never have kids. Every time she thought of that gaping hole in her life, she'd remember the black car with the tinted windows coming at her. Terror and rage would rise in her, again and again.

No way could she tell Mason about her hysterectomy. He was a family man, through and through. Solid, steady and stable, he was suited for a long-term relationship. That didn't work for her, but she was fairly sure that he'd be happy with a no-strings-attached affair. Most men were.

It wasn't her nature to have casual relationships, but her only other choice was to shove him out the door and insist on a less charming bodyguard. She didn't want to do that. She and Mason were most definitely attracted to each other. The moment he walked through the door, the air in the room had changed. The pheromones were flying. The snug fit of his jeans and the black T-shirt under his plaid shirt made her heart beat faster. Her fingers longed to embrace the breadth of his shoulders and slide down his muscular chest and abs. The timbre of his voice drew her closer.

He sat at the counter, sipping his lemonade and waiting for her to explain what she'd meant when she said that someone had tried to kill her. It was her turn to speak, and she knew it. But her throat had become a rusty hinge, holding back the words she needed to say.

"I'm not ready to talk about it," she creaked.

"Let's start with something easy," he said. "Why did you take out all those weapons?"

That, she could talk about. "I was in the gym when I got this creepy phone call."

"Ha-ha," he said.

"A really nasty voice," she teased, "ugly and evil. Then I went to Command Central, and I saw a rope dangling. I needed to check it out and didn't want to go in unarmed."

"You lost me. Let's go back to the gym."

"I'd love to."

"Can I see it? The admiral sent me blueprints of the security system and the house. The gym is huge, and I know Prescott would have the best equipment."

"Let's go. This way." She led to the staircase leading down. "I need to get my shoes, anyway."

Mason was a big man, several inches over six feet, but his hiking boots hardly made a sound when he walked across the wood parquet floor. Silence accompanied his movements. Not stealth. He had nothing to hide. But there was a stillness that came from his sheer, unshakable confidence.

At the foot of the stairs, he made a detour, turning right and opening the door to Command Central. Apparently, he already knew his way around the house. As he stood in the doorway, his gaze flicked from screen to screen, taking in all the dials and knobs. Again, he seemed to know how everything worked without having her explain. Why shouldn't he? Security was his job, after all.

"Show me where you saw this dangling rope."

Taking a seat at one of the consoles, she flipped though several views from cameras outside the house. She paused and pointed. "There it is. That's the north end of the house near the kids' bedrooms."

"It goes up to the roof," he said.

"But there haven't been any break-ins. If any of the windows or openings onto the roof were tampered with, an alarm would go off."

"I'm familiar with this system." He leaned over her shoulder to tap the keyboard, and the warmth of his body wrapped around her. His citrus and nutmeg aftershave teased her nostrils.

"What are you doing?" *Other than smelling good and driving me crazy.* "The screen went dark."

"I'm doing a rewind," he said. "I programmed it to go backward in twelve-hour jumps. Good eye, by the way. I never would have noticed the rope."

A picture on the screen came back into focus. The shadows and light were different, but nothing else had changed. The rope still dangled.

There was another picture and another and another. He leaned even closer. His cheek was even with hers. If she swiveled her head, she'd be looking directly into his ear.

He pointed to a time stamp in the corner of the screen. "This is Tuesday morning."

The next picture filled the screen. Together, they said, "No rope."

Using the keyboard, Mason had both arms around her, though the low back of the office chair separated them. It would have made sense for her to move, but he hadn't suggested it, and she liked being nestled in his arms. He played forward on the screen until he found Tuesday at four o'clock. The long shadow from the house almost obscured the appearance of a man dressed in jeans and a black Windbreaker. He wore a cap with the visor pulled down. His features were hidden.

Mason put the image on pause while he juggled dials to improve the resolution on the screen. "His jacket says CIA across the back."

"Tuesday was when Agent Collier and his men from the CIA were at the house, searching for the Damascus Cache. This guy could have been any one of them."

"To your knowledge, were they outside the house?"

"No, but I wasn't keeping track of what they were doing. You need to talk to Collier for verification."

As she watched the intruder, her muscles began to tense. The dangling rope indicated that someone had been there, but she was hoping for an innocent explanation. The intruder had a hook attached to the rope. He tossed it onto the roof three times before it caught. Then he used the rope to scale the wall.

"He's fast," Mason said. "That didn't even take five minutes."

"And we still haven't gotten a clear look at his face."

Mason straightened and stepped back from the console. His demeanor had changed; he'd gone from light to dark. "Do you want to know the worst thing about a risk assessment?"

"I think I know," she said. "Sometimes you find danger."

He nodded, then hit a button to pause the playback on the screen. "I'd like to see the gym before we finish the assessment."

She padded barefoot down the hall to the keypad outside the gym. "The code is B-U-N-S and never changes.

We have the room locked to keep little Todd and Stella away from the heavy equipment."

He trooped inside behind her. Helena's Pilates equipment, mirror and ballet barre were of little interest to him. His eyes lit up when he saw the array of weights and punching bags.

"Beautiful," he murmured with undisguised lust. He rubbed his palm across his close-cropped blond hair and turned toward the sunlit forest outside the wall of windows. He inhaled a deep breath, and his muscular chest expanded inside the black T-shirt. A wide smile stretched across his face.

It would have felt good to have him look at her with such naked longing. She huffed. "Do you love it?"

"I could live here."

"A gym rat, I knew it."

"I haven't always been that way." Bouncing on the balls of his feet, he went to the speed bag and punched it a couple of times with his bare knuckles. "When my brother was killed, I needed something to get rid of the tension, know what I mean?"

She did, indeed. Lexie relied on her karate exercises to relieve stress. She crossed the gym to the more feminine side and slipped into her red sneakers.

He shucked off his plaid shirt, picked up a ten-pound dumbbell and did a few curls. "I used to exercise until I could barely stand up. I'd stagger home, fall into the sack and my eyes would pop open. Couldn't sleep. My brain wouldn't shut down. I kept thinking that Matt wasn't really dead. It must be a case of mistaken identity. I couldn't let him go… Still can't."

She'd been so caught up in the tragedies of her life that she'd forgotten about him. When the SecNav had commended his brother's heroic action, she'd seen the pained and haunted look on Mason's face. A Purple Heart was a great honor, but he'd rather have his brother back.

Not that Mason was the type to indulge in a pity party. Automatically, he transferred the weight to his other hand to balance the exercise as he strolled toward the covered lap pool and hot tub. "Do you ever use these?"

"Yes for the tub. Not often for the pool. It takes thousands of gallons of water to fill and when the little ones are around, it's not safe." She wasn't ready to drop the subject of his brother. "How old were you when he died?"

"He was killed," Mason said. "Saying he died implies that there was something natural about it. Murder is an unnatural act. Six years ago, he was murdered in Afghanistan. I was finishing up college, deciding if I should go for my master's."

She hadn't pictured him as a college student. "What was your major?"

"International studies." He continued to pump the dumbbell as he walked the perimeter of the long lap pool. "Back then, I was young and innocent and thought I could make sense of the world. I learned that no single country can take credit for being the worst mess. They're all bad, even us."

"I could've figured that out." She wanted to know more about him, more details. "How did you get into security?"

Standing in front of her, he stopped pacing and dug into his jeans pocket. In his hand, he held a key chain. The brass fob was a four-leaf clover with TST Security written in a half circle across the top. Three of the leaves were a lucky-Irish green. One was red.

"I don't remember who came up with the idea," Mason said. "Me and Matt were buddies with Sean and Dylan, and we thought we'd be outstanding crime fighters. Just before Matt was killed, we sat down and talked about the possibilities. Sean's the oldest, and he had done a stint in the FBI. Dylan is a computer whiz, which is necessary for security work. Matt had top-notch military training. And I was a political wonk who could get by in seven languages."

"Seven? I'm impressed."

"Don't be. With language, you've got to use it or lose it, and I haven't kept it up. I turned into a gym rat. Now I'm the muscle in the group."

He was so much more than muscle. Not that she had any complaints about his body. But she found herself being drawn to his mind and the unique way he saw the world. For sure, he was cynical. But there was a redeeming ray of hope that kept him from being bitter.

With her forefinger, she pointed to the three green leaves. "These stand for you, Sean and Dylan."

He raised the red leaf to his lips and kissed it. "This stands for Matt. He's always watching over us."

If he was trying to seduce her, he was sticking to an extremely low-key approach. And yet she wanted him. She wanted him desperately. Maybe because she hadn't been dating much for the past year and a half, Lexie was ready to pounce, to drag him off to her bedroom and get sexy. Better yet, they could strip down right here in front of the mirror. Practically panting, she asked, "What comes next?"

"I'm not finished with my risk assessment."

Inwardly, she groaned.

He continued, "The dangling rope indicates that somebody might have tried to break in. But I need to talk to Agent Collier and find out if he sent one of his men up onto the roof."

"Then what?"

"I should familiarize myself with the house and make sure all security functions are working properly."

Following someone around and watching while he did

his job wasn't her idea of a great time. Besides, she seriously doubted that she'd be able to trail him all the way around the massive house without tearing off his clothes. "I'll leave you to your work."

As she went down the hall toward the staircase, she heard him call after her, "We have a date at five."

"How should I dress?"

"You decide."

She had a few ideas for her outfit. Maybe she'd go casually seductive with shorts and a bare midriff. She had a fancier outfit with a plunging neckline. Maybe she should go for a wraparound dress that could be removed with one light tug on the sash. Or she might decide to wear nothing at all.

Chapter Twelve

While he was exploring the main floor of the house, Mason's call to Agent Collier finally went through. He went into the formal office with the locked gun cabinet and sat at the massive, carved desk. Being in a classy office/library like this made him feel like a high-ranking officer. Tilting back in the swivel chair, he stretched out his legs and rested the heels of his hiking boots on the desk blotter.

"I'm at Admiral Prescott's house," Mason said. "Lexie told me that you and your men were here on Tuesday."

"Yes, I brought four agents." Collier's accent sounded thicker over the phone. "We discovered evidence that we weren't the first to go through the house."

"What did you find?"

"An infestation of bugs." He chuckled at his pun. "There were twelve listening devices planted throughout the house. Also, we found three cameras that weren't part of the Prescott security system."

The blueprints showed three cameras inside the house: one in the hallway outside the children's bedrooms, one in the kitchen where there were French doors and one in the lobby. "Are there more than three cameras inside the house?"

"That is all," he said. "While we were there, we made a thorough search, except for one room."

"Which room? And why not?"

"In the lower level, there is a safe room with a combination lock and a key. According to the magnificent Helena Christie Prescott, her husband possesses the only key. He was still at the Pentagon."

Keeping it locked was counterintuitive. A safe room was supposed to be entered easily by the people who lived in the house. Once they were safely locked inside away from any threat, the room should be impregnable to outsiders.

He jolted forward to sit upright in the chair and spread the blueprints for the house across the desktop. "I'm assuming they don't actually use that room as it was intended. Is it storage?"

"Helena says yes." Collier mumbled a few words that might have been curses. "Extreme valuables are kept there—artworks, statues, antiques."

"What about deeds and paperwork?" The safe room seemed like the ideal place to hide the Damascus Cache. The admiral was from an older generation where papers and documentation were all carefully stored in locked boxes in banks or in safes.

"Helena would not say more. But I suspect she has a key. Among the valuables, there must have been jewelry. *Her* jewelry."

"She stonewalled you."

"It was disturbing," Collier said, "to come all the way to Aspen only to be denied full access to the premises."

"It's not a bad trip."

"Marvelous scenery," he agreed, "and the gym is among the best home facilities I have ever seen."

Tracing with his forefinger, Mason found the safe room on the blueprint. It was located on the lower level at the opposite end of the hallway from the gym. The house butted up against a cliff with one floor stacked on top of another. At the northern end, the safe room would be underground. The level on top of it was the wing with the children's bedrooms, where the rope had been left dangling. Mason wondered if there was any connection.

"In your search," he said, "did any of your men go outside?"

"No, nor did we search the outbuildings, including the horse barn or the garage or anywhere that an outsider could approach without help from someone inside the house. We operated under the theory that the AC-CD believed the admiral had hidden the cache, and it was probably smaller than a matchbox—the size of a computer flash drive."

"Can you think of a reason why anyone wearing a CIA Windbreaker would want access to the roof?"

There was a moment's silence. In a moment like this, Mason wished he had Sean's training with the FBI. Sean had studied criminal psychology and profiling; he knew the various techniques of questioning. Sean would have known if Agent Collier's moment of hesitation had any significance. It seemed logical that he was hiding something. Was it guilt? Was Collier after the cache for his own nefarious purposes? Or was he embarrassed about his men breaking protocol?

"I require an explanation," Collier finally said. "Why do you think my men were on the roof?"

"One man." Mason leaned forward, resting his elbows on the desk. He wished he could see Collier. It was easier to catch someone in a lie when you were face-to-face with the liar. "An outdoor surveillance camera shows a man in a CIA Windbreaker throwing a grappling hook onto the roof and climbing up a rope attached to the hook."

"Not one of my men. Did the camera show this man coming down?"

"I haven't bothered to look," Mason admitted. "None of the alarms for the windows or the rooftop openings were activated."

"Of course they weren't. We shut them down."

"What? You turned off the security system?"

"Not all day. Occasionally." His voice was faster, his accent heavier. "We accidentally set it off twice. Then we made the decision to turn it off when we were searching."

Panic shot through Mason. He surged to his feet so quickly that his head whirled. How could he have been so careless? He should have known that the CIA would turn the system off. The intruder might have entered the house through the attic. *He might still be here.* "I've got to go. Thanks, Collier."

He dashed out of the office, down the hall and into the foyer. Lexie's bedroom was somewhere on the second floor, north end, but he didn't know which one was hers. He flew up the staircase, taking the steps two at a time. The landing stretched into a balcony that overlooked the foyer. Leaded glass windows above the front door admitted a splash of natural sunlight.

He called her name. "Lexie, are you here? Lexie?"

Skylights overhead kept the long hallway from being too dark, but he flicked a switch that lit sconces along the wall. Afternoon light poured through the window at the end of the hall, which was where they'd spotted the rope dangling.

His fingers drew into fists. He wasn't sharp enough to handle this job. Sean's deductive skills would have been more useful. Or Dylan's cleverness with computers. If anything happened to Lexie because of him, Mason would never forgive himself.

"Lexie?" Where was she? Did she step outside for a

walk? She would have told him, wouldn't she? He should have laid down ground rules. "Lexie?"

He took out his phone and punched in her number. It rang six times and went to voice mail. He charged down the hall and back again. Maybe she'd gone to the gym.

He hit redial for her phone. As he stalked down the hallway, he heard her ringtone, a song from *Mary Poppins*. The cheerful, perky music was coming from inside a room. He paused outside the first door to the right of the staircase and listened. "Just a spoonful of sugar…"

"Lexie!"

Without waiting for her to answer, he shoved open the door. She was nowhere in sight. Her phone in the center of the bed gave a final chirp and went quiet. The little red sneakers she'd been wearing peeked out from the edge of her comforter beside her neatly made bed. Her room was a good size, with a large window and a view of distant snow-capped peaks.

Where was she? He wanted to tear apart the bed and fling open the closet door. Then he heard the rumble of the shower from the adjoining bathroom. In a whoosh, he exhaled the tense breath he'd been holding. *She's fine. In the shower. Perfectly fine.* The classy thing for him to do would be to exit, close the door and knock on it until she answered.

Shower steam rushed from the bathroom door when she opened it a crack and poked her head through. "Mason? What's up?"

He strode across her bedroom. Without saying a word, he pulled her close against his chest and nuzzled her wet hair.

"Is something wrong?" She wriggled in his grasp.

"It's okay now." He held her closer. Obviously, he owed her an explanation, but all he wanted right now was to feel her energy and know that she hadn't been hurt. There was nothing between them but a bath towel, and his behavior was totally inappropriate. He didn't care.

Her arms wrapped around his torso and her wiggling subsided as she settled into a comfortable stance. In spite of the twelve-inch difference in their heights, their bodies fit together nicely. Her soft curves molded to his hard edges.

After a final squeeze, he took a step back. She managed to grab her towel before it fell, but not quickly enough that he didn't catch a glimpse of her left breast and the dusky rose of her nipple. As wardrobe malfunctions went, this was modest.

Still, she blushed. "Have you lost your mind?"

If he stood here and tried to make sense of his tension, panic and guilt for having failed her and failed at his job, Mason was fairly sure that he'd dissolve into an incoherent, babbling mess. All he could do was stare at the towel and wish for it to be gone.

"In the hall," he managed to choke out. "You get dressed. I'll be in the hall."

He made a crisp pivot and went out the door. In the long hallway, he was unable to make himself stand still. He paced up and down, trying to burn off the emotional shock he'd felt when he realized that the intruder could still be in the house. Though it was extremely unlikely, he and Lexie had to go downstairs to Command Central and play through the tape until they found him climbing down. Mason cursed himself. Why hadn't he done that in the first place? *What goes up must come down.* It was child's play to recall that simple formula.

Sean would have told him that you should never trust the security system. People relied too much on electronics. On the other hand, Dylan would have put his faith in the computerized security and pointed out that if it weren't for the outdoor surveillance camera, they wouldn't have seen anything.

Lexie joined him in the hall. She had on her cutoffs and a fresh T-shirt with hummingbirds on the front. She'd stuck her feet into flip-flops that displayed her multicolored toenails. Her damp hair was tucked behind her ears. She smelled like a garden of lilies, lilacs, roses and honeyed flowers.

She cleared her throat. "The last thing I remember you saying is that you were going to call the CIA."

"Agent Collier was helpful." He gestured for her to come with him as he descended the grand staircase into the foyer and the less grand set of stairs into the lower level. "Collier didn't send any of his men onto the roof, so our intruder must have swiped a Windbreaker so he could walk around unnoticed. A simple disguise."

"Or not," she said. "One of his agents could be a traitor."

"Correct." He liked that she was smart and saw all the possibilities. "The worst part is that Collier had the security turned off at various times during the day while he was searching. We never saw the man on the roof climb down."

"And you thought he might have gotten into the house?" Her tone was incredulous. "That he was hiding out in the attic?"

"It's possible."

"Since the weekend, there have been more than thirty people coming into and going out of this house. Managing to hide out from that mob would take some fancy footwork."

"Humor me, okay? Let's just see if he left."

They were in Command Central. He sat in front of the screen where they had watched the intruder climbing onto the roof. As Mason started running the images in fast-forward, she peeked over his shoulder, bringing that delightful fragrance with her. He inhaled deeply, trying to identify all the scents. The rose was from a soap from a hotel he knew in Grand Junction. Lilies and lilacs—the purple tones— were from a shampoo a former girlfriend had used. The honey sweetness emanated from Lexie herself. "Honey," he murmured.

"What?"

"You smell like honey."

"Honeysuckle," she corrected. "It's the fragrance of a moisturizing cream I use on my arms and legs. Is it too strong?"

"I like it."

"Colorado is the worst for dryness. I'm always smearing on moisturizer and guzzling water."

Whatever beauty regime she was using, it worked. Fresh from the shower, her clean skin glistened. The freckles across her cheeks were more obvious than those on her tanned arms and legs. She hadn't hidden any of those polka dots under layers of makeup.

"There." She pointed to the screen. "The guy in the CIA jacket is climbing down the rope."

Mason verified the time stamps on the footage and mentally calculated. "Our intruder was on the roof for less than an hour. We should go up there and see what he was doing."

"Do you need me to help you?"

To help him? Not really. But he wanted her to be with him until he was one hundred percent certain that the house was secure. "You're coming with me."

With her fists on hips and her legs slightly akimbo, she planted her feet as though taking a stand. "You want my help, right?"

"Sure." He didn't want to argue. When he'd thought she might be in danger, he used up his adrenaline spurt of panic tracking her down to the shower. His current energy level was more laid-back, less intense. "I'm not letting you out of my sight until I'm certain that it's safe."

"That's not fair. I'm—"

"Coming with me," he said, finishing her sentence. "What's the fastest, easiest way to get to where the rope is dangling?"

Her slender shoulders twitched in a shrug. She went to the door and turned left. "This way."

She marched down the hallway in the lower level toward the north end of the house. He could track their depth by the shape of the windows. At the southern point of the lower level—the gym—the windows were floor to ceiling. Heading toward the staircase, the windows were garden level. Then they were near the ceiling. In the last forty feet, there were no windows at all.

"We're underground," he said. "Is the safe room down here?"

"How did you know about the safe room?"

"I have blueprints," he reminded her.

The hallway ended in a T-shape. To his right was an open archway leading to what appeared to be storage. Lexie went past him and closed it. "This isn't supposed to be open. Not a good place for the little ones to play."

The door directly in front of him was matte black and mounted in a metal frame. There was a dial on the front and a door handle. "Have you ever been inside there?"

"When I first took the nanny job, Helena showed me how to get inside. It's really safe but scary. Going in there is a last resort."

"They don't call it a panic room for nothing."

"The Prescotts use it as a safe for their important papers, the furs, jewelry and a couple of paintings and sculptures." Her eyes darted nervously. "You know, stuff like that."

Lexie's furtive behavior made him think she was hiding something. Maybe the artworks hadn't been purchased legitimately. If so, it made sense that Helena didn't want Agent Collier and his men poking around in there. "Can you show me how to open it?"

She eyed him suspiciously. "Planning to steal a mink and a tiara?"

"I was thinking it might be useful to have a safe room. In case the bad guys show up."

She reached over and twirled the dial on the front of the door. "The entry code is different from the rest of the house, and it resets after every time it's opened. I can track the number down by accessing household computer files."

Access to the panic room was meant to discourage anyone from going inside. If there had been any reason to suspect Helena of hiding the Damascus Cache, Mason would look in this room first.

At the left end of the T-shape at the end of the hall, she punched numbers into a keypad and opened the door. She skipped up a flight of stairs, and he followed. They were in the forest.

Sunlight dappled the leaves of chokecherry shrubs and grasses while the breeze whispered through the high branches of surrounding pines. He loved being in the mountains. The air tasted fresher here. The light was clearer.

He hiked up the slope to where the rope was dangling. Though it was only a one-story climb to the roof, Mason stayed below Lexie. If she slipped, he'd catch her. Using the rope, she ascended quickly.

Standing on the rooftop, she spread her arms to take in the wide vista. "Great view. The admiral is thinking about putting in solar panels."

Far below the high cliff where the house perched, the

relatively flat land of Henscratch Valley stretched to another jagged ridge. A small herd of cattle grazed. A hawk swooped across clear blue skies. He inhaled and exhaled slowly. This was a king of the world moment. He was overwhelmed by the spacious grandeur and would have preferred sitting and soaking in all this natural beauty.

But he had a job to do. His footing on the thermal asphalt shingles felt solid. The landscape of the roof was slants, slopes, gables and skylights, which Lexie scrambled over like a mountain goat in flip-flops.

Mason concentrated on figuring out why the intruder had climbed up here. As far as he could tell, the wiring on the windows hadn't been tampered with. The alarm system appeared to be intact.

About halfway down the north wing—an area that was directly above the children's bedrooms—he noticed a small but potentially lethal device tucked against the edge of a skylight.

It was a bomb.

FROM HIS PERCH fifteen feet off the ground, Tony dropped his binoculars into his lap and leaned back against the thick trunk of the tall pine tree he'd chosen for his surveillance point when he followed them outside. While they were in the house, he was able to keep track of them using a heat-sensing infrared camera that showed their images in red outlined against the cooler green of their surroundings. He'd been watching when Lexie and the bodyguard went in different directions…and when they came together for a steaming-hot embrace.

Tony almost felt sorry for the guy. He was falling for Lexie, which meant she'd wait until she had him wrapped around her little finger, and then she'd dump him. That was what she did. He wasn't the only guy in Texas to get booted from his relationship by little Miss Francine Alexandra.

On the rooftop, she scooted toward the escape rope. The bodyguard warned her to get away; he'd located one of the tiny, cell-phone-activated bombs Tony had planted.

This guy didn't know much about explosives. These bomb charges weren't big enough to do serious damage. They were meant to be used as a distraction.

Tony wasn't going to blow up the house. Directives from the leader were clear: no one was to be harmed, especially not the kids. *And isn't that too bad?* Tony would have enjoyed inflicting harm on those spoiled brats, enough harm that they'd understand that they couldn't have everything they wanted. Sometimes your mama promises a kiss but you get a slap in the face.

He'd leave a few scars behind to remind them...like the scars on Lexie's legs.

Life wasn't all sunshine and butterflies. Why was the leader protecting these people, treating them as if they were special? Tony was sick and tired of pussyfooting around.

Being cautious wasn't getting the job done. If they didn't get their hands on the Damascus Cache soon, they'd miss out on a big payday. And there were other ways than kidnapping the admiral and trying to get him to talk. Tony had presented an idea about using Lexie as a hostage to leverage the admiral into giving up the cache.

Getting his hands on her would be easy. All he had to do was get that damn bodyguard out of the way. He closed his eyes and imagined Lexie all trussed up, naked and helpless. He'd take his time getting to know her body again, seeing her quiver when he squeezed her soft breasts, hearing her moan when he traced the folds between her legs.

She'd cry when he slapped her face. She'd fall to her knees and beg for his mercy.

Tony was tempted to put his plan to kidnap Lexie into effect. The leader could deal with the consequences. That would be his problem.

Chapter Thirteen

The Aspen fire department had done such an excellent job that Lexie wished the kids were home to watch. Less than twenty minutes after she'd called in to report the bomb, the shiny red truck pulled up to the front door with sirens blaring. Fortunately, she and Mason had been standing by to open the door, because the local firemen and one woman were armed with axes and ready to hack their way through to the nonexistent flames.

Their search of the roof had been eventful. They found six small cell-phone-activated charges, none of which would result in a major explosion. "More like fireworks than a bomb" was how the chief explained the devices. "More like a bomblet." But those nasty little bomblets were a fire danger and needed to be removed.

The fire department crew had used a long, basket-like tool to scoop up the bomblets and then deposit them in a shiny metal sphere called a blast chamber. This marked the first time they'd used the blast chamber. When all the devices had been collected and the chamber had been locked up tight, the threat was contained.

The crew seemed happy to have a new piece of equipment to play with. They were cheerfully discussing procedure for setting off the explosives when the chief pulled Lexie to one side and gave her a report sheet to fill in and sign. Out of respect for the admiral, he wouldn't conduct a formal investigation, but he would appreciate being kept in the loop. He was concerned because of the attack at the hotel, but the fire chief didn't have a beef about jurisdiction. He'd rather not be in charge.

Before he and the crew drove away in their shiny red truck, he'd consulted with Mason. As she watched the two men, Lexie realized that her bodyguard hadn't changed from the clothes he wore when he arrived, minus the plaid shirt. Not that there was anything wrong with the way he was dressed. She liked the simple, masculine look of his black T-shirt and jeans and hiking boots. But was it date appropriate?

The sun slipped lower in the sky, and Lexie checked her phone for the time. It was 4:35 p.m. Mason hadn't mentioned their date. Nor had she.

It seemed that the idea had simply faded away. Why bother dating when they had a mansion to themselves? If they wanted, they could fill the hot tub or watch a movie in the downstairs theater or make themselves a gourmet dinner. There was no need to go out, and he hadn't said a word about where they'd be going. She exhaled a disappointed sigh. It wasn't important.

She entered the house, climbed the staircase and went to her bedroom, where she sprawled facedown on the queen-size bed with the pale blue striped comforter. Lazily, she dragged her fingers through her shoulder-length hair that had dried in messy tangles. She should have done a quick blow-dry, but Mason had been in such a frantic hurry when he pulled her from the shower. He'd been afraid that something bad had happened to her. In his eyes, she had seen the glimmer of real fear.

In spite of the muscles, he had a sensitive streak. If he needed to kick ass, he could. But he was smart—smart enough to know that not all problems could be solved with his fists or by running away. Mason didn't fit the stereotype of a muscle head with a great bod and no brain. That was as unfair as the myth of the dumb blonde or the fiery redhead.

There was a rap on her door.

She sat up on the bed. "Come in."

Smoothly, Mason stepped into the room and closed the door. "I wanted to let you know that I'm going to be a few minutes late for our date."

"Is it still on?"

"I didn't cancel."

"If you don't want to go out, we don't have to bother."

"Not a bother." He crossed the room and lowered himself on the bed beside her. "It's my pleasure."

"Why?"

And why was she looking this gift horse in the mouth? If a man wanted to be nice to her, she ought to let him. She was always quick to throw up her defenses, maybe too quick.

"I like you," he said. "Dating is what happens when a man likes a woman. It's a great American ritual. Part of our culture."

"Our culture?" That description seemed a bit too grand. "You might be overstating."

"As an international studies major, I'd argue that American dating habits are one of our biggest exports. Going out with one boy, one girl and one car—it's the American style. No chaperones. No arranged courtships. And we definitely don't require dowries or bride tokens."

"What's a token?"

"A payment I'd make to your father for your hand. You know, a golden goblet and six goats."

"Only six?"

"You're sort of skinny."

"You pig." She smacked him on the arm. His easy conversation was relaxing her. The defenses were falling. "It's terrible that families used to do that to their women, selling them off for livestock. It shows no respect."

"Or is it the other way around? Their daughters are so precious that they demand payment for them."

"If it was acceptable, my dad would be like that. He'd ask such a ridiculously high price that nobody could pay it, and I'd never leave home."

"Did you get a chance this week to talk to him?"

"Not really." She collapsed backward on the bed. She'd talked to her dad but hadn't told him everything. She hadn't confronted him about the crash, about how it was his damned fault. It didn't seem that there was anything positive to be gained from that confrontation.

Mason stretched out beside her on the bed. Lying side by side should have felt intimate, but she was doing her best not to put him in that category. She wanted Mason to be a friend, someone she might know two years from now. Not a boyfriend. Her lovers came and went as fast as a revolving door.

"Did you tell him everything?" he asked.

"What do you mean?" Had Helena blabbed to him, too? "What do you know?"

"Only what you've told me," he said. "He was treating you like a child, saying that you had to come home at the first sign of danger."

"Right." Now she understood why her dad had been so concerned about her safety. "I kept a few things to myself."

"Like what?"

"He's so anxious to interfere in my life now, but there was a time when he should have protected me but didn't."

"That doesn't sound like a marine."

Though her bed was queen-size, the space seemed to shrink around them until it was as small as a camping cot. If she and Mason were going to have any sort of relationship, she needed to trust him and tell him the whole story. She scooted around until she was sitting cross-legged beside him, looking down at his handsome face.

There was something she'd wanted to do from the first time she saw him, and now seemed like the right time. She reached out and rubbed her palm back and forth over his buzz cut. His short, razor-cut blond hair tickled.

He caught hold of her wrist. "Is there a reason you're petting my head like a dog?"

The bristly haircut actually did remind her of a sleek-coated dog, like a Great Dane. "I wanted to see how the buzz felt."

"This is your one and only warning. If you treat me like a dog again, I will get you good." He released her wrist and lay back on the bed, staring up at the ceiling. "This thing with your dad, did it happen a long time ago?"

"It was the car crash when I was twenty. I told you about it." His teasing kept her from sinking into depression when she talked about the worst trauma of her life. "I always thought it was an accident, even though they never found the guy who ran into me. A hit-and-run accident. And I was lucky that another driver came along to help me and to call for assistance."

She shook away the dark, terrifying images. She'd seen the car coming at her. Through the dark-tinted glass, she couldn't make out the features of the driver.

Mason's large hand rested on her knee. Again, he wasn't trying to be sexy. His touch was meant to soothe her and offer comfort. When she gazed into his blue eyes, they seemed to absorb and reflect her pain at the same time.

"The driver," she said without a tremble, "was sent by

enemies of my father. He attacked me as a warning for my dad, a warning for the whole CIA, MI6 secret-agent community. They struck at me. I paid the price for all the other families."

"Finally," he whispered.

"Finally what?" she snapped irritably. "What are you talking about?"

"One of the first things you said to me was someone tried to kill you and very nearly did. Then you made a hundred and one excuses not to tell me. Now you trust me enough to tell me."

"Maybe I trust you. Maybe a little."

"Did your father know that you were the intended target of a hit?"

"No." At least, she didn't think so. "He couldn't have known. If he had, my brothers would be protecting me."

"When he was informed, what did your dad do?"

"The bad guys wanted him to quit the exercise he was involved with. He did. Then he took early retirement, left the marines and came home to take care of me."

So many emotions swirled inside her that she couldn't tell her anger from her fear from her guilt. Had she ruined her father's life, causing him to leave the work he loved? Or had he ruined hers by placing her in the line of fire?

"We never talked about it," she said. "He doesn't know that I know about the terrorist and how he quit to protect me."

Mason sat up on the bed. Gently, he stroked her hair off her cheek and tucked it behind her ear. "It's not your fault that your father chose to leave the marines and put you first. And it's not his fault that you were in the crash."

"Then who do I blame?"

"The hit-and-run driver. He's the one who directly hurt you. But you could also blame the larger organization that sent him. Blame the war. Blame the ongoing struggles. Blame humanity."

"It's not fair."

"And there's nothing you can do to change it. It's in the past."

With a frustrated little sigh, she leaned into him and rested her cheek against his broad chest. Holding her, he slid back into a reclining position. They were crosswise on the bed with one of his legs halfway off and his foot on the floor. She snuggled into the nook below his chin, rubbing her cheek against his soft T-shirt.

"I want the past to be different," she said.

"Good luck with that."

She wanted to be whole and complete. If he wanted children, she wasn't the right woman for him. *Keep your distance, Lexie.* It was smarter to end this relationship right now, before she got too wrapped up in him, before he became a part of her and dumping him was as painful as tearing off a limb.

She disentangled away from his embrace and got off the bed. Straightening her shoulders, she asked, "What should I wear for our date?"

LEXIE WAS GLAD she'd paid no attention to his suggestion of an outfit with a very short skirt and a casual but very low-cut top. Her choice for their date was skinny jeans with cowgirl boots and a turquoise blouse under a short, light-weight leather jacket. She'd be warm and comfy and looked pretty good with her hair held back by a thin gold band.

Mason had showered but hadn't shaved. The stubble on his chin was darker than the hair on his head and made him look a full five years older. Adding five years balanced out his youthful buzz cut, which made him look younger. She had calculated his age at twenty-seven or twenty-eight, which was a good match for her at twenty-five. On the drive to the restaurant in the hills outside Aspen, she'd been studying his profile. He had a classic Roman nose, but otherwise his features were Scandinavian, like a Viking's.

It was half past six when he pulled out her chair and tucked her into her seat at the table. After his lecture about the proper rituals of dating, he'd better be sharp about performing all those jacket-holding, door-opening jobs. No surprise, he was skilled at acting the role of a gentleman, which made her feel so ladylike that she crooked her pinkie when she lifted her water goblet, took a sip and looked at him over the rim.

"Did you ever complete your risk assessment of the house?" she asked.

"If I hadn't completed it, we wouldn't be here. In spite of the bomblets on the roof, the security system is intact and effective. Between the electronic surveillance, the alarms and Command Central, nobody is getting into that house without announcing their presence. The admiral told me his system was state of the art, and he didn't lie."

"Which makes me wonder." She set down her glass and smoothed the linen tablecloth. Since this was a nice dining establishment that was geared toward adults, not children, she hadn't been here. "If he's not really worried about security, why hire you?"

"Ever heard the phrase 'CYA'?"

"Cover your ass."

"I'm thinking the admiral wanted to settle his conscience, especially since you were attacked and targeted as a young woman. He wants to be sure you're protected. Just like your dad, the admiral carries his share of guilt."

"It's not necessary. Feeling bad never does any good."

He raised an eyebrow. "That sounds like something they teach in nanny school."

"Oh, my God, you're right. I sound like Mary Poppins."

"At least you get to fly."

"But I don't want to be a turn-of-the-century spinster who takes care of other people's kids." Those words were truer than he would ever know. "I'm changing my ringtone."

The waiter appeared and rattled off a list of special dishes ranging from chicken paprika to schnitzel and kraut. Without having to worry about watching the kids, she could choose adventurous foods. She selected something with potatoes and something with venison that she'd never before heard of. And they both ordered beer from a huge selection.

"This dating ritual is a little bit fantastic," she said. "I usually don't drink."

"Glad to oblige."

"I have an idea." She was still thinking about security and the cache. "We should do some crime solving. We're sitting in the middle of this great big web of intrigue and spies."

"So you're not Mary Poppins anymore."

"I never was."

"Now you're Nancy Drew."

"We might as well try to figure it out."

"It's not the worst idea I've ever heard," he said. "The anti-conspiracy people think the cache is in Prescott's house, and we're the only ones with access."

She hadn't forgotten that her father's name might be included in the cache. When it was located, he might be in danger. She wanted to find it, to end this threat. "The problem is that we're not cops. We don't have the authority to make people talk to us."

"But we hear a lot."

His knowing glance sparked her enthusiasm. In her role as nanny, nobody paid much attention to her. She never ever eavesdropped, but she couldn't help overhearing things. She knew that the handsome Agent Collier was having an affair with his fifteen-years-older CIA boss with the sexy shoulder-baring dress. She'd heard a couple of captains talking about someone else who had been fired. His name was Ackerman. Where had she heard that name before?

Their waiter returned with a basket of warm, fragrant bread and two frosted mugs filled with the restaurant's brand of beer brewed with local hops. "These drinks are from the two gentlemen sitting by the window."

She looked over and saw Hank Grossman and Sam Bertinelli. What were the NSA agents doing here?

Chapter Fourteen

Mason noticed that Grossman and Bertinelli had only a couple of beers on their table—no leftover plates from dinner—and their silverware sat neatly on their linen napkins. They hadn't been in the restaurant for long, had probably arrived within minutes of when he and Lexie got here. Had the NSA agents been following them?

Lexie waved to them across the dining room and smiled. "Should we go over and talk to them?"

"If we don't," he said, "they'll come to us, plant themselves in chairs and refuse to leave."

"I don't want to spend my date with Grossman." She popped to her feet. "Also, this is an opportunity to investigate."

Mason wasn't the sort of guy who leaped before he looked. Jumping feetfirst into an investigation without considering the information they needed might be dangerous. "Be careful."

She shrugged. "It's just Grossman and Bertinelli."

Her cavalier attitude came from having high-ranking officers and federal agents passing through the Prescott home. Most people would be plenty scared if confronted with two men who worked for the National Security Agency. A little fear was smart. Either of these agents could be involved with the AC-CD group. They might know more about the Damascus Cache than they admitted in the meetings. Mason considered it likely that they had information they hadn't shared. The NSA had more covert ops than any other US intelligence service, both at home and abroad.

He followed Lexie across the half-full dining room and waited while she gave each of the NSA agents a hug. Mason shook hands. He nodded to Grossman and saved his comment for Bertinelli, who was by far the less offensive of the two. "I'm surprised to see you gentlemen here. This place has a reputation for being romantic."

"German food?" Grossman answered for his partner, pulling a frown and holding his nose in a not-so-subtle indication that he wasn't a fan of the cuisine. "There's nothing sexy about kraut."

"We came for the beer," Bertinelli said. He seemed nervous, as though he'd been caught in a lie. It pleased Mason to have that effect. "This place has a great selection of beer."

"I wasn't aware that you were staying in the area," Mason said. "What are you working on?"

Grossman slouched down in his chair. Though the waiter had poured some of his beer into a glass, he drank from the bottle. "I could ask the same question, Mason. What made you come back to town?"

He rested his hand on Lexie's shoulder. "We're on a date."

"That's real sweet," Grossman said in the exasperated tone he might use to say *I've got a flat tire*. His patience for civil conversation was just about spent, which was sad because it hadn't taken much to wear him down. Pretty soon they'd be hearing the full-out, probably obnoxious truth about why the NSA was in town and why they'd been following Mason's car. Good old sloppy Hank wouldn't be able to keep his mouth shut.

Bertinelli straightened his posture. He was more corporate in his attitudes, more economical with his words. But it was obvious that he didn't like playing a cat-and-mouse game, trying to figure out what the other guy was doing without asking a direct question. He reached up to his throat to adjust his necktie, but he wasn't wearing one. He had on a pullover sweater and a shirt with a button-down collar.

He fiddled with the buttons. "We heard you had some excitement at the house this afternoon."

"We did," Lexie said with the sweetest of smiles. "Who did you hear that from?"

"I can't remember. Maybe the guy at the gas station. Was there an accident at the house?"

"It's all taken care of," she said.

"Perhaps we could help," Bertinelli returned.

"The fire department was terrific," she said.

"It sounds dangerous," he said.

"We have things under control."

"Never hurts to have someone else check it out."

The two of them were lobbing comments back and forth like a tennis match. Mason was pretty sure that Bertinelli wanted to wangle an invitation to the house so he could take a look around for himself. Mason didn't know what motivated Lexie, but she appeared to be enjoying herself. Her cheeks were pink, and her dark eyes glistened.

"That's enough," Grossman grumbled. "We all know what's going on here. We've been running surveillance on the house."

"Shocking," Lexie said.

"We saw the fire department and followed them back

into town to observe their use of the blast chamber, which was very groovy."

Mason had figured the detonation would be fun; watching stuff blow up usually was. He wouldn't have used the word *groovy*, though. "You followed us here tonight."

Grossman looked over at his junior partner. "I told you he picked up on the tail."

"I don't think so. I was careful." Bertinelli looked hopefully toward Mason. "Did you see me?"

Mason didn't want to squash this last grasp at competence. "I didn't see you following, but I knew you were surveilling. Your arrival here is too coincidental."

Lexie stamped her foot. In her little cowgirl boots, she was adorable. "Why were you watching us and following us?"

"We've got no leads," Bertinelli said. "The CIA team didn't find anything that would lead us to the cache. None of our informants know anything, which isn't surprising, because most of them are in the Middle East."

"Yeah, it's a problem." Grossman took a long glug of his beer. "There aren't many spies or snitches in the high Rocky Mountains."

"You don't have to creep around the house," Lexie said.

"No?" Bertinelli's brows went up.

"I'll check with Helena and the admiral to make sure it's okay, and you can come over tomorrow around two in the afternoon. You can poke around to your heart's content."

As they returned to their table, he wished she hadn't been so generous with her hospitality. He didn't trust those two. From what Mason understood, the Damascus Cache was worth a lot of money to the right people—enough money to tempt someone like Grossman, who didn't have many years left as an active agent. Bertinelli might opt for a big payoff so he wouldn't have to be under Grossman's thumb.

Mason held Lexie's chair for her again. She turned her head to look up at him, and her grin widened. "That was fun."

He sat opposite her and sipped his beer from the frosted mug. "How was it fun?"

"For one thing, we were just too cool for school. We were, like, good cop and bad cop."

"Which one were you?"

"I'd like to say I was the bad cop, but I kind of invited them over to the house."

The idea of this cheerful, open-faced woman being a stern interrogator tickled him. "And you'll probably feed them cookies and milk."

"I'd like to point out that my method worked. Grossman admitted everything. I'm a little peeved that they've been snooping near the house with binoculars."

"If I were you, I'd make certain my curtains were always closed."

"What about you?"

If somebody was spying on him, Mason would stand at the window naked, waving and making rude gestures. "It's different with guys."

"I grew up with three brothers." She cocked her head to one side. Her gaze softened as she took a sip. The dark beer left a trace of froth on her lips. They seemed to be moving into the dating part of their evening, when the conversation turned more personal. "You just had the one brother, right?"

Matt was several years older, and Mason sometimes felt like an only child. He remembered when he was seven and saw the sign at Elitch Amusement Park that said you couldn't ride until you were a certain height.

"You must be this high." He held out his hand beside the table. "That's what I felt like as a kid. Matt was on the roller coaster, and I was on the sidelines waiting to grow. Then I did. And the age difference didn't matter."

"Did your family always live in Denver?"

"We spent a couple of years near San Francisco in Silicon Valley." His dad was a computer guy and had brushed up his skills with a stint at one of the big software companies. "How about you? Where have you lived?"

"Everywhere." She stretched her arms wide apart. "When you're a military brat, you get accustomed to shuffling from one place to another. Mostly, I've been in Texas. I'm a countrified woman. I grew up knowing how to ride, shoot and hunt. I'm not scared of snakes or spiders. And I love beef."

He liked her résumé, even though their childhoods didn't have much in common. He'd been a city kid who shot hoops, played sports, jogged and spent every Saturday morning with the chess club before discovering the gym. "I always wished I'd lived in the mountains. I'd have a whole different skill set."

"Like snowboarding and skiing."

"Rock climbing and kayaking."

She flashed one of her upturned smiles. "I'd like to learn how to do those things, but it's impossible while I'm being a nanny and need to watch out for the kids."

"Maybe while I'm here," he said, "we could learn together."

"I'd love to."

Their dinner was served. He couldn't argue with the portions. With the side dishes, including a container of pickles, the plates covered the whole surface of the table. He hadn't realized how hungry he was until he dug in. The beef was so tender it could be cut with a fork, and everything else—even the sauerkraut—was perfectly seasoned.

As their official date progressed, he learned more about her. Almost all her fond memories about her mother were from when she was a little girl. With her dad being deployed, her mom was lonely and her daughter was her only company. Her mom cried a lot, and Lexie tried to make her happy. She'd dance around with a goofy smile on her face or tell a joke or make up a nonsense song.

The two NSA agents came over and said goodbye before they left the restaurant. If they had the okay from the admiral and his wife, they'd come to the house tomorrow and make their own search for the cache.

"I should warn you," Lexie said to Bertinelli, "there's no way that Helena will let you go into the safe room, and I don't know how to open that door."

"Nobody has ever searched in there," he said.

"And nobody ever will unless Helena gives the okay." Big smile. "I don't think any judge will issue a search warrant for Admiral Prescott's private papers."

"Is that what's in there?"

She shrugged. "Could be."

As soon as the agents left, he reached across the table and took her hand. "We're going to search in the safe room tomorrow morning, aren't we?"

"Absolutely. It feels sneaky to do that to Bertinelli. He's not a bad guy."

"We don't know that. Don't know hardly anything about him."

"I do." She squeezed his fingers and reclaimed her hand. "Sam Bertinelli with his neat black hair and pretty hazel eyes wanted to go out with me, and I got curious about him. He's from Chicago, was an accountant for an oil exploration company before he joined the NSA and is twice divorced, no kids. He's also forty-seven, which is old enough to be my father. He was annoyed when I told him no. Then he pushed, and I hinted very subtly that the age difference bothered me. And then he was seriously angry."

"Gee, I wonder why."

Her cute smile twisted into an evil smirk. Sweet little Lexie wasn't a wide-eyed innocent. "Age isn't the only reason I didn't want to date him. There was a whole list of problems."

"I hope you're not holding any of those nasty bomblets for me. Maybe you hate men with blond hair. Or you never date guys whose first names start with *M*."

"I don't *enjoy* rejecting guys." There was a dark undertone to her voice, a mixture of anger and sadness. "But I don't see any point in getting started with a relationship that can never work."

"Not every relationship is going to end in marriage."

"I know." She scowled. "There are a million different kinds of relationships. Friends. Colleagues. Coworkers. You and I could be partner detectives."

"A lot of possibilities," he said. But there was one relationship he wanted with her. Pure and simple, one word, he wanted to be her lover.

EVER SINCE THE CRASH, Lexie had preferred vehicles with substance. Mason's ten-year-old Land Rover fit the bill. Leaning back in the passenger's seat, she felt a pleasant sense of security that wasn't entirely due to the muscular SUV wrapped around her. Mason would keep her safe. He was her protector.

She noticed that he was taking a different route back to the house and wasn't using his GPS device. "Do you think Grossman and Bertinelli are trying to follow us again?"

"Probably not."

"Why are you going this way? It's longer."

"Since I'm going to be here for a couple of weeks, it's useful for me to know my way around."

She gazed through the window at the twinkling lights of Aspen to her left in the distance. Though it was just after nine o'clock, there wasn't much traffic outside town. An occasional car or truck zipped past the Rover on the two-lane road. A truck had been following them for a few miles, but when Mason made a left, the truck stayed on the main road.

He drove into a wide, rocky canyon with cute little cabins on either side. She lowered her window so she could hear the burble of the narrow creek that had dictated the winding path of this road.

"What's this creek called?" he asked.

"It's the Little Wapiti. That's the Shawnee word for elk." She felt another grin coming on. "Actually, it means white rump."

"So if you told the kids you were going to spank them on their little wapitis…"

"Oh, I've told them that before. I never could bring myself to hit them. The threat is usually enough. You know what's crazy? I kind of miss the little beasties."

"That's not crazy. You love those kids, even the twins."

"I guess I do."

Casually chatting, they drove out of the canyon into the open expanse of Henscratch Valley. In the distance, the looming hills, dark pines and jagged rocks seemed alive in the shifting shadows and moonlight. It was a beautiful night, and she realized that she was having a good time. This date was a success. The food was good. The conversation was interesting. Would it end with a kiss? Should she invite him into her bedroom?

The Rover glided onto a section of road that zigzagged

up the side of a cliff in sharp hairpin turns. Mason checked his rearview mirror. "Damn."

A ripple of fear went through her. "What is it?"

"The truck behind us. It's the third time I've seen him."

"Are you sure?" She turned and stared out the back window. A filthy truck was two car lengths behind them. "Lots of people drive trucks around here."

"Look at the license plate."

She wriggled around in her seat as much as she could without unfastening the seat belt. "I can't see it."

"Because he's covered the number with mud. On the front and back. Unidentifiable, he's just another beat-up old truck."

And the driver wants to kill us.

Chapter Fifteen

Remembered terror from her first devastating car crash sluiced through her veins and joined with a newer version of fear. Not again, not another crash.

Mason pushed the accelerator, and the Rover responded, leaping forward in a burst of speed. Though the narrow asphalt road ascended on a steep incline, their vehicle seemed to be going faster. They gained traction. The rear end fishtailed as they took the first of three tight curves.

The landscape whirled past her like a kaleidoscope. Her mouth was open to scream, but she couldn't make a sound. Her throat constricted, strangled by fear. Her heart thumped hard against her rib cage.

Even faster than the first curve, Mason swiveled the Rover around the second. The tires skidded but only a bit. He had control. He was a better driver than she'd ever been. With Mason at the wheel, they might survive.

If she had a choice, she might want to die rather than going through the physical agony of another bone-wrenching crash with injuries on top of injuries and days of constant surgeries. They said what didn't kill you made you stronger. Not true. Not for her.

It had taken every shred of her willpower to get through her painful physical therapy. She'd used up her lifetime allotment of courage battling the naysayers who told her she'd never walk again. But she would never choose death. She couldn't do that to her father.

There was only one more hairpin on this stretch. The vehicle behind them was so close that his headlights flashed in the Rover's rearview mirror and blinded her. Her hands flew up to cover her eyes. She couldn't bear to watch.

The Rover took the final curve at a fearsome speed. At the same time, the truck bumped the fender. They skidded and drifted across the center line. She heard gravel from the shoulder kick up and batter the undercarriage. Then the Rover straightened out.

Mason was driving so fast that she didn't dare peek at the speedometer, but she dropped her hands to her lap. "Is he gone?"

"Not yet."

The upper ridge of this cliff was above timberline; there were no trees blocking her view when she turned to look for the truck. He'd fallen back quite a distance. "Is something wrong with his truck?"

"It'd be a damn shame," Mason said, "if he damaged his vehicle while he was trying to kill us."

Her pulse was still racing, and she was breathing in frantic gasps. But they'd made it this far. She had reason to hope.

"What happens on the road ahead?" he asked. "It looks like we're headed into a forest."

"The trees are close on both sides of the road. It's a gradual descent, not a lot of huge drop-offs."

"I don't want to get trapped in there."

"No?"

"Hell, no. We're taking the fight to him."

But she didn't want to fight. She was happy to see the truck falling even farther back. "It looks like he's given up."

"Brace yourself."

The Rover rounded a gentle curve. For a moment, their vehicle was hidden from the truck behind a rocky mound. Mason tap-danced between the accelerator and brake, throwing them into a spin in the middle of the road. The Rover came around one hundred and eighty degrees. He killed the headlights. They sat and waited for the truck to approach.

She had no trouble screaming, "Are you insane?"

"This time, we'll get him."

"'This time'? What do you mean 'this time'? It's not the same guy who hit me before."

It couldn't be. That was in a different area, at a different time. The first attack was for different reasons. Why was Mason putting the two together?

She saw the headlights approaching.

Mason revved the engine.

She couldn't believe he'd try to take out a truck with his SUV. Land Rovers were sturdy, but this wasn't a Hummer. On the hopeful side, it was possible that Mason knew exactly where to strike the truck to disable it. His one-hundred-and-eighty-degree turn had been impressive.

He stopped revving and sat back in his seat as his hands dropped from the steering wheel. "It's not him," he said.

A Volkswagen bug chugged around the curve and kept on going. She asked. "How did you know?"

"The beams from the headlights were too low for a truck." He turned toward her. "We need to go after him. Keep your eyes open. He might have pulled off on a side road."

"No." She reached over and grabbed his arm as though restraining him could stop the car. "This is where we need to remember that we aren't federal agents or detectives. Here is where people like you and me have to back down and let the police take over."

"The guy who attacked us—the guy in the truck—is a lead. We can't let him get away."

"What if he's waiting for us? What if he's armed?"

Mason patted the shoulder holster he wore under his sports jacket. "So am I."

Turning her head away from him, she folded her arms below her breasts and stared straight ahead through the windshield. Arguing wouldn't do a bit of good. Mason was as stubborn as the men in her family. Once they got a course of action set in their minds, they couldn't be stopped.

He tapped the accelerator, and the Rover rolled slowly forward. The car eased around the edge of the mound. The high mountain road stretched before them. There wasn't another vehicle or human being in sight. Nothing but grasses and junipers and a single lodgepole pine that reached up toward the Big Dipper.

Instead of taking up the chase, Mason made a three-point turn. The Rover was headed back toward the house. "You're right. I have no business chasing after that guy."

She was grateful that he'd changed his mind. "Thank you for listening to me, for hearing me."

"I'm not a cop. It's wrong for me to put you in danger. My job is to keep you safe."

He activated his hands-free phone and called the chief investigating officer from the Aspen police, whom he'd met at the hotel.

She sat in silence, chewing her lower lip and wishing that she didn't like Mason as much as she did. *I don't want to hurt you. Don't make me hurt you.* The near crash reminded her of the past and made many things clear to her. After dinner, she'd been pleased with their date, thinking about their relationship and wondering if this evening should end with a kiss…or something more interesting. But that was wrong. Intimacy wasn't an option.

A committed connection with Mason would never work. She couldn't provide him with a family, and she knew he wanted kids. A bright energy emanated from him when he talked about his brother and growing up with his buddies Dylan and Sean. Mason was comfortable with the Prescott kids. He couldn't help chuckling when he was around little Princess Stella, and he was cool with the older boys. A natural-born family man.

She glanced over at him. He was watching the road and talking on the phone, describing the truck that looked like hundreds of other trucks in this area. There'd be a dent in the truck's front fender, passenger side and in the grille. He gave their location with pinpoint precision.

He would have made a good cop, but TST Security probably paid better and he had more freedom. The downside of TST was getting stuck with a prickly client like her. She needed to end this budding whatever-it-was right now. It was the smart thing to do.

WHEN THEY ARRIVED at the Prescott house, Mason was glad he'd insisted on parking in one of the four spaces attached to the house. Climbing the hill from the larger parking garage would have meant unnecessary exposure. The guy in the truck might have a cohort watching the house, a sniper.

But it seemed unlikely, because none of the attacks had been lethal. The charge on the bomblets had been too small to cause serious damage. The truck had given up too easily. The only thing accomplished by the chase on the mountain roads was scaring Lexie half to death. He'd watched as her fear rose up and overwhelmed her. He'd seen her pain.

When he parked in the garage and the lights came on,

she had her seat belt off in seconds. She reached for the door handle.

"Wait," he said.

"What for?" The harsh overhead light made the freckles stand out on her face. Her usually sparkling eyes were dull and tired.

"Just wait."

"Fine."

He came around to her side of the Rover and opened the door for her. "I won't pretend this date is ending the way I'd hoped, but it doesn't have to be all bad."

"I agree." Her forehead pinched in an unfamiliar scowl. "We're going to be together for a while, like it or not. Might as well try to get along."

"I wanted to say…" This wasn't an apology. He wasn't sorry that his first impulse had been to go after the bad guys. "I can't begin to understand the pain you suffered in that first crash. You're a brave woman, a strong woman. I respect you and your opinions. And I never should have suggested chasing down that truck."

Her features softened a bit. "I know why you were tempted. I'm as anxious as you to have this threat over with."

She left his car and walked toward the house. At the entry, Mason punched in the numerical code that was synced with all the other security systems. Feedback indicated that nothing had been disturbed, but he would make a visual sweep before they went to bed. The attack on the road meant he needed to step up his regular procedures. "Lieutenant Hough from the Aspen police is going to stop by tonight to take our statements."

"Can't it wait until morning?"

"He wants to get the details while they're fresh in mind. My car insurance company can wait."

After they moved from the garage to the house, he rearmed the alarm and followed her on a winding trek through the huge house to the kitchen.

She tossed a comment over her shoulder. "How are you going to explain to the insurance people that you couldn't exchange information at the scene of the accident?"

"Maybe they have a box I can check for lunatic psycho." He shrugged. "The Rover has been battered worse than this. She's a tough little car."

"She?"

"Rhonda," he said, "as in 'Rhonda, you look so fine.'"

She went to the fridge, got waters for both of them and placed the plastic bottles on the counter. Some of the tension had left her shoulders. Her posture was more relaxed.

He hated to do anything that would upset her again, but he couldn't let this slide. "I'm going to have to notify the admiral about this."

"I suppose."

"You know what that means."

"My dad."

"You have to call him, Lexie. He nearly went berserk the last time he thought you were in danger. A car chase seems even more directed, more personal."

She pinned him with a sharp gaze. "Is that what you think?"

"There's something weird about it." He pulled a stool up to the counter and sat. "How does running us off the road connect with the admiral and the Damascus Cache?"

"It might have been a warning. Like the first time I got crashed."

"But there's no clear message. What kind of threat is it to attack the nanny and a bodyguard?"

As her scowl deepened, her freckled nose twitched.

The woman couldn't help being adorable, even when she was deeply worried. "I don't suppose the admiral would be convinced to talk because you and I were hostages."

"He's got six kids. Any one of them would be a better hostage."

"Maybe not the twins." She tried to grin, but the attempt failed.

"Your dad might have some ideas," he said. "I'm sure he knows more about your first crash than anyone else."

"You can forget that line of questioning. I will call my dad and inform him that someone bumped your fender, but I'm not going into any details about the cache."

"Didn't you say his name was in it?"

"Yes, but…"

"Do you want me to call him?"

Her face lit up with pure, beautiful relief. The veil lifted from her eyes. Her smile came back. "I should be able to take care of this myself. Let me think about it."

"Think fast," he said. "It's ten o'clock here and an hour later in Austin."

Taking his water bottle, he went down the hall to the richly furnished office and sat behind the desk. It wasn't so much that he needed privacy, but he wanted Lexie to have some space to think. The call to her father was going to be difficult, no matter who made it.

He took out his phone. He wasn't pleased to be sending separate text messages to the admiral and Helena. This was his second message in one day—his first day on the job. The way he saw his security position was to keep the house and Lexie protected and not to bother the people who hired him. The Prescotts shouldn't have to worry, and he felt like an alarmist when he texted them about every little thing. But when emergency personnel, like cops and firemen, came to the house, the Prescotts needed to be informed.

He sent the texts, leaned back in the swivel chair and put his feet on the desk blotter. He waited.

Lexie appeared in the open doorway. "Make the call."

Chapter Sixteen

"Sergeant Major DeMille, this is Mason Steele from TST Security. We've never met, but you might have known my brother. He was a marine, stationed in Afghanistan. His name was Matthew Steele."

"Sorry, I don't recall the name." Lexie's dad cleared his throat. "I'll tell you what, young man. I'm giving you ten seconds to explain why you called in the middle of the night."

"I work for Admiral Edgar Prescott as a bodyguard." He put the call on speakerphone so Lexie could hear. "I'm at the Prescott home in Aspen with your daughter."

"Is she all right?" The anxiety was evident.

Mason imagined DeMille jolting forward, fully awake. "Yes, but there was an incident earlier tonight."

"Put her on the phone. What did you say your name was? Mason Steele? Listen up, Mason Steele, you put my daughter on the phone right now."

No doubt about it, Sergeant Major Danny DeMille was an intimidating person, a real hard-ass. But Mason had already backed down for Lexie and wasn't in the mood to do the same for her dad. "Your daughter asked me to explain."

"Did she, now?"

Mason started right in. "After dinner, we were driving back to the Prescott home in my Land Rover."

"What year is your Rover?"

"It's a 2003 Land Rover Discovery with the square top."

"Nice, that's a car that looks like a car."

Why was DeMille being chatty about vehicles? Trying to be friendly? No way. He might be trying to distract Mason. Or he might be nervous. This conversation about his daughter had been a long time coming.

Mason looked over at Lexie. At the far end of the tan leather sofa, she was curled up in a ball with her knees pulled up to her chin. Her eyes were squeezed shut, but she was still listening.

"Driving back to the house," Mason continued, "we came to a series of hairpin curves. A truck pulled up behind us."

"Had you noticed being followed before that?"

"Yes, sir, but the truck was maintaining a safe distance. This was a narrow mountain road with no exits. Evasive driving tactics were not possible."

"Anything's possible," he growled, "if you've got the guts to do it."

"The truck was on my bumper, going too fast. At the curve, he smacked my rear fender. I recovered and we reached an open stretch of road. I pulled far ahead."

"The truck didn't keep up?"

"No, sir, he fell back. When I got to a place where I could turn, I did a one-eighty and got ready to ambush this guy. But he was gone."

"Did you pursue?"

"My job is to keep your daughter and the Prescott home safe." He nodded to Lexie, acknowledging that the retreat was her idea. She didn't see him. Her eyes were still closed. "We immediately came back to the house, where the security system is fully activated. The police will come here to take our statements."

"Well, Mason, it sounds like you're doing a fine job. Put my Franny on. She's listening to this call, isn't she? Francine Alexandra DeMille, you pick up the phone."

Mason didn't give her the chance. He wasn't letting this guy off the hook until he got some answers. "What can you tell me about the Damascus Cache?"

"Sorry, son, that information is above your pay grade. It's none of your business."

"When somebody tries to run me off the road, it becomes my business. Why would somebody who's interested in the cache come after Lexie? Could there be a connection to her earlier accident?"

"Whoa, there. I never said these two incidents were connected. You're jumping to conclusions."

"She knows." He paused for a moment, allowing those words to sink in. "Lexie knows that the first accident was a warning to the intelligence community in the Middle East. She knows that she was hurt to prove a point. Helena Prescott sat her down and had a heart-to-heart talk."

"Damn it, Helena had no right to shoot off her mouth."

"Your daughter has a right to know." Her eyes were open, staring at him. He couldn't tell if she was angry or on the verge of tears.

"It was my fault," DeMille said. "My baby girl was almost killed because of my job."

"Like father, like daughter. Lexie blames herself for taking you away from the work that you love." He could have been angry with these two. They were so busy trying to protect each other that they didn't realize how much they were hurting themselves. "I've never known a family so anxious to take responsibility. You and your daughter must love each other very much."

"She's the light of my life." His voice caught, and he exhaled a ragged breath. "Tell me the truth, Mason. Is there any way I could help if I came to Aspen?"

"The investigation has run into one snafu after another. Prescott has no idea where the cache might be, and the Anti-Conspiracy Committee for Democracy thinks he's lying and has the cache hidden in the house. The CIA has made a search. The NSA is coming tomorrow." He decided not to mention the bomblets on the roof. "There's a serious lack of evidence."

"You're grasping at straws, young man. That's why you asked me about connections between Lexie's accident and this truck that bumped your fender."

"The truck was in serious pursuit. But he quit after one tap. Why?"

"The real question is, why do you think I'd know?"

"Because you probably know more about Lexie's first accident than anyone."

"You're right about that. I researched the hell out of the accident, got real serious about forensics and watched every interview with every suspect," he rambled on, describing a desperate yet futile investigation where he was riding the detectives every step of the way. "As you know, they never caught the bastard who did it."

"Did you work up a profile?"

"You know I did."

"Will you fax it to me?"

"I'll do better than that, Mason. I'll make a copy of the whole file and ship it express. There might be some detail that helps your investigating."

"Technically, I'm not an investigator."

"But you're in this up to your elbows." He chuckled. "Now will you put my daughter on the phone?"

Mason handed over the phone and left the room. As he closed the door, he heard her say, "I love you, too."

AFTER THE BEST talk she'd ever had with her dad, Lexie came out of the office to find Mason. She checked the time on her phone. She and her dad had only spoken for fifteen minutes, but she felt deeply loved by a man whose gruff manner couldn't completely conceal his open heart.

Not in the kitchen. "Mason? Where are you?"

"Upstairs."

She skipped down the hall and across the foyer toward the sweeping staircase that climbed to the second floor. Mason was unpacking the few belongings he'd brought with him in the best, largest bedroom suite in the house. Twice the size of the other bedrooms, this guest suite also had a sitting room with a huge sofa and chairs. There was even a desk by the window. The decor was a classic southwestern style. Two woven rugs with deep blues, sienna and turquoise decorated the floor. The rough-hewn coffee table held a round, fat cactus.

"Nice room," she said.

"I thought so."

"You think you're pretty hot stuff."

"There's a reason I'm taking this room. We're both going to sleep in here."

"Me? With you?" She didn't dare! Being that close to him would be too tempting, and she was determined to keep their relationship at the friend level. "I don't think so."

"It's not a choice," he said. "I can't protect you if we're sleeping in separate rooms."

"Oh, please. Do you really think somebody is going to get past all this security and sneak up on me?"

"After talking to your dad, I'm not going to take that chance."

Her father had that effect. "Yeah, if anything happens to me, you're a dead man."

He pointed to the extra-long king-size bed. "There's

plenty of room. You could fit all the Prescott kids and a small pony in that bed."

On this issue, she had to put her foot down. No way were they sleeping in the same bed. "There's the sofa. If you insist on being in the same room, you can sleep there."

"I suppose you know there's a tub with massaging water jets in the bathroom."

"On occasion, I've been known to take a nice, long soak in there. It uses less water than the hot tub."

"And you can be naked." He wiggled his eyebrows. "How did the rest of the conversation with your dad go?"

"Great! I forgave him and vice versa. He's still worried about me, but not so much with you being here. He's already looked up TST Security on his computer, and he believes you're qualified."

"Good to know."

"He checked out your photo. Likes your buzz cut."

"I don't wear it this way to impress retired marines," he said. "I like it short in the summer because it's efficient and cool when I'm outside."

"Apparently, there's a photo of you and your Land Rover on the TST website. He said to tell you it was a good vehicle."

"Ha!" He sank onto the sofa that would be his bed. "Your dad is a sneaky old codger. That's why he was asking about my car. First thing he did when we started talking was to look me up."

"'Sneaky old codger'?" She nodded. "That would be accurate."

From downstairs, she heard the familiar doorbell chime: "Yo ho ho, and a bottle of rum." She left the room. "That must be the cops."

"Lieutenant Hough," he reminded her. "Be nice to the guy. He's going out of his way for us."

"Don't go into the house," the leader said. "That is a direct order, Tony."

"What if I could slip in there for a few minutes and plant some bugs?" He'd had listening devices all over the house before the CIA came through and cleaned them out like a bunch of high-tech maids. "Or a camera."

"I don't want you to take the risk of getting caught. I need you. You're my best man."

"Damn right, I am."

"But if you ever pull a stunt like you did earlier, I'll get rid of you. No more easy paydays. No more fun."

"But there was no harm done."

"You ignored my orders. Never do that again."

Tony ended the call and dropped his glowing cell phone on the seat of the used sedan he'd bought in Denver when he knew he'd be spending time in the mountains. He didn't want to lose his easy paycheck.

Chasing down the bodyguard's Land Rover wasn't the first time Tony had disobeyed a direct order from the leader. There had been the incident in Montreal when he was supposed to grab a Russian drug lord off the street and rough him up. The guy was a loudmouth jerk. Tony had shut him up for good.

Ultimately, it turned out to be a good thing that he'd eliminated the threat from the Russian, but the leader had been angry when it happened. The same way he was mad at Tony for crashing into the Land Rover when he was only supposed to keep an eye on Lexie.

Tony hadn't set out to break the rules, hadn't planned it. He just couldn't stop himself.

When she and the bodyguard left the house, he'd been surprised. If Tony had been locked inside that mansion with a sexy little babe like Lexie, he wouldn't go anywhere. They had plenty of food, booze, a pool table, video games and a swimming pool. Hell, they even had their own movie theater in the basement.

He had watched them drive away. He didn't have to tail them because he'd already attached a GPS tracer to the bodyguard's car, but he followed, anyway. And he noticed another car watching. They were forming a damn parade.

That was when he got the idea of running them off the road. It'd be ironic. Five years ago, he'd almost killed Lexie with a car crash. It was one of his first assignments from the leader. At first, he thought the crash was a dumb idea. He'd told the leader that a bullet was more efficient, and he'd been right. She survived the accident. Apparently, that was the best outcome, after all. A bunch of the undercover ops and agents came to visit the sick little girl, and they could all imagine their family members going through a struggle like hers.

A year and a half ago, he'd arranged to meet her. He'd been expecting an invalid. At the very least, she'd be wheelchair bound or limping around on a cane. Instead, he found this energetic little fireball. She was hot. She was tough. And she owed her life to him.

He was ready to collect that debt. His first car accident failed to kill her. This one would succeed. If not, he had his rifle. He'd stolen a truck and waited. By the time they left the restaurant, he was pumped.

Making sure they didn't have another tail, he followed at a distance. At times, he let them get out of his sight and tracked them on the GPS. They wouldn't suspect a thing until…

Tony closed in at the first of the hairpin curves. That damn bodyguard was a good driver. His car was in control. When the first hit failed to even slow them down, Tony fell back. His plan was to wait for them to come to him.

He would have shot the bodyguard and kidnapped Lexie. But they never showed. Cowards.

The way he figured, she owed him one.

Chapter Seventeen

The detective from the Aspen police was cordial and efficient and offered very little hope of finding the driver who ran into them. The truck might have been stolen. Or the dirt obscuring the license plate might be legitimate grime. It could be local teens messing around.

It was frustrating not to get answers, but she understood. Everything about this case was baffling. Top agents in the CIA and NSA were stumped. Why should she expect local law enforcement to figure it out? It was clear that the Aspen police chief was backing away from this mess as quickly as possible. The five guys who were arrested at the hotel had already been transferred to federal custody and were being charged with attempted terrorism…or something like that.

After the lieutenant had recorded her statement, her interest waned to a mere sliver. Mason and the cop went into the garage to look at his crumpled fender, and she didn't bother to tag along. Though this hadn't been a physically taxing day, not compared with her usual chasing around with the kids, which kept her on her feet, she was tired. Today weighed heavily on her emotions.

From her first trickle of fear when Mason arrived to finding the bomblets to the car chase that had been horribly reminiscent of what happened to her five years ago.

She recalled what Mason had said. *This time, we'll get him.* What did he mean by that? It couldn't be the same driver, it couldn't be.

After they'd said good-night to the lieutenant, she trudged upstairs. Mason followed, making sure that she was going to bed in the large guest suite instead of her own cozy room.

As he watched, she dropped her nightshirt—a gift from Princess Stella that was covered in pink unicorns—at the lower end of the king-size bed and pulled back the gazillion-thread-count mauve duvet. "You know, movie stars have slept on this mattress. Famous people, fabulous people."

"Anybody I'd know?"

"I don't know. What kind of movies do you like?"

"I like when stuff blows up." He gave her a sheepish grin. "And zombies, yeah, I like zombies."

She named two older actors who starred in a zombie franchise. "And we've had vampires. And aliens."

"That must be fun."

"Not so much," she said. "These people are Helena's friends. They like visiting here because of the skiing. Since I'm not much of a skier or snowboarder, they have more in common with the guy who drives them to the slopes."

"Skiing is one of those things you never learned in Texas," he said. "I'm not great, but I could show you a couple of moves."

"Too bad there's no snow."

"But there will be in a couple of months," he said. "Winter always comes around too fast."

"I hope you're not planning to stay here as my bodyguard for the changing of the seasons."

"Maybe I wouldn't be your bodyguard."

"Stop!" She threw up a palm. "I don't make long-range plans. Leave the future to take care of itself."

She snatched up her nightshirt and stomped into the bathroom. Too bad she'd forgotten her toothpaste and brush from her bathroom down the hall. Her dramatic exit was ruined when she stomped past him again.

When she returned with her bathroom supplies, he was sprawled out on the sofa with his long legs stretched out straight in front of him. "I have an idea for our investigation, Nancy Drew. You want to hear it?"

"Toothpaste first."

"It's always something," he grumbled.

She returned to the room, went to the desk by the window and closed the laptop computer she'd placed there earlier. Then she perched on the desk chair, which just happened to be the farthest spot away from his sofa. "Okay, what's this big idea?"

"Let's agree that we can trust the admiral. That means he's not hiding the cache and hasn't seen it in years."

"Okay." She liked the way he laid things out logically.

"But the AC-CD group is certain the cache is in this house. That means someone else brought it to the house. And there's an informant who talked to AC-CD."

"This all makes sense," she said. "So we have to figure out who planted it and find the mole. When you break the problem down, the solution seems easy."

"Then you add in the dozens of people who have visited this house recently. You estimated that there were thirty in the past four days."

She started taking a tally on her fingers. The admiral and his entourage, including Josh and bodyguards, had flitted through on their way to the Pentagon. Helena's hairdresser and stylist came by before she left for California, because there was no way she intended to face her hunky ex-husband without looking fabulous. The older kids had had friends over. There had been a playdate for the little ones with three friends and their parents. The cook and her assistant received food and wine deliveries. The maids came through on Wednesday. The housekeeper had an appointment with an accountant. "At least thirty."

"We need a chart like the one downstairs that you made to keep track of the family's vacations. It'd show who came to visit, how long they stayed and if there was overlapping timing."

"I can use records from the housekeeper and the cook to put that together." His idea was proactive, and she'd much rather be working on that than sitting and waiting for the next weird assault. "I see only one problem with this. After we have everybody listed, how do we know who's guilty?"

"One step at a time." He hopped off the sofa and crossed the room to the desk where she was sitting. He leaned down and lightly kissed her forehead. "We'll take it one step at a time."

She wasn't sure if he was still talking about crime solving or their possible relationship.

Both, she hoped.

LEXIE WAS IN the middle of a nightmare, but she wasn't really scared because she knew she was asleep. The scenario was too obvious. A faceless driver dodged through a thick forest to chase her. He kept gunning the engine of his truck. *Vroom, vroom, vroom.* He was coming closer, and she was running but not really hard, not struggling. Then the scenery changed.

She was on a beach with the surf crashing and receding on hard sand. When she looked over her shoulder, the car was gone. A man was running toward her.

Even though he was far away, she recognized Mason's muscular shoulders and buzz haircut. He was running hard and wearing red trunks like the guys on *Baywatch*. *Vroom, vroom, vroom*. As Mason got closer, he was joined by members of the old cast, tanned men and gorgeous women in red suits. Over the sound of the surf, she could still hear the revving of the truck. *Vroom...*

She blinked and was awake. What did that dream mean? She was afraid of the car coming after her. That much was clear. But was she also afraid of having Mason pursue her? Or maybe her nightmare was about crime. Maybe it was telling her that David Hasselhoff was the faceless driver in the truck.

Squinting, she could see across the large room to the sofa where Mason curled on his side, unable to stretch out all the way. In contrast, her body barely made a ripple under the duvet on the huge bed. It really wasn't fair for her to have all this wonderful space to spread out while he was cramped. She ought to offer to trade for the rest of the night.

She slipped from the covers. The big room was cool at night, which was good for sleeping but not running around. She padded across the woven Navajo rugs to his sofa. If he was sound asleep, it meant he wasn't uncomfortable, and she'd leave him there. *Let sleeping dogs lie.* His eyes were closed.

On tiptoe, she approached and leaned over him, hardly daring to breathe in case she woke him. His dark eyelashes made crescents above his heavy cheekbones. His jaw and mouth were relaxed, making his lips appear fuller and softer. Glancing down, she noticed that he wasn't wearing a shirt.

A shiver of awareness went through her. She wanted him, wanted to feel his warm flesh against hers. It had been over a year since she'd been intimate with a man, and she felt a familiar need.

Lexie had never been a prude. Maybe because she grew up around men, she'd never learned to play flirty games like other girls. She enjoyed sex, and she was surprised when others complained about how they never got satisfaction from the act. She did, multiple times. A low groan escaped her lips. She missed it.

His eyes popped open. Even in the darkness of the bedroom, that flash of blue was startling. Before she could do or say anything, he grabbed her and pulled her on top of him.

He kissed her. His arm encircled her. His large hand cradled the back of her skull, holding her so she couldn't move, couldn't escape while his mouth ravaged hers. Usually, she didn't think in those terms. *Ravage* wasn't a word she used, but there was nothing else she could call it when he was so demanding and so dominant.

It was purely impossible for her to hold back. She flung herself against his bare chest. He was so toasty warm. She kissed the hard column of his neck and the hollow of his throat while his musky scent coiled around her. She glided her fingers down his arm, tracing the ridges of his thick, hard muscles under his supple skin.

She groaned again, arched her back. His hands were all over her, pulling up her unicorn nightshirt. He almost reached her breast. She stopped breathing, waiting at the peak of anticipation.

Then…he stopped.

He opened his arms wide.

She scooted away from him so quickly that her bottom landed with a thud on the floor. She pushed her hair off her face and glared into the darkness. "What?"

"I didn't mean to grab you like that," he mumbled as he sat up on the sofa. "I thought I was dreaming."

If they had both been asleep, sex would have been appropriate. There would be no messiness, no strings attached and no thoughts of their potential for a future life together. "But we're not sleeping."

"What are you doing all the way over here?" he asked.

"I felt sorry for you, all squished up on the sofa."

"Thank you." Before she could say that she no longer had any qualms about making him sleep here, he was on the move. He threw off the sheets and blankets. She was glad to see that he wasn't sleeping naked, but had on gray jersey boxer shorts. He shivered once, acknowledging that it was chilly in here, and then he charged across the room. In seconds, he was under the duvet on the opposite side of the bed from hers.

He exhaled a huge sigh as he snuggled into the pillows. "Oh, yeah. This is heaven."

Though she couldn't see his face, she knew he was smiling. She couldn't interpret the meaning of a sigh, but she knew he was happy. And she didn't have the heart to throw him out.

As she got under her covers, she said, "You have to stay over there."

"Not a problem."

"I mean it, Mason. Don't come sneaking across the bed in the middle of the night."

To emphasize her words, she constructed a wall of pillows using the ones on the bed and running back and forth to the sofa.

When she had them all piled up, he peeked over the top. "Is this supposed to stop me?"

"It's supposed to get your attention," she said. "Then

you'll notice that you're not sleeping and you'll stop yourself. Because you're a gentleman."

"Right," he drawled. "How is it that you don't have a custom-made chastity belt?"

She delivered a serious karate chop to the pillows. "I never needed one."

"Good night, Lexie."

She rearranged the duvet. With Mason in the bed—on the other side of the pillow wall—she fell asleep quickly and wasn't aware of any other bad dreams. When she woke, sunlight was streaming around the edges of the drapes. The digital clock showed the time as 7:22 a.m. She heard the thrum from the shower in the attached bathroom.

He'd interrupted her shower yesterday. Turnabout was fair play. She ought to sneak in there and steal all the towels. But no, she didn't want to encourage him.

Last night, their kiss had been accidental. At least, she could pretend that she'd never meant for it to happen, that she'd somehow been sleepwalking and had fallen on top of him. And all her groaning and groping was part of a nightmare where she was wrestling an octopus.

There was no excuse for that very hot, sexy kiss and embrace. She couldn't deny that she had wanted him. But she didn't need to mention it, either.

They were going to be spending a lot of time together over the next few weeks. She had to make sure their friendship didn't turn into anything more serious.

A romantic relationship would never work. Not only was there the whole issue of her not being able to have kids, but they were set on different paths in their lives. He was determined to make TST Security a success. She liked being a nanny.

There couldn't be anything between them.

Chapter Eighteen

Lexie marched resolutely to her bedroom, avoiding the temptation of lolling around in the king-size bed and watching Mason emerge from the shower with a towel slung around his hips. Nothing was going to happen between them. They were working together to find the cache. Other than that? *Nada.*

In her own small bathroom, she splashed water on her face, brushed her teeth using an extra brush she found in her cabinet and applied the tiniest bit of makeup. Just because she wasn't trying to seduce him, she didn't need to look like an escapee from one of those zombie movies he liked.

She made a mental note to tell him about the unique feature of the movie theater downstairs. Helena had wanted it to show films, but the admiral wanted a privacy room where no technology could reach him. He could flip a switch in the theater and create white noise so no one could listen with a bug. An invisible-to-the-naked-eye spectrum of light masked the presence of anyone in that room, and it could even fool infrared technology. Being able to disappear might come in handy.

She dragged a brush through her hair and pulled it up in a ponytail. For clothes, she put on sweats, a long-sleeve T-shirt and a fleece vest to ward off the morning coolness.

Nothing sexy or cute about this outfit. Then she bounded downstairs to make coffee.

Mason beat her to it. He stood over the coffeemaker and muttered, "Come on, how long does it take? Come on."

She took a mug from the shelf and joined him at the counter. "I heard you in the shower. How'd you get dressed so fast?"

"I air dried."

That would have been fun to watch. It seemed that he was one of those people who took a while to wake up. One of her brothers was like that—half conscious for the first hour of the day, totally unaware and funny without knowing it. "You must really need your coffee."

He rubbed his hand against his jaw. "Didn't shave."

His stubble came in fast. She guessed that he could sprout a full beard in a week or so. Apparently, he'd gotten the memo about not dressing up. On top, he wore a University of Denver sweatshirt that had been red about ten years ago. The sleeves stopped above his elbow and looked as if they'd been torn off by a grizzly bear. He wore baggy gray shorts on the bottom. No socks. Beat-up black moccasins.

Though he appeared to be inches away from homeless, there was still something appealing about him. The blond fur on his forearms and calves was probably longer than his buzz-cut hair, and she had a crazy urge to stroke him like a hound.

The coffeemaker was done, and she poured cups for both of them. He stumbled around the counter to a stool, sat and took a long sip. He scowled. "You're wide awake."

"Almost eight o'clock, it's time to get started. I should call the admiral and tell him about Grossman and Bertinelli coming here to search. Plus I'll report about the chase."

"Be sure to tell him that we talked to your dad."

"I will." That was her main reason for calling. Her talk with her dad had been great, and she didn't want Prescott calling him and saying anything that would make him worry.

"I texted both the admiral and Helena last night. You're aware of that, aren't you?"

"That was *your* business—bodyguard business. When I talk to them, it's more about family." She sipped her coffee. "And I want to get started on the charts we talked about."

His expression was blank. "Charts?"

She pointed to the listing on the wall that he'd used as an example last night. "We talked about this. The chart would show people who have been to the house, when they came, how long they stayed, et cetera. Then we can figure out who brought the cache here and hid it."

As she continued, he seemed to remember. He nodded, drank coffee and nodded faster.

"A spreadsheet for suspects," she said.

"And the room," he said. "You're going to open the safe room for me."

She wished he'd forget that little promise. To access the safe room, she needed to use Helena's personal computer. It felt like prying, and she was afraid of running across something private and secretive, like the time she'd accidentally opened the diary Helena had written when she and Prescott were dating. All doodled with hearts, everything was sweet and sexy and it was none of Lexie's business. But once she'd taken that first peek, she couldn't look away.

Mason finished his coffee and went down to the gym for a morning workout. Two hours later, she found him back in the kitchen, eating a bowl of granola cereal with a banana and, of course, more coffee. He looked like a new man. The stubble was gone, and he was dressed in layers for a spring day in Aspen with cargo shorts and hiking boots, a T-shirt on top and a plaid flannel over that.

"Wow," she said drily. "You look like the centerfold for an L.L.Bean catalog."

"Hey, this is how I dress. I've lived in Colorado for a very long time. I'm outdoorsy."

"Just keep telling yourself that, city boy."

His grin brightened the whole room. Then he shoveled in another spoonful of granola. "What have you got there?"

She flipped open her laptop. "I transferred records from the cook and the housekeeper to make a list of visitors for the past year. Taken one day at a time, it doesn't seem like much. But over a twelve-month period, there have been over three hundred people in the house."

"Can you break it down?"

"Already did. I eliminated locals, like delivery people and repairmen. Then I took out friends of the kids and social groups, like a charity board who met here to discuss their event."

"Did you keep those people on a separate list?"

"As a matter of fact, I did." It had taken some effort to compile these names, and she didn't want to dump them until they were sure they didn't need them. "Why?"

"A delivery person who appears innocent might be your faceless driver who tried to crash into us. Or might have planted the bomblets on the roof. Or could be searching for the cache."

She hadn't considered that possibility. Randy, the local florist who could whip up a centerpiece at a moment's notice, took on a more sinister aspect. How did he know Helena's favorite flowers were white roses?

She scrolled through the pages. "The last two groups are the movie people and the government types."

"Helena's friends." He turned his right palm up as

though he could hold these directors, actors and the starving writers as one group. "And Edgar's associates."

"I've been concentrating on the government types," she said. "There's not much I know about their backgrounds. It might be helpful to figure out who knows who."

"No problem. The computer guy at TST can take care of the research."

"Dylan," she said, recalling the lanky guy with the ponytail at the hotel. "He seems decent."

"A real peach."

He scraped the last nibble of cereal into his mouth, took his bowl to the sink, rinsed it and put it in the dishwasher. The easy way he went through these motions made her think that he was in the habit of cleaning up after himself. Mason was good at planning ahead, a trait that suited him well as a bodyguard. And he was tidy, almost obsessively.

The man was perfect husband material. Too bad she wasn't looking for a spouse.

"Okay," he said, "let's do the safe room."

MASON FOLLOWED HER up the stairs to the bedroom suite that belonged to the admiral and his lady. It wasn't any bigger than the bedroom they'd slept in last night, but the Prescotts' room had a sultry, sexy aura. The colors were deeper, richer, and there were lots of subtle personal touches. Helena's fancy bottles of lotions and perfumes mingled with his clothing brushes, aftershave and an opened bottle of single malt. There were chocolates in a container that looked like the Eiffel Tower and a cigar humidor with a couple of Cubans. She had a book on her side of the bed. From the steamy cover, it had to be a romance.

That was what the guest room lacked: romance. It was clean and attractively furnished, but there was no passion. By contrast, the Prescotts' suite was loaded with charac-

ter. There were two desks by windows on either side of
the bed. Helena's desk was strewn with knickknacks, including three acting awards, and her computer. Her husband had a filing cabinet on wheels. Mason went over and
flipped the lid open. It was jam-packed with paperwork.

"It looks like the admiral hangs on to everything."

"This is a huge improvement," she said. "His assistant
convinced him to do a monthly sweep to dump the junk.
Last month, Josh found a warranty for a Betamax player
from 1977."

"I guess it makes sense that Prescott would be in possession of the last remaining copy of the Damascus Cache.
It's strange that his office downstairs is so neat."

"You love that office," she said.

"I do. I like to put my feet on the desk and pretend that
I'm ruling the world."

"Yeah, well, the people who really rule the world don't
operate like that." She crooked a finger at him. "You've
got to see this."

"Where are we going?"

"Not far." In the hall, they took a sharp right turn. She
pushed open a door, turned on the light and stepped aside
so he could enter first. "The office downstairs is just for
show. This is where the admiral does his real work."

Chaos reigned. The working office held dozens of cabinets and a huge scarred and battered wooden desk. Every
flat surface was covered with papers and weird objects,
like model cars and navy caps. The walls were hung with
photos; unlike the posed shots downstairs, these were
mostly snapshots.

Lexie slipped inside behind him. "I think this represents
what's going on inside his head. It looks like a wild jumble,
but the admiral knows where everything is. He can walk
in the door and lay his hand on whatever he's looking for."

"What did Collier and the CIA guys say when they knew they had to search this room?"

"I wasn't close enough to hear the exact words. Helena told me there were a lot of French curses being thrown around." She gazed directly into his eyes. "An office like this would drive you crazy."

"I like to see the surface of my desk," he admitted. "But there's something I've always wanted to do with an office like this."

"Set fire to it?" she sweetly suggested.

"I'd like to do one of those one-armed sweeps and knock everything onto the floor. Then I'd grab the girl." He suited the action to the word. He cleared a space, took hold of her arm and spun her around. "Then I'd put her on the desk."

He leaned her backward on the wood surface. Though she hadn't resisted him, he saw the fire in her eyes. Her lips pulled back from her teeth.

"That's enough," she snarled.

"Then I'd take off her glasses."

"I don't wear glasses."

"You're beautiful, Lexie." He wasn't playing anymore. Looking down at her, he was struck by a realization so sudden that it had to be true. She was everything he had ever wanted. She was the woman he'd been waiting for. "You're so damn beautiful."

She sat up quickly. "The admiral isn't going to like that you touched his stuff."

"He won't mind when I tell him what I was doing."

"You wouldn't!"

"Don't worry. I'll claim it was an accident. Better yet, I'll blame Collier."

As she stomped from the room, he wondered at her reaction. She liked him, he knew she did. When they were on their date, they were enjoying each other. Why was she constantly pushing him away?

Carrying Helena's computer, Lexie returned to the office and set it down on the counter. After fiddling around on a couple of different sites, she wrote down a six-digit combination to open the safe room. She carefully tucked the note into her pocket and headed for the stairs. "I can't share this with you, Mason."

She wasn't sharing much. The atmosphere between them grew colder and colder. They'd be together for a couple of weeks, at least. There was time enough for him to be patient with her. But he didn't understand. Had he done something to make her mad?

At the door to the safe room, he stayed all the way down the hall so she wouldn't think he was sneaking a peek at the supersecret combination. Carefully, she turned the dial in the middle of the door. When the last tumbler clicked into place, she grabbed the door handle and pulled. The heavy door slowly swung open.

This time, she went first. At the flick of a switch, a cool overhead light came on. The rectangular concrete room was as carefully packed as a shopping boutique. The free-standing wardrobe hangers held several see-through bags, some of gowns and others of fur. Metal lockboxes were stacked on shelves. Three wooden crates marked "Fragile" lined the far wall. Storage racks covered with muslin or plastic held several paintings.

"It's cold," he said.

"The temperature is steady between fifty-five degrees and sixty, which is optimum for the furs. The humidity is set at twenty percent, which is best for the oil paintings."

"If the family ever had to use this room for an extended time, their combined body heat would throw off the storage temp and humidity."

"Here's hoping that Helena never needs to choose between her children and her furs."

He pushed the door closed. A chill intimacy surrounded them. It was just the two of them, tucked away from the rest of the world. Mason had never been a guy who worried about his relationships and dating. But here she was...the girl of his dreams. Getting close to Lexie meant opening himself to the possibility of losing her. She'd made it real clear that she didn't want anything long term

But he did.

There was trouble ahead. He sensed the impending explosion. The fuse had been lit and the bomb was ticking down to zero hour. He wanted time to duck for cover.

"Is something wrong," he asked, "between you and me?"

"Why? Because I wouldn't have sex with you last night?"

"I wasn't even thinking of that." He paused. It was best to be honest. "Well, yeah, I was thinking about you in bed and how cute you looked in the morning with all those pillows around you. But that's not what I'm talking about. You seem angry."

"I told you before, Mason."

"Got it," he said. "No long-term commitments or relationships. I don't want that, either."

"You don't?"

Now she sounded hurt. He couldn't win! "Are we going to search in here or what?"

She went to the shelves and took down a metal box. Sitting at a small table, she unfastened the latch. Inside, she found an incredible brooch in the shape of a flamingo, a tiara with a huge blue stone, a diamond bracelet and a couple of rings.

When she looked up at him, a tear slipped down her cheek. She quickly dashed it away. "I never thought my life could be like this. I'm juggling diamonds and rubies, and I think the blue one is tanzanite. This is a good job, it pays well and I like the kids. I don't want anything to change."

"Never?"

She carefully returned the jewels to their box. "I'm not going to be a nanny forever. But I'm definitely not leaving a job I really like because some man wants me to."

Not making any sense. She'd gone back to angry. Now she was referring to him as "some man," and her tone implied that man was a jerk. "Fine."

"You bet it's fine."

He took down a box and opened it. More jewels.

Another was marked "Important Papers." Inside were legal documents, deeds, car titles and other stuff. He sat at the table to sort through it.

Lexie was far from calm. She flipped through the paintings in the storage racks. "I suppose I should take each of these paintings out and feel around the edges for a flash drive."

"Not necessary," he said.

"I want to be thorough."

He placed another metal box on the table and lifted the lid. It was filled with cash—mostly hundreds. With relish, he plunged his hands into it and felt around. "I can see why the Prescotts didn't want the CIA searching down here."

"And not the NSA, either." She went to a wooden crate that was taller than she was. "Should we break these down and see what's inside?"

"I don't think so." He closed the money box and put it on the shelf. "We're done in here."

"Why?"

"Reason number one—the Prescotts aren't deliberately hiding the cache, and this safe room is always closed.

Number two—the Damascus Cache is not a flash drive or a microdot."

"Hold on." She waved her arms. "That's what everybody has been looking for, a drive that plugs into a computer."

"Do you think the admiral knows how to use a flash drive?" He asked the rhetorical question and didn't wait for an answer. "From everything I've seen, this is a man who loves documents and disdains technology. If someone wanted to give him a copy of the cache, they'd bring a paper copy of the original."

Her eyes got wide. "You're on to something."

Finally, an acknowledgment. He bowed from the waist. "Thank you, Nancy Drew."

Mason might not be a detective and might not have the right stuff for a long-term relationship, but he was smarter than people expected.

Now he knew what to look for.

Chapter Nineteen

At two o'clock in the afternoon, Grossman and Bertinelli rang the sea chantey doorbell at the Prescott house. Instead of taking them into the cozy kitchen, Lexie escorted them to the huge, sprawling front room with the magnificent furniture that Helena brought to the marriage. There were two Degas paintings on the wall, perfectly maintained and perfectly lit, but the artwork was nothing compared to the view through the arched windows.

This was a breathtaking room; very impressive. She'd purposely brought the NSA agents here so they wouldn't dismiss her as the nanny or a pesky Nancy Drew. She wanted them to take her seriously, and she had learned—by watching Helena—that a display of wealth almost always got respect.

"Gentlemen, please sit. Have some lemonade. Before we get started, I want to set parameters for your search. And I have a few questions."

"This isn't a quid pro quo," Bertinelli said. "You don't get to ask. Our work is classified."

She'd expected a prissy-pants response from him. For one thing, he didn't like her. For another, he was frustrated by having to answer to Grossman, who was sort of a moron. She smiled and said, "I'd never expect you to betray classified secrets."

She sat on a Scandinavian-style chair beside the sofa. On the coffee table was a tray holding a pitcher of iced lemonade, alongside bowls of strawberries, cream and scones. Though Bertinelli held back, Grossman didn't hesitate before digging in. He sloshed the lemonade on the tray when he poured and loaded a delicate china plate with scones and one strawberry.

"I'm guessing," Grossman said, "there are places the admiral doesn't want us to search. I'm sure he's got private stuff. We all do."

"You have permission to go anywhere," she said, "but Mason and I will accompany you."

Mason came forward and shook hands with both men. Before the NSA agents arrived, she and Mason had decided not to be friendly. He had told her repeatedly that he didn't trust them.

"I should mention," he said, "that the CIA swept for bugs and cameras after their search. And I've gone through the house again. If I find any electronic devices after you leave, I'll have to assume they came from the NSA."

"Why would I bug you?" Grossman asked.

"Doesn't make sense to me," Mason said. "But you boys staked out the house. And you followed us to the restaurant. We must be doing something that you find interesting."

Ignoring the napkin, Grossman wiped his mouth on the sleeve of his beat-up sweatshirt. With his messy steel-wool hair and sloppy clothes, he was dressed for searching in dark corners of the garage and going through crawl spaces. He looked toward his neatly dressed partner.

"I forget," Grossman said. "Why are we watching them?"

"I thought it was your idea."

Lexie got the sense that Bertinelli was more in charge

than the senior agent. She cleared her throat. "The admiral asked me to put together a list of all the people who have been in and out of the house in the past year."

"That's got to be a significant list," Bertinelli said as he finally sat down. "How many names?"

"Over three hundred."

"I want a copy," Bertinelli said.

She pinched her lips together so she wouldn't blurt out what a jerk he was. Why should it be okay for him to get information from her but not the other way around? "Of course, after I get the okay from Admiral Prescott."

"Why do you want it?" Mason asked.

"You never know what might be useful in an investigation," Bertinelli said. "Information is power."

She centered her laptop on the coffee table in front of her. "I'm hoping you can give me details about the people whose photos I'm going to show you. The kind of thing I wouldn't find in a casual search on the internet."

"The dirt," Grossman said. He popped another scone in his mouth.

"I don't mean to gossip," she said.

"Sure you do. When you come right down to it, that's what we do as federal agents. Track down rumors and mine for gossip. Show me the pictures."

She started popping up the pictures on the laptop screen. Mason's computer genius partner had already found ID photos and provided minibiographies. She wanted the gossip. Among all these people, many of whom were tied to the intelligence community, who would have access to the Damascus Cache? Why would they drop it off with the admiral?

Grossman had a lot to say about the handsome Agent Collier, who was sleeping with his supervisor, Margaret Gray, and had bedded three or four other undercover agents.

"Under the cover of his sheets," Grossman said with a laugh.

She'd slipped in Josh Laurent's photo to see if she'd get a reaction. Grossman pointed at the screen. "Isn't that Prescott's assistant?"

She faked surprise. "Oh, you're right. That must have gotten in there by mistake."

"Or maybe not," Bertinelli said. "We've been looking far and wide for suspects. Maybe we should stick to our own backyard. Josh does a lot of whining about why he hasn't been promoted. He's a fan of conspiracy theories."

"Good to know."

It would be ironic if this AC-CD scheme had been engineered by the admiral's pointy-nosed assistant. Josh had the intelligence to create a complicated plot, but she didn't see him as someone who could organize other people. AC-CD was run by a mysterious figure called the leader. Josh? She doubted he could inspire followers.

One of the faces on her laptop belonged to Al Ackerman. Lexie didn't remember him from his visit. The housekeeper had made a note about special food requirements for his Saudi princess bride, but the new wife canceled and didn't make the trip. In her eyes, Al Ackerman became only another one of a group of spies. He had passed away this year.

"Murdered," Grossman said darkly.

She corrected him. "His bio says he died from complications after a heart attack."

"Sure, if those complications included a bullet. Everybody knew Ackerman, especially after he married the princess. In our business, that's dangerous."

Lexie had obtained all the information she wanted from

these two agents. She closed up her laptop and resigned herself to spending the rest of the day shepherding Grossman and Bertinelli around the house. No big deal.

She glanced over at Mason and winked. They were handling their investigation like a couple of ace detectives.

AFTER DINNER, MASON followed Lexie into the dramatic front room. It was easy to imagine this house filled with classy, cosmopolitan guests, from Helena's Hollywood contacts to the admiral's acquaintances from the world of international diplomacy. The Prescotts lived large.

Not a lifestyle he envied. Mason didn't need or want all that bustle and noise. The machinations of big money and international business fascinated him, but he was a behind-the-scenes guy. He liked to see how things worked.

He stood behind Lexie by one of the arched windows. Through the glass, a spectacular mountain sunset was unfolding with intense shades of crimson and gold. "So this is how the top one percent lives."

"It is," she said. "I've learned a lot in the past year."

Though he wanted to stroke her shoulders, he kept his hands to himself. "Is this what you want for yourself?"

"No." Her response was fast. "Living like this is way too high maintenance. The best part of the Prescotts' life doesn't have anything to do with money. They're a kind, caring family. And, best of all, Edgar and Helena are truly in love."

He didn't know them well, but he saw signs of their romance throughout the house and also when they were together. "Is that what you're looking for?"

She spun around to face him. "Are you sure I can't go for a walk outside?"

Her lightning-swift change of subject didn't escape him. Lexie would not be drawn into anything resembling a talk about relationships. He answered her question, "Until I'm sure there's no threat aimed at you, you're housebound."

"When will you be sure?"

"The Aspen police haven't found the truck that hit us. Basically, they've got no clue. If my back fender wasn't crumpled, they wouldn't believe it happened."

She paced in front of the window as though trying to simulate a walk in the forest. "Maybe tomorrow?"

"Maybe." There was no need for her to feel trapped. This house was like a very high-class amusement park. He selected the toy he'd most like to play with. "How about a soak in the hot tub?"

She beamed. "You're on."

Upstairs in the giant bedroom, he changed into olive green board shorts. If it had been up to him, he would have gone in the hot tub naked, but he was pretty sure Lexie wouldn't go for it. Before he dashed down to the workout room, he grabbed his shoulder holster. Even though he downplayed the danger, he kept in mind their suspects as well as the person driving the truck. Somebody wanted her dead. It was his job to make sure that didn't happen.

They went downstairs to the gym together. Her coral-colored one-piece bathing suit was just about the sexiest thing he'd ever seen. It wasn't skimpy, but the color was close to her skin tone. When she dropped the towel she'd wrapped around her waist, she appeared to be naked.

He had used this type of hot tub before and got the water started. Before he could play around with adjustments to the temperature, Lexie informed him that the maintenance for the hot tub and the pool was taken care of by the maid service.

A nice perk. There were some things about living large that he could get accustomed to.

The tub was designed for six, so there was plenty of room for him and Lexie to bob around while it filled. It would have been nice to use the lap pool as well, but he understood her concern with wasting water. Drought was a consistent problem in the West. This house had its own well and septic system, but the water table was only so large. Conservation was necessary.

Lexie backed up to a water jet and moaned with pleasure as the water massaged her back. "I can never get enough of this. When I was recovering after the first crash, my dad bought a hot tub. I scolded him about wasting all that money. He laughed and said, 'What makes you think I bought it for you?'"

"Did he use it?"

"Constantly. And so did I."

She ducked her head under the frothy water and then popped up like a cork. She laughed and giggled and splashed as she bounced through the hot liquid. At one point, she burst from the water and darted across the floor to the light switch.

The gym went dark. There was enough glow from the tall windows beside the hot tub and pool to see what they were doing, and he knew when Lexie came back into the water. The great thing about the darkness was being able to look into the forest. The vertical trunks of pine trees formed a backdrop for the leafy thickets and occasional wildflower. Far away, he saw the shadow of the mountains.

"Ackerman," she said.

"What?"

"The guy who married the Saudi princess and was murdered this year. Ackerman. My dad mentioned him."

It was another connection between the past and the

present, between the first attack on her and the recent crash. Were they related? He had plenty to think about. For right now, he was content to relax with Lexie and to keep her safe.

Chapter Twenty

Three days had passed, and Lexie hadn't seen anyone but Mason. She'd talked on the phone to other people, but no one had come by the house, and she hadn't been allowed to leave. Not while the truck driver who tried to kill them was still on the loose.

When she considered her enforced alone time with Mason, she should have been bored, but they'd found plenty to do. This house offered a number of amusements. They'd spent time in the gym, watched movies in the theater and taken baths in the hot tub. Last night, she'd baked a pie from scratch. He'd trounced her on all the computer games, and she'd defeated him in chess.

Even more surprising, they hadn't run out of things to talk about. The investigating and her suspect spreadsheet took up some of their conversation, but mostly they talked about themselves, their families and friends, their hopes and dreams. Mason was the most comfortable man she'd ever known, except for one thing.

She missed sex.

He had respected her repeated statement about not wanting a relationship. They could be friends but nothing more. Ha! She wanted a lot more. His muscular body was a constant temptation, and the magnetism was about more than the way he looked. It was his easygoing smile. The way he moved when they did tai chi together. His laughter made her happy, and his rich baritone tickled her desires.

In the middle of the afternoon, she got off the phone in the kitchen and went in search of Mason. He was hanging out in the fancy downstairs office. On the desktop in front of him, he had three framed snapshots that he'd rescued from the chaotic upstairs office.

"Take a look at this," he said. "Here's our suspect, Agent Collier, with his arm around another suspect, his supervisor, whose name is Margaret. They're standing by the fireplace downstairs. I can't tell for sure, but it looks like he's patting her bottom. Grossman thought this was gossip, but they're out front about the attraction."

"That was at a luncheon on New Year's Day," she said. "I was just in the kitchen and—"

"This picture is five agents from NSA. They're a chummy group, but notice this. Bertinelli is glaring at Grossman like he wants to slit his throat."

She really didn't want to talk about suspects. "I had a phone call from Josh."

"One more photo. It's another group scene." He pushed it toward her. "Over on the right side is Ackerman. It looks like he's presenting something to the admiral. Can you tell what it is?"

She peered at the photo. "It's an Arabian vase made of brass that looks like Aladdin's lamp, only it's bigger and taller. I know exactly where it is."

He glanced up at her. His eyes were an unreal shade of blue. His lips moved and her attention shifted to his mouth. She heard him say, "Why do you know where the vase is?"

"I made it disappear." As she spoke, she gathered her self-control so she wouldn't fly across the desk and attach herself to him like a limpet on steroids. "The admiral had it downstairs in a place of honor because it was a gift from his buddy and the princess. Helena hated it. I've got to say, I'm on Helena's side. The vase is cheesy. She asked me to get it out of her sight. So I moved it to the admiral's office."

"Then it's nothing important?"

"Probably not."

Mason shrugged. "Did you say something about a phone call?"

"It was Josh. He told me that Helena was stopping by the outdoor camp in Oregon to check on Stella."

"What's wrong with the munchkin?"

"She's feeling sick," she said. "Then Josh told me that he's coming back to Aspen and staying at the house. His arrival is tomorrow at eleven thirty."

Mason's grin faltered. "We won't have the place to ourselves anymore."

She hadn't been planning to make a decision so quickly. For the past three nights, she'd spent many sleepless hours on her side of the pillows, trying to make up her mind. But now it hit her: a sudden, certain revelation. Nothing had ever been so clear. They needed to have sex before the house was invaded by Josh and others. They needed to have sex now.

She reached across the desk and took his hand. Her voice dropped to a husky whisper. "We should take advantage of our time alone. There's not much left. Come upstairs and help me move some pillows."

He vaulted out from behind the desk. "It's about time." He pulled her out to the hallway and into the foyer. "I've been obsessed with your pillow wall. I want to destroy it." He started on the staircase, taking two at a time. When she couldn't keep up, he yanked her off her feet and carried her. "Let's set all these damn pillows on fire."

He dropped her in the middle of the bed.

She grabbed a pillow with each hand and flung them onto the floor. "Down, wall, down."

Leaping up beside her, he got rid of more pillows.

In seconds the bed was cleared. They were standing on top of the mattress where famous people had slept, staring at each other and breathing hard. Mason unclipped his holster from his belt and carefully placed the gun on the bedside table. With an evil grin, he turned toward her. He lunged and tackled her and they crashed down together.

Lexie was not inexperienced when it came to sex, but Mason's kisses made her feel as if this were the first time. He was so eager, nearly desperate. His mouth was everywhere. His hands roamed wildly over her body. And she was the same way, unbuckling his belt and groping until she touched his hard erection. Her self-imposed drought was over. *Let it rain.*

Gradually, they slowed to a less frantic, more sensual pace. His long fingers combed her hair back from her face until he reached her ponytail. With a deft twist, he unfastened the band she used to hold her hair back.

Her curls tumbled free, and he paused, rising over her on the bed and gazing down. "You're a beautiful woman, Lexie."

How could she respond to that? To say yes would be arrogant. No was a sure indication of poor self-esteem.

"Same to you," she said. "I mean, not a woman. And *beautiful* probably isn't the right word."

"I know what you mean."

"I thought you might."

They had much in common, but they weren't a perfect fit. And there were still reasons why they shouldn't take this relationship to the next level. But she wasn't going to stop.

She stroked down his chest to the edge of his T-shirt,

and then she slipped her hand under the fabric and pulled it up, baring his torso and his rock-hard abs. She stroked and fondled and tweaked, and before she knew it, his shirt was off.

When she got dressed this morning, she hadn't consciously thought about having sex, but she'd worn the perfect outfit for a simple strip: a striped blue blouse with buttons and a front-fastening bra.

He pushed her back on the bed and went to work on the buttons. In a few practiced moves, he had unhooked her bra and pushed the flimsy lace aside. Slowly, he lowered his head and suckled at her breasts. With every lash of his tongue against her tight nipples, an electric surge shot through her body.

"The rest of these clothes need to be gone," she said. "Right now."

"You think?"

She looked down the length of his body. His belt was unfastened and his jeans were pushed down to show a glimpse of black jersey boxers and a very large bulge. Farther down... "You still have your boots on."

"And an ankle holster."

Going to bed with an armed man was never a good idea. Was this a warning? Was she making a big mistake?

Removing the rest of their clothing wasn't graceful, but when their bodies came together, she felt as beautiful as he'd said she was. Having sex with Mason felt like a dance with different rhythms and textures than she'd ever felt before. Smoothly, he guided her through the steps, and she was happy to let him lead, right up until the moment when he rose above her and parted her thighs.

"Wait," he whispered.

She knew what was coming, knew what he would say.

She knew she wasn't going to like this. Still, she asked, "Why?"

"I have a condom in my wallet."

She didn't need one, would never need one again. There were other health protection reasons, but she never needed to worry about getting pregnant. She stiffened in anger. The dance was over. Reality had intruded.

Though he had been ready to mount her, he had changed positions. On the bed beside her, he cuddled her against his chest as though he could protect her by absorbing her sadness and rage.

"Something's wrong," he said.

"I'm okay."

She'd come this far and it had been amazing. She refused to turn around and go back, not even if she was leading him into a lie. Couldn't she pretend, just for a moment, that they were a normal couple? Couldn't she have this pleasure, just a thin slice of happiness to cut through the darkness?

She turned so she was facing him. It wasn't a lie. As long as she didn't do something stupid and tell him that she loved him, she wasn't making a promise.

Her frustration channeled into passion. As she threw herself into sex, every muscle in her body tensed. Her breasts flattened against his chest. She clenched her legs around him.

"Easy, now," he whispered.

"I don't want to go easy."

But he was much stronger, and he was in total control. He soothed her, cajoled her with slow caresses. So patient, so sweet, he entered her slowly, almost cautiously, as though she might shatter. His kisses were soft and gentle as he eased into a simple tempo.

Again, she was trembling. Goose bumps prickled her

arms. This time, the earthquake that rattled her body came from pure satisfaction and relief. When she fell back onto the bed, her smile was real.

A happy sound—sort of like a meow—came through her lips. It wasn't anything she'd heard from herself before. "You know, Mason, I wouldn't mind having a pillow."

"Only one," he said.

He pulled up a pillow, set it against the headboard and arranged the duvet so they could lie comfortably in each other's arms. In this cozy position, with an orgasm still resonating inside her, she wondered why on earth she kept pushing him away.

"It'd be nice to have servants," she said.

"Is there something you want?"

"Dinner."

The cook had left the freezer filled with prepared meals that only needed to be microwaved to be ready, but Lexie felt too blissfully lazy to even turn the microwave dial. She hadn't been so utterly relaxed in ages.

There was a noise from downstairs. Mason heard it, too. In two seconds, he pulled on his black boxers, grabbed his gun and went to the door. He eased it open and slipped into the hallway.

She fumbled from one side of the huge bed to the other, trying to find her clothes. She didn't hear gunfire from downstairs. *A good sign.*

She'd just zipped her jeans when the bedroom door flew open and Stella dashed inside. Lexie managed to get two buttons fastened before she wrapped her arms around the little girl and scooped her off the floor.

"Hey, cutie pie. What are you doing here?"

Stella poked out her lower lip. "I'm sick."

Helena charged through the door with Mason following. "I don't know what she has, but I wanted her to see her regular doctor, so I pulled her out of camp."

Lexie nodded. "Okay."

Stella pointed at Mason and giggled. "He's got no shirt."

"Pretty funny," Lexie said.

"Hysterical," Helena said as she glanced between them. Lexie wasn't sure if her boss approved or disapproved. Probably the latter.

Stella hopped down and went toward the messy bed. "Lexie, were you taking a nap?"

"You caught me."

"I don't like naps," Stella said as she meandered around the room. "I'm too old for nap time. Lexie, does Mason take naps with you?"

She swallowed hard. This would be complicated to explain.

"Let me," Helena said as she made a dramatic swoop toward her daughter. "Sometimes, when a boy and a girl like each other a great deal, they sleep together."

"In the middle of the day?" Stella wrinkled her nose at the ridiculous idea.

"And at night, too."

Helena cast a radiant smile at all of them. The actress actually believed that her quick thinking had averted the crisis, and she wouldn't have to explain to Stella in more detail. Lexie knew better. This little girl asked question after question. She wouldn't give up so easily.

Hoping to create a diversion, Lexie charged through the bedroom door into the hallway. "Let's bring your luggage inside."

Standing behind Lexie at the top of the staircase, Stella asked, "Lexie, do you like Mason?"

"Sure I do."

"Do you love him? Are you going to marry him?"

And there they were: the two sentences she wanted most to avoid. Sometimes she just couldn't catch a break.

Chapter Twenty-One

The explanations to Helena weren't difficult. While Lexie thawed dinner, tossed a salad and chatted to Stella, who was playing in the family room, Mason told Helena about the threats to the house and possibly to Lexie.

"The only way I could be sure she was safe all night was to sleep in the same room," he said. "That's why we took the larger suite."

Helena nodded and sipped the vodka martini with two olives that he'd made for her. Mason and Lexie weren't drinking.

"I'm too tall for the sofa," he said. "Lexie graciously allowed me to join her in the bed. She set up a wall of pillows between us."

"Then the wall came tumbling down," Helena said. "It's all right, Mason. If the other children were here, we might have to come up with another explanation so we wouldn't give the impression that we approve of or condone premarital relationships. The older boys would be quick to use that as ammunition when they bring girls home."

He remembered what it was like to be a teenage boy. Eddy Jr. was nearly ready to start driving. The twins were sneaking up on puberty. He didn't envy the situations Helena and the admiral would soon face. "Stella seems to accept that Lexie and I like each other and take naps together."

Helena cast a worried glanced in her daughter's direction. "She was running a temperature yesterday. When it continued into today, I felt like she needed to see the doctor. Stella is usually such a healthy child."

In the family room, the little princess sat at a kid-size table and colored in a book about Cinderella. Lexie peeked over her shoulder. Subtly, she felt Stella's forehead and frowned.

"What did your doc say?" Lexie asked.

"His office is running tests. If she's all right, I'll take her back to camp tomorrow. If not, she'll have to stay here." She confronted him directly. "Is this threat real?"

"As real as the dent in my bumper."

"We'll need to find somewhere else for Stella to stay. And for Lexie, as well. I had no idea how dangerous this was."

"We'll be all right tonight," he said firmly. "I'll contact my office and have another two guards sent for tomorrow."

She finished off her martini and asked for another. In his brief acquaintance with Helena, he hadn't seen her as a drinker. This was a different side of the actress's personality. She seemed a hundred times more subdued. Her voice was deeper. She looked tired.

That night in their bedroom, he asked Lexie about the change in Helena. "Is this a case of maternal concern?"

Lexie stuck her head through the open door and looked down the hallway toward the Prescotts' suite, where Helena would be sharing her bed with her youngest daughter. Talking in a low voice, Lexie said, "Yes, she's worried about Stella. Helena is a busy woman with her fingers in a lot of pies, but the kids are important to her. She told me that the drinking and the bummed-out mood are for the role she's playing. She's also trying to drop ten pounds in three days."

"By drinking martinis?"

"I don't ask," Lexie said.

She threw back the duvet and got into bed wearing one of her child-appropriate nightshirts. This one had row upon row of flamingos. She had left the door to their bedroom open so he could hear any disturbance and do his body-guard thing.

His gaze devoured her. "How am I going to lie beside you and not make love?"

"Helena locked the door to her suite. Maybe they won't hear us."

Their first act of passion had been loud and energetic, involving the throwing of pillows and moans of pleasure and tackling and grabbing. The memory made him smile broadly. "We might be able to tone it down."

"Stella is only six. But I think she'll know the differ-ence between napping and what we were doing before."

"I'm going to take that as a challenge. Silent sex." Now that he'd had a taste of the incredible passion that had been growing between them, he wasn't going to stop. "Aren't there religious sects that do that?"

"We can try."

That was all he needed to hear. They would be very quiet and very, very hot.

THE NEXT MORNING, Lexie was annoyed to find Josh stand-ing at the front door before nine o'clock. He pushed a pair of horn-rimmed glasses up his nose and gave her a terse smile. "I caught an earlier flight."

"I didn't know you wore glasses."

"There wasn't time this morning to put in my contacts."

He dragged his suitcase across the threshold. "Did Helena get here with Stella?"

"I didn't know she was coming yesterday," Lexie said. "A heads-up would have been nice."

"When I talked to her she hadn't made firm plans about pulling Stella out of camp. I hope she didn't catch you in the middle of a wild party or anything."

You little beaky pervert! That was exactly what he'd been hoping—that Lexie would get caught. She'd come within minutes of having that be true. Helena wasn't upset now, but if she'd walked in on them while they were... It would have been bad.

"Where are you going to sleep?" she asked him.

"If Helena stays, I'll take the basement."

There was a small, plain, windowless bedroom in the basement near the safe room. Josh preferred it to the second- and third-floor guest rooms when the kids were at the house, because he liked the privacy. She'd never asked why he needed to be private, just assumed it was something creepy.

"Put your suitcase in the hall closet," she said. "We'll figure it out later. Right now I need to get breakfast."

In the kitchen, Mason sat at the counter. He saluted their entrance with a mug of coffee, which she figured must be his second, because he seemed wide awake.

"Good to see you, Josh. How are things at the Pentagon?"

"Every time the admiral goes there, he gets pulled into more meetings, totally unrelated to his main concerns. Our only solid information on the Damascus Cache is that all copies were destroyed years ago in a computer purge."

Mason exchanged a look with her. "What if there was a hard copy?"

"On paper? Nope, no way." Josh had noticed their sly

glance. His head swiveled like a woodpecker's as he looked from her to Mason and back again. "What did you find out?"

"We were speculating," Mason said. "We didn't locate the cache. Neither did a team from the CIA or two agents from NSA."

Wrapped in a silky robe, Helena joined them, pouring herself a mug of coffee. "Stella's still running a fever. I thought I'd let her stay in bed as long as possible."

"Good plan," Lexie said.

Since they were all at the counter, she decided to do breakfast like a short-order cook, with a menu of any-style eggs, toast and bacon. Helena and Mason both wanted scrambled with cheese melted on top. Josh wanted over easy, which meant he'd get served last.

Josh pointed to the chart on the flat screen on the wall in the family room. "What's that?"

Lexie winced. She hadn't changed the screen back to the usual display of family schedules. "It's a spreadsheet for suspects."

Mason took over the explanation, detailing that these were all the people who had been through the house and why they were there.

"Amazing," Helena said. "I didn't realize we did so much entertaining."

"Why is my name up there?" Josh asked. "Am I a suspect?"

Lexie wanted to tell him that he was their number one suspicious person and would, no doubt, spend the rest of his miserable, pointy-nosed life in a federal prison cell. But she opted for honesty. "We're just being thorough."

"I'm impressed," he said. "Can you run me off a copy?"

"I'll send the list to your email."

"Me, too," Helena said. "What else have you been doing?"

While Lexie served them breakfast and made up a plate for herself, Mason used the remote control to scroll through photos of their various suspects. Every time Helena made a comment, he slowed to study the person. He paused on Ackerman.

Helena exhaled a melodramatic sigh. "That poor, sad man. Lexie, do you remember that dreadful vase he gave us?"

"I made it disappear into the admiral's upstairs office."

"Perfect. Ackerman wanted Edgar to have it. And I don't have to look at it."

She also had a comment for Collier. "A ladies' man. He has women crawling all over him."

Josh finished eating, shoved his empty plate toward Lexie and dashed to the front closet, where he'd left his computer along with his suitcase. He returned to the kitchen, laptop in hand. "I'll need all this information. All the photos."

"Not so fast," she said, remembering her conversation with Bertinelli. "Let's try a bit of quid pro quo. What have you got that I might find interesting?"

"This isn't a game," he said with a haughty air of entitlement. "You should give the information to someone who can use it."

"And I could say the same to you."

"Fine." He tapped a few keys on his computer. "I just sent you a couple of my files. One of them is a brochure for AC-CD."

She really didn't care what it was. She just wanted to win. If this international incident involving the Damascus Cache was going to be solved because of work she and

Mason had done, she wanted credit. Maybe even a raise. Maybe she should have a change in status. She could be a nanny/investigator.

Chapter Twenty-Two

While Josh stormed off to parts unknown in the huge house, Helena's cell phone rang. She squinted at the caller identification. "It's the doctor's office."

Helena strode away from the counter, holding the phone to her ear, and Lexie looked toward Mason. "Multiply this by six kids and you have a typical morning at the Prescott home."

"With one major difference," he said. "All the kids are more mature than Josh. He's so damn whiny."

"He's supposed to be real smart," she said, "but you and I were the ones who made up the spreadsheet of suspects."

Mason took out his phone—which was synced with hers—and pulled up the files that Josh had transferred. "He's got basically nothing here. Places where AC-CD has been active, members of the group who are in prison. Here's their brochure."

He held his phone so she could read the sheet that was put together in a simple format. The first thing that struck her eye was the motto under the logo for Anti-Conspiracy Committee for Democracy: Information Is Power. It was attributed to Thomas Jefferson, but she'd heard the words recently. "Did you see this? That's what Bertinelli said."

"He could be the AC-CD leader," Mason said. "Under

his snotty, obsessive-compulsive exterior, he's a smart guy."

Had he been purposely giving them a clue? Or was he setting Lexie and Mason up to look foolish? "I don't like these games of one-upmanship. Why can't people just say what they mean?"

"Everybody lies," he said.

"Is that something you learned in international studies?"

"As a matter of fact, it is. But I also learned it in life."

"How?"

"Whether it's a fib about remembering somebody's name or a fake alibi for murder, we all dabble in misdirection. Even you."

She couldn't argue.

WHEN HELENA STRODE back into the room, her eyes were red-rimmed and bloodshot. Mason thought she'd been crying, but he couldn't be sure that she wasn't practicing for her upcoming role. The actress was hard to read.

"I'm a terrible mother," she said.

"You're not," Lexie said as she hugged Helena tightly. "What did the doctor say?"

"My darling little Stella has a strange variety of measles that's running rampant in Europe. She must have been exposed when we were in New York for a fashion show."

"Is it serious?" Lexie asked.

"No, she's been vaccinated so the case will be mild, and the doctor will contact the pharmacy and have meds delivered. He gave me the okay to leave." She gave a loud sob. "When I heard the doctor say that, I was relieved. That's why I'm a bad mother. I was glad that I didn't have to worry about my child and I could carry on with this movie role."

"That doesn't make you bad," Lexie said.

"I should cancel the movie."

While Lexie escorted Helena into the family room and they put their heads together, he had his own reaction to the news. If Stella had measles, the family surely wouldn't want Lexie to take care of her. He'd always heard that young women were supposed to avoid measles, mumps and rubella. She'd probably already been vaccinated, but he wanted to know for sure. Before he could pry her away from Helena, the house alarm went off. It gave one blast, then another, and then it went silent.

He ripped his gun from the holster and dashed to the foyer entrance. Inside the code box that disarmed the alarm was a schematic. He checked the blinking light. The alarm had originated from downstairs—from the door near the safe room.

Lexie and Helena appeared in the foyer. "Upstairs," he ordered them. "Make sure Stella is okay. Stay in Helena's room. Door locked."

He raced down the staircase.

Josh was coming down the hall toward him, waving both hands in front of his face. "Sorry, sorry, I set it off by accident."

Mason didn't put his gun away. "Why did you open that door?"

"I wanted to go outside and catch my breath. Lexie got me all flustered with her quid pro quo. I forgot the code for a moment, but then I remembered."

"I'll be making a thorough search of the house." Mason watched Josh to see if he had a guilty reaction. There was nothing. "I need to be certain we're secure."

"Like I said, sorry."

Mason pivoted and ran upstairs to tell the ladies that all was clear and Josh was an idiot. At the door to the Prescotts' suite, he tapped on the door. Helena opened it.

"False alarm," he said. "Josh wanted to go outside and accidentally set it off."

"I don't know which is more incredible—Josh being outside or Josh being sloppy enough to forget the code."

Beyond her shoulder, he saw Stella leaping across the bed toward Lexie. The kid didn't look sick at all. He waved to her. "Hey, princess."

"Mason is a basin," she yelled to him.

"Stelly is made of jelly."

"I'm not Stelly."

"Grant me some poetic license, kiddo. You're sweet like jelly."

She flopped on the bed. "Okay."

He took Lexie's hand and directed her away from the room and the germs in it. "We need to talk. Ladies, will you excuse us?"

As soon as they were in the hall, she asked, "What's wrong?"

He took her into their bedroom, closed and locked the door. "Stella has measles. I'm not sure what happens with the variety she has. According to Helena, it's some new variety from Europe. In any case, you should check it out before you expose yourself."

She shook her head. "I don't understand."

"This might be an old wives' tale, but I heard verification when we studied international pandemics in college. Measles can cause infertility in adults."

Realization hit her like a splash of cold water to the face. She gasped. Then she burst into tears. Her legs crumpled and she was on the floor, sobbing.

"I'm sure you're okay," he said. "We can go to the doctor right now."

"It doesn't matter."

"If it didn't you wouldn't be so upset."

She raised her tearstained face. "Fertility isn't an issue for me. After my first car crash, I had a hysterectomy. Mason, I can't have children."

"Then we don't have to worry about exposure."

"Did you hear what I said? I will never have kids. If you and I have a relationship, it'll never be what you want. I can't give you a family."

"I don't care."

"But I do."

LEXIE FLED FROM the bedroom and rushed down the staircase, not knowing where she was going. Her world was falling apart. She'd finally found the right guy, the man her dad would have wanted her to settle down and raise a family with. Mason was a partner, a friend and the best lover she'd ever known. He deserved children.

In the foyer, she blindly lurched toward the lower level. She needed to be alone, locked in the safe room where no one could hear her sobs. Could she remember that combination from yesterday? Doubtful. Instead, she went into the movie theater—the room the admiral had made soundproof and invisible to electronic searches.

She flung the door open and ran inside. The curtained room resembled an actual theater with well-padded seats that had footrests and separate snack tables. Four risers went all the way to the back wall. At the front there was a stage the kids used for performances. There were two screens, one that lowered and one huge flat screen.

She spotted Josh's head in one of the front row seats. He was just sitting there, motionless and in the way.

"Get out!"

He didn't move.

"Get out, get out, get out."

She ran toward him, ready to forcibly eject him if necessary. She wanted privacy for her breakdown. When she stood in front of him, she stopped. The handle of a hunting knife protruded from Josh's scrawny chest. The front of his shirt was covered in blood.

"Hello, Franny."

She whirled at the sound of his voice. "Anton Karpov."

"I go by Tony now—Tony Curtis, like the actor." He held his hands wide, gesturing to the stage he stood on. In his right hand, he had a Glock. "And you go by Lexie."

"Why are you here? How did you get in?"

"You can figure it out. You always were a smarty-pants. One plus one."

"Josh let you in."

She noticed the blood on the sleeve of his denim jacket. "Why did you kill him?"

"He's not dead, not yet. Wiggle your fingers, Josh. Show her that you're okay."

She noticed the slightest bit of movement. "He's lost a lot of blood. We have to get him to a hospital."

"Not until he gives me what I want." He strode across the stage as though he were lecturing her, schooling her on how to be a violent psychopath. "Our little Josh found the Damascus Cache. And the first thing he did was call the leader of AC-CD and tell him. It seems Josh has been blackmailing our leader for quite some time, and he forgot how to show the proper respect, the proper amount of fear."

Was it only a year ago that she'd dated Anton? How could she have been so blind? Yes, he was good-looking, with his blue eyes and his thick Tony Curtis hair. But his inner ugliness made him grotesque.

At the time, she hadn't thought she could do better than Anton, hadn't thought she deserved better. Mason had shown her a different way. He could care about her. But there was no future for them.

Anton said, "As soon as Josh gives me the cache, I'm gone. And you can take him to a hospital. What do you say, Josh? Do you want to live?"

His lips twitched. "Vase."

"I know what he's talking about." The Arabian vase from Ackerman, hidden in the admiral's office. "I know where it is. Should I take you there?"

"As soon as I get within karate range, you'll attack."

It was gratifying to know that he was still scared of her, but it was inconvenient. "Then you have to let me go and get it."

"So you can bring reinforcements? I don't think so."

"Rock and a hard place, Anton. What are you going to do?"

Muttering to himself, he paced back and forth on the stage. She watched him carefully, measuring his stride, plotting a possible move. If he hadn't been armed, she could have taken him. But she knew Anton, and he was an ace marksman.

"I should have killed you before," he said.

"Were you driving the truck that smashed Mason's fender?"

His smile was ice-cold. "That was my second try at vehicular homicide. The first time, I was in a black car, and you were on the road near Buena Vista. In that little bronze sedan you crashed off the cliff."

Her heart stopped. "You're lying."

"It was me, Franny. I've been working for the leader for years. He was disappointed that you didn't die." He bent at the waist and stared at her. "When you think about it, I did you a favor. The person you really want to hurt is the leader."

"Sam Bertinelli," she said. Bertinelli had quoted the motto of AC-CD. He had been spying on her. He was stronger and smarter than he acted while hiding behind his junior agent pose.

"Good guess," Anton said. "But not a smart guess. I want Bertinelli to keep paying for these jobs, and if you accuse him, he'll be out of business."

He lowered his gun and took aim. "I'm afraid you're going to have to die."

"No way, psycho."

She dived across the row of chairs and flattened herself on the floor while he fired three shots. She heard him moving and dodged to a different place. He fired again.

Her hope was that Mason would hear the gunfire. Not even the best soundproofing could muffle the concussive explosion of a bullet being fired, which was why Anton had used a knife on Josh.

Reaching the top row, she ducked underneath the risers. And there it was. The brass vase holding the Damascus Cache was right there on the floor at the back of the room. She wouldn't let Anton have it.

He dropped to the floor opposite her. His hard, cruel eyes peered through the scaffolding under the risers. "I see you, Franny."

She vaulted up and onto the risers again. Holding the handle of the brass vase, she dashed across the row of seats.

He'd taken too long to climb back up. She was close enough to fight him. Her flying kick hit him in the arm, but he didn't lose his gun.

She heard the door to the room open. Mason stood there, aiming his weapon with both hands. "Drop it."

She looked down at Anton. "Do as he says."

When he hesitated, she swung hard with the vase and connected with the side of his skull. Anton hit the floor, unconscious.

Mason had her in his arms. "Are you okay?" He kissed her forehead. "Were you shot?" Another kiss and another.

"I'm okay. But Josh is at death's door. We should call 911."

"Already did. As soon as I heard gunfire, I told Helena to get the cops and the EMTs."

"How did you know we'd need an ambulance?"

"I know you, Lexie." He smoothed the hair off her forehead. "If there's ever a confrontation, you'll kick somebody's butt hard enough that they need a doctor."

"I guess that's true."

"It's one of the things that make you special. I love you, Lexie."

"I'm not the right woman for you, remember? We can be friends, maybe even lovers. But we can't ever have a family."

He took his wallet from his pocket. "Have I ever shown you a picture of my brother?"

She took the official Marine Corps photograph from him. His brother was handsome in his uniform and his cap. "He's African-American."

"We were adopted, both of us. That was the family I grew up in, and it's the kind of family I want."

She knew how much he adored his brother. Adopted? "You don't care if the kids aren't your own?"

"But they are," he said. "If I raise them, they're my kids. I'm their dad. You're their mom. You don't need to have a baby to be a good mother."

She held him close. "I love you, Mason. And I always will."

"Let's clean up these scumbags and get out of here."

"Were you planning to go somewhere?"

He picked up the brass vase. "I think our first stop

should be the Pentagon, where we can drop this off with the admiral. And maybe we'll drop off Stella, as well."

"What about us?"

He suggested an elopement followed by a honeymoon in Paris, but she wanted her dad to meet the man she married before the ceremony. They were off to Texas and on their way to happily ever after.

* * * * *

MILLS & BOON®

INTRIGUE
Romantic Suspense

A SEDUCTIVE COMBINATION OF DANGER AND DESIRE

A sneak peek at next month's titles...

In stores from 14th July 2016:

- **Six-Gun Showdown** – Delores Fossen *and*
  Hard Core Law – Angi Morgan
- **Stockyard Snatching** – Barb Han *and*
  Single Father Sheriff – Carol Ericson
- **Deep Cover Detective** – Lena Diaz *and*
  Be on the Lookout: Bodyguard – Tyler Anne Snell

Romantic Suspense

- **The Pregnant Colton Bride** – Marie Ferrarella
- **Beauty and the Bodyguard** – Lisa Childs

Available at WHSmith, Tesco, Asda, Eason, Amazon and Apple

Just can't wait?
Buy our books online a month before they hit the shops!
visit www.millsandboon.co.uk

These books are also available in eBook format!

MILLS & BOON®

Mills & Boon have been at the heart of romance since 1908… and while the fashions may have changed, one thing remains the same: from pulse-pounding passion to the gentlest caress, we're always known how to bring romance alive.

Now, we're delighted to present you with these irresistible illustrations, inspired by the vintage glamour of our covers. So indulge your wildest dreams and unleash your imagination as we present the most iconic Mills & Boon moments of the last century.

Visit **www.millsandboon.co.uk/ArtofRomance** to order yours!

MILLS & BOON®

Why not subscribe?
Never miss a title and save money too!

Here is what's available to you if you join the exclusive **Mills & Boon® Book Club** today:

* *Titles up to a month ahead of the shops*
* *Amazing discounts*
* *Free P&P*
* *Earn Bonus Book points that can be redeemed against other titles and gifts*
* *Choose from monthly or pre-paid plans*

Still want more?
Well, if you join today we'll even give you
50% OFF your first parcel!

So visit **www.millsandboon.co.uk/subscriptions**
or call **Customer Relations on 0844 844 1351***
to be a part of this exclusive Book Club!

*This call will cost you 7 pence per minute plus your
phone company's price per minute access charge.